# MOM,
# I'll Stop Crying,
# If You Stop
# Crying

*Best Wishes,*

*Bob Lamm*

# MOM,
# I'll Stop Crying,
# If You Stop Crying

## A COURAGEOUS BATTLE
## AGAINST A DEADLY DISEASE

### ROBERT SAMARAS

VALMAR PUBLICATIONS
ST. CLAIR SHORES, MICHIGAN

Valmar Publications
9003 Harbor Place Drive
St. Clair Shores, MI 48080

PUBLISHERS DESIGN SERVICE
PROJECT COORDINATION: ALEX MOORE
COVER DESIGN: DEBRA ANTON
TEXT DESIGN: MARY JO ZAZUETA

Printed in the United States of America

1  3  5  7  9  10  8  6  4  2

Publisher's Cataloging-in-Publication Data
Samaras, Robert, 1927
Mom, i'll stop crying, if you stop crying:
a courageous battle against a deadly disease
/ Robert Samaras. – St. Clair Shores, Mich.
: Valmar Publications, c1995.
p.    cm.
Includes bibliographical references.
1.Samaras, Valeri, 1961-1991.  2.Thalassemia–
Patients–Biography.  3.Thalassemia.  4.
Anemia–Patients–Biography.
I.Title.
RC641.7.T5S2    1995
616.152'09–dc20        94-62183

ISBN 0-9644441-0-0

*I dedicate this book to the memory of my precious Valeri.
May her indomitable courage in pursuit of a happy,
high-quality life against seemingly insurmountable
odds serve as inspiration for those who suffer
from debilitating disease.*

*I also wish to recognize the caring families and guardians
of similar sufferers. I commend – and deeply thank –
the medical professionals who devote their lives to
research and treatment of Thalassemia and
other dread diseases.*

# CONTENTS

RAISING a child is challenging indeed. But if that child is a victim of a killer disease, the challenge is magnified a thousandfold. The parents of a stricken child must seek uniquely strategic ways to help their child develop physically, emotionally, psychologically, socially, and spiritually. In order for parents to be able to do this, it is vital that they have the support of friends and family. The child must be enabled to learn to cope with the disease and strive to function as normally as possible within society. How well that child learns to do this will determine whether or not (s)he will live a reasonably happy life. This book has been written from the very depths of my overflowing heart. It is about my dear daughter Valeri's life – and death. It tells of her desire to find love and happiness despite being born with a deadly disease.

When Valeri's mother – my wife, Marietta – was a young girl, she asked her father if there really is a heaven and a hell somewhere. Her father responded: "There is a heaven and a hell: right here on earth. We make our own heaven or hell here, according to how we live our lives."

Her father's words provided the code by which my wife has lived. When, as an infant, our Valeri was diagnosed with Thalassemia (Cooley's Anemia), a condition where the bone marrow can't make enough healthy red blood cells, her mother and I decided right there and then that we would make her life the closest thing to a heaven-on-earth that we possibly could, for however long we would be blessed to have her with us. Due to her disease, Val had to receive a monthly blood transfusion. According to medical predictions, the many complications caused by the anemia would inevitably render her life painful and short.

It wasn't until Valeri was about ten years old that she realized her life depended on her transfusions, and that the shadow of death always lurked over her. Fortunately, by this age she had developed many admirable qualities, not the least of which was an extremely positive attitude. She was an up-beat youngster who loved and enjoyed life immensely, despite her illness. Thus, she was well-primed to fight for her life, and she fought valiantly.

As you'll note as you progress through these chapters, one of Valeri's favorite coping-methods was to write in her journal. In order to remain optimistic and positive, she got rid of some of her more dismal thoughts and feelings by writing them down. In a journal entry from her freshman year at the University of Michigan, she expressed her feelings about going to the hospital for a transfusion:

> The drive to the hospital brings a barrage of thoughts and emotions to my mind. The highway is long and desolate. A dull gray covers my entire surroundings. I cannot distinguish the road up ahead from the dreary sky. My disposition is also a dull gray. I do not utter a single word to the driver seated next to me. I remain secluded in my own world. The weather, too, says nothing. It remains indifferent to the whir of cars. I blend into this gloomy atmosphere. In fact, it seems to devour me. Each passing street sign seems to get lower and lower as I approach my destination. The words slowly begin to be distinguishable, and the signs become bolder and more outstanding next to the dingy sky. The letters on the final sign are overwhelming. "ST. JOSEPH'S HOSPITAL NEXT RIGHT" flashes like lightening and sends shivers through my body.
>
> The massive city buildings loom all around, and I suddenly feel hemmed-in by walls and concrete. The tall buildings cast shadows of doom on the car-worn streets.

I get the same terrible feeling of doom in the pit of my stomach.

Finally, my mom and I arrive at the hospital. It looks somber standing against the murky sky. As I exit from the car, the wind howls ferociously. It holds me back, making it seem impossible for me to advance toward the sterile hospital doors. The snow crunches sharply under my heavy steps. Finally, I enter the building.

Immediately, I feel reassured by the friendly faces in the white uniforms. After I receive my treatment, I begin to feel physically and spiritually better. I realize life really isn't that bad. As I leave the health sanctuary, I see the clear night sky sparkling with stars. The radiant moon leads my mother and me peacefully home.

In the pages to come, I share the complete chronicle of her brave life. Thus, you will also have the privilege of knowing my Valeri.

# ACKNOWLEDGEMENTS

I would like to express my gratitude to many friends whose support and encouragement were vital to the completion of this book. Addamae Akin, Nick Cheolas, Debra and Brian Dittmer, Dr. John S. Kastran, George Kordas, Pete Kotsis, Jim Kotsonis, Christ Petrouleas, Nikki Rahaim, Bill Venettis, and Louis Vlahantones all lent financial support to the printing.

G. Deno Skuras contributed advice on technical aspects of the manuscript preparation. Bill Schade gave advice on audio-taping the initial manuscript. Teresa Jurkewicz typed the original copy from the audio tapes. Carol Horn typed and edited the second copy.

Special thanks to Dr. Leon A. Lande, retired professor from Wayne State University, and currently an outstanding baseball hitting coach, for displaying his writing talents by editing the very rough first draft of this manuscript.

Their help was invaluable in bringing my long labor of love to fruition.

# MOM,
# I'll Stop Crying,
# If You Stop
# Crying

# *Heartache*

T HE funeral service for our daughter Valeri is about to begin. It is 11:00 a.m. on Friday, March 29, 1991. We are at the Assumption Greek Orthodox Church in St. Clair Shores, Michigan. Valeri looks beautiful and peaceful lying in the mahogany casket. A small icon of the Virgin Mary holding baby Jesus sits in the left front corner of the casket.

We have been lifetime members at Assumption. Reverend Father Demetrios S. Kavadas and Reverend Father Costas Makrinos appear at the Great Altar Entrance, signifying that it is time for the ceremony to begin. Father Kavadas will officiate. He has known Valeri since she was one year old. Father Makrinos, who will assist with the service, visited Valeri in the hospital during the last few days of her life, and consoled the family immediately after her passing.

The Greek Orthodox funeral service includes three different segments. First, the ceremony takes place. This includes prayers, hymns, and the blessing of the body. The Eulogy is the second segment. For the third segment, the priest invites the people to come up front and view the body of the deceased for the last time. The procedure in this segment is to have the people come up in single file, beginning with those in the back pews of the church. As each passing individual views the body for the last time, he/she may kiss the icon in the casket, if so desired.

As the organist plays a hymn, both priests approach the casket and the service begins. I can't help thinking about our wonderful family and relatives who are sitting in the first two pews. Valeri loved them so much.

Sitting next to me is my wife, Marietta. A strong and creative individual, she was always a loving and supportive mother to Valeri. Marietta passed these traits onto Valeri, who used them to get the most out of her life of 29 years, 10 months, and 10 days. Sitting next to Marietta are Valeri's two lovely sisters. Debra is six years older than Valeri; Nikki is four years older than Valeri. I am Valeri's father, Bob Samaras. I am a heartbroken man.

As I gaze upon the congregation, I see Valeri's grandmother, Ianthie Christofis, her only living grandparent. Marietta's older sister and brother-in-law Mary and George Backos; Marietta's brother Mike Christofis and his wife, Marilyn; and Marietta's youngest sister Toni Christofis and her daughter, Andrea are seated in the first row. As I look at the second row, I notice Rena Venettis and her husband, Mark. Rena is Valeri's godsister and closest, beloved, lifelong friend. Sue and Steve Schucker are also seated in this row. Sue was a best friend of Valeri's since junior high school.

I glance across the aisle to the first row where the pallbearers are seated. Six of Valeri's cousins accepted the invitation to participate in the funeral. They are: Nick Backos (who was very close to Valeri) and his brother, Dean; and Brian, Mark, Jeffrey, and Gary Christofis.

Father Kavadas and Father Makrinos, with the assistance of a cantor who chants the hymns to the background organ music, perform a very dignified service. Father Kavadas blesses the body, and it is now time for the Eulogy by Dr. John S. Kastran. Dr. Kastran, who was honored by our request to present the Eulogy, is the principal at Grosse Pointe North High School. He and Valeri became very close friends when Valeri worked as the school's yearbook sponsor for three years.

Father Kavadas granted us a special favor by allowing Dr. Kastran to make his presentation. In our religion, it is only by a special request that a lay person can give the Eulogy. Our request was granted because Dr. Kastran was Valeri's godfather.

Dr. Kastran begins: "Valeri's life evoked the word 'courage' for us all. She had an ingrained capacity for meeting persistent difficulty with fortitude and resilience. Valeri was born with a genetic blood disease called Thalassemia, which is common in Greeks, Italians, and other people from the Mediterranean area. She struggled through the years with a great number of illnesses and injuries, and had to have a blood transfusion almost every month of her life in order to survive. Talk about spirit! Valeri was a young woman who possessed a quality of temperament that enabled her to maintain a high morale, even though her life was frequently threatened. I think of the appalling nature of her last nine days, when life itself was slipping away. Marietta, Val's sisters, her relatives, and friends marveled at her will to live - and how hard Val struggled to regain her health so that she could continue her wonderful life with us on earth."

Dr. Kastran continues, "Here was a kid who overcame many tribulations and persevered to achieve. She had mettle and courage to succeed; and succeed she did. Valeri Samaras is gone now, but her inner spirit -

which was her gift to us - is her legacy. No one ever heard Valeri complain. We should all be reminded of how Valeri Samaras, a very special person with a very special purpose in life, handled the hazards of life. We should let that be a strength within all of us."

Listening to Dr. Kastran gives me the feeling that Valeri is with us in church, and that at any moment we are going to hear her lovely, infectious laugh. Probably one of the things we will always remember most about Valeri is that she was either smiling or laughing. No matter what happened, she always looked at the brighter side of life.

Dr. Kastran returns to his seat, and Father Kavadas steps up to the microphone. He looks down at the floor for several seconds before beginning his comments. As he begins to speak, my mind drifts back to the comment Dr. Kastran made about how nothing was easy for Valeri. I think of the physical, emotional, and social problems she encountered continuously. She always had to prove herself. After graduating from the University of Michigan, Valeri tried to seek employment and ran into even more frustrations. Because of her illness, Valeri was considered handicapped and even qualified as a handicapped employee. However, this did not help her obtain employment, as employers were reluctant to hire a person who had a major health problem. She tried hard to find a job in order to accomplish one of her primary goals: being an independent person and a useful member of society. Somehow Valeri would meet failure with a positive outlook and a smile, ready to try again.

In his commentary, Father Kavadas highlights the following theme: "God sent us an angel to take care of; her parents, friends, and family did this - and then God took her back again. She was a wonderful person, the angel; a wonderful person to know and to be a part of our lives. God sent us an angel and God took back his angel."

Next, Father reads a poem that I had given him. I often recited this anonymous poem at the end of presentations I made at athletic award night banquets for athletes and their parents. It reads:

> *There is a destiny that makes us brothers.*
> *None goes his way alone.*
> *Whatever we put into the lives of others*
> *Comes back into our own.*

The poem epitomizes Valeri, because she contributed positively to others' lives by way of her personality, attitude, enthusiasm, and personal relationships.

Father Kavadas now reads my comments: "I am grateful to you who are present; you who loved, encouraged, and supported Valeri. It was this give-and-take relationship that ignited the spark and maintained the flame and desire for life that characterized Valeri's existence. I want to thank you all for doing this for Valeri."

Father finishes. It is time for the next segment of the funeral service. This is when the people can view the deceased for the final time and pay their last respects. Afterwards, they leave the church to go to their automobiles in preparation for the funeral procession to the cemetery. This is a very emotional part of the service. Since it is the final farewell, people usually feel strongly about wanting to participate.

I sit here with Marietta and our daughters and family, watching this scene of depressing sadness. Many friends are crying, some hysterically. Most touch the casket, while others touch Valeri's hand. Still others kiss the little icon on the corner of her casket. Many have to be assisted by a priest or a member of the funeral director's staff to move away from the casket. I feel honored that so many of her friends are here to view her for the last time - and that they are willing to show their emotions so publicly. Valeri did many wonderful things with so many of these fine people.

Suddenly I think about Chris Garkinos, who is not here. After visiting Valeri in the hospital the last two days before she died, he had to return to his job in California. He could not make arrangements to return for the funeral. Chris was one of her best friends. Although Chris is not here physically, I know that he is here in spirit.

It is now time for us to pay our last respects and to view Valeri for the last time. First our relatives go to the casket, then our daughters. They are crying as they kiss their sister and stand near her casket. Marietta and I begin to cry. We both touch Valeri's hand, kiss her cheek, and say good-bye. Then, we just stand by her casket, crying.

Finally, Father Kavadas says it is time to go. We step away from the casket and watch Father Kavadas recite a prayer, bless Valeri, and close the casket. The pallbearers carry the casket out of the church. Marietta, our daughters, and I follow. The pallbearers place the casket in the hearse, while we sit in the limousine behind the hearse.

There are fifty-eight cars in the procession to the Clinton Grove Cemetery in Mt. Clemens. Marietta breaks the silence in the limousine, "Valeri was born in Mt. Clemens and she is going to her final resting place in Mt. Clemens." The four of us talk about the funeral service, and about how we selected Clinton Grove Cemetery. I remember that it is the non-Greek Orthodox Good Friday. This determined when and where Valeri would be buried.

When I had called the proprietor of the cemetery recommended by our clergy, I was told that the cemetery's policy did not allow any burials on Good Friday. She had suggested that we wait until Monday of the following week for the burial. This was not acceptable to Marietta and me; so, I telephoned the director of sales at the Clinton Grove Cemetery (which was the cemetery where Marietta wanted to have Valeri buried in the first place), Jim Krause, to ask if they had the same policy. They did not. The director said that he would make all of the necessary arrangements. Marietta and I appreciated his kindness and willingness to help us solve our dilemma.

Another topic we discuss on the way to the cemetery is Valeri's love for the Palm Sunday, Wednesday Holy Unction, and the Good Friday services. A highlight of this celebration was the Saturday Midnight service, which commemorates the rising of Christ. This service included a post-assumption liturgy that lasted until about two o'clock in the morning, which was followed by a feast in our community center. The feast was very much a favorite of Val's, as she would socialize with all of her friends. And, over the past few years, she would organize a group of peers to go downtown to Detroit's Greektown, to continue celebrating into the early morning hours.

The funeral procession arrives at the Clinton Grove Cemetery. The hearse is parked in front of the mausoleum. The pallbearers carry the casket inside the large chapel, as our family and friends follow it. Father Makrinos prepares to perform the final ritual, a brief farewell to the deceased. The casket remains closed. He chants several brief prayers, then finishes with the official prayer, "May her memory be eternal," which is repeated three times. He asks all of us to place a flower on the casket as we leave the chapel.

After placing a flower on the casket, Marietta and I decide to go to the burial plot and watch as the casket is lowered into the earth. We mention our intent to Mr. Krause, who supervises the moving of the casket to the plot. "Of course," he says. "Our maintenance staff is going there right now." The limousine takes us to the site, located a few hundred yards from the mausoleum. We are surprised to find that many of our relatives and friends are there. They do not want to leave Valeri at the mausoleum either, but wish to see her casket placed in its final resting place.

After watching the casket placed into the plot, some of us drop flowers onto the casket. We then return to the limousine to be driven to the community center of the church for the funeral luncheon. It is a tradition of our religion that a luncheon be held to commemorate the ascension of the deceased person's soul into heaven.

The feast is held in the community center's banquet room. Over two hundred people attend. Our immediate family, along with both Father Kavadas and Father Makrinos, sit at the head table. After completing our meal, Marietta and I sit at the table, talking with our daughters. Father Kavadas looks at Marietta and I. "Now you and Bob have joined the club and are part of us. It is very heartbreaking to lose a child." We understand. His son, Steve, had become ill and died suddenly about ten years earlier. Steve was twenty-four years of age at the time.

After the meal, people pay their final respects and condolences to us before they leave. We thank both priests for the service, and thank the banquet hall staff for the fine meal. We leave for home. Some friends and family members will join us at our house, to console us. This support is also a tradition of our religion.

Later that evening, we find ourselves home, alone. Our daughter Nikki and her six-year-old daughter, Alexandra, who live with us at this time, are in another part of the house. In the family room, Marietta and I discuss the events of the last three days. We talk about the two days that Valeri's body laid in state at Peter's Funeral Home, and the lovely flowers that filled the room. Valeri loved flowers and would have been pleased at the many beautiful arrangements. We felt honored that over one thousand people visited the funeral home to pay their respects. So many talked about how Valeri was such a lively, happy, and active young lady who never dwelled on her illness. Somehow she would find the fortitude to confront her health problem and get back on her feet quickly. Over and over we heard people say the same thing, "'discouraged' was not in Valeri's vocabulary." In fact, many people did not know the seriousness of her disease. She was too busy enjoying life.

We discuss the many blood transfusions Valeri received. They were her lifeline. We acknowledge the many outstanding and dedicated medical professionals who served Valeri so well. Their care, along with new medical techniques and treatments resulting from outstanding research, gave Valeri an opportunity to live an extended life.

Next, Marietta and I focus on Valeri's many accomplishments, while she lived a quality life. Not only did Valeri earn a bachelor of arts degree from the University of Michigan, but she also pursued a master's degree in education and earned a teaching certificate from Wayne State University. Later, she worked as the school yearbook sponsor for Grosse Pointe North High School.

Valeri loved to travel and went on many trips. A stylish dresser, one of her favorite pastimes was clothes-shopping. And - the Dodge 600 convertible that she buzzed-around town in fit her personality perfectly. Val's enthusiasm and happy outlook were evident and infectious. Her zest for living and positive approach to life affected all of us, guiding us in our personal and business lives.

Debra, Nikki, and Valeri were very close, developing an even more intimate relationship as adults. Rarely a day would pass when they didn't speak with each other. They would meet for lunch almost every week. Actually, between family functions and other meetings, it seemed that the three of them were always together.

Marietta and I continue to reflect on Val's life. She acquired an outstanding knowledge of the communication and entertainment industries - music, television, radio, and the movies were a big part of her life. At a very young age, Val developed a great fondness for sports, especially football, baseball, and basketball. She was an ardent fan of the Detroit Lions, the Detroit Tigers, and the Detroit Pistons. Our final thoughts center on Val's love for human relationships. She participated in many weddings, baptisms, and other celebrations. She was a maid of honor on several occasions, a bridesmaid many times, and a godmother for two infants. Very involved in church social functions, Val served on many entertainment committees.

The theme, "Seize the Day," which she used in the last yearbook she sponsored at the high school, described her perfectly. (This theme was borrowed from the actor Robin Williams' quote in the movie: *The Dead Poets Society*.)

The key to Valeri's life was a comment that she made to her mother a long time ago. It was during one of her transfusions as a very young child. Both Marietta and Valeri were crying. As Valeri lay in bed, with the IV needle stuck in her hand, she said: "Mom, I'll stop crying, if you stop crying." This was to be her philosophy for the rest of her life.

## 2

# *Another Lovely Daughter*

L ET us return now, in flashback, to May 16, 1961. That day promised to be an eventful day in the Samaras' household. Dr. Arthur Rothman, Marietta's obstetrician, had informed her that she could expect to give birth to our third child sometime that day. However, since the actual time of the birth was not predictable (what child has ever arrived at a specified time?) we agreed to keep to our daily routine. This meant that Debra and Nikki would go to their classes at Roxana Park Elementary School, and I would teach and coach my students at Eastern High School in Detroit.

The day began with Marietta making breakfast, at which time she reiterated her desire that I be the one to drive her to the hospital. Of course, I felt the same way and assured her that as soon as she telephoned the school, I would rush home to take her to St. Joseph's Hospital in Mt. Clemens; about fifteen miles from our home. And, in case Marietta was not able to contact me (while I was en route to the baseball field) we formed an alternate plan: for Marietta to contact my brother-in-law, George Backos, who could always be counted on to help. He was available today because it was his day off from work. Both Marietta and I were comfortable with our plans.

After breakfast I left for Eastern High to teach my two morning classes. There was no word from Marietta, and the morning passed quickly. At noon, I met the baseball team and we prepared to drive to Northwestern Field to play our 3:30 p.m. game against Cass Tech. The team knew that my wife was expecting to deliver our baby today. We even formed a plan to have Coach Don Miller go to the game, so that he could take over the coaching duties, if and when I received the call from Marietta.

We left for Northwestern Field - about six miles away from the school. Everything fell into place nicely: the warm-up, the batting practice, and the infield practice. The game began promptly at 3:30 p.m. We scored a run in the first inning, to take a one to nothing lead.

As I sat on the team bench watching the game progress, I heard a voice behind me, "Bob! Bob! I have to talk to you!" It was Miss Gormley, our art teacher. "Bob, your wife called the school a short while ago and said she was ready to go to the hospital."

The game continued. At the top of the fifth inning our team still held the same lead. We were at bat. Marietta was on my mind, but I felt it would be all right to stay. A few minutes later, along came coach Dick Sunday, the head basketball coach at Northwestern High School. He was a good friend of mine. As he approached the bench, he said, "Bob, I was just informed from one of your school office staff members that your wife was on her way to the hospital. George was taking her there." I thanked Dick and told him that I was planning to stay, but I'd hustle to the hospital immediately following the game. Dick smiled and walked to the bleachers.

The last half of the fifth inning began. Runs began streaming across home plate. With two men on base, two outs, and Cass Tech leading six to one, the next player hit a single to left field. His hit led to a close play at home plate. The umpire called the man safe. I disagreed. I rushed to the plate to argue with Benny the Ump (as he was referred to by the league coaches). Benny was the best umpire in the league, having the ability to calm even the most irate coaches quickly. As I approached Benny, I said, "He was out by a mile."

Benny lifted his mask. "Bob, what are you doing here? Your wife is in the hospital, ready to deliver the baby. You'd better get going if you plan to be there for the birth."

I looked at Benny and thought, "That did it, this is the last straw." So I walked back to the bench and said to Don Miller: "I'd better get going. Take over!"

When I arrived at St. Joseph's Hospital, I rushed up to the Maternity Ward and into Marietta's room. She was in bed, waiting impatiently. "No baby yet, Bob," was her first comment. "How was the game going? I am glad you are here." Before I could answer her question, she continued, "I am having contractions about every five minutes, so there is still some time before I will deliver."

Dr. Arthur Rothman entered the room and greeted us. He asked Marietta how she felt and how many minutes between contractions. She answered, "I feel much better now that Bob is here. The contractions are five minutes apart." Dr. Rothman was a marvelous doctor and a wonderful, warm human being. He practiced in our small town, East Detroit. We always felt so lucky to have him as our family doctor.

"Well Bob," Dr. Rothman said, "it will be about another forty-five minutes. I'm going to give Marietta an IV to speed things up." I said fine, and he proceeded to insert the needle to start the IV. Shortly after, the contractions came on more rapidly and Marietta was taken into the delivery room. I stayed in the waiting room. (In 1961, it was not the norm for fathers to participate in the actual birth of a child.) Less than a half an hour later Dr. Rothman came out into the waiting room. He was holding a beautiful baby. He looked at the baby, then at me, and said: "Bob, it is another girl. That makes three." Of course Marietta and I thought it would be nice to have a boy, but we agreed a girl would be fine. I thought to myself, we now have three wonderful daughters. Maybe our next child will be a boy.

The first thing I said was: "Dr. Rothman, is she healthy?"

"She is perfectly healthy and weighs seven pounds, one ounce," he answered. Then he gave her to me. It was a very exciting moment and I was overwhelmed with elation. As a coach, I knew the thrill of victory in an athletic contest, but it didn't compare to holding your newborn child.

I went into Marietta's room and put our daughter in her arms. "Sweetheart," I said, "this beautiful baby is our Valeri!" She looked like a Valeri, the name we had selected for her. In the Greek Orthodox tradition, children are named after their grandparents. My oldest daughter Debra was named after my mother, Demetrula. Debra was the English interpretation of Demetrula. Our middle daughter Nikki was named after my father-in-law, Nick. We also gave Nikki a middle name, Cynthia, after my mother-in-law, Ianthie. Valeri's Greek name was Vasilia, after my stepfather, Vasili, which in English is interpreted as William.

After a few minutes Marietta said, "Bob, it's another girl."

I looked at her, smiled and said, "That's okay, Sweetheart, the next five will be boys!" and we both laughed. We sat there and looked at our lovely, little baby for a few moments, until a nurse came into the room and took Val away for her first bath.

Later that evening when Marietta was feeling stronger, we talked about my day. I explained what had happened at the game, and how I was told by three different people to go to the hospital. We both had a laugh.

The phone rang. It was Coach Don Miller. He informed me that the players put forth a supreme effort to win the game, but fell short, losing eight to seven when Cass Tech's outfielder made a fine catch to end the game. That was gratifying news for me. I realized how hard they tried to win the game on my behalf.

The rest of the evening at the hospital was spent notifying family members and friends of our little Valeri. We telephoned Debra and Nikki to tell them about their new sister. Nikki was happy to hear that Valeri was going to share her bedroom. Our home had three bedrooms. Debra, being the oldest, had her own room and we had the other room. Both sisters expressed their desire to see Valeri. We explained that Mom would be home in a couple of days, and then they would see plenty of Valeri. (In the 1960s it was standard for mothers to remain in the hospital for several days after giving birth. This allowed them to rest before returning home to care for both the newborn and the rest of the family.)

This eventful and happy day climaxed when Marietta and I went to the nursery to look at our Val prior to my departure from the hospital. We looked at her as she slept, and we agreed that she had a special glow about her, just like our other two daughters did when they were first born. Of course, as all parents, we were prejudiced about our children. We were just about the two happiest people on earth.

As I drove home that evening, I felt happy that in a few days our family would be together again.

3

# Thalassemia: What's That?

MARIETTA and Valeri came home. Everyone adjusted to having an addition to the family, and everything was going very well. Val's habits and needs were normal, with the exception that she wasn't obtaining sufficient sleep at night or during her naps. We tried to compare her sleeping habits with those of her sisters' when they were infants. Debra started sleeping through the night when she was only two weeks old; and Nikki, who had colic as an infant, didn't sleep well until she was four months old. Valeri, on the other hand, was a mixture of both of their sleeping habits. During her early months, sometimes Valeri slept well; at other times she had difficulty sleeping.

We began to notice that Valeri didn't appear as strong or active as our older children. Our understanding was that the youngest child in a family was usually more active, even in the first month of infancy. But, since Val was a very happy and affectionate baby, we didn't pay much attention to her limited activity. We thought that things were okay. Even Val's six-month check-up proved her to be a healthy baby. Our lives were content.

However, about a month later, things didn't seem normal. Valeri's complexion was pale compared to her red-cheeked sisters'. And, more importantly, she became more lethargic. Marietta called Dr. Rothman and told him about our observations. He told us to watch her for a couple of days, and if there was no evidence of improvement, to bring Valeri into his office for an examination. A couple of days later, we saw no improvement and Marietta took Val to see Dr. Rothman.

After examining her, Dr. Rothman still felt that Valeri was healthy. He did instruct us, however, to continue to monitor Val closely and to keep him posted about any negative changes in her appearance or behavior. Two weeks passed. It became more and more apparent to Marietta and me that Val's health was deteriorating. She was sleeping and eating less. She was very lethargic, irritable, and her complexion continued to pale.

One evening, as I was caring for Valeri while Marietta was out with a couple of her friends, I tried to feed her. Valeri refused to eat any of her baby food. This was uncharacteristic, as eating was a favorite pastime for her. It seemed almost painful for her to swallow. Later that night, Val became extremely irritable and began a very painful type of crying.

Marietta and I discussed Val's behavior and decided to take her to see Dr. Rothman again. We visited him the next day. This time when he examined Val, he noticed that her abdomen was swollen, and he also heard her painful cry. After finishing the examination, Dr. Rothman turned to us and said, "Val is not well. There is definitely something wrong with her, as indicated by her symptoms and by her swollen abdomen. Also, she has lost two pounds since her last examination. I feel that it's serious enough for you to take her to St. Joseph's Hospital now." We were upset by this news, especially since Dr. Rothman was not an alarmist.

Upon arriving at St. Joseph's Hospital, we learned that Dr. Rothman, an obstetrician, wanted to transfer Valeri's case to a pediatrician. He suggested Dr. Howard Charbeneau. We agreed with Dr. Rothman's recommendation.

Later that evening, we met Dr. Charbeneau when he came in to examine Valeri. Dr. Charbeneau was an excellent choice. He resembled our wonderful Dr. Rothman in many ways. Dr. Charbeneau was a low-key person who seemed very knowledgeable, caring, and attentive. He tried to comfort us by explaining his plans. "First we are going to give Valeri a series of tests. As of now, we don't know what is wrong with her. You may call me any time during the next few days while the tests are proceeding. I will keep you posted with the test results daily." His reassuring attitude gave us confidence that Val was in good, capable hands.

Shortly after his examination, Val was placed in a room with another infant. We stayed with her until it was time for us to go home. It was difficult for us to depart, as she was very attuned to the fact that we were leaving her and that she was in a strange place. As we headed for the elevator, we could hear Val's cry. We turned around and went back into the room. Marietta picked her up and both of us comforted her with soft words and cuddly touches. Again, Marietta put her down. Although Val cried again, we left for home.

That evening Marietta and I decided on the routine that would be kept while Val was in the hospital. I would go to work at the high school and coach the basketball team, then proceed directly to the hospital after practice. Meanwhile, Marietta would send Debbie to school and Nikki would stay home under the supervision of her grandmother, who would also care for Debra after school. This schedule would allow Marietta to spend the day at the hospital attending to Val's needs and overseeing her care.

Although I felt obligated to perform my duties as a teacher and basketball coach, my mind was continually on Valeri and what the tests would find. My thoughts ranged from feeling that everything was fine except for a minor, curable problem, to a fear that she had something very serious and incurable.

By Thursday, the tests had not revealed the nature of Valeri's illness. All of the test results were normal except for one of the blood tests which indicated a low red blood cell count. Normally, a hemoglobin or red blood cell count is translated by its percentage in relation to the white blood cells and platelet cells. For simple analysis, the percentage is then converted to grams per deciliter. Children normally have a ten to twelve hemoglobin gram count, women have an eleven to fourteen count, and men have a thirteen to sixteen hemoglobin blood count. Dr. Charbeneau told us that Val's count was low and that it was necessary to do some more testing to find out her exact count. If her count was too low, a follow-up treatment would then be planned. The new blood test results would be finalized by Friday morning.

That night, Marietta and I felt that there was something seriously wrong with Valeri. I decided to accompany Marietta to the hospital on Friday.

It was a difficult day at the hospital. Dr. Charbeneau was to inform us of the test results as soon as he received the report from the laboratory. The morning passed without any news. Throughout the afternoon there was no word from Dr. Charbeneau. Finally, after seven o'clock that evening, a nurse told us that Dr. Charbeneau would be in soon to discuss the results of the blood tests.

Marietta and I were very apprehensive. Although both Dr. Rothman and Dr. Charbeneau had talked to us every day, they never mentioned what they suspected might be wrong with Valeri. As Marietta and I talked about the upcoming discussion with Dr. Charbeneau, we watched Valeri lying in her crib. She was very weak and listless, as she had been all week. She had not eaten much for several days, and she wanted to be held often. Whenever Marietta put Valeri back in her crib, Valeri would cry the same painful cry we were now so familiar with.

A short time later, Dr. Charbeneau came into the room. He appeared very serious. At his request, we stepped out into the hallway, just outside Valeri's room, so that we could talk privately. Both Marietta and I were extremely anxious. He began by repeating that although all of the other tests were normal, Valeri's hemoglobin test showed a very low red blood cell count. More importantly, he emphasized, further testing showed that the red blood cells had a slightly different appearance. Consequently, the diagnosis was made that Valeri had a blood disease called Thalassemia, also known as Cooley's Anemia. (Dr. T.B. Cooley from Children's Hospital in Detroit discovered the disease in the late 1920s.)

Dr. Charbeneau explained that Thalassemia was a genetic blood disease common among Greeks, Italians, and other people from the Mediterranean region. This is why it is often called Mediterranean Anemia. Due to inter-ethnic marriages in America, the disease was not that common here, where only about one in a million people contracted it. Thalassemia is the type of disease where both parents must carry the minor anemia or the trait. It can then be passed on, according to genetic law, to one out of four children. When the symptoms are classified as Thalassemia Major, it is a very serious disease. The Minor (trait) Thalassemia is not serious. The Minor victims have low blood counts and may tire easily, but suffer no bad effects. Victims of Thalassemia Major cannot produce enough healthy red blood cells to allow enough oxygen to be passed throughout their bodies. This leads to the destruction of their vital organs and tissue. Bone marrow cannot produce enough red blood cells for the person to survive. Unfortunately, Valeri was diagnosed as having Thalassemia Major.

I asked Dr. Charbeneau if this disease was curable. "No, it is **not** curable," he answered emphatically. "Often children die by two years of age; some might live to puberty."

Immediately, I felt weak. "Doctor, I think I am going to pass out," I said. "I need to sit down."

"I feel the same way," Marietta added.

Dr. Charbeneau quickly called for a nurse to bring us two chairs. We both sat for a couple of minutes, trying to overcome our horror. After several minutes, we asked him to continue. He told us that there is a treatment for Thalassemia. This instantly made us feel better. Victims can be given blood transfusions on a regular basis. The transfusions would be restricted to packed red blood cells, instead of whole blood. These periodic transfusions would give Valeri a high enough red blood cell count so that her body could function somewhat normally. Beyond that, he didn't know what would happen. He had never seen a Thalassemia victim before (only three or four victims of this disease lived in the Detroit area), and he knew little about what to expect.

We then asked Dr. Charbeneau a flood of questions. How often would Valeri need a transfusion? How many pints of packed cells would be needed? How long would she have to stay in the hospital? Was it easy to transfuse an infant? Will she have reactions? Will there be other complications?

Dr. Charbeneau took his time and tried to answer each question, but he also admitted that he just didn't have all of the answers. Finally, he said, "Here is what we plan to do. Because Val's red blood cell count is so low, around three grams, we must give her an immediate transfusion. A blood count of only three grams is very dangerous. Most people with a blood count that low can hardly lift their heads or move. You should see a big improvement in Valeri after the transfusion. She should be well enough to take home. The next thing I want you to do is to set up an appointment to see Dr. Wolfgang Zuelzer at Children's Hospital in Detroit. Dr. Zuelzer is a protégé of Dr. Cooley's and knows more about this disease than anyone else. He has been researching the disease and treating patients for many years. He should be able to give you a detailed account of the disease and Valeri's prognosis." Dr. Charbeneau wanted this appointment to take place within a week after releasing Val from the hospital. At this point he left.

We sat there quietly for several minutes, just staring into space, with tears in our eyes. My thoughts centered on my family. I had two brothers, Gus and Peter. Gus and I were healthy. But, my brother Peter had severe health problems from infancy and died at the age of eleven, from the same symptoms as Valeri. Peter was weak and often hospitalized. Eventually, his heart enlarged to such a degree that doctors had to remove two of his ribs so that his heart could beat properly. He died in the early 1930s, a couple of years after this operation. I remembered that Peter would be sent to a sanitarium following his release from the hospital, so that he could secure more rest. Upon leaving the sanitarium, he would remain healthy for some time, but he was never very active or very strong. In spite of his illness, Peter was a happy child.

I often thought about my mother taking Peter to Children's Hospital in Detroit for check-ups, the same hospital we planned to visit. My mother was widowed, raising three sons and caring for her mother, who also lived with us. (Later, she would marry my stepfather, William Samaras.) I often thought of the years prior to my mother's remarrying, when she had to carry Peter from the bus stop to the hospital located several blocks away. By the age of nine, Peter was very weak, and only home for short periods of time. I felt sorry for him, though he was always in a good mood and never complained. It suddenly occurred to me, as I sat there, that Peter suffered from Cooley's Anemia. Unfortunately, the only treatment for the disease at that time was rest.

At this point, my mind shifted back to the reality of the current scene. I thought of one important factor: with periodic transfusions there was a good chance for Val to be quite normal. I turned to Marietta, who was in tears, and said: "Honey, at least there is a treatment available today that wasn't available in the past, and research of the disease will be ongoing." (I decided to talk about Peter at another time.) "Let us do first things first. Val should receive a transfusion and then be examined by Dr. Zuelzer at Children's Hospital."

We walked into the room and looked at Valeri. She was lying quietly with her eyes closed and appeared to be sleeping. As we approached her bed, she immediately opened her eyes and held out her hands to Marietta, indicating that she wanted to be picked up. Marietta lifted her into her arms and began to cry. Val looked at her Mom's face and also began to cry. Marietta immediately started sweet-talking to Val and told her everything was all right. Almost instantly, Val stopped crying. Soon it was time to go home. After comforting Valeri for a few minutes, we left.

Once at home, we told Marietta's mother what the doctor had explained to us. Needless to say, she was very upset. She told us that Marietta's father had several brothers born in Greece with a mysterious disease. All of them had died at young ages.

Marietta and I then explained to Debra and Nikki that their sister Val was going to have a transfusion, and she would then come home in a day or two. That seemed to satisfy their curiosity. We then made many telephone calls to family members and friends.

Later in the evening, we finally found time to be by ourselves and to recap the occurrences of the day. We both felt optimistic about Valeri's chances to get well and to have an opportunity for a quality life. I told Marietta about my brother Peter and my family. She quickly acknowledged that Peter didn't have a chance to live any kind of an eventful life; but, with transfusions, Val did have a much better chance. She also felt that together we could give Valeri family experiences that Peter didn't have during his life.

Early the next morning, Marietta called the hospital. The nurse on the floor said that Valeri was being transfused and that it would take all day because she would receive three pints of blood at a very slow rate. We decided to go to the hospital around noon. When we arrived, we found Valeri lying in bed quietly with an intravenous needle penetrating her right hand. A bulky bandage held the needle in place. The tubing led up to a high stand with two plastic bags, one on each side of an extended rod. One bag held the blood and the other held a sterile water solution. The tubing connected to the blood bag was turned to the "on" position, which meant that Val was receiving her needed blood. The other bag would be turned on at the end of the transfusion to keep the vein open while waiting for another bag of blood to be hooked up to the tubing. Then the sterile water content would be turned off and the blood line would be turned on. Each pint took about three hours to empty into Val's vascular system. The heart-rending sight made us catch our breath. Marietta bit her lip and tried valiantly not to cry.

We spent all day Saturday at the hospital with Val. The final pint was finished in the early evening. Next a blood sample would be taken, followed by a check-up on Sunday morning by Dr. Charbeneau.

After attending church in the morning we returned to the hospital. We walked into Valeri's room and Marietta yelled: "Look! She's standing up! It's the first time that she ever stood up!" Seeing her standing for the first time made us ecstatic! Our family and friends were also thrilled to see Val moving around energetically.

When Dr. Charbeneau came in, we told him what had happened. He said that Val's blood count was at a normal range and that she would have a normal amount of energy for now. He explained that she would develop strength, but she would also lose energy as the red blood cells began to die. That meant that her blood would have to be replenished with another transfusion. The average life span of a blood cell is about 120 days. Val's body would create some red blood cells, but not enough to sustain her.

The doctor said that everything else checked out normally and we could take our Valeri home. We were to make an appointment to see Dr. Zuelzer within a week, so that he could give Val a complete examination, verify the diagnosis and recommend further treatment. Since Dr. Zuelzer was the Cooley's Anemia expert in Michigan and had a great deal of experience working with youngsters suffering from anemia, Dr. Charbeneau asked us to consider having Dr. Zuelzer become Val's physician, and to have Val receive all transfusions and treatments at Children's Hospital. We thanked Dr. Charbeneau for his medical advice, treatment and care. The nurses helped Marietta dress Val, and we left for home.

Val seemed very happy in the car. It was great to see her act like a healthy, happy baby. Both Marietta and I agreed that we felt very comfortable with Dr. Charbeneau's low-key approach and optimistic manner. We were confident of his abilities to treat Valeri.

# 4

# *The Thalassemia Expert*

OUR scheduled appointment to visit Dr. Zuelzer was set for Monday, eight days after Val's release from the hospital. Our family spent a very happy week preceding this visit. Val was very active and did things that she hadn't been able to do before, such as move around and pull herself up in her crib, talk, and eat. She ate more than ever before! She laughed and played, and was very much aware of what was going on around her. The three girls played together and enjoyed their new relationship. Of course, Marietta and I were tremendously happy to see this happen.

Our family seemed to be like any normal American family. I tried to block out the fact that Val had a health problem and that we had a very important meeting with Dr. Zuelzer coming up. Marietta and I particularly wanted our family to enjoy this time when all seemed well, as there certainly would be enough problems and worry to dominate our lives later.

The night before our appointment with Dr. Zuelzer, I lifted Val into my arms, looked at her face, and suddenly noticed that she had red, rosy cheeks. The paleness was gone. I called my wife and said: "Marietta, look at her rosy cheeks!"

Marietta looked at Val and said, "Oh, my goodness!" and began to cry. "Do you think that the diagnosis is wrong and Val is cured of whatever ailed her? Or, that it was just something minor that was wrong with her?" she asked.

"Let's hope so," I answered. It was difficult for us to believe that there was something seriously wrong with Val. Later that evening when our three lovely daughters were tucked away for the night, both Marietta and I could feel the tension mounting, as we both anticipated the appointment with Dr. Zuelzer.

We got up early, dropped Debra and Nikki off at my mother-in-law's home, and headed for Children's Hospital.

After we registered Valeri, a medical technician needed to extract samples of Val's blood. Val cried when the needle was inserted, but she soon quieted while the technician filled four large vials with her blood. I thought that this was a great deal of blood to extract from such a small person. (Little did I realize then that this would take place over 1,500 times in the years to follow.) A nurse asked Marietta to put a gown on Val so she could be placed in a crib. Val had a desperate look on her face as Marietta changed her and laid her down in the crib. We were then taken into Dr. Zuelzer's office.

It was a small room with medical books on many of the shelves. Dr. Zuelzer was sitting behind his desk and stood up to greet us. After he introduced himself and asked us to sit down, I couldn't help but notice the pictures on his desk. They included his wife and three grown daughters. Of course, they reminded me of our three girls.

In some ways Dr. Zuelzer was friendly and understanding, yet in other ways he seemed arrogant and impatient. He discussed how he had studied under Dr. Cooley. Since Dr. Zuelzer appeared to be in his early fifties, I had the impression that he had worked rather extensively with Dr. Cooley, who had since died. He explained that he was committed to working primarily with Thalassemia, Sickle Cell Anemia, and Leukemia patients, as well as researching these diseases. He then questioned us about our family background. I told him about my brother Peter. Dr. Zuelzer was convinced that Peter had had Thalassemia, but this could not be verified since all patient records that were twenty-five years or older were destroyed. He told us that the blood sample results would be available in a few minutes, at which time he would continue the discussion.

A few minutes later a nurse gave Dr. Zuelzer the results of Val's blood tests. As he looked at the sheet of paper, Marietta and I held hands and looked at each other nervously. After reading the report, Dr. Zuelzer looked up at us and said, "I am very sorry, but our reports indicate that your daughter Valeri has Thalassemia Major."

Upon hearing the terrible news, both Marietta and I were in a state of shock. Those dreaded words shattered all of our hopes. After a few moments, I finally asked him what the disease involved. We had a good idea, but we didn't know all of the implications. He said Thalassemia Major was also known as Cooley's Anemia or Mediterranean Anemia, and that all three names were used interchangeably to identify the same disease. He explained that it was a genetic disease which was incurable. Val's bone marrow couldn't produce sufficient numbers of red blood cells, nor healthy red blood cells. Her bones wouldn't develop normally and she would be shorter and weaker than most youngsters.

I asked him to please give us more details about the blood. He explained by telling us that there were four parts to the blood. The first was plasma, which is the fluid part of the blood; second, the platelets, which are cells that cause the blood to clot. The white blood cells, which are the cells that fight antigens, are the third part; and finally the red blood cells, which carry oxygen to all the tissues in the body, make up the fourth part. In a healthy person, there are many more red blood cells than white.

He went on to explain that the hemoglobin in the red cells produces the color and carries the oxygen to the body. Anemia is a condition where there are too few red blood cells or too little hemoglobin in the cells. If the anemia is mild, there is a minor problem; if severe, the problem is major. A gram table is used to rate the anemia. Grams per deciliter of hemoglobin dictate the severity of the anemia. Minor anemia is a gram count of nine to eleven, whereas severe anemia is below eight grams of red blood cells per deciliter. The doctor told us that Val's red blood cell count would continue to drop. If she went untreated, in a short period of time she would die. I asked him why the disease didn't show up for so many months. He answered that infants are protected through an immunity by the mother for approximately six months. Once the infant depends on its own system, it cannot produce sufficient numbers of red cells or enough hemoglobin in the cells. It is then that the anemia becomes evident. Infants appear to be normal for approximately six months. In Val's case, it was eight.

"Although it isn't curable, it can be controlled," Dr. Zuelzer continued. "Transfusions can help a victim lead a relatively normal life, but for how long, is not really known. Some patients survive into their teen years, although puberty is a very difficult time for a Cooley's Anemia victim." He then added a positive point about Cooley's victims being very intelligent.

"On the other side of the coin, victims are more susceptible to infections, and worst of all, there is an iron build-up from transfused blood that remains in the body. This iron build-up eventually destroys the vital organs. Often the first organ to be affected is the spleen, which is being overworked, since its main function is to destroy old and defective red blood cells. The endocrine system is initially affected, which causes the liver to swell. Eventually, the heart is affected and the whole body breaks down, causing inevitable death." He sighed and concluded, "Your daughter is in for a very difficult time. And, of course, so are you."

I sifted through the information given to us by the doctor and one obvious question came to mind: "What is the chance for a cure in the near future?"

Dr. Zuelzer looked at us for a few seconds, then began, "You know Sputnik, the Russian missile that went into space and circled the earth recently? Finding a cure for Cooley's Anemia Major is like people in ancient times thinking of when they could put a missile into the air and orbit the earth. We now know about as much about curing the anemia as they did about building a Sputnik and sending it into orbit. That's how far away we are from a cure."

This was disheartening to hear and very depressing to both Marietta and me. He tried to make us feel a little better by mentioning that there was more emphasis on researching Thalassemia, but it looked impossible for many, many, many years.

I questioned him about Valeri's physical development. He said she would develop much slower than other children her age. Probably she would be very short, under five feet in height; have a protruding stomach, because of a swollen liver; be very pale; and lack energy. This was demoralizing for us, even though Marietta and I were typically very optimistic in our outlook on life's problems.

Marietta asked about the transfusion treatments. Dr. Zuelzer said he would like to have Valeri as a patient and to treat her at Children's Hospital, where he could watch her carefully - and should anything new surface, we could take advantage of the situation. He explained further that he would like to keep Valeri at a high gram count - somewhere around twelve. That would mean blood transfusions every three weeks of either one, two or three pints, as necessary. His plan was to admit her to the hospital for three days with limited visiting privileges until the transfusion was completed. The reason for limited visiting was that young patients became upset when their parents left and would cry to go home. I asked if this was standard policy for the very young. He explained that it was very difficult to find a vein for the transfusion in a youngster, so it was best to keep the vein open until the treatment was completed. Consequently, it was better to keep the child in the hospital until the treatment was completed. He repeated his desire to maintain a high gram count with Val.

We asked questions about Val's school and social activities. He answered that she could take part in everyday activities. Even though Valeri's life would be tied to transfusions and she would lack stamina, we should try to keep her active. We asked whether transfusions would be painful. He answered, "Not really." Asked if there were reactions to the blood transfusions, he said "Yes, but the staff would try to protect against any reaction and would stop the treatment if it became apparent that the reaction was becoming severe." At this point, Dr. Zuelzer glanced at his watch, looked up and said, "I have several other duties to look after. Are there any other questions?"

I glanced at my watch and noticed that the discussion had lasted about an hour. "We have no other questions," I said. We thanked him for his time and for his offer to be her physician. As he walked toward the door, he told us to feel free to call him whenever we needed to - for any reason.

When he left the room, it suddenly occurred to us that we didn't know what was going to take place immediately. Was he planning to keep Valeri in the hospital for three days? How many pints of blood would she receive if a transfusion was planned? Would we be able to stay in the hospital for the day? We had forgotten to talk about the immediate health plan.

I asked a nurse where I could find the doctor. She told me he was downstairs on his way to the Pediatric Ward. I hurried down the stairs and saw him walking with a young female resident. I walked up to him and asked to talk with him for a minute. He appeared a little perturbed. He impatiently asked me what I wanted. I asked about the health plan for the day. He informed me that a resident doctor would give me the details and take care of Valeri. After she received at least two pints of blood, Dr. Zuelzer would evaluate her condition and decide the next step. At that point, he would also inform us to the length of Val's stay in the hospital.

I returned to the room where Marietta was waiting and relayed the information to her. We were then escorted to a lobby by a nurse who said that she would let us know where Val was and when we could see her. Marietta and I sat down and began reviewing the whole scenario. At times, both of us became emotional. We were very, very upset.

Soon a woman approached us and told us that she was the Chair-woman of the Leukemia Foundation. She had heard about Val, and she told us that the Foundation was quite an active organization to help family members of children afflicted with a serious blood disease. She explained that the organization was formed to help people share their problems with other people, to raise money for research, and to keep people informed about advances in the medical treatment of various blood diseases by way of a newsletter. She also told us about her two children, who were victims of Cooley's Anemia. One child was a five-year-old boy and the other was a three-year-old girl. We asked how often they received transfusions. She gave us a great deal of insight about their daily lives and the problems both the children and family endured. We expressed our gratitude to her for sharing this information with us. We wished her good luck as she left to visit her children.

Marietta and I talked about the misfortune of having two children with Cooley's Anemia and how difficult that must be. The thought occurred to us that of the six or seven children with Cooley's Anemia in the whole state of Michigan, two were in the same family. Marietta looked at me and said, "I don't think we should plan on having any more children. The chances are too great that the anemia could crop up again."

Shortly afterwards, a nurse came to the lounge and told us we could visit Val. We were so happy to see Val, and she to see us. Marietta picked her up and at the same time asked a nurse's aide in the room if Val had eaten anything. It was around noon and Val had not had breakfast because she had to fast for the blood tests. The aide said that Val had not yet been fed but that she would get her some food. She left the room and returned a few minutes later with a dish of tuna fish salad, some bread, cake, and a glass of milk.

Marietta looked at the tray and said, "No, she can't eat this kind of food," and in a disgusted voice asked the aide to please find her some baby food, like cereal, vegetables, fruit or milk. The aide left and returned about a half hour later with some baby food, which we fed to Val.

Later that afternoon, Val took a nap. We decided to find out what was going to take place, so we went to the nurses' station to talk to Val's nurse. She informed us that Val would be given a transfusion that night. Then Val would receive another pint of blood the next day, at which time a decision would be made regarding a third pint. I asked the nurse which doctor would take care of Val. She answered that a resident would, but that Dr. Zuelzer or Dr. Lusher would examine her every day to make sure that things were progressing normally. I thanked the nurse for the information and asked if we could stay with Val until evening. She replied, "Of course." So, we returned to Val's room.

Marietta and I sat there for several hours. We tried to put everything in proper perspective. and to make plans on how we were going to cope with Val's problems. There were many implications we had to resolve. Our final conclusion was that, first, we had to learn more about the disease; second, about the treatment; third, about potential complications; fourth, about establishing a suitable routine for her transfusions; and finally, to decide which doctor should handle her case. Marietta preferred St. Joseph's Hospital in Mt. Clemens over Children's Hospital. Her thought was that St. Joseph's was a smaller hospital, where the pace seemed slower and the nurses were more attentive. But, she did not want to make that decision yet.

An hour later it was time to go. Valeri seemed happy playing in her crib, as she was smiling and making pleasant sounds. It was comforting for us to see her so active. Marietta picked her up and we both kissed Val good night. When Marietta put her down in the crib, Val sensed that we were leaving and began to cry. Believe me, it was a heart-shattering experience for us to leave. But, we had Debra and Nikki to consider, and the transfusion plans were set in place. Besides, we planned to call later that evening to check on how the transfusion was progressing.

The following day, I went to work. Marietta would pick up her mother and go to the hospital to stay with Valeri all afternoon. I would join Marietta at the hospital that evening, after coaching the basketball team.

Later that morning, I happened to have a free hour in my teaching schedule and decided to make a quick visit to the hospital, which was only a short distance from the school. I hurried to my car and drove to the hospital.

When I arrived and walked into her room, I saw Valeri wrapped with a bandage from her neck to her toes. It looked like she was in a cocoon. She had a needle sticking into her forehead and was tied to the side of the crib by a bandage near her waist. She was lying in a position facing the far wall, away from the door. Since Val was sleeping, I went to find her nurse to ask her what was taking place. The nurse explained that infants often pulled the needles out or moved around so much that the needle would fall out of the vein. Consequently, this type of bandage was standard. "Additionally," she explained, "it is very difficult to find a vein in a young child."

"Wow!" I said. "It looked so uncomfortable for her, especially since she was also tied to the side of the crib." The nurse reiterated that this was the procedure and it worked quite well with infants. I was upset, but told myself that if this was standard procedure, I should accept it. I decided to talk with Marietta before questioning the doctor about using another technique.

I walked back into Valeri's room and saw that she had awakened. She hadn't seen me enter the room. I walked over to the bed, opposite the direction that she was facing and said softly, "Valeri, Sweetheart, it's Daddy!" She immediately recognized my voice and squirmed to turn around. When she couldn't move, she contorted her neck in a way I had never seen before, looked at me, and gave me a big and affectionate smile. It was such a heart-warming moment.

I walked around the crib and sat in a chair next to her. She could see me easily and I put my hand on her shoulder. I stroked her head softly and began talking to her gently. Although she didn't understand what I was saying, she did understand my tender hand-movements on her head and back. She was obviously happy to have me there. A few minutes later, realizing that I had to return to school, I leaned over the crib bar, kissed her on the forehead and said, "Daddy has to go to work. I will see you later." She looked at me with tears in her eyes. As I left the room, she again twisted her neck to take a final look at me.

That afternoon, I was teaching a swimming class, when the assistant coach, Marty Keck, came into the pool and said, "Bob, you have a phone call from Marietta." He seemed very upset, and I became apprehensive. After thanking him, I ran up the two flights of stairs leading into the office where the phone was located. My heart was pounding as I picked up the receiver. I was concerned that something serious had suddenly happened.

I heard Marietta crying on the phone, and asked her what was the matter. Now wild thoughts began racing through my mind. She answered, "I am taking Valeri out of this hospital. Valeri is receiving her blood and I am here with her. I can't stand this room, and I can't stand the lack of attention by the staff. I can't stand seeing Val wrapped up in this cocoon-type bandage, and I can't get any information from anyone. I feel the treatment here is inhumane. Even though the medical people think differently, I am taking her out of this hospital, and felt you should know." Marietta is a headstrong person and will always take action when she feels it is necessary. Although strongly opinionated, she has good judgment, plus she is willing to assume responsibility for her actions. Marietta continued, "I don't care what you say, I am pulling her out of this hospital."

"If you want to take her out, that's fine with me," I said.

"I told the nurse how unhappy I was to see Valeri bound up and tied to the side of the bed," Marietta explained. "Nobody would tell me the number of pints of blood Valeri needed. The nurse would only repeat that Dr. Zuelzer would tell me later. Meanwhile Valeri was sobbing continuously. I told the nurse that I had had it with the hospital's procedures, and with Dr. Zuelzer's ideas for treatment. So I insisted that the nurse remove the bandage and needle and prepare Valeri to go home. When the nurse refused, I threatened to do it myself. About this time a resident passed by the door and I grabbed his arm and asked him to remove the IV needle, as I wanted to take Val out of the hospital. He said he couldn't do this, as Valeri was Dr. Zuelzer's patient. The resident also told me that Dr. Zuelzer is an outstanding doctor and knew exactly what to do for Valeri now and in the future. Once again, I threatened to remove the IV needle and bandages. The resident informed me of my liability and responsibility for Valeri. After both the IV needle and bandages were removed, the resident left the room while I dressed Valeri. The resident then returned with a form for me to sign, which he said prohibited us from ever bringing Valeri back to Children's Hospital. I told him of my plans to return to St. Joseph's Hospital. I agreed for us to be responsible for taking Valeri out of the hospital and away from Dr. Zuelzer. I then picked up Valeri and we left."

I listened to her detailed description of the incident and thought about it for a few seconds. I finally said, "Marietta, whatever you decide is fine with me because we do have our Dr. Charbeneau and he will work with Dr. Zuelzer if necessary. I am sure Valeri will receive better care at our hospital, where we will feel much more confident and relaxed." I looked out a window and added, "Marietta, it is snowing outside; please be careful driving home."

I sat in the office for a couple of minutes thinking of the conversation that had just taken place. I felt Marietta had made the right decision.

I called home after basketball practice that afternoon. Marietta and Valeri were safely home. Marietta said it was very difficult driving in the blowing snow and sleet. She said that Valeri was playing on the floor and seemed to be very happy, smiling and laughing all the time. This was very comforting to me.

When I came home that evening Marietta told me that she had already been in contact with Dr. Rothman and Dr. Charbeneau. "I explained the incident to both of them. They said that they would be happy to take care of Valeri. If there was ever a need, they would contact Dr. Zuelzer for assistance. Both doctors also suggested that I try not to worry so much."

The plan we agreed on was for Dr. Rothman to examine Valeri and to test her red blood cell count. Then, when necessary, he would send her to St. Joseph's Hospital to have Dr. Charbeneau follow up with transfusions or any other treatment. Both doctors would observe her progress.

The next few weeks were very happy ones for the Samaras family. Debra and Nikki liked having Valeri home, and Valeri enjoyed the same things that the other two did at her age. Marietta was very happy to have the family on a stable emotional level. I enjoyed coaching and found it easier to concentrate on my task of preparing our basketball team to win a fourth straight city championship.

We knew that in a short while it would be time to have Valeri examined to see if her red blood cell count had dropped significantly. After receiving the transfusions at St. Joseph's Hospital and Children's Hospital, her count was at a high of eleven grams. On several occasions Marietta and I discussed how to best help Valeri develop normally. This concern was on our minds continually.

Meanwhile, several events took place during these happy weeks. A group of friends learned that Valeri would need blood transfusions quite often, so they organized a blood drive. At that time it was customary to have a blood bank reserve to replace the number of pints of blood given to a specific patient. A good friend, Lambros Milonas, recruited some of the young people from our church and organized the blood drive. An article in the local newspaper disclosed the need for blood, and over one hundred people responded to the call. Of the hundred volunteers, less than fifty could give blood as a result of the restrictions made by the Red Cross.

Since I had Cooley's Anemia minor, and Marietta had minor anemia, we did not qualify as donors. This was very upsetting. Our daughter needed blood transfusions to combat her disease, and as her parents, we could not even help her by giving a single pint of blood.

One of the first to give blood was John Kastran, a dear friend, who later became her godfather. Bob Roehl, a friend and a fine sports referee living in the Detroit area also was quick to donate blood. My brother-in-law, George Backos, gave blood the first day and many times thereafter. All of the young people from our junior and senior Assumption Church basketball teams donated blood. Many members of our church softball team also offered to do so, as did our friends and relatives, my fellow teachers, and fans who followed our Eastern High School athletic teams. The fifty pints of blood were sufficient to last for many transfusions.

Marietta and I were grateful for the wonderful generosity on the part of all the donors. It was an eye-opener for us, realizing how helpful and kind people could be when called upon for assistance. We would experience such kindness several times during Valeri's life.

Other things that happened evolved around the advice we were given by people. Most suggested ways to help Valeri. However, one thoughtless person remarked: "It is too bad you have a daughter with a serious disease. She really cannot have much of a life."

"What do you think we should do?" I asked him.

He thought for a minute then answered, "I don't know."

"I know we can help her enjoy a relatively happy life!" I quickly responded.

Some relatives even thought that we should give Valeri whatever she wanted - so that she would stay happy! In the end, all of this advice was valuable, as it forced Marietta and me to do some deep soul-searching. We knew that Valeri would endure many obstacles in her lifetime. So, we agreed that the best way to help her was to treat her as though she was a normal child. We would encourage her to pursue an active life and to have high expectations of herself. We agreed that we would help keep her as healthy as possible, stay in touch with all current research, and expect her to uphold the same standards as other children. She must have an opportunity to have a life of her own. We also agreed to develop an optimistic attitude that a cure would be found. Life would be more fulfilling if she had to earn her way. We felt very comfortable with our decision.

We took time to explain our decision to Debra and Nikki, then added that Valeri would have to go to the hospital periodically to receive blood transfusions. We asked them to respect Valeri and each other, and to play and share with her. We could have a family life much like any other family. Both daughters were very receptive and seemed to have an excellent understanding of our plan.

The following day Marietta called Dr. Charbeneau's office and requested a conference with him and Dr. Rothman to help us in both short- and long-term planning. Marietta and I felt that we were ready to go on with our lives and that we could meet the challenges of everyday life constructively.

# 5

# The Bargain

URING the six weeks that followed the visit with Dr. Zuelzer at Children's Hospital, Val looked and acted healthy. She developed so well physically, emotionally, and socially that Marietta and I once again wondered if Valeri really had a physical problem. Maybe her condition had been misdiagnosed? Valeri appeared very normal during this time, and actually gained four pounds. This made us think that maybe the doctors were wrong. Perhaps Val had a temporary blood problem that had cleared up with the transfusions. Our hopes that perhaps she would outgrow her problem began to rise.

The next week, our hopes were dashed. Val began to look pale, and she was losing her appetite and energy. All of the doctors had told us that these were the symptoms indicating a loss of red blood cells and the need for a blood transfusion. These negative symptoms, plus others, were indicative of severe regression in her physical condition. It became apparent that we should make an appointment to visit Dr. Rothman to have her red blood cell count checked.

We visited Dr. Rothman the following day. The nurse took a blood sample, then placed it on a slide and inserted the slide into a small instrument that resembled a flashlight. This instrument made it possible for the nurse to determine the red blood cell count. After viewing the blood sample, she looked up and said, "Let's go into the next room and see Dr. Rothman."

Dr. Rothman looked at the results of the test and said, "The red blood count is down to six and a half grams. Remember, we want to keep Valeri between a seven and ten red blood cell count which would be a safe count for her, even though it is below a normal ten to fourteen count for the average child." So he called Dr. Charbeneau's office and made arrangements for Valeri to receive a blood transfusion at St. Joseph's Hospital the following day.

We went to the hospital the next morning and had her admitted for a transfusion, a trend which was to last for almost thirty years. Even though we knew what to expect, Marietta and I were very apprehensive. We were not sure what the protocol was nor what to expect from the medical staff.

A technician began the process by drawing four vials of blood from Valeri's right arm. I again thought: "Wow! Four big vials of blood from our little Valeri. That will certainly remove a lot of red blood cells from her small body." The next step was a waiting game. Nothing took place for a couple of hours until Dr. Charbeneau came in to give Val a physical examination. During the physical, Sister Jerome, a nun in charge of the Pediatric Ward, came into the room. (St. Joseph's Hospital was administrated by nuns for many years, until a non-sectarian group assumed the administration.)

Sister Jerome was assigned the task of inserting the IV needle into Valeri's hand in an attempt to find a vein for the blood to be transfused. This was a formidable task. Not only is it difficult to find a viable vein in a small child, but it is also difficult to keep the vein open for the length of time needed to complete the transfusion. Marietta and I were asked to leave the room when Sister Jerome was ready to begin her task. Valeri looked nervously at us as we left. We stood out in the hall near the doorway and heard Valeri begin to cry. A few minutes later, both Sister Jerome and Dr. Charbeneau came out of the room. She told us that the IV was in place and that we could go back into the room. Dr. Charbeneau explained that the blood was being prepared and that the transfusions would begin shortly. Val was scheduled for one pint of packed red blood cells, he said; then, he turned and left.

When we went into the room, Val was crying - so, Marietta picked her up and held her until she quieted down. While being held by Marietta, Valeri looked around the room, then at the IV pole which held a small bag of sodium chloride, which was dripping through a long tube to the needle that was inserted in her arm. The needle was held in place with two strips of tape and covered with a bandage. The expression on her face was interesting. She had a suspicious look that something was going to happen, and yet, a confident look that indicated that everything was going to be okay.

Preparation of the blood included removing the red cells from the plasma and placing the blood into a plastic receptacle to be fastened onto the IV stand. It was around noon when the pouch of blood was brought to the room and hooked onto the IV stand. The transfusion started.

During the next three hours Valeri ate her lunch and took a couple of naps. Marietta read a magazine and napped in her chair while I sat and designed some basketball plays for the team. My favorite pastime was to fiddle around with basketball offensive and defensive plays on paper.

Occasionally, I would look at the blood dripping into the tube that fed into Valeri's arm. The drip, drip, drip made me realize that with each drop of blood Valeri was getting stronger. It was her lifeline to health. At times I would count the drops per minute and then compute whether the transfusion was proceeding normally, too quickly or too slowly. A rate too fast could be dangerous for Valeri, and one too slow could allow the vein to shut down and the transfusion would terminate. If either took place, I would call the nurse immediately.

Marietta cried from time to time, seeing the needle stuck in Valeri's arm. Valeri would join her mother in crying, but both would stop after a few minutes and the situation would appear to be normal again.

The transfusion ended later that afternoon. The nurse closed off the valve that allowed the blood into the tubing and opened the valve permitting the sodium chloride to enter. This was done to keep the vein open, in case more blood was needed. A technician then drew a vial of blood from Valeri's arm. A short while later, the nurse closed the sodium chloride valve and removed the needle from Val's hand. Val was tired and she slept for a couple of hours. She regained her pink complexion, which made us happy.

After resting, Val ate her supper. Dr. Charbeneau called on Valeri later that evening and informed us that her blood count had jumped up to ten grams with one pint of red cells. He was pleased, because it appeared that she could do well with one pint of blood, which would minimize the danger of iron buildup at this time.

We had a lot of confidence in Dr. Charbeneau's judgment in keeping Valeri's gram count low. He felt that a buildup of iron caused by multiple transfusions would be less prominent if Val received fewer pints of blood per transfusion, thereby causing less damage to her vital organs over the years.

I asked Dr. Charbeneau if the low count was better than a high count, since it would reduce her energy level. He told us that he felt Valeri would do well with a low red blood cell count. He also said that she would not be as active as other children, but that she would find her own level of activity, just as water seeks its own level. All of his ideas sounded logical to us and we confidently agreed to abide by his decision.

Since this was the first transfusion under Dr. Charbeneau, he kept Valeri in the hospital overnight to make sure everything went the way he thought it should. He wanted to make sure there were no complications, such as a fever, a viral infection or an allergic reaction to the blood. Everything checked out fine when Dr. Charbeneau examined her the following morning. Marietta went to the hospital and brought Valeri home. Marietta, Debra, Nikki, and I were happy to see Val so active and affectionate.

The stage was set for a routine that was to be repeated over and over for many years. A loss of energy. A trip to the hospital. A blood test. A blood transfusion. Rest. A blood test to affirm a high blood count. A check for complications. Home to rest for a day. A return to a normal lifestyle. Then again, a loss of energy. We learned to accept this routine, and more importantly, Valeri accepted it. Our only problem was thinking about all the painful needles she had to endure.

We soon realized that the few weeks following a transfusion could be quite normal. Consequently, we felt compelled to take advantage of them. We encouraged Valeri to make the most of this opportunity and to live her life to its fullest. If we kept Valeri as healthy as possible and nurtured her emotionally and socially, we could help her enjoy a happy, normal life.

This routine went on for over a year-and-a-half with excellent results. Valeri developed nicely physically, emotionally, and socially; although as expected, her physical development was a little slower than normal for a child of her age. It was evident that our system was working quite well.

Marietta took Val to the hospital almost exclusively at that time, because I was working two jobs. I was a counselor at Pershing High School in Detroit and head basketball coach at Windsor University in Ontario, Canada, which was located across the Detroit River. Usually my day began at eight o'clock in the morning and ran into the late evening hours.

Even after three years, it was still common for Marietta to cry during the treatment process. Valeri would look and see her mother crying, and then she would also cry. During one of Valeri's transfusions, as she was lying in bed, Marietta began to cry. This upset Valeri and she also began to cry. Suddenly, Valeri looked up at her mother, who was sitting on a chair next to her bed, and she said: "MOM! IF YOU STOP CRYING, I'LL STOP CRYING."

Marietta looked at her and asked, "What did you say, Valeri?"

"Mom, if you stop crying, I'll stop crying," Valeri repeated.

Marietta immediately hugged Valeri for several seconds and kissed her. Then, she looked affectionately at Valeri and said, "Okay, honey! I will stop crying. That is a promise." And, they both stopped crying immediately. Marietta thought to herself: "Gosh, our darling little daughter gets upset when she sees me cry. I am not doing her justice and I shouldn't permit myself to display these emotions. Certainly, there will be times when I'll need to cry, but this is not one of them." Through the years, Marietta kept her promise. Although there were times she did cry, it was never again in the presence of Valeri.

Valeri and her mother had made a bargain, and Valeri too, did not cry anymore during her transfusions. She always found something useful to occupy her time, such as to color pictures, read a child's book, watch television, talk to a roommate, or play with a toy or game.

When Marietta told me what Valeri had said, I felt Valeri's was trying to say: "Let's move on. I have better things to do than to lie here feeling sorry for myself. Enough of this. Let's begin doing other things. This blood is going to help me. I feel sad when I see my mother cry. We should both try to be happy." Val had made a very profound statement. We had to count our many blessings. A treatment was available and we should move forward. There were many positive things to minimize the pain in our lives.

Valeri's comment helped me take a good look at my coaching philosophy and led me to develop one that helped me to become a much better coach and teacher. That philosophy was to place more emphasis on the proper priorities and to keep striving toward quality goals. Life, health, and death are the important things that keep everything in the proper perspective.

In the years to follow, Valeri's comment was also enlightening and inspirational to Marietta when she began a teaching profession, and for Debra and Nikki.

# 6

# *First Major Crisis*

A LTHOUGH there were several occasions when Valeri had to be hospitalized, most were for minor problems, such as a virus or cold - and usually only as a precautionary measure. Her first major crisis occurred a couple of months before her fourth birthday.

We noticed that Valeri's blood count was beginning to drop faster than usual. Instead of getting a transfusion every five weeks, she needed a transfusion every three weeks. Dr. Charbeneau decided that a test should be taken to see how her spleen was functioning.

The tests ordered by Dr. Charbeneau confirmed that the spleen had enlarged and was not functioning properly. It was not only destroying old cells, which was the spleen's primary function - it was also destroying defective new red blood cells, which were still useful. To make matters worse, the spleen would destroy the platelets, and some of the white blood cells. Dr. Charbeneau consulted with the chief hematologist at the hospital and decided that it was time to remove Valeri's spleen. He referred us to Dr. Peter Kane, a fine surgeon on staff at the hospital.

I arrived home that night after coaching the Windsor University basketball team, to find Marietta very upset and crying. "I talked to Dr. Kane concerning the operation," she said. "He wants to operate in about a week. He also mentioned that Valeri might not survive the operation. Complications during the operation could cause an infection, which could be toxic to her system and kill her."

Naturally, we were both upset by his comments. We decided to call Dr. Rothman. Needless to say, Dr. Rothman was not pleased. He said, "Marietta, do you think for one minute that I would permit Dr. Kane to perform this operation if Valeri's chances for survival were minimal? I am telling you that her chance for survival and the complete healing of her body is predictably one hundred percent." Both Marietta and I felt much better after speaking with Dr. Rothman.

The next morning Marietta called Dr. Charbeneau to relate her conversations with both doctors. Dr. Charbeneau reiterated what Dr. Rothman had said. He would talk with Dr. Kane, whom he considered more of an alarmist than most doctors. "But," he added, "Dr. Kane is an extremely competent surgeon."

We then made an appointment with Dr. Kane to determine the operation date. This time Dr. Kane told us that he felt quite sure that Valeri would survive the operation with limited problems. The operation was set to take place two days after our appointment.

Valeri entered the hospital the night before the operation for pre-surgery prepping. Horrendous thoughts went through our minds. We worried all night about our little daughter undergoing a major operation, and about the unknown future effects of losing her spleen.

We arrived at the hospital early in the morning to be with Valeri for a short time prior to the operation. The orderly brought in a stretcher, put her on it, and was ready to take her to the operating room. We both kissed her and promised that we would see her in a little while. Once again, she probably knew that something different was going on, but yet she had a look of confidence. Valeri gave us a big smile and was then wheeled down the hall to the operating room.

Marietta and I waited anxiously for over two hours. Wild thoughts ran through our minds. We were tremendously worried and extremely nervous when Dr. Kane suddenly appeared. He said, "Bob and Marietta, the operation was successful. Everything went well. Valeri is resting in the recovery room and you should be able to see her shortly." He then showed us the spleen that he had removed and wrapped in gauze. It was over eight inches long, compared to a normal three- or four-inch spleen.

Val was brought back to her room, where we were waiting. For drainage purposes she had a tube extending from her nose. To supply her with blood lost during the operation, she had an IV in her hand. Valeri was wide awake and had a panicky look in her eyes. She held out her hand for Marietta to hold. We both kissed her and told her that she was going to feel fine and strong again.

She looked at me with a faraway and dazed look, smiled, then closed her eyes and fell asleep. We sat at her bedside all afternoon as she slept. Later, we went to eat our evening meal.

I was bothered by the expression on Valeri's face when she returned to her room after the operation. How traumatic it must have been for her to undergo an operation of that magnitude. I could sympathize with children who had major health problems - and with their parents. How difficult it is for parents to see their children suffer during a major health catastrophe. Val's look haunted me for several days.

Shortly after we returned from our meal, Valeri awakened. Although she appeared to be uncomfortable, Val was alert and smiled at us quite often. Several relatives came to the hospital to see her, and also to give us moral support. Our daughters weren't allowed to come into the hospital, as children under twelve years of age were not permitted. Still, we called them several times to update them on what was happening. Most of our time was spent in the waiting room with our relatives, since only two visitors were allowed in Val's room at any one time. After everyone left, Marietta and I sat in Valeri's room until the late evening, as Valeri slept.

Valeri bounced back rapidly after her operation. Marietta would be with her all day and I would join her in the evening after basketball practice or in the afternoon if our team played at night. Many friends and family members visited Valeri. She seemed to respond nicely to seeing people. She was quite a "people person."

For the first three days following the operation, Valeri did not have much energy or appetite. Then suddenly on the fourth day, she became very active. That evening when Marietta offered her some jello from the restricted diet, Valeri pushed it away and said, "Mom, I want to eat good food, because I am hungry."

Her appetite had returned and she ate heartily during the rest of her hospital stay. A week after the operation Valeri was energetic, walking around the room and playing with the toys. Her appetite was excellent. She was alert and would ask about home and her sisters.

The nurse told Marietta earlier in the day that Dr. Kane planned to send Valeri home. Dr. Kane was very attentive, visiting and checking Valeri twice a day. After checking her, he said, "She is doing fine and can go home tomorrow."

"That's great!" I answered. "Can she resume normal activities soon?"

He responded, "Yes." A strange, sad look came over his face. After some hesitation he continued, "You know that children with Valeri's anemia only live to about ten years of age." This statement stunned both Marietta and me. Marietta asked him to explain his comment.

He said, "As the anemia causes havoc in the body, there will be many complications that will have an affect on her. I am telling you this, so that you know what to expect." We were both disheartened. I wondered if he knew something that the other physicians did not.

After he left, Dr. Charbeneau visited Valeri again. I told him what Dr. Kane had said. For the first and only time I can remember (and Dr. Charbeneau was Valeri's doctor for twenty-five years) he became excited, perturbed, and upset. His complexion turned bright red as he said, "I am Valeri's physician and I feel that what Dr. Kane said was out of order. I am going to mention it to him. I feel that with the continued use of transfusions we can keep Valeri as healthy as possible, and that she will enjoy many, many years of life. Please believe me when I tell you this." With that, he turned and walked away. Both Marietta and I felt confidence in Dr. Charbeneau and relieved with his prediction.

The following day Marietta thanked the hospital staff - especially Sister Fredericka - who had taken Sister Jerome's place as director of the Pediatric Ward a few months earlier. Sister Fredericka also was a very outstanding person and nurse.

Marietta took Valeri home. Val was very happy to be home again, smiling, laughing, and playing with her older sisters. They were also elated with Valeri's return and sensed that everything would be fine again.

A week later, Dr. Kane removed the stitches from the operation and told us that she was completely healed. The blood Valeri had received after the operation had boosted her blood count up to eleven, and it showed in the ensuing weeks when she seemed to make great physical progress.

However, there were times during those weeks when I thought of a comment Dr. Zuelzer had made years before: "The sooner a patient has a spleen removed, the more serious the anemia." This thought stayed in the back of my mind for a long period of time, but I was very optimistic that he could be wrong. Our job was to do what Dr. Charbeneau had said - to keep her as healthy and happy as possible and to hope for the best. I figured our commitment was to focus on Dr. Charbeneau's comment.

With her Mother's excellent cooking and superior care, the love of her family and friends, and a happy play routine with her sisters, Valeri enjoyed good health for several months after her splenectomy. The high red blood count made it easier for her to keep up with everything happening around her. She bounced around, having the time of her life.

# 7

# A Fun Trip

OUR life was going along beautifully. My newly-published book, *Blitz Basketball*, was selling at a best-seller rate. The basketball season at Windsor University ended with our team again winning the National Canadian College Championship. It was time to prepare for our trip to Maryland University so that I could participate in the Guidance Counseling Institute. Marietta, as usual, did all of the planning and preparation for the trip. Shortly after the school semester ended in June, we packed everything into our 1964 Pontiac and the family headed for Maryland.

Prior to leaving, Valeri received three pints of blood - raising her blood count to over twelve grams. This insured that she would not need any blood for the seven weeks we would be gone.

Our drive to Maryland was enjoyable. We played various games with the children, and the scenery was picturesque. I noticed that Valeri really enjoyed travelling. Her lovely big eyes became even bigger when she saw different things along the way. She was fascinated by the farm animals, farms, bridges, tall buildings in the cities, and the rivers. This first trip set the stage for her love of travelling later on in life.

We arrived at College Park and located the mobile home which was to be our home for the next seven weeks. It was so long that it had two flats. Each flat contained a small kitchen, a living room and two bedrooms. Just by accident, no one had rented the other flat, so we had the entire trailer to ourselves. It gave us an opportunity to invite some of our friends to come and visit us for a few days during our stay.

Each day while I attended classes Marietta went through her household chores and visited with other counselors' wives and children. Our daughters visited the local pond with the other children. It was interesting and exciting for Marietta and me to see Valeri take part in the activities with her sisters and the other youngsters. She loved the pond and often returned home with wet clothes, just like her sisters. Marietta said Valeri enjoyed watching the frogs and other little animals that visited the pond, along with throwing rocks into the water, etc. We ate out every day and evening. The children enjoyed being served many tasty meals.

Often during the evenings, we travelled to Washington, D.C. to see the sights. There were so many beautiful and historic places for us to visit. The White House and Capitol and the Washington, Lincoln and Franklin Memorials were very interesting, as were the Washington Zoo, the Smithsonian Museum, and so many other sites. Our children enjoyed them all.

One of the highlights of the trip was when we decided to go to the top of the Washington Memorial. On hot evenings we often sat at the base of the Memorial and people-watched. One evening, however, we decided it was time to climb to the top! We boarded the elevator, which took us only part way. Then we had to climb the stairs to reach the top. I carried Valeri because I felt it was too difficult for her to climb the several hundred steps. When we arrived at the top, I noticed how much Valeri enjoyed the view. I was elated to know that she was having such a good time.

Another highlight was when Jim and Ann Skuras and their daughter, Rena visited us for a week. All of us "did our thing." I attended school and played golf with Jim; Marietta and Ann went shopping; Debra and Nikki played with the neighbor's children; and Valeri and Rena played together. All of us spent a wonderful week together.

Soon after the Skurases left, the Cheolas family visited. Nick and Christine brought their children Steve (Debra's age) and Nancy (Nikki's age). During their stay we visited the Naval Academy. The children enjoyed seeing the midshipmen and watching the ships enter and leave the harbor. After the Cheolases left, Marietta's cousin, Jim Panagis, stayed in the flat. He was wonderful company and we did many things together.

It seemed that the seven weeks flew by and it was time to start for home. We had so many enjoyable moments on that trip, that we actually forgot about Valeri's health problems. We would usually end our evenings by buying the homemade ice cream from the College Dairy. It was the best ice cream we had ever tasted.

One thing stood out in my mind: Valeri was a real tiger on the trip. In fact, some children couldn't keep up with her. I realized that when she had a relatively high red blood count, there was no holding her down.

The children talked about their trip to Maryland for many years. The model was set for us to plan frequent trips.

# 8

# Early Happenings - Painful and Happy

ONE of the first sad occurrences to take place in Valeri's life was the death of my stepfather, William (Vasilio) Samaras. This happened in January 1966. He enjoyed playing with our three daughters and had a close bond with each of them. Marietta had taken the girls to visit their grandparents a couple of evenings before he died. After his fatal heart attack, my mother told us how he had played with Valeri that evening. They both had a good time.

Only Debra and Nikki attended the wake and funeral. We felt that it would be better for Valeri to remember her grandfather when he was still living. Valeri asked what happened to her Pa Poo (grandfather in Greek) and was told that he went to heaven and wouldn't be with us anymore. She accepted this explanation, but was saddened by his death.

Later that spring our family went to Grand Bend, Canada, to spend Memorial Day weekend with Jim and Ann Skuras, and their daughter, Rena, and John and Dolly Kastran (Valeri's godparents), and their three daughters Nikki, Diane, and Lydia. A couple of years earlier all of us had started the tradition of spending Memorial Day, the Fourth of July and Labor Day weekends at a cottage we rented from Jim Skuras' friend. The six adults and eight children were all comfortable in the cottage, even though several children slept on the floor in sleeping bags. On occasion other families would visit for a day or two, which only added to the festivities. The Grand Bend experience continued until Valeri and Rena were in their late teens.

The good thing about Grand Bend was that each individual had something to do. The men would go golfing. Occasionally the women would golf, but typically they spent more time on the beach or shopping in the interesting stores. The older children spent time on the beach and attended the carnival in town or went on hikes. The two young ones, Valeri and Rena, would play on the swing set in the backyard or go to the beach with an adult. There were many times when everyone went to town as a group. The evenings were highlighted with a cookout, with everyone present. Later, all of us would sing around a fire or do our own thing again until it was time to retire.

It happened that on the Sunday before Labor Day the men were out golfing, the women were grocery shopping and the older children had journeyed to town to the public beach. Valeri and Rena were left alone to play on the swing in the backyard. They were both told by their mothers not to go to the beach until an adult had returned. The two girls were well-disciplined and could be trusted to be alone.

It wasn't until several years later that we found out what had happened to Rena and Valeri that afternoon, while they were home alone. Both girls were playing on the swing set in the back yard. Valeri got off the swing to play with another toy. Rena, meanwhile, had decided to see how high she could swing. Valeri watched Rena go higher and higher. Suddenly, the swing set tipped over, trapping Rena underneath the heavy bars of the set. A support bar was on her chest and another was on her neck. Rena couldn't breathe. She was being choked by the bar on her neck. Rena's eyes bulged. She tried to lift the heavy swing set, but to no avail. Meanwhile, Valeri saw Rena struggling to get free and ran over and grabbed the swing set. Valeri tried to lift it up, but the set was extremely heavy and too difficult for her to lift, especially since she was shorter and lighter than most children her age. On her first attempt, Val could not lift the set high enough to free Rena. Valeri screamed for help, but there was no one else around. She then grabbed the bar again and strained with all of her strength to lift the set. Somehow, Val managed to lift the set high enough for Rena to quickly slide out from beneath the bar that was choking her. Valeri had saved Rena's life.

They both regained their composure. Rena was bruised, but not hurt seriously. They decided not to tell us what had happened, fearing that they wouldn't be allowed to play together by themselves anymore, which they enjoyed immensely. Later, they tried to lift up the set, but couldn't. In fact, Rena found that she couldn't lift the set by herself, even though she was bigger and stronger than Valeri. Later that evening, Jim and John picked up the set and stabilized it in another part of the yard. Rena enjoyed telling the story many times during her adult life.

In September 1966 Valeri began kindergarten at Roxana Park Elementary School in East Detroit. She loved attending school from her first day in kindergarten, and her affection for education remained with her throughout her life. She enjoyed the teachers, the activities, the administrator, and the children. The only time she missed school was when her health forced her to stay away or when she had to go to the hospital for a transfusion. Actually, she was an outstanding student and her attendance was excellent considering all of her health problems.

When Valeri began attending kindergarten, she was doing well physically. At this time, she was receiving transfusions of one pint of blood almost monthly. They kept her blood between a seven- and nine-gram count. Although we tried to observe her energy level to make sure she wasn't run-down physically, there was one time when we waited too long before having her blood checked.

Although Valeri's complexion was pinkish, which was an indication that her blood count was normal, she complained that her teeth hurt. We thought perhaps it was a cavity, so we contacted our dentist, Dr. Emmanuel (Manny) Rothis, my friend for many years. We told him about the pain Valeri was experiencing. He told us to bring her in immediately, which we did. Val did have a cavity in a tooth which he proceeded to fill. Dr. Rothis mentioned that her gums appeared gray, which was an indication of a low red blood cell count. He suggested we have her checked immediately, as he knew of Valeri's anemia.

Shortly after leaving Dr. Rothis' office, the anesthetic had worn off and Valeri began crying because of the pain in her gums. We called Dr. Charbeneau from home. He wasn't in his office but his answering service notified him. (We could call Dr. Charbeneau anytime and he would return our call shortly. He always kept an open line of communication for us to call him about any problem Valeri might encounter.)

Shortly after our call, Dr. Charbeneau contacted us and we informed him of Valeri's symptom of pain in the gums. He told us to give Valeri a Tylenol®, let her rest at home, and bring her into the hospital for a blood test in the morning. If necessary, she would receive a transfusion the following day.

We took Valeri to the hospital in the morning. Her blood test showed a red cell count of 3.1. This was extremely dangerous. She was rushed into a hospital room and given two pints of blood. Dr. Charbeneau discussed the danger of allowing her blood count to drop too low. One was possible heart failure. Sometimes the red cells transfused into Valeri's body would be mature, meaning that many of the cells would die off much earlier than the potential 120 days of life for a young blood cell. Perhaps that was why Valeri's blood count dropped so low, because there were too many adult blood cells. Needless to say, we vowed to never become careless again about having her blood tested. Val felt much better after the transfusion and returned home that evening.

In January 1968, Valeri returned to school after the holidays. One morning later that week, as I was working at Pershing High School as a counselor, I received a telephone call from Marietta. She informed me that Valeri had slipped and fallen on the wet floor in the school hallway and had fractured her right arm near her shoulder. Marietta had called Dr. Charbeneau and he made arrangements for Dr. Stanton, an orthopedic surgeon, to treat the injury.

That afternoon, instead of going to Windsor University to coach the basketball team, I went home to determine what had happened to Valeri and to see how Dr. Stanton was treating her injury. I always found it difficult to concentrate on anything other than helping take care of Valeri whenever an emergency occurred. Upon arriving home, I found that Valeri was already there. She was sitting on the couch with a full body cast on her upper body and upper arm. A full body cast was necessary because the upper part of the humerus bone was fractured and the upper body cast was the only way to immobilize the bone. There was our little darling with yet another health problem.

After a single day's rest at home, Valeri insisted on returning to school. So, the next morning she did. Fortunately, except for a little inconvenience, Valeri adjusted to her injury and kept moving along in school academically, without allowing her injury to affect her performance. The cast, with many signatures on it, was removed two months later. Valeri regained full use of her arm in a short period of time.

Soon after her injury, the inevitable happened. Valeri was due for a transfusion, and her mother informed her that she would have to go to the hospital the following day. The next morning when it was time for Marietta to take her to the hospital, Valeri looked at her and said, "I am not going to the hospital." She continued, "Debra doesn't go to the hospital. Nikki doesn't go. You don't go. And Dad doesn't go. So, I am not going to go, either. I am not going to get blood. Why do I have to go?" So she sat on the couch, folded her arms, and stared into Marietta's eyes with a determined look.

Marietta, a quick thinker, carefully selected her words. She said, "You have a problem that we don't have. It can be a serious problem, but with blood transfusions you can be healthy just like the rest of us. I am sorry that you have the problem, but the transfusions can keep you strong and healthy. It is like the little girl in your class with sugar diabetes. You know that she has to inject herself with a needle and give herself insulin every day to stay healthy. She has the misfortune to be a victim of sugar diabetes and her brothers and sisters are not. But she is willing to accept the shots of insulin every day to remain healthy. You have to receive blood from time to time to be healthy, just as she needs her shots. I know it doesn't seem fair, but it keeps your body strong by keeping your red blood cell count elevated to the proper level. We all love you so much we want to help you continue to be healthy and strong. It is the only way. You have been wonderful to be so cooperative."

Valeri stared at her mother for a couple of minutes while she thought over what had been said. Then, Valeri answered reluctantly, "Okay, I guess if I have to go, I will go."

Marietta thought about Valeri's comment several years earlier: "Mom, I'll stop crying, if you stop crying." Val went to the hospital with her mother, and she never again questioned why she had to go. She just seemed to make up her mind: "If I have to go, I have to go." It seemed that she just wanted to receive first-hand rationale as to why she was different and to ask if there was an alternative to her problem other than to have the blood transfusions.

I left my positions as secondary school counselor at Pershing High School and head basketball coach at Windsor University in the fall of 1968 to accept a position as head baseball coach and assistant professor of Health and Physical Education at Wayne State University. We decided that if I accepted the position at Wayne State University, then Marietta could teach full-time in the East Detroit Public School system, as she had a strong desire to return to teaching.

This change in work schedules allowed me to drive Valeri to school in the morning and Marietta could pick her up afterward, since the school where Marietta taught was only five minutes away from Valeri's school. It also meant that I could see Valeri every morning. I would have the opportunity to see how she was feeling, and to spend more time with her each day.

That December I decided to take our family to Florida to enjoy the warm sunshine for two weeks during the Christmas holidays. We drove down in an automobile borrowed from a driveway company. They furnished the gas and oil, and my job was to deliver the car to the owner in Miami Beach, Florida. It was free transportation to Florida.

The trip down was hard because we ran into a terrible snow and ice storm in Tennessee. Eventually, the weather cleared and we had no more trouble driving the next two days. We stayed in Miami Beach on the Atlantic Ocean.

It was a fun-filled vacation and we spent many hours on the beach, swimming and sunning. Valeri developed a nice tan. She enjoyed the waves in the ocean and spent many hours in the water. Swimming was one of Valeri's loves. It was the second time she swam in the Atlantic Ocean, the other being at a beach in Baltimore during our Maryland experience three years earlier.

Our return trip was to be by airplane, since the car I drove down was kept by the owner for his four-month stay in Florida. The day we were scheduled to leave was the first time it rained while we were in Florida. We arrived at the airport an hour before our flight. To pass some time, Valeri and I went outside for a walk to watch the planes taking off. After we saw two of them, Valeri looked up at me and said, "Dad, I am afraid to fly in an airplane."

She had a frightened look in her eyes. I sat down and put her on my lap and explained how airplanes fly, and how safe and comfortable they are. We then joined the others and boarded the plane. Once on board, I asked the flight attendant if the children could look in the cockpit prior to take-off. She said, "Of course, come with me," and led the three girls and myself to the cockpit.

The pilot greeted them and showed us the instrument panel. He talked to us for a couple of minutes before the flight attendant escorted us back to our seats in preparation for flight. The girls were very excited on the take-off. It was the first flight for Debra and Nikki, too. All three enjoyed the trip immensely. They were especially impressed with the fact that it took us three days to drive to Florida, but only three hours to fly back home.

The next couple of years went along smoothly for all of us, especially Valeri. She developed a normal growth pattern and her energy level was usually high. Except for an occasional viral infection, she was healthy. In fact, Valeri seemed to be the last member of the family to contract a viral or bacterial infection.

Her schooling was progressing very well. Her grades were excellent and the teachers were very complimentary of her as a student and as a young lady. Valeri's good friend Kathleen Ritter, who lived next door, switched from St. Basil's Elementary to Roxana Park Elementary. As I drove both of them to school it was interesting to hear them share their interests and ideas. Since Kathleen was having difficulty learning multiplication tables, Valeri decided to help Kathleen learn them, as the other children were making fun of Kathleen. So, every morning on the way to school Valeri would quiz Kathleen and explain the multiplication tables to her. She did a fine job of teaching; Kathleen soon learned the tables to perfection. They had a great deal of fun together on our morning rides, as well as on other occasions.

One morning I told Valeri and Kathleen to wait in the car while I ran an errand. When I returned and opened the door - I was shocked! The radio was on full blast, the heater was turned up to maximum heat, and both the windshield wipers and lights were turned on! I didn't know what to turn off first. When quiet and order were restored, Valeri and Kathleen laughed hysterically. Finally, Valeri said, "Dad, I wish you could have seen the expression on your face when you entered the car."

"Okay, now I owe one to you both," I replied.

Valeri celebrated her tenth birthday in an unusual manner. We had a party for her and invited our relatives, John and Dolly Kastran, the Skuras family - Jim, Ann, Billy and Rena - and a couple of her friends. After singing and cutting the cake, Valeri, Rena and Kathleen went to Valeri's bedroom to play.

While the adults were visiting in the living room we heard Valeri scream. It was a painful, ringing scream. Rena came running into the living room and said, "Something is sticking in Valeri's knee!"

I jumped off the chair and raced into the bedroom to see what it was. I was surprised to see a needle with some thread in it sticking in her knee. Valeri was crying. Apparently she had been on her knees playing a game, when the needle lodged itself in her knee. (Earlier that year, we had installed shag carpeting throughout the house, which was a mistake as anything we dropped would be difficult to find, especially small items.)

"Let me look at it, Valeri," I said. She turned her knee toward me so that I could get a good view of the needle and thread. I gently touched the needle. It was deeply imbedded and would not dislodge easily. I told Marietta to call Dr. Charbeneau, which she did. He told us to take Valeri to emergency immediately and not to touch the needle.

We bid everyone farewell and took Valeri to the Emergency Room at St. Joseph's Hospital. A doctor in the Emergency Room took one look at the needle and said, "I am not going to touch this needle because it is imbedded too deeply. Instead, I will call Dr. Peter Kane (the fine surgeon who removed Valeri's spleen) and ask his advice." He made the call and requested help. Dr. Kane arrived at the hospital about an hour later.

Dr. Kane examined the needle in Valeri's knee and said, "I think we better operate tomorrow morning."

Valeri was admitted into the hospital and placed in a room. A nurse put a cute note on the needle which said, "Please do not attempt to remove the needle from the patient's knee." She feared that a nurse on the next shift might try to dislodge the needle. Actually, Valeri spent most of the evening laughing about the needle, thread, and note. Out of curiosity, many nurses and patients visited Valeri's room to see the little girl's "knee-needle."

The next morning Marietta and I arrived at the hospital early so that we could be with Valeri before she went into the operating room. She was still laughing about the needle and the attention she had received during the night.

Dr. Kane performed the operation. He came to the waiting room to inform us that everything was fine and that Valeri was in the recovery room. The needle was in fact imbedded deeply into the bone. Luckily, it was removed without any complications, even though Valeri's bones were more brittle than other childrens' as a result of her anemia. "Her knee was fine," he said, "and she should not have any problems."

He examined Valeri's knee that evening and sent her home the following day. Valeri mentioned on the way home how nice Dr. Kane was and that she appreciated his special effort to take care of her. Although the knee was sore for a few days, she had no further problems and the incident was soon forgotten.

Over the years Valeri established a pattern of working hard to complete a task successfully; she enjoyed being challenged. This pattern was used in school, social, sport, and recreational activities. In many cases, her participation in sports was limited, but she wanted to try everything, even if it was on a limited basis. Dr. Charbeneau was exactly right when he said many years before, "She will find her own level of activity."

Valeri worked hard at learning new games and sports, albeit at a slower pace. She loved swimming, ice skating, roller skating, kick-ball, and other children's games. Running was difficult for Valeri, as she didn't have the stamina to run very far or very fast. In school, when an activity was too strenuous, the teacher would make her the official score keeper. She loved gym class.

Valeri developed a fondness for sports, especially for basketball. I often took Valeri and her sisters to sporting events, including many basketball games. One day Valeri asked if I would teach Kathleen, Suzy, and her how to shoot a basketball. I said I would. (A couple of years earlier, I had installed a backboard and rim on our garage.) I began teaching the three of them how to shoot, beginning with the same shot that I taught my elementary school children when I was a physical education teacher at Richard Elementary School in Detroit. That shot was accomplished by holding the ball with both hands with the arms extended down between the legs and knees bent. Then, with a vigorous motion, the arms would be brought up toward the basket, while releasing the ball.

The other two girls, being bigger and stronger than Valeri, could easily reach the rim (which was set at ten feet off the surface). They even came close to making a few baskets. Valeri could only throw the ball about two feet over her head - and that took a supreme effort. The first lesson ended.

I continued to work with Valeri several times after that. She learned the shooting technique, but still could only manage to propel the ball approximately four feet above her head. One afternoon, when Valeri was practicing with Suzy, Kathleen, and a couple of other small girls from the neighborhood, I walked out to them and said, "Tell you what, Val. I will give you ten dollars when you make your first basket."

It was interesting watching Valeri practice her shooting from time to time. She was getting the ball higher and higher into the air, but I felt my money was safe for the time being. Ten dollars was quite a sum of money at that time. Meanwhile all of her girlfriends would occasionally make baskets.

One summer afternoon, while I was writing an article on basketball in our basement, I heard screaming in the backyard. It was an excited scream and I thought to myself, "I wonder what happened?" As I was running up the stairs, the side door suddenly opened. Before I could reach it, Kathleen Ritter screamed: "Mr. Samaras! Mr. Samaras! Valeri made a basket! Valeri made a basket!"

I went outside the door into the backyard where Valeri and the other girls were standing. The girls continued to yell, "Valeri made a basket! Valeri made a basket!" Valeri had a big smile on her face and her eyes were lit up. Then the girls in unison said, "You owe Valeri ten dollars. You owe Valeri ten dollars!"

They finally quieted down enough for me to speak. I was smiling from ear to ear when I said, "Okay, I'm going in the house to get my wallet to pay Valeri the ten dollars." I went in, picked up my wallet, took out a ten dollar bill and went back outside. I then made a formal ceremony of presenting the money to Valeri. I announced, "It is with pride and joy that I offer this ten dollars to Valeri, in full payment for her first basket." I then hugged and kissed her, and said, "Let me see how you did it, Valeri." We all followed her to the basket and watched her make two baskets out of three attempts. All of us clapped. I was thrilled to give her the reward, considering how hard and long she had worked to achieve her goal.

Baskets came easily for Valeri after that day. She became a good shooter. In fact, it cost me one hundred dollars a couple of years later when she attended one of the sessions at my Bob Samaras Basketball Camp at Notre Dame High School in Harper Woods. Valeri was shooting baskets, while I was nearby talking to Walter Studinger, a high school coach, prior to starting a session. Valeri yelled to me, "Hey, Dad! How much will you give me if I make a basket?"

"Ten dollars," I replied. Meanwhile, Walt and I continued our discussion. I saw Valeri make a basket and hollered out, "Double or nothing, Val." She made another basket and I called, "Ten dollars more or nothing, Val." She made another basket. I then said, "Keep going, Val, same bet." I was then distracted by a couple of players and didn't pay much attention to Valeri; although I heard her saying fifty, sixty, seventy, eighty and ninety. Suddenly it occurred to me that she was making consecutive baskets. I said, "Hey, Valeri! What's going on?"

"You owe me ninety dollars, Dad," she said.

"Ninety dollars," I repeated. "I tell you what, Valeri. Let's make it a hundred dollars or nothing." She nodded her head in agreement. By now there was a crowd of players watching.

She picked up the ball and repeated, "One hundred dollars or nothing." She aimed the ball, shot, and it went swish! through the hoop. She jumped up and down with glee and the players all cheered.

I then said, "Okay, Valeri, one more shot for double or nothing."

She looked at me and said, "Thanks for the offer, Dad, but I will settle for a hundred dollars. No use in getting greedy." All eyes were on me to hear my answer.

"Okay, Sweetheart, you earned it. One hundred dollars it is."

I made good on my bet a week later, when I gave Valeri one hundred dollars to go to Eastland Shopping Center to buy some clothes. I was always so proud of her moment, too. Valeri felt such happiness whenever she succeeded at a task. The gratified look on her face was always one of the joys in my life.

# 9

# An Angel's Voice

I T IS interesting how we learn about important things in life by accident. That is how I discovered the existence of the Thalassemia Blood Clinic at Cornell University Center in New York, and its director, Dr. Virginia Canale. She had more clinical knowledge about Thalassemia than anyone else I had met.

Each year our baseball team would travel to New York City to compete against Long Island, St. John's, and Fordham Universities. In the spring of 1972, as we were returning home from the competition, Bill Kriefeldt, our sports information director at Wayne State, was sitting next to me, scanning a newspaper. (Bill would buy any newspaper he could find and scan it for information regarding sports and local news).

He looked up and said, "Hey Bob, look at this article." He handed me the newspaper. I looked at the picture and article, and read the caption under the picture. It said that Dr. Virginia Canale, the Director of the Transfusion Clinic at Cornell University Center, helped many victims of Thalassemia and their parents. They were treating over one hundred patients. In my excitement, I had to read the article twice before I could comprehend it. In the article, Dr. Canale talked about the functions of the Clinic, the disease itself, the victims of the disease, and their parents. The types of treatments were highlighted, and the article stated that Dr. Canale welcomed calls from any victim or parents of victims.

The article explained how the victims would enter the outpatient clinic early in the morning, receive a blood test, then be transfused, checked physically, and sent home - all in the same day. It also stated that a night clinic was available for the convenience of the victims who attended college or worked during the day. Key to the operation of the Clinic was a hot line to be used for emergencies and to contact Dr. Canale anytime of the day or night.

The final point made in the article was extremely important. It was about the "washing of the blood" to prevent reactions during a transfusion. Reactions to blood were common during transfusions, and Valeri had had her share. When this happened, the transfusion had to be stopped either temporarily or completely. Not only was it frightening, but it was very uncomfortable for Valeri. The symptoms would include chills, fever, nausea, and some swelling in the arm. "Washing of the blood" was a system of cleaning the bacteria by adding saline solutions to the blood. This system was put into effect at St. Joseph's Hospital a short time later, which eliminated further reactions to the blood by Valeri.

I was thrilled by this marvelous article. Now I knew that there was a hospital where many Thalassemia patients were treated. It meant that Dr. Canale and her staff had a wealth of information about this disease: its complications, the treatments for these complications, the physical development of the victims, and the progression and prognosis of the disease.

I felt the Clinic could be a great source of information for Marietta and me, and for Dr. Charbeneau, especially when medical problems arose. I would be able to telephone Dr. Canale to receive an accurate assessment of any problem, for my peace of mind. I was always grateful to Bill Kriefeldt for giving me the article.

Although I didn't call Dr. Canale immediately upon arriving home, I did have occasion to do it a few months later. It was October of that same year when Valeri began showing signs of being exceptionally run down and tired. As usual, we began to worry and wondered what problem she was experiencing. It appeared to be a virus, but when Dr. Charbeneau examined her he couldn't find anything wrong.

A couple of days later, Val's complexion looked paler and yellowish. I called Dr. Charbeneau and was told to bring her to his office immediately. After examining her, he concluded that Valeri appeared to be slightly jaundiced. Jaundice is associated with liver problems. I became very concerned, as I remembered that the anemia would affect the liver, glands, and the heart. The doctor gave us a prescription for medication and sent us home. He wanted Marietta and me to observe Valeri, and to inform him immediately if she continued to display this condition, as it would mean that hospitalization was necessary.

On the way home, Valeri and I were conversing about her not feeling well and about what the doctor had said. Valeri then changed the topic of conversation to my deceased stepfather and cemeteries. She asked if, in the near future, we could take a ride to the cemetery where her grandfather was buried. I questioned why she wanted to visit her grandfather's grave. She answered, "I don't know, Dad. I guess I just want to see what it is like. I have never been to a cemetery before." Although I wondered what her thoughts were, I assured her we would visit the cemetery someday.

That evening Valeri's jaundice worsened. Marietta called Dr. Charbeneau early the next morning and was told to take her to the hospital for tests. Both Marietta and I escorted Valeri to the hospital and stayed with her all day, while she underwent a series of blood tests, x-rays and a liver function test.

By the time Marietta and I arrived home that evening, we were extremely upset and worried. I decided to telephone Dr. Canale in New York. I made the call and found that she was not available, but that she would call us back soon. It was around midnight when the phone awakened us. It was Dr. Canale. In a very pleasant and friendly voice she said, "This is Dr. Canale. You called me regarding your daughter. How can I be of help?" I explained what had happened to Valeri. She replied, "Oh, don't worry about a thing. It sounds like hepatitis. Our children all acquire hepatitis from time to time, usually as a result of the blood, or sometimes it is caused by the needle used for the transfusion. In fact, they can even turn yellowish right in front of your eyes. It is frightening, but not serious, and it should pass in a week or so with rest and an antibiotic. You should not be too concerned. The liver is a very sturdy organ with great recuperative powers. It will heal very nicely after this infection has subsided."

Listening to Dr. Canale was like hearing an angel from heaven speak! To hear her explain Valeri's condition so reassuringly alleviated our fears and put us at ease instantaneously. I thanked her profusely. Dr. Canale encouraged me to call anytime I felt a need and also suggested that I have Dr. Charbeneau do the same.

The next day I told Dr. Charbeneau about the phone call. He said fine, but he would continue to do some further testing and keep Valeri in the hospital for a few days. A week later, as Dr. Canale had predicted, Valeri recovered and was released from the hospital.

I wrote a letter to Dr. Canale, thanking her for giving me the medical information and advice. I also sent her a picture of Valeri and a $25.00 donation. A few days later, I received a brief letter from her in which she wrote:

> *Thank you for the check. I shall use it to buy some sweets for the Halloween party we will be having in the transfusion clinic next week as the children receive their transfusions. From the photograph, Valeri appears to be a rather healthy child. Her facial features are not very prominent which indeed is an asset to her. I put her picture on my bulletin board with all of my other children.*

It was my feeling that the pipeline I had established with Dr. Canale would be vital in helping us care for Valeri. I decided to correspond with her by phone or letter intermittently, to ask if Valeri was progressing normally, if there were any new discoveries in treating the disease, what problems to expect, how to cope with various physical problems, and if Dr. Charbeneau was pursuing the proper care for each problem. Dr. Canale always responded immediately by mail and answered all of my questions. This contact gave Marietta and me considerable peace of mind for the next several years.

In November 1972, I read an article about the Cornell University Center Thalassemia Transfusion Clinic in the health section of *Time* magazine, which included comments from Dr. Canale about the nature of the disease. The article stated that a thirty-year-old woman was the oldest living patient at the clinic with Thalassemia. This was encouraging to us. Although the average life span for people with this disease was eighteen years, it indicated to us that it was possible for a victim to live past the age of thirty.

When I wrote to Dr. Canale in the summer of 1976, I did not receive a response. It seemed strange, but I didn't bother to follow up until the next summer, as Val was doing quite well. I wanted information concerning the Vitamin E experiment in England. Several weeks later, I received a response from a Dr. Alicejohn Markenson, who introduced himself as the new director of the Thalassemia Transfusion Clinic. He informed me that Dr. Canale had gone to Italy to marry a medical doctor from that country and planned to live there. I never heard from her again, but I always felt she was continuing to help people with problems with that wonderful "voice-from-an-angel-in-heaven" telephone call.

# 10

# Sports, Travel, and Fun

A S Valeri neared her eleventh birthday, her health was generally very good. Her transfusion regimen was changed from one to two pints. This was predictable, since she was growing physically and her body needed more red blood cells for her to remain healthy and strong. Dr. Charbeneau told us that with the onset of puberty, we could expect Valeri to need three pints per transfusion.

In March 1972, just before entering the hospital for a transfusion, Valeri contracted a cold. She was always most susceptible to infections when her blood count was low. Dr. Charbeneau prescribed an antibiotic for her. After several days, the symptoms became more pronounced and she appeared to be tired. Her temperature reached 103 degrees and her chest hurt when she coughed.

We immediately took Valeri to the hospital that afternoon. By evening, she was a very sick youngster. Obviously, the antibiotic wasn't working. A culture was taken to find what pathogenic organisms were affecting her. Two days later the diagnosis was reported. Valeri had a case of pneumonia. The culture test identified the exact organisms, and a new antibiotic was prescribed. When we were told it was pneumonia, Marietta and I became very frightened, as we knew that pneumonia was considered life-threatening to a Thalassemia victim.

After Valeri had been on the new antibiotic for three days, she was smiling and able to sit in a chair. It was heartening to see her feeling so well. After receiving her scheduled blood transfusion, Valeri was released from the hospital.

This was the first time Valeri contracted pneumonia, although she would contract it again on two other occasions. Each time we worried excessively because of the danger of this disease. (Fortunately, many years later a vaccine was discovered that eliminated the most common type of pneumonia and diminished Valeri's chances of contracting it again.)

I was happy that Valeri recovered rapidly from her bout with pneumonia, as our Wayne State University baseball team was going to Jacksonville, Florida for eight days to train for the upcoming season. I had planned to take my three daughters with me, since I knew they would love to go to the Sunshine State during their spring vacation from school. All of the plans were in place. Marietta would stay home and the girls would enjoy a vacation in warm weather while watching the baseball games. Debra was designated to be responsible for caring for her sisters when I was busy working with the team. She was very reliable, and Nikki and Valeri were very cooperative.

We flew to Florida. I loved having my daughters with me. All three enjoyed attending the baseball games. They also spent a lot of time swimming in the pool at the motel, and we took several trips to the carnival on the ocean beach, only ten miles away. For Valeri, the highlight of the trip was learning more about baseball, and getting to know the baseball players. Several players enjoyed kidding her and playing shuffleboard with her and her sisters. All in all, it was an outstanding experience for the girls.

In June 1972, we moved to a house in Grosse Pointe Woods. It was a lovely, large colonial home with four bedrooms. The house was much larger than our ranch home in East Detroit. The one thing that disturbed me about our new home was the stairs. I felt they could be very tiring for Valeri to climb up and down. But she didn't seem to mind and never complained.

Valeri enrolled in the Ferry Elementary School, and Debbie and Nikki attended Grosse Pointe North High School. Valeri enjoyed attending Ferry School and made a rapid adjustment to a much larger school than Roxana Park, her former school in East Detroit. She enjoyed the teachers, classmates, and multiple activities.

Although Valeri soon made many new friends at school, she missed Kathleen Ritter, Suzy Ricevuto and others from the old neighborhood. So, we had her friends from there visit Val often that first year, and we also took Valeri back to visit them. Of course, Rena Skuras visited often, as did Valeri's cousins Dean and Nick Backos. Valeri was a gregarious youngster and enjoyed being with friends. With continuous visits from her friends and cousins, Valeri adjusted to our new neighborhood.

With the arrival of the football season, Valeri and I found a use for the big living room. It made a perfect football field. I loved watching football and Valeri and her sisters would often watch it with me out of necessity, since I controlled the television set during a game.

One evening I said to Valeri, "Come on, Val, we are going to play football in the living room." I always felt it was beneficial for youngsters to occasionally participate in physical-contact games. The living room seemed like a perfect place to play football, since it hadn't been repainted yet and didn't have any furniture.

Valeri was very enthusiastic about my desire to play football in the living room. We established the rules and were set to start. "Where is the ball, Dad?" she asked.

"I'll find one," I responded. I went to the basement and brought up a miniature football. It was now game time. I kicked the ball to Valeri and waited for her to retrieve it and tried to tackle her (half speed, of course), while she attempted to run to the other side of the room. Valeri really enjoyed the excitement and the contact of running with the ball and being tackled. We both laughed heartily when she would try to grab my ankles in an attempt to tackle me. Often I would drag her across the carpet with her hanging on and trying to trip me with her other hand or foot. Somehow it always turned out that she would win, mostly because if I happened to win, she insisted that another game be played immediately. No way would she stop playing if she lost. Needless to say, we had a great deal of fun - until the furniture arrived.

Valeri's two sisters were always protective of her, although only when it was necessary. Valeri did not want us to tell people about her health problems. She figured many children had problems and that hers was not that serious. She wouldn't mention her disease to her friends, because she wanted to be accepted as any other child and not pitied.

However, some kids can be cruel, and on occasion she was called "The Green Monster or the Yellow Monster" because of her paleness immediately prior to needing a transfusion. Or Val would be called "pregnant" because of her enlarged abdominal area, from her enlarged liver. On other occasions, students would harass her with other comments. Valeri learned to cope with these taunts by not paying attention to them. Usually the offender would eventually stop, as the taunts did not bring any reaction from Valeri, and her many friends in class would pressure the agitator into using better manners.

Once a boy in her class started provoking her in school. He continued to do this for several days. At first, Valeri didn't pay any attention to him, but the continual assault began to wear heavily on her. She mentioned it to us and we suggested she tell the teacher. She was reluctant to do this, feeling that it would be better if she could resolve this problem without the teacher's assistance.

The next day the boy started his usual assault. He even continued after school was dismissed, shouting in her face at close range as she left the school. He began running around and shoving her. Meanwhile, Val's sister was waiting in a car at the curb to drive her home. Debbie spotted Valeri walking and saw the boy bothering her. Debbie quickly got out of the car and ran over to Val. She grabbed the boy by his jacket collar and lifted him off the ground. Debra, a low-key, passive person, was very angry. She looked into his eyes and said, "If you ever, **ever** bother my sister again, you will have to answer to me. Do you understand what I am telling you?"

The panic-stricken boy, with fear in his eyes, looked up at Debbie and said in a weak voice, "Yes, I understand."

Debbie put him down and let go of us jacket. "Now, scram!" she said. Valeri and Debra got into the car and took off. Needless to say, the boy never bothered Valeri again. The only thing he did in class was to greet her with a smile and a quiet "hello" on occasion. It was ironic, because Debbie had never shown that much anger before. Valeri described the incident to us at supper that night as Debbie giggled. She said, "I don't know what happened to me, but I saw red when that obnoxious boy was harassing my sister."

After attending Ferry Elementary School for one year, Valeri moved over to Parcells Middle School, located about a mile from our home. As in the past, I would drive Valeri to school in the morning and Debbie would pick her up in the afternoon. Val enjoyed a period of good health and physical progress during those two years.

One of Valeri's fond memories centered around a trip she took with her eighth grade class to Chicago to visit the famous Science Museum. The class departed early in the morning, visited the museum, had supper in a very nice restaurant, and returned to the school parking lot shortly after midnight. I waited for the bus to return. When it arrived, the sleepy students began unloading. Several students said: "Wait until you see what Valeri brought back with her!" When all the students were off the bus except Val, I saw this huge dog doll coming down the bus steps. I looked closely and there was Val carrying the doll. It was as large as she was.

She yelled out to me, "Dad! Look what I won at a drawing at the museum!" She loved that dog doll and kept it for years.

The highlight of her stay at Parcells was meeting Sue Fattore. Sue lived in Harper Woods, about two miles from our home. She and Valeri struck up a lifelong friendship. Sue was a darling young lady and an outstanding friend. They attended middle school, high school, and the University of Michigan together and remained very close friends after graduation.

During Christmas vacation of her eighth grade year, Valeri asked, "Say Dad, when are we going to Florida with the baseball team for spring training? I want to ask Rena to come along."

"Florida?" I replied. "Wait a minute. What do you mean, Florida? That was a one-time shot last year. Besides, maybe your Easter vacation is different than our spring break at the university."

"Oh, no!" she exclaimed. "I have checked and they fall on the same dates. Besides, Debbie, Nikki, Mom, and I voted that we should go. That's a democratic procedure, you know. And, you must respect the democratic process." So, I checked the dates and found that indeed she was right. "I know you will take us, Dad," Valeri exclaimed, "because you are such a nice guy!"

What else could I do, but say, "Okay, you girls can come."

"Remember, Rena, too. And by the way, Jeanne Ricevuto plans to go to keep Debbie company." Val was developing a nice way of selling her ideas to us. Besides, when it was feasible, I always enjoyed taking my daughters and their friends with me. So, later that winter, the baseball team, my daughters, their friends, and my assistant coach, Christ Petrouleas, and I departed for the Sunshine State to start our spring training season.

For the girls this was old stuff. After last year's trip, they knew all about the facilities at the Royal Inn Motel where we were quartered, and they knew the routine of our practices and game schedule. As usual, Debbie was in charge of the younger girls whenever I was not able to supervise them.

Rena and Valeri had a nice time together. They both served as bat girls for the team. Rena wasn't too keen on the idea of being a bat girl, but Valeri loved "the position" - as she referred to it, and she went about her duties as though it was the number one job in baseball. She showed a tremendous amount of enthusiasm and excitement, cheering the players on and sympathizing with them whenever a player made an out or an error. She enjoyed the good innings and suffered through the bad ones. This experience helped Val understand the dynamics of the game of baseball and it made her a dedicated fan of the "National Pastime."

Valeri got to know several of our fine young players, including Jim Saros, one of our Greek parishioners. Val developed a lifelong crush on Jim. He would kid her as she performed her bat girl duties, and both Val and Rena appreciated his sense of humor.

Soon it was time to return home. A nasty storm front had arrived, and it was getting worse. There was even talk about a possible tornado. We went to the airport that evening and boarded a 747 jet, the biggest commercial airplane made in our country. As the plane took off, the visibility was excellent, although it was raining hard. Our immediate destination was Atlanta, Georgia, where we would change planes before resuming our flight to Detroit.

As we reached cruising speed and altitude, the storm intensified. A few minutes later, the plane began bouncing up and down and moving from side to side. This went on for about half an hour. I began feeling airsick and became very nauseous. I looked around and realized that there were many people experiencing the same symptoms or worse. Even some of the flight attendants were ill. I began worrying about the players and the kids, especially Valeri. I decided to check on our group. Some players were not feeling well, but most were sleeping. Rena was awake and nauseous. I looked at Valeri. She was sleeping like a baby. Finally, after what seemed like an eternity (but in reality was only an hour and a half) we landed at the airport in Atlanta.

After our group left the plane, we were told by an airline representative that our flight to Detroit was originating from a gate on the other side of the airport, a relatively long distance from where we had just gotten off the plane. Upon arriving at the correct terminal, we noticed a large crowd by the gate. I went up to the desk and asked the attendant what time our plane would be leaving. He answered, "I'm sorry to say that due to tornadoes in our area, the plane won't leave until six o'clock tomorrow morning." We now had a seven-hour wait, as it was only eleven o'clock in the evening.

I told Christ Petrouleas about the delay and that we didn't have any money in our budget to rent hotel rooms for the night. He replied, "Oh well, Coach, the floor in the airport is carpeted so there shouldn't be any problem."

At first I thought, "No way!" - but then I saw many other people sleeping on the floor. I called our group together and informed them about the comfortable bed they would have for the night. Next, I began to worry about Valeri and the girls. After eating in the cafeteria, I suggested they find a spot on the floor to put their coats and try to sleep. All of the girls did just that! And boy, did they ever sleep! They were dead-to-the-world for almost seven hours! I awakened them with just enough time to get washed up before boarding the plane. Almost everyone in our group slept soundly, but the "old coach" just couldn't sleep a wink all night.

The flight home was perfect with no other problems. On our drive home, the girls raved about the wonderful time they had had on the trip.

A result of this trip was that Valeri developed an interest in baseball. After the college season ended, Valeri said to me one day, "Dad, I want to go and see the Detroit Tigers play." It was customary for me to take Debbie and Nikki to several games each summer, as each year I received two free Tiger passes to any game. Also, I could call up my friend, Bill Lajoie, a Tiger scout and later general manager, to ask him for additional tickets. We made use of the opportunity often. Valeri's request to go to a Tiger game pleased me because I wanted her to become attached to our beloved Tigers, too. We set a date for her to attend a night baseball game. She loved the Tigers from the first pitch. She reacted to every pitch and every play, and she cheered loudly and exuberantly for her Tigers that night. She was hooked. They were her team.

Throughout the years, we spent many nights watching the Tigers play. Customarily, we would sit in our seats in the grandstand when the games started. As the game progressed, we moved to seats closer to the field, until finally, in the late innings, we were sitting in a box seat.

When Valeri joined the Junior Greek Orthodox Youth Association (G.O.Y.A.) chapter at our church, it opened up a whole new era for her. The G.O.Y.A. is a national youth organization for boys and girls between the ages of thirteen and eighteen. The goals of the Junior G.O.Y.A. were to help Orthodox youth to understand their religion, to serve their church and community, and to have social functions where they could enjoy each other's companionship. The sponsors of our chapter at the Assumption Greek Orthodox Church at that time were Betty and Gus Nichols, whose daughters Madeline and Lydia were also members of the organization.

Valeri was fourteen years old when she joined. Although she knew some of the youngsters in the organization, she made new friends very quickly. She also helped plan various functions and took part in many of them, like singing Christmas carols at St. John Hospital, hay rides and youth dances. The Junior Goyans also assisted at various church functions, including the annual Greek festival, which was a three-day event held by our church in August beginning in the middle 1970s.

Valeri met a boy in the organization named Christos (Chris) Garkinos. She often said she didn't know what the attraction was, but just something about him was special. He was friendly, nice, and shared many similar interests with Val. Most of all she could talk with Chris and had a lot of fun discussing the social club, world affairs, rock music or whatever topic they chose. He was three years younger than Valeri and actually became a Junior Goyan a little before he was twelve years old. At that time, Chris was actually a little shorter than Valeri, who by now had almost grown to her five-foot, one-inch adult stature. Ultimately, Chris grew to be six-foot-three-inches.

Chris lived just a few blocks from our home and attended the same schools that Valeri had attended. One of the things she liked about Chris was his fine sense of humor. Valeri loved to laugh and enjoy the things around her, and so did Chris. Valeri had a great perception and understanding of people, and she knew that Chris was a special person. Being older, she nurtured him as life went on.

Another person she met and developed a fine friendship with was Vasilia Chambos. Vasilia's family were lifelong members of our Assumption Church, as was our family. She lived quite far from church (in Warren, Michigan), but would see Valeri at club meetings, in church on Sundays, and at other church functions. They would communicate by telephone quite often. Vasilia was of diminutive stature, like Val. In fact, she was slightly shorter. They hit it off almost from the first day that they met and did many things together in the ensuing years. Valeri loved the way she could communicate with Vasilia and talk about anything. They understood each other and shared many similar interests. During the week, they would often plan their Sundays by phone. Their Sundays included taking care of the pre-nursery class at Sunday School. Valeri spent many happy hours taking part in the Junior G.O.Y.A. activities throughout the years. Especially rewarding was her friendships with both Chris and Vasilia.

Valeri's first opportunity to take part in a wedding occurred in July 1975, when her oldest sister Debbie married Joe Bellomo. Nikki was the Maid of Honor and Valeri was Junior Bridesmaid. The wedding ceremony was set for July 15th at our Greek Assumption Church on Charlevoix in Detroit.

There was a great deal of excitement around the Samaras household for several months before the wedding. With all the preliminaries completed, the wedding was ready to take place. The big day arrived and all the participants met in the back of the church (the Narthex), ready for the big event to begin. Nikki looked lovely in her yellow gown, as did Valeri in her peach gown.

Valeri was a beautiful young lady, just like her sisters. She had long, curly auburn hair, big, beautiful brown eyes, lovely high cheek bones, and fine facial features. The dress fit her perfectly. She looked like a living doll.

The organ music started, signifying that the wedding was about to begin. The ring bearers began walking down the aisle. Valeri, being the junior bridesmaid, followed. As I stood there with Debbie, watching Valeri walk down the aisle with so much poise and class, I couldn't help think what a wonderful day it would be when I would have the opportunity to escort Valeri down the aisle to her future husband. The bridesmaids followed Valeri, one-by-one, and then it was my turn to escort my lovely daughter, Debbie, to her groom.

When I walked her to the altar, I stopped, kissed her, and gave her hand to Joe to hold. I moved over to the first pew with Marietta and took my place in preparation for the ceremony to begin. Father Demetrios Kavadas performed the marriage ceremony. As we stood there, watching, I couldn't help but notice that Valeri was clearly enjoying the event.

Following the ceremony we headed for The Gourmet House for the reception. We followed Debbie and Joe in the lead car, beeping the car horn all the way.

Four hundred people had been invited to the wedding. We formed the reception line immediately after arriving at the hall. The wedding reception was wonderful, beginning with the meal, and ending with dancing and socializing.

Nikki and Valeri taught Joe's sisters, Pauline, Patti, and Nan some of the steps in Greek dancing, and they all had fun participating. There was also some Italian dancing in which his sisters helped our girls take part. Of course, there was ballroom dancing. Everyone seemed to be having a wonderful time. The reception lasted into the early hours of the morning. When we finally made our way back home, Marietta, Valeri, Nikki, and I sat and talked about all the wonderful things we had been through that day. Valeri talked about the wedding for a long time and raved about her wonderful, wonderful experience as a junior bridesmaid.

# High School Days

G REAT changes occur in the lives of teenagers, during the years between puberty and young adulthood, when they are between fourteen and eighteen years of age. Significant change occurs physically, emotionally, socially, intellectually, and spiritually. There is a constant need for adjustment during this time. The individual progresses from being dependent on other people to becoming an independent citizen.

For Valeri, her high school years were exciting and loaded with fun. She took advantage of the opportunities offered to her. She made huge, positive strides in her intellectual, physical, social, emotional, and spiritual development. To her, life was one big, wonderful, adventure. She realized that you must live every day to its fullest and never take things for granted. She wrote in her journal:

> *We take things for granted. I know I am fortunate enough to have*
> *kind, understanding and loving parents, who mean a great deal to me,*
> *more than I can say. Don't take your parents for granted. Their love*
> *is a great treasure. Enjoy every moment you can.*

Val felt that many young people were so busy during their teens that they often took their parents' care for granted.

Valeri displayed a great deal of enthusiasm when she began Grosse Pointe North High School in September 1975. The teachers, facilities and programs were ideal. Valeri was eager to take advantage of this situation. Her attitude was: "You get out of something what you put into it." She wanted to put so much into it so that she would receive a whole lot in return.

Valeri was an excellent student and participated in many extracurricular activities. She had a strong allegiance to Grosse Pointe North High School and felt very much a part of their total program.

During her freshman year, Valeri developed close ties with four life-long friends. They were: Sue Fattore, whom she had met at Parcells Middle School; Jill Haley, who had taken a liking to Val because she was a little shorter than Val's five-foot-one stature; Lynn Ekstrom, who Val could talk to about confidential things; and Prov Vitale, who was a very serious and outstanding student. The five of them spent much time together, enjoying high school and social activities.

In the harsh reality of life, pain can be inflicted by a spoken word. Such an incident took place early in Valeri's freshman year in a drama class. She loved the acting and entertainment field and decided to enroll in a beginning drama class her first semester. She felt that the drama class could meet her needs in learning about acting. About halfway through the first semester there was a call for students to try out for the school play, which would take place the following semester. Valeri attended the organizational meeting. The teacher, Mr. Barr, indicated a need to find a leading actress. He requested all of the pretty girls who wanted to try out for the lead to go to the right-side of the stage, and all of the other girls who wanted a part to go to the left-side of the stage.

Valeri wanted to try out for the lead part, so she began walking over to the right-side of the stage. Mr. Barr looked at her and yelled, "No! No! Young lady, you go over to the left-side of the stage." Valeri quietly moved over to the indicated side.

Later she remarked, "Of course there were many pretty girls trying out, but I wanted to try out for the lead too." She was hurt for two reasons. First, because she wasn't even considered for the lead part, and secondly, because Mr. Barr had implied that she wasn't very pretty and had embarrassed her in front of the other students. But, Valeri went along with the teacher's request, made a supreme effort, and landed another role in the play.

During the rest of the semester, Valeri decided she would take a different approach to drama. She decided to take advantage of the class and of Mr. Barr's knowledge, and to learn about script writing, in which she excelled later on. She also learned stage preparation, stage management, production, editing, stage props management, and other facets of the entire drama field. She developed a deep respect for Mr. Barr, despite how their relationship began. He developed a fondness for her and respected her hard work in his class.

Valeri joined the Valkyries Club during her freshman year. The object of this club was for students to serve as hosts at school plays, parents' nights and teas, and to assist in any way at school functions. She also joined the French Club, as she was enrolled in a French class and someday wanted to visit France, particularly Paris.

In addition to these activities, Val joined the yearbook staff. The school yearbook was named *The Valhalla*. During her senior year, she became editor of the yearbook.

In addition to her club activities, she loved attending many of the sports events, as well as other social and academic functions. A key factor in helping her to become completely involved in all of the school activities was her assignment as a roving reporter for the school yearbook. This assignment included taking pictures and interviewing people during different events, and then writing about them. She welcomed this difficult task because of the exposure to so many students and school organizations.

The roving reporter role also enticed her to learn more about cameras and photography. She loved taking pictures, but realized her limited knowledge of cameras. So, the logical step, she felt, was to enroll in a camera and photography class at our Assumption Cultural Center. To enroll she needed a quality camera; which Marietta and I bought for her.

As she progressed through high school, Valeri was very excited and happy with her life. She expressed her feelings when she wrote in her journal:

> *One person's idea of life can be so different from another's. My life is a very good life, although at times I don't think so. People would think my life is horrible because I have to go to the hospital and I can't do certain things. I have more happiness than the "jock of the year." To me, this is my life, and I love it!!!*
>
> > *Life is full of joys and fears,*
> > *Full of laughter and tears.*
> > *When I think of life, I start to cheer*
> > *because to me my life is oh, so very dear!*

These comments reflected Val's feelings, which were typical for a high-powered, emotional, young female of that age.

There are things that students are compelled to think about during high school. A most important one concerns an occupational career. Sue Fattore and Valeri were quite successful in their earth science and biology classes at Parcells Middle School. This led them both to settle on the idea of wanting to become physicians. Valeri's idea came from the contact she had with so many fine medical people. She wanted to share in and become a part of this profession. She thought helping people would be an excellent venture in life.

Both she and Sue signed up for chemistry, which was a college preparatory course necessary for those who had any plans of later attending a university and studying medicine. Each girl found the content of the class, including the charts of elements and the study of compounds and formulas, to be quite confusing. They knew the lab work would be difficult as well. Sue insisted that they get separate lab partners who could help them with their lab work. After a couple of weeks, they both realized that chemistry was going to be very difficult and they elected to find ways to entertain themselves, rather than to actually learn the content of the class.

One thing they did was to bring candy into the classroom and lab. They offered the candy to their classmates, and laughed about doing this while the students would eat their candy. Another thing they did, in lieu of studying chemistry during class, was to compose songs. Valeri wrote words to fit the music "I Am a Wanderer." They called it "The Chemistry Song." It went something like this: "Valeri, Sue Marie, Chemistry, Eck! Eck! Eck! Eck!" Every time they bumped into a stone wall and couldn't move forward in chemistry, they would get together and put their arms around each other and sing that song.

Both Sue and Valeri laughed at and kidded their classmate, Rick Zenn. During class lectures, he would relax to a point of almost dozing off, and he appeared not to be paying any attention to the teacher. Much to their surprise, he excelled in his lab work and received outstanding grades on his exams. They felt he was some sort of genius and nicknamed him "Mr. Genius." (Rick later became a medical doctor.)

Needless to say, it all caught up with Sue and Val in the end, when both of them barely survived the class with C- grades. That was the end of their aspirations to become medical doctors. Val and Sue would laugh about the chemistry class, and realized they had to start thinking about a different profession. Later on in high school, Sue decided she would like to go into the business world, and Valeri realized her love for the stage and theater could be met, in some ways, by entering the communications field. With these new aspirations, they tried different types of classes to better prepare them for their chosen careers.

One of the things that Sue liked about Valeri was her sense of humor, especially the way Val could make someone laugh when they were depressed. Sue felt Valeri had a very infectious laugh, and could look at the brighter side of life and find the humor in events taking place around her. Sue described herself as a "Donny Osmond" type of person; that is, she wanted to do everything perfectly, and she didn't permit herself to fully enjoy experiences and events. She considered Valeri outgoing and adventurous - ready to try something new at the spur of the moment.

Sue felt that both Valeri and her were naive in many ways, especially in the area of boys and forming relationships with them. Both girls felt that this was an interesting aspect of life, but that they would take a very conservative approach, compared to other girls in school.

Sue always got a kick out of hearing Val describe her math teacher, Mrs. Roads. As the story goes, it was the custom of Mrs. Roads to write a math problem on the blackboard and try to explain it. If Mrs. Roads decided that it wasn't written on the board the way she really wanted it, she would promptly take her open hand and erase the problem. Occasionally, Mrs. Roads' fingernails would scratch the board, causing Valeri to cringe. After erasing the problem, Mrs. Roads would then wipe her hand on her skirt or blouse, and proceed to write another problem on the blackboard. Again, if corrections were needed while she was lecturing, she would wipe the board off with her fist or hand, scratch the board with her nails, and once again wipe the chalk onto her blouse or skirt. This habit was very amusing to Val and Sue.

Valeri would mimic Mrs. Roads for Sue, Jill, Prov, and Lynn. They would laugh heartily as Val demonstrated Mrs. Roads' actions, and Val would always cringe when she talked about Mrs. Roads wiping the board and scratching it with her fingernails.

One of the things that Val's girlfriends always kidded her about was the fact that she was a "night owl." Valeri was a slow starter in the morning and seemed to pick up energy as the day progressed. She would shift into second gear after supper and could go into the wee hours of the morning with her added source of energy. This caused humorous conflict with her friends. It seemed as though her friends liked to get up early and get a fast start. However, as the day continued, they would slow down, and were ready to call it a night by nine o'clock in the evening.

It was common for Valeri to go over to Sue's house to do homework or to just socialize. Sue would then say, "Val, it's nine o'clock. It's getting near my bedtime, so maybe you should call your dad and have him take you home."

Valeri would call me up and say, "Hey, dad, come on by and pick me up. Sue's conked out on me again." I could hear Sue laughing in the background.

When I would pick up Valeri at Sue's and begin the drive home, she would say, "Hey Dad, how about stopping at Big Boy's and getting something to eat?" This became quite a ritual for several years. I enjoyed it as much or more than Valeri, as we had extra time to talk and be in each other's company.

When Valeri finished her freshman year in high school, Marietta and I marveled at all of the wonderful things she had done in such a short period of time. We were thrilled with her involvement in so many activities, and with her interest in education.

At times, though, we worried that she would overextend herself. If we ever said anything to Valeri about her being too active, she would reply, "Oh Mom and Dad, don't worry. I'm not getting too tired. I'll let you know if I do."

In her sophomore year, Valeri followed a pattern similar to her freshman year. Everything seemed to fall into place once Val understood the high school routine. She had the feeling of being a high-rated sophomore, not a lowly freshman. Val gained more confidence during her second year. She continued her involvement with the clubs and other extracurricular activities and expanded her role as a roving reporter. She became deeply involved in taking pictures and conducting interviews at many of the athletic contests, and she started to take the teams' victories and losses to heart. She definitely built a loyalty to the athletic program, especially since she knew so many of the participants.

The summer following her sophomore year, Valeri became increasingly active with her friends. Sue was a tennis instructor at the Harper Woods Recreation Department and invited Valeri, Jill, and Lynn to visit her there, so that Sue could teach them the rudiments of tennis. Soon, Val decided she wanted to learn how to play tennis, even though it was difficult for her to move quickly. Plus, it was a good way for Valeri to spend time with Sue.

One day, Val and Lynn decided to visit Sue, and to have a tennis lesson. Sue said, "Well, now that we've finished our lesson, let's go to Kavaan's," a very popular restaurant on the east side of Detroit that served delicious sandwiches, french fries, and strawberry shortcake.

So the three girls went to Kavaan's and ordered their lunch. They decided to eat double hamburgers and a double order of French fries because they were hungry after the tennis lesson. After consuming the sandwiches and fries, each ordered a strawberry shortcake. It didn't take them long to devour their desserts. When the waitress brought the bill she said, "My goodness! I can't believe you girls ate all that food!"

Val answered, "It was quite a bit, but I'm still slightly hungry." They all laughed.

The waitress looked at them and said, "I swear, you three are real eating machines." So they adopted that nickname and would use it from time to time and laugh.

They'd say, "Let's go, eating machines. It's time to go somewhere and eat."

Valeri loved eating. She enjoyed all types of foods, especially fried foods and desserts - particularly chocolate. I was always a little apprehensive about her diet. I knew that it was common for Cooley's Anemia victims to have gall bladder problems and, in many cases, to develop sugar diabetes. Although I wouldn't make an outright statement of this fact, I would hint, at times, and ask her to not overeat sweets or fatty foods. Val had a wonderful appetite, and it was great to see her enjoy eating so much.

During the summer it was common for Valeri and me to take our dog, Schatzie, for a walk after supper. Then, we would go to Big Boy's for a snack. Often, she would see some of her school chums there, and socialize with them. We often reflected on what had happened during the day, and we discussed the activities we were going to participate in as the summer progressed. Valeri's routine was to order fried calamari and wash it down with a malted milk shake. For dessert she'd have her favorite hot fudge sundae with chocolate ice cream.

Later in the summer, Valeri went to our Orthodox Youth Camp, near Rose City, with her friend Vasilia. They spent a wonderful week at camp, participating in a number of activities with their Orthodox Youth friends. Chris Garkinos also went to camp that year, and both Vasilia and Valeri watched over him, since he was younger than them. It was a very good experience for all of them, especially the girls.

When Valeri began her junior year in high school, she and her friends appeared to be much more sophisticated. They began to wear high-heeled shoes to school more often and dressed in better clothing. They were also more involved in co-ed activities, and became more serious in getting to know boys.

One day after school, the four girls decided that they would go to the Baker Shoe Store at Eastland Mall, and that all of them would buy the same style of shoe. They each bought a pair and went over to Santa Land to pose with Santa Claus for a picture. They laughed about this for a long time - Santa and the four girls with the same shoes.

Marietta is a very stylish person, and she passed her fashion-consciousness on to our three daughters. Valeri made it a point to learn about fashion, and she became knowledgeable in hair styling, facial make-up, and clothes. *Vogue* was one of her favorite magazines, although she would occasionally buy several women's magazines to study the different styles of dress. Her attire was always up-to-date, as she followed the clothing trend quite closely, and she often was the first one to try out a new fashion or dress.

Valeri was really excited and grateful when shoe manufacturers started to make platform shoes, as she looked much taller in four-inch heels. She and Sue used to kid each other about "moving up" in the world. Sue would say, "Hey Val, let's put on our stilts and go out tonight!"

It was during her junior year in high school that Dr. Charbeneau suggested that we take Valeri to the University of Michigan Hospital to have her examined for physical development and maturation. She was five-feet, one-inch tall, and he thought it would be advantageous to know if Valeri had completed her growth, as well as to determine the condition of her bone structure, and gauge the functioning of her glands.

So we made an appointment at the hospital with Doctor Bacon, an expert endocrinologist, and a friendly and accommodating person. He ran a series of tests on Valeri, then gave us the results a few days later. Dr. Bacon told us that Valeri was developing nicely and that whatever we were doing we should continue doing. Except, there was one problem: the parathyroid glands weren't functioning anymore. These glands give off a hormone which produces calcium for the bones. Of course, this was tied in with her anemia. However, he said that if we treated Valeri with Dihydrotachysterol (DHT), she would develop normally, since this medication is the same hormone that a normal body would produce. Marietta and I were quite pleased with Dr. Bacon's findings. We were encouraged that Valeri seemed healthy and was progressing quite normally in her development. We also hoped that she would remain healthy, and that, perhaps, a cure or a better treatment would be found for her disease in the near future.

Sue was always impressed with the rhythmic movements Val had when she danced. She noticed this when they attended a couple of the school dances. "Boy, I sure wish I could do that. I move like a plow horse," Sue said. She talked Val into taking a dance course with Ken Geogle, a popular dance instructor. He taught them quite a few steps, and Valeri loved "the stroll." It was a dance where persons could express themselves and have rhythmic movements as they moved down a long aisle made up of men on one side and women on the other. Sue asked Val to teach her some creative movements for the stroll. Val worked with her and tried to help. She felt that Sue was really learning to dance quite well, but Sue would say, "No way! Once a plow horse, always a plow horse." And, they would laugh. By the time the class was over, Sue had learned to be a relatively good dancer, and both of the girls thought they had gained by taking the fancy dance classes from Ken.

Sue always kidded Val about the first concert they attended together. Sue and her boyfriend, Steve Schucker, Jill, Lynn, and Valeri attended a Billy Joel concert. It was the first concert any of them had attended. Billy Joel put on a tremendous performance, and the group felt it was very exciting to watch him go through his gyrations, while also playing such wonderful music. They decided to cap off the evening by going to Greektown for a late evening meal. Greektown was, and is, one of the lively places in Detroit. Many other Detroit entertainment spots had been closed, but Greektown was always active, with people eating at the restaurants and walking up and down the streets until the early hours of the morning.

Steve drove and parked near the restaurant area. Once in the restaurant, Valeri said, "Well, we're in a Greek restaurant. We might as well order lamb and rice or some sort of combination of lamb with vegetables. Since we are in Greektown, we must eat lamb."

Steve and Lynn concurred. "Sounds like a good idea to us."

Sue said, "No, I'm not much of a lamb-eater, so I'll just have something else, maybe a hamburger."

So Valeri spoke up again and said, "Come on, Sue. Join us and have a real Greek dinner of lamb and rice." But Sue and Jill were reluctant. The waiter took their orders. Three of them ordered lamb and rice, while Jill and Sue ordered hamburgers.

In a Greek restaurant, lamb and rice is served in tremendously large portions, along with soup and a loaf of bread. Steve, Lynn, and Val ate everything on their plates.

The next day Val told Sue that she didn't feel very well. Obviously the food from the night before had not agreed with her, as she had vomited. Later, Sue received a call from both Lynn and Steve. They had the same symptoms as Valeri. Meanwhile, Sue and Jill felt great. The two of them laughed about this experience for a long time. The next time they went to Greektown, Sue joked and asked, "Well, how about lamb and rice tonight?" There was no response from her friends.

During January of Valeri's junior year, she decided to learn how to drive an automobile. Soon, she would be sixteen, eligible to take a driver's education course at the high school, and she lacked the perception of what it was like to drive. Valeri had never paid too much attention to automobiles prior to this, other than to ride in them. Now, she realized it was time to get behind the wheel and begin driving.

Valeri asked her mother if she could learn to drive. "Of course, Valeri," said Marietta. "Talk to Dad and we'll see if he can work something out for you. Even though it's illegal for you to drive without a permit, let's see what we can do."

Val came into the family room and said, "Dad, how would you like to do me a big favor? How about taking me someplace where I can try to drive our car. I am afraid that with my limited knowledge about automobiles, it will be difficult for me in the driver's training class. All I know about cars is that they have a steering wheel, a motor, and four wheels. How about it, Dad?"

I thought it over for a few seconds. "You know, Val, I think we can go to the high school parking lot on Sunday when there won't be any cars, and I can spend time helping you learn how to drive."

That winter there was a considerable amount of snow in the area. When we went to the high school parking lot that Sunday, we noticed the snow was piled up on the outer edges of the lot. In a way, this was advantageous as it was like a private driving arena. I started the driving lesson by explaining the different mechanical parts of the car, how the car ran, the shifting system, and everything else connected with driving. Then I told Valeri to climb into the driver's seat and give it a try.

Our car was a little four-cylinder Pontiac Sunbird, with power steering. It was very easy to handle and a perfect match for Valeri - the small car and her small stature. We worked hard for a couple of hours and Val began to develop the technique on how to drive. Except for a couple of incidents when she drove into a snow bank at slow speed, everything worked out quite well.

We spent the next several Sundays going to the lot so that Valeri could practice driving forward and backward, stopping, and parking. Quite often the car would slip and slide, because she would put the brakes on too hard or turn too fast on the still icy pavement. She named them "the-slip-and-slide practice sessions."

Learning to drive was a very happy experience for Valeri. She looked forward to the day she would be independent, and would have her own automobile.

The highlight of Valeri's junior year came in early spring, when we offered to send her to Paris for a week with the French Club. She said it was like a dream come true. She was thrilled at the thought of going to

Paris and speaking French, experiencing all of the beautiful sights that she had read about, and seeing the high-fashion clothes that the cosmopolitan people in Paris would be wearing. She felt it was a nice reward for her very concentrated effort to learn the language, and she was grateful that we would sponsor her trip.

Soon the time had arrived for Valeri and the group to depart. Angie Rothis - Manny and Betty Rothis' daughter - was also going along. It was comforting to know that Angie, a senior, was going, because she knew Valeri.

The big day arrived. We drove Valeri to the airport that evening, to make a nine o'clock departure. After arriving at the airport and meeting the excited group in the lobby, we walked to the gate where the plane was being prepared for take-off. Excitement reigned supreme with the students and their parents. Valeri had a happy, anxious look on her face and we knew that she was really excited and ready to go on this new venture.

The time arrived for the students to board the plane. We hugged and kissed Valeri good-bye, then watched as she and Angie joined the other students. As they boarded the plane, Marietta had tears in her eyes. She said, "Bob, Manny and Betty, let's stay here by the window and watch the plane take off."

We all agreed and stood there, watching as the plane left the gate and taxied toward the runway. With our hearts pounding, we waited for the airplane to pass our window. We heard someone holler, "There it goes!" and watched as it gained speed and lifted off the ground, heading into the night and out of sight.

The airplane was older and had a narrow body, which meant that the passengers would be quite crowded in the limited space available. Right after the airplane faded from sight, Manny turned to me and remarked, "I can't believe that we put our daughters on that little old airplane to fly across the Atlantic Ocean all the way to Paris." We all laughed as he said this.

Betty added, "How true."

"Oh, I feel it's a safe airplane," chimed in Marietta. "After all, if the pilot is willing to get on and fly it, he must be confident that it's in good shape. So, we really have nothing to worry about." We laughed again and said, "Yeah, I hope so. I hope you're right."

We bid the Rothises good-bye, went to our auto, and drove home. I couldn't fall asleep easily that night. I kept thinking about Valeri, Angie and the other kids on the airplane, wondering what part of the Atlantic

Ocean they were over. I was very apprehensive, but eventually fell into a solid sleep. When I woke up in the morning for breakfast I heard Marietta say, "Well, Bob, they're in Paris now. I bet they're really excited."

Valeri called two days later from Paris, as we had planned. She was excited and happy! They were staying at a nice little hotel near the outskirts of Paris, and the group had spent time sightseeing with their teacher, Miss Poquette, who had planned a heavy itinerary for the next few days.

The week flew by and soon it was time for us to return to the airport to pick up Valeri. We drove out during the evening and met the Rothises again. We walked to the gate and waited anxiously for our daughters. The airplane was about an hour late in arriving. As the students exited, there was a lot of kissing and hugging by parents, relatives, and friends. Finally, at the end of the line, we saw Angie and Valeri. Both had big smiles on their faces. Tears came to my eyes at that moment. I felt so good that Valeri could feel so happy, going through a new adventure in life and having enjoyed it to such a degree.

On the way home, Valeri told us how much she enjoyed the trip and Angie's companionship. She said that Angie would just crack her up with off-the-wall remarks. They had many good laughs together. Val couldn't believe the comments that Angie could invent out of the clear blue while they were sightseeing.

Once we arrived home, Valeri began unpacking. She had souvenirs for Marietta and me, her sisters, and a couple of friends. The three of us enjoyed talking about her adventures, and we conversed until the wee hours of the morning.

Later that week, Valeri picked up the pictures she had taken. She had many photos of beautiful sights in and around Paris, including the Eiffel Tower, the Arc de Triomphe, the River Seine, and Notre Dame Cathedral. She would talk excitedly about her experiences at each site. One day she finally said, "You know, Mom and Dad, I'd love to go back, and, I want you two with me so you can see the beautiful sights of Paris, too."

During her junior year, Valeri worked extremely hard on the school yearbook. It was common for her to come home late at night around eleven, twelve, or even one o'clock in the morning. I worried about her extensively, feeling that it would leave her in a run-down condition, but she just loved doing it and said, "Dad, I really relax when I'm working on the school yearbook. It's very enjoyable and I don't find myself getting too tired. I just love doing it. I will be sure to get my rest. The difficult work will be over soon, and then the book will go to print."

The summer following her junior year Valeri became even more so-cially active. But even with her busy schedule, she set time aside to baby-sit for her one-year-old niece, Michelle. Michelle was the daughter of her sister Debbie. Val loved caring for Michelle, whom she adored. Michelle was an alert and active baby, and took a liking to her Aunt Valeri.

Just prior to the beginning of Valeri's senior year, Steven Lazurenko, the newly-elected yearbook editor, was killed in an automobile accident. Valeri was to have been his chief assistant on the staff that year. After his death, Valeri was then given the assignment of yearbook editor. She was hit hard by his death because she liked him very much. Valeri always received satisfaction from Steve's comments when things were in a tur-moil. He would say, "Don't worry, Val, I have everything under con-trol." He was sorely missed by Valeri and the entire yearbook staff.

When the school year began, Valeri had to immediately go to work setting the plan for the year. Another staff member, Mary Sanders, was elected to be the chief assistant with Val. Val was very happy about this because Mary was a hard worker.

Valeri and her friends were much more daring during their senior year. They found several ways of adding excitement and adventure to the routine of school life. When Sue was campaigning for class presi-dent, Valeri played a large role in the campaign. Wearing an election sandwich board with all kinds of nice comments about Sue, Val would walk up and down the halls, advertising for the campaign. Val would also wear the sandwich board to any functions after school. Although Val bore the brunt of many student wisecracks, she had a lot of fun doing it. And, her efforts were well-rewarded, as Sue was elected class president.

Valeri's group would occasionally meet in the morning at the Big Boy's Restaurant for breakfast. Then they would attend their classes, and at noon they would jump into one of the girls' cars and head out to a restaurant for lunch. They felt that they were beyond the "school lunch-room" scene. Often they extended the lunch hour, returning to school late for their classes. Val would tell her teacher that the elevator which was available for handicapped students wasn't working properly - or she conjured up some other excuse. Val had a permanent hall pass, since she was a member of the school yearbook staff. Sue, who was the class presi-dent, could convince her teacher into allowing her to return without any penalty, as could Jill and Lynn. Actually, they could get away with this tardiness because they were excellent students. The extended lunch hour gave them time to try many different restaurants in the area.

In high school, Sue and Val had many crushes as they agreed that there were quite a few boys who were real heart-throbs. Even though Sue was beginning to date her eventual husband, Steve Schucker, she and Val still attended stag parties, etc. They designed a unique rating system to evaluate their crushes, and received a great deal of satisfaction from doing this.

Valeri enjoyed reasonably good health throughout her high school years. She still received blood transfusions about every month, which meant that in five years, between the ages of fourteen and eighteen, she was in the hospital about sixty times. Occasionally she would suffer viral infections, but basically she was at an optimum health level for a Cooley's Anemia victim. She didn't dwell on her health and never talked about her condition with anyone in high school, other than with her very close friends Sue, Lynn, and Jill. Actually, most people didn't even know that Valeri was suffering from any kind of serious illness.

Naturally, in the back of my mind, I would often consider Valeri's anemia, and that even with her good health, we didn't know what the future would hold for us. Of course, we were always hopeful that somehow she would overcome her disease. Valeri seemed to have so much more energy and endurance than many of her friends. At times, we wondered why.

Obviously, Valeri did quite a bit of thinking and reflecting about her disease. She wrote in her journal:

> *I don't really remember when I first realized that I had to go to the hospital. It always seemed natural. My mother told me that when I was five, I came to her and said I don't want to go to the hospital. She explained that I had no choice and this would always be a part of my life. Life, huh? That word is so strange. I remember going to the hospital and all the time I spent there. That was about the worst part. I can take the pain. In fact, I hardly notice the pain, and that only lasts a second, but the process takes so long. When I was younger I remember them jabbing me several times and still having no luck. They often had to stick it in my feet. That was when I dreaded that hospital most.*

At this point in time, Valeri knew her capabilities. She was aware of what she could and couldn't do. She adjusted very well to her life.

Often, when Valeri and I took our evening walk with Schatzie, we would talk about different things regarding life. Val was so impressive, because she seemed to have things "together" so well. She had a wonderful understanding of life and people. It was always interesting to listen to her reflect about life. In fact, many times I would relate some of the problems I had at work or coaching, and she had the unique ability to understand. On many occasions, Val was able to help me develop insights into resolving my problems.

We formed a very close relationship at this time, especially since Nikki was living away from home, attending Eastern Michigan University. Valeri was wonderful company. We did many things together, similar to those I had shared with Debbie and Nikki in earlier years. We went to baseball games, football games, basketball games, and social events. We often went out to eat in the evening. Valeri was also a fine companion for Marietta. They spent much time shopping, attending social events, and doing other things that mothers and daughters do together.

Valeri felt that there was a void in her life because she didn't have a steady boyfriend, nor did she date very often. She had many friends who were boys, but she yearned to be asked to go out on dates more often.

She did have a really good friend in Chris Garkinos, who, as a freshman, was three years younger. Valeri would talk to Chris daily, and they did go out on many unofficial dates to athletic games, local restaurants, and other events. They had a nice relationship and enjoyed talking about so many different activities and events.

Valeri invited Chris to join the yearbook staff, which he did. In fact, it was kind of cute, because Valeri, being older, could drive; and Chris, being younger, could not. So, she would drive him around in her car. He was a good friend and companion for Val.

Valeri and some of her girl friends compensated for not having boyfriends by participating in other types of social activities and by doing unusual things together. Val and her friends found humor in a popular song called, "Close the Door, Baby." For those days, the lyrics were quite suggestive. Valeri quickly adopted the idea that whenever they saw a foxy, sharp-looking guy, she'd look at her girlfriends and say "Close the door, baby." They eventually developed it as a humorous theme for most of the senior year. If a friend was in a room with Val and an attractive person came into the room, Val and her friend would stare at each other, look up at the ceiling, and they'd each know what was meant: "Close the door, baby!"

As mentioned before, Valeri was a stylish dresser. One time she and Sue decided to change their hair color. Valeri had long, light-brown, curly hair. Sue had light-black hair. So, they went to a drug store, looked through the hair color section, and finally chose the color they each wanted. They went back to Sue's house, mixed the colors, washed their hair, and added the dye. When their hair was dry, they discovered that Sue's hair was now a nice, light color, although they couldn't distinguish what color it actually was. Valeri's hair was orange! They didn't know what to do, except laugh. Valeri kept the orange hair for only one or two days, then she dyed it back to her original color.

Another hair incident took place shortly thereafter. Sue was a business co-op student and worked at the Renaissance Center (RenCen) in downtown Detroit. She found a hair stylist she liked at the center and told Val about him. His name was Francis Bolas. He had a great reputation for being a creative hair stylist.

Over the next few years, whenever Valeri wanted a haircut, she'd go to the RenCen to see Francis. He enjoyed having the girls come down for their haircuts, but especially enjoyed Val because she was so daring. Whenever he had an idea for a creative style, he would suggest it to her and she would say: "Go ahead Francis, do your thing. I'm ready." She loved his work. He was an outstanding stylist and would often make her look extremely attractive with his ideas.

October through February of her senior year, Valeri was immensely busy producing the school yearbook. During its production there were many deadlines to be met, which meant that the staff and Valeri would have to work past midnight or later. Marietta and I were frequently very upset at this. We asked her if there was some way she could get home earlier, but she always responded, "Please, Mom. We have a deadline and it has to be met. Don't worry, I'll be okay."

As often happens with high school yearbook staffs, many student members quit - and the big responsibility lies on the sponsor, the editor, and the assistant editors. Valeri and Mary Sanders put in many hours meeting the deadlines in preparation for publishing the yearbook. When the yearbook was finally completed, Marietta and I were relieved because it took the pressure off Valeri and enabled her to relax more and enjoy the remainder of her senior year.

For Valeri's senior year spring break, Marietta and I decided to take her to Florida. We selected Vero Beach as the destination, because some friends, Terry Vickrey and her daughter Cindy, would be there, as well as Stephanie Daskas and her daughter Christina. Also, Vero Beach is the spring training camp of the Los Angeles Dodgers baseball team. "Dodger Town," as it is known, has a nice reputation in the baseball world.

By the time we arrived, spring training was in full bloom. We attended many exhibition baseball games, obtained autographs from the players, swam in the ocean, built sand castles, and basked in the warm sunshine. A highlight of the trip for Valeri was acquiring an autograph from Sandy Koufax, the Hall of Fame pitcher and coach. After ten glorious days, we returned to Detroit, tanned and ready to weather out the remaining cold.

Later that spring, the high school homecoming dance was scheduled. Valeri and her friends were anxious to attend. Sue was asked by her boyfriend, Steve Schucker; and Jill was invited by a friend. Prov, Lynn, and Valeri were not asked to the dance. Val yearned to go and felt frustrated. As with most teenagers who were shunned, it depressed her. She vented her feelings by writing in her journal:

> *Often I wonder why I don't have a boyfriend. On last Saturday, March 11, at our church there was a disco. All weekend there were basketball tournaments. I had to cheer. I went to the disco after the game. There were hundreds of guys there of all ages and sizes. There were so many foxes. With all those guys there, not one asked me to dance. Why? I just don't understand. Not even the players who I cheered for, asked me to dance. That drove me crazy. All right, I don't have the best figure or the most gorgeous face, but there must be something about me a guy could like. They don't give me a chance. Two girls have fifty guys fighting over them. Why? They're not gorgeous. Guys just like them because they have good bodies and act like they're the new Farrah Fawcett. Only Farrah Fawcett's prettier and probably nicer.*

When Valeri felt depressed about boys she wouldn't say much to us, but she would vent her feelings with her friends. She also had this quote in her journal about being depressed:

> *When I feel depressed and need someone to talk to, besides my parents, I call Vasilia. She always gets me laughing. It's funny, I get her laughing when she's depressed. I just sing to her my theme song "Just a little ol' ant thinks he can move a rubber tree plant." I'm grateful to have such a true kind of friend like her. I don't know what I'd do without her.*

Actually, the problem of the homecoming dance was resolved quite nicely. Valeri decided that she would talk to Chris about going with her to the dance. He was pleased that she had called. "Yes," he said. "I'd be happy to go. I wouldn't mind going, even though I'm only a freshman."

Final arrangements for the dance were completed. Marietta and I were amused by Valeri's plans, especially when she returned to our house after picking Chris up, so that we could see them dressed up before they went to the dance.

Val and Sue enjoyed the evening, but they didn't find it too exciting. They noticed that many of the couples were showing affection for each other. Both Val and Sue, who were conservative, thought this was amusing. After a while, Sue got tired of seeing all of the emotional activity going on. She looked at Val and said, "Hey Val, what the hell are we doing here?"

They both laughed and said, "Come on, let's go grab a snack to eat. After all, you know that's our favorite pastime." Val enjoyed the homecoming dance, and appreciated Chris for going with her.

Time was running out for the seniors. The next big dance, the senior prom, was fast approaching. Sue was invited by Steve. Valeri wanted to go, but wasn't invited. Nor did she feel right about imposing on Chris a second time.

Although disappointed by not being asked to her prom, Valeri decided that she would arrange a "girls' night out" for Lynn, who also wasn't invited, and herself. On the evening of the prom Val and Lynn visited several different night-spots in the Metropolitan area. They dined, danced, and had a few beers. They both had a good time and often talked about the night of the senior prom.

Graduation was fast approaching. It was time for the seniors to complete their final high school semester and to receive their diplomas. Valeri and Sue planned to attend the University of Michigan, Lynn chose Wayne State University, and Jill selected Capitol College in Ohio. Prov was planning to marry early, so she decided not to attend college. It was time to think ahead and plan for the future.

Val and her friends decided to "live it up" one more time during graduation week. They planned to paint comments on one of our cars, wear their caps and gowns, drive around and sound the horn, and do all kinds of things to let the world know they were graduating and ready to move on to the next phase of life.

The decision as to which car Valeri would use for graduation week depended on her sister Nikki. Nikki drove an old Maverick back and forth to Eastern Michigan University, but since she was going to graduate from Eastern that semester, Nikki felt that she needed a better automobile. So Nikki asked to use our newer Pontiac Sunbird. Now, Valeri was a little perturbed with this, because she wanted to use "her" favorite Sunbird. In a moment of disappointment, Val wrote in her journal:

> *Tonight at dinner, Mom and Dad asked me and Nikki if we could have graduation parties together. I said yes, but Nikki said no, it's not fair. She's crying the blues about how she gets treated unfairly. I hate when she's home because my Mother gives her what she wants. I wanted to use the little car. My Mom usually says yes, because the old one is so hard for me to drive. Now since Nikki complains, she gets to take the little car.*

The old Maverick was difficult for Valeri to drive as she could hardly see over the dashboard. It drove like an old truck and was very difficult to steer because it didn't have power steering. Actually, Valeri's friends didn't mind riding in the Maverick as they had fun helping her steer when she was making turns. It was really an old clunker, but it beat walking. The scene was set. Valeri would use the Maverick, and Nikki and Valeri would have separate parties.

All systems were go for Seniors' Day. Finals were completed. Valeri drove the car over to Sue's house, and the girls secured some water paints and painted on funny quotes. Sue painted "Shit Shaker" on one side. They laughed and laughed about that phrase, as they agreed: "It's an exact description." However, Sue and Val quickly washed it off, as they didn't want to offend anybody - especially their parents. Some of the painted words that stayed on the car were: "79" for their year of graduation, "GPN" for Grosse Pointe North, "Good Dude," "Snob," "Comrades," "Wild Ones" with arrows pointing in, "Goose," "Take Me There," and on the door, "Exit." They spent several other days that week driving around town. The four friends attended many of the "hot bashes," and cruised up and down Lakeshore Drive along Lake St. Clair in Grosse Pointe Shores, which was one of their favorite pastimes.

Lakeshore Drive is lined with huge mansions and is a very beautiful drive. One day the girls decided to drive Sue's father's Cadillac into the driveway of one of the mansions and take pictures of each other standing there. They decided to repeat this a couple of times, and Sue agreed. At the final stop, the girls left the car, walked to the house, and had their pictures taken. When they returned to the car, Sue let out a big scream: "Oh no! I left the keys in the car and the motor is still running!" This predicament was especially upsetting as Sue had to go to the Renaissance Center to work at her co-op business shortly. There stood the five girls, staring at the car, listening to the running motor, unable to get into the locked car. Sue began to panic since she still had to go home to change clothes before going to her job. One of the girls suggested they knock on the door of the home to ask permission to telephone Sue's brother Steve and have him bring another key. Sue thought this was a good idea, but didn't know how the homeowner would react to her knock.

Valeri walked with her up the stairs. They knocked on the door. Very innocently they looked at the person who answered the door. Sue began, "We have a problem. Could you please allow me to use your telephone to call my brother to come and help us open the door of our car? I left my keys in it and the motor is still running!"

The woman at the door began laughing heartily and answered "Okay, I'll do you graduates a favor. Come on in and make your call." Sue telephoned her brother, and then thanked the woman. Sue and Val went back to join the other girls at the car. A short while later Steve showed up with the keys and the girls finally got into the car and took off. Sue did make it to work on time that day.

Marietta, Nikki, Debbie and her husband, and I attended Valeri's graduation ceremony. Both Marietta and I were emotional, but in a quiet way. We were both thinking about what Valeri had gone through to get to this point in her life. We were so happy to see her sitting there in her cap and gown, ready to receive her diploma.

Sue, the class president, made an excellent speech about what high school meant to her and of how proud she was to be graduating from Grosse Pointe North. Prov, the class Valedictorian, also made a brief speech concerning her high school experiences. Sue, Jill, Lynn, and Valeri were all cum laude students.

The reception after the graduation ceremony was a favorable experience, yet sad in many ways. The students were hugging each other, crying and laughing at the same time. For many people, graduation is an interesting time, as it combines pleasant memories of the past with anticipation for unknown future experiences.

Valeri and her friends decided to go out and have a lively evening to celebrate one last time their graduation from Grosse Pointe North High School. That night, I noticed Valeri's school yearbook was on the table. I picked it up, sat down, and began looking through it. It was a wonderful book. I was so proud to know that our Valeri was the editor of this book. I then turned to its front pages and read some of the things her friends had written about her.

*Val, you're such a super sweet, super person. You've been a friend on yearbook at the same time you got me moving. I'll miss you next year, especially if I join the yearbook. I won't ever forget you. Love, Dann (Lil-stem)*

*Val, thanks for all the help with Valhalla over the years with the hard work you did in room B-325. You really motivated me in the darkroom. Well, have fun in college and have a happy life. Good luck. Don Wishart.*

*Val, words just can't express all the things I'd like to tell you. It has been a memorable experience. All those late nights, phone calls to Modern Mrs. Miller's. We need you now!!! Well the book is finally here and it looks like we have worked hard at it. Of course the color section is the best. Thanks for all the great times. Good Luck at U of M. You better keep in touch. Love Always, Mary Sanders.*

Vasilia, although not a student at Grosse Pointe North High School, also wrote in Valeri's book. She and Val used to call themselves "Laverne and Shirley" after the TV sit-com at the time:

*Laverne, Well, sweetie, what can I say? You're the best sister a woooman could have. You bring out the worst in me and I love it! Thanks for being everything to me and for everything you do for me. Well, when you go to Ann Arbor don't get so caught up in the dudes that you forget about little old me. I'll be up there every weekend, and you better write to me and come home whenever you can. I'm sure gonna miss you, Vernie. Well, here come the tears again. Good Luck and don't do anything I would do 'cause you'll get in trouble. Behave! I love you always. Love, Vasilia.*

Val's friend Chris Garkinos wrote on the back cover:

*Val, Howdy! I don't believe I'm writing this novel because this means you're going to be away. What am I going to do? We've had such great times this year - Homecoming, G.O.Y.A. (when you were there) and of course yearbook. We had incidents that I'll never forget, Miss Sopranowicz' grandson, me trying to help you drive your sister's truck, or us going on the racers at Kings Island. I can never repay you for all the rides you gave me, unless I p-a-y for all the gas. Now it's been fun putting down people, if you know what I mean. Seen any fat straw lately? It looks like I'm not going to take up all your space so thanks for being a sister to me, I love you, Chris.*

There were many other comments by classmates and friends throughout the book.

Valeri was very happy for the opportunity to work on the yearbook staff during high school. She wanted to express her thanks as editor of the final yearbook to all involved under "acknowledgments" on the last page. This is what she wrote:

*Well, we did it! We, the Valhalla staff, produced a book that we hoped would please everyone, especially Steve. Just before the beginning of the 1978-79 school year, a tragedy occurred: we lost someone we admired and loved, Steve Lazurenko. Steve was to be the editor, and I was to be his assistant. Suddenly, after the accident, I was faced with the job of editor. I always kept Steve in my mind and endeavored to create a book which he would love and be proud of. Thanks to many, many unselfish people whom I could never have done without, we made this book a cherishable reality. Miss Marsha Hall - Thanks for the tanks. They helped us develop a wonderful book. The Science Department - Thanks loads for the darkroom privileges. Peggy Levan - Thanks for finishing the three necessary pictures in a lickety-split. Modern Yearbook - Thanks for designing and opening and fulfilling my aspirations. Mrs. Martin, Mrs. Rogers, Mrs. DeSantis - "Hi, can I use the phone?" "Hi, can you give me her sixth hour class?" "Hi, I need fifty of these run off." Thanks for putting up with these requests, for early sixth-hour dismissal. These three ladies have the patience of saints. Chris Garkinos - Thanks for revitalizing body copy, replenishing cut lines, and rejuvenating spirits when you could have been relaxing at home. WNIC - Thanks for the last minute support. Madeline Nichols - Thanks for being my buddy, chum, pal! Mary Sanders - It's been great having you as an accomplice in the opening section, in divisions, and sixth-hour dismiss antics! To all my section heads, Madeline Nichols, Maureen Stemmelen, Sue Barr and Jim Martens. Thanks for devotions, determination and defending Valhalla's HONOR. Thayer Carlson - Thanks for keeping the money rolling in as I kept spending it! Jack Spzytman and Dan Wishart - Thanks for the super job. The Valhalla staff never had to suffer from the "I-am-*

*waiting-for-my-enlargement" syndrome. Thanks to the entire, truly
100 percent Valhalla members who gave all they had and more!
Thanks to Miss Nancy Smith who was a master in exhibiting all the
qualities of a champion yearbook advisor. I have obtained a galaxy
of journalistic knowledge, understanding of people and perseverance
from working as editor under Miss Smith. Mr. and Mrs. Samaras -
Thanks for having the true patience that only parents could have!
Thanks to you the reader. After all, there's no business like Valhalla
Business! LOVE YOU ALL, VAL.*

I realized as I sat there that it was a great finish to a wonderful four years
in high school for Valeri. It was a happy milestone in her life. Valeri
accomplished so much and opened so many avenues in all aspects of her
life, making it possible for all the nice things to happen.

Valeri was accepted as a student at the University of Michigan and
would attend in the fall with her good friend Sue Fattore.

After graduation, Valeri enjoyed a restful, happy-go-lucky summer.
In mid-summer, she would return to the Greek Orthodox Camp with
her good friend Vasilia. They had attended camp the previous summer,
and were going to go back for two weeks this year to serve as junior
counselors. But, as Val was getting ready to go to camp, Vasilia called and
notified Val that she would only be able to stay at camp for one week.
Valeri was disappointed because they always had such a wonderful time
together. Val pulled out her journal and wrote:

*I called Vasilia and she told me that she cannot go to camp for two
weeks. We were supposed to leave a week from today. She said her
mother doesn't want her to go. She can only go for one week. I would
say okay, but we had it all planned. Now she changes everything. I
didn't mean to seem angry, but I couldn't help it. I couldn't understand
how a person (her mother) could just change like that. Her mother
said because of her allergies. Well, she only had a stuffed up nose.
There's a nurse at camp if she needed anything. I'm so glad my
mother doesn't treat me like that. I mean I have Mediterranean
Anemia and my mother worries about my going, but she doesn't
pamper me. I tell her that I'm going. She understands that I have to
get away and shouldn't be treated any differently from other kids.*

Valeri and Vasilia went to camp. Valeri stayed for two weeks; Vasilia only
one. In her journal, Val described how beautiful it was at the camp and
the fun she had with the children and counselors. She really enjoyed it.

By summer's end, Valeri didn't spend very much time with Sue, as Sue was busy working and getting ready to attend the University of Michigan. Instead, Val began spending more time with Lynn Ekstrom. One night, after being with Lynn, Valeri wrote in her journal:

> *Tonight Lynn and I had a plain talk and it was very good. I feel I have gained a new, dear friend, one whom I can talk to and not feel stupid. I am very happy to have found her.*

That summer Mr. G. Bruce Feighner, the principal of Grosse Pointe North High School, called to inform us that Valeri was awarded a five hundred dollar scholarship by the Crisis Club in Grosse Pointe. The scholarship money would be applied toward her tuition at the University of Michigan. He sounded as happy as we were about the award. Mr. Feighner had always been supportive of Valeri throughout the four years, and was very understanding whenever she had any kind of problem. He congratulated Valeri on an excellent effort in high school and wished her the best of luck at the University of Michigan.

# 12

# The Big Step: College

V ALERI spent a restful and tranquil summer at home after graduating from high school. She enjoyed the interim period between high school and college. Although she had wanted to work during the summer, Marietta and I insisted that she enjoy her free time and not take on a job. So she did just that. She drove to our old East Detroit neighborhood to visit her friends, she socialized considerably with the Junior Goyans, and she spent lots of time with Sue, Jill, and Lynn.

Valeri and I spent many evenings that summer taking walks with Schatzie, and talking about life in general and her plans for the future. Val also spent a great deal of time shopping for clothes with her mother and looking at the latest styles in the shopping centers.

This freedom from assigned responsibilities seemed to benefit Valeri's health. The only time she knew that anything was wrong physically was when she went in for three transfusions. Otherwise, she experienced another healthy, enjoyable summer.

Vacation was winding down rapidly, signifying a need for Valeri to make final preparations to attend the University of Michigan in Ann Arbor. There were many things she had to buy and things to pack in preparation for the oncoming semester. Marietta, a master at vacation-planning, helped Valeri immeasurably in readying herself for college.

Val and Sue Fattore made dozens of telephone calls back and forth deciding what they were going to take with them. They were both extremely anxious and excited about the future, and they enjoyed all of the tasks necessary to prepare for university life.

Marietta and I didn't know why Valeri chose to attend the University of Michigan. While it is one of the finest universities in the country, it also has a very complex campus with a varied student body. We thought Valeri might be better off attending Wayne State University, where I worked, or one of the smaller colleges closer to home. But Valeri insisted that she wanted to be a graduate of the University of Michigan, since it had a wonderful communications program, which was her intended major.

Of course, the thought of Val's going away to school with Sue was very intriguing. We were concerned about her attending such a large university, but we realized that Ann Arbor was only one hour away from home. Also, Valeri wouldn't get lost in the hustle and bustle of the big campus life. She would balance her schedule to enjoy the university, and still would have considerable time for academics, relaxation, and socializing. Since Valeri preferred an active life this scenario seemed ideal for her.

Although Valeri welcomed the opportunity to attend the University of Michigan, she did have some apprehensions. On August 4, 1979 she wrote in her journal:

> *I am very frightened yet excited. I graduated on June 14, 1979. It was a very strange experience in high school, yet with a great deal of amusement. Soon I will be attending the University of Michigan. I am both scared and excited. I am scared because I will be alone with Sue. Classes will be difficult. Everyone keeps asking me are you sure you want to attend. You can always go to Wayne. It is a new experience and therefore I don't know what to expect. I will have to give the most that I possess and try my best. I'm going to make the most of this experience and hopefully it'll pay off in the end.*

It was now time for orientation week. Orientation week gives new college students the opportunity to familiarize themselves with the university in general, to check into their rooms, to take a series of tests, and to find out about campus life. It is also a time to meet once or twice with the other freshmen as a group.

Valeri and Sue drove back and forth to Ann Arbor several times throughout orientation week. One advantage the two of them had was that Sue's two older brothers, John and Steve, were already attending the University.

Sue visited Couzens, her dormitory, which was located some distance from the Diag, the center of campus. Valeri had requested a single room in the Betsy Barbour dormitory, located next to the Student Center and across the street from the Diag, where a number of activities take place. Also, many of the classroom buildings were located nearby. In addition, there were clothing shops, restaurants, and a theater within a short walking distance of the Betsy Barbour dormitory.

During orientation week, Valeri's small stature got her into a serious, but peculiar, situation. Many of the freshmen had gathered on the mall between several of the dormitories. They had an old parachute top (without the ropes) and were looking for someone to put on it for a parachute ride. The parachute ride is executed when several people hold the circular chute and pull outward on a given signal. The chute becomes taut, propelling a beach ball high up in the air. Val stood by, innocently watching, when someone said, "Let's put a person on the chute and see if we can make him fly up in the air." They looked around and someone else said: "Here's a nice, small, young lady," pointing to Val. "Let's see if she'll fly."

Valeri laughed while objecting, "No thanks, I'll do my flying in an airplane." But the gang holding the parachute insisted that she volunteer. Although she objected, they escorted her onto the parachute, while Sue was standing there laughing. Finally, Valeri consented to try it. She got on the parachute, still doubting that she was doing the right thing. Several fellows grabbed the parachute, counted: "One, two, three, GO!" and they all backed up and pulled the parachute toward themselves, which put tension on the parachute. Up flew Valeri, about six feet in the air! She immediately came tumbling down, and landed hard on her side. She hit the ground and rolled over, then sat up laughing. Sue was frightened and worried as she ran over to Val, thinking that maybe Val had been hurt. Val stood up and everyone applauded as she smiled and waved and walked off with Sue.

"Oh, my goodness Val," said Sue, "I was so worried that you were hurt."

"You think *you* were worried," replied Val. "I was really concerned when I went flying through the air and didn't know how I was going to land or what was going to happen. Please, Sue, if you see any other groups having fun doing weird things, don't talk me into going over to see what's going on." They both laughed about that incident whenever anyone mentioned orientation week.

Student activities for orientation week ended on Friday. Saturday and Sunday were the two days that students could move into their dorms to prepare for classes that would begin on the following Monday.

On Friday evening we spent some time talking with Debbie, Nikki, and Valeri about college life. Nikki had just graduated from Eastern Michigan University and was giving Valeri tips on how to adjust to the college scene. Val seemed to be in good spirits and listened intently. Marietta and I received some satisfaction from talking about the future, and we also found humor in many things that Val would probably do at school. Additionally, it was comforting for all of us to know that friends at the University of Michigan were ready to help Valeri should there ever be a problem.

Regardless of all the plans being finalized, Marietta again made Valeri the offer to stay home and attend Wayne State University. "We will not worry about deposits applied towards the room at the University of Michigan or anything else!" Marietta said.

"Oh! Mom! Please don't worry," laughed Valeri.

Valeri, being very conscientious and thoughtful, discussed in her journal her feelings about her last night at home before leaving for the University of Michigan. She wrote:

*September 4, 1979, 12:20 a.m. In seven more hours (approximately) I will begin a new life. I will be moving up to the University of Michigan, leaving my parents, Nikki, Lynn, and Vasilia. Today was very sad. Vasilia and I went shopping and when I had to say good-bye, I could not. It will be so hard not being able to call her every night and not to have that special friend who always makes me laugh and knows exactly what I am thinking - just a call away. Also, it will be hard to live on my own, not having my parents around to talk to; yet, they are only a phone call away too. I am very, very grateful that they're giving me this opportunity. I am very, very lucky to have such wonderful parents. I want to make the most of this opportunity. **I want to succeed.** I want to have fun and get a good education and do well in all my classes. I am going to try my best to do this!*

Marietta and I felt a lot of apprehension, too, that night, as we thought about Valeri leaving us and going to the University of Michigan. There were a lot of thoughts running through our minds as we tried to sleep - thoughts about the pressures she would be under and whether or not her health would permit her to continue attending until graduation.

It wasn't long before the alarm clock went off and it was time to get up and drive to Ann Arbor. En route, Marietta made one last comment. "Valeri, you still have a chance to say no to the University of Michigan and yes to Wayne State University. It wouldn't hurt our feelings if you wanted to change your mind right now." (Marietta always had a way of belaboring a point.)

Valeri just laughed and said, "Okay, Mom. Nice try, but it's too late." Soon after, we arrived at the Betsy Barbour Dormitory entrance, only to find that there was no available parking. After driving around the block several times, we realized it would take some time for me to find a place to park the car or I would have to park a distance away. So, I took the suitcases out of the car and put them on the front step of the dorm. Marietta told Valeri that we would drive around, find a parking place, and come back to see her in a short period of time. Meanwhile, Valeri was to go in and register for her room and determine where it was located. We would then help her unpack her clothes and put them away.

After finally parking the car, Marietta and I made our way back to the dormitory. We walked to the main desk and asked in what room we could find Valeri Samaras. We were told she was in Room 103, immediately outside the main lobby door in the vestibule. Marietta was very upset with the location. I suggested that we wait and see where the room was located before worrying. When we walked to Val's room we found that indeed it was just outside of the dorm lobby. As we entered the building, there were two rooms off to the side. They were formerly used for storing maintenance equipment, such as brooms. We found Valeri inside, staring at her room, which was very, very tiny. She couldn't quite open the door because it bumped into the bed. "Surely they don't expect me to live in a room as small as this one!" Needless to say, Marietta and I were upset, too.

Marietta immediately proclaimed: "Valeri cannot live in this room."

All of us went to the main desk. Marietta asked whom we could talk to about changing a room. She was told that we would have to go to the Housing Director's office and talk to one of the people in charge. We proceeded to that office and spoke to Miss Brown. She explained that, unfortunately, due to the big crowd of students attending the University this year, there were no other single rooms available in Betsy Barbour and that Valeri would have to stay in that room.

"No way!" Marietta immediately replied.

So, we asked to see the Director of Housing. We were told that we had to make an appointment to see him later in the day. The Housing Director informed us that there was nothing we could do about Valeri's room. So, we asked to see his boss. The Director said the Vice President of Housing was the person we sought. He gave us the Vice President's name and telephone number. We then called and visited the Vice President of Housing. He was a very polite gentleman and understood our feelings. He said he would try to help us, but that it would take a week or so before he could do anything.

Although we were unhappy with his comments, we decided that there was only one alternative at this time. We went back to the miniature room and helped Val unpack and get situated. Marietta commented that because the room was away from the regular dormitory and the windows were close to the ground, someone could very easily break into the room through the window, creating yet another threat. I told Marietta not to worry, and that eventually everything would work out. Actually, Val didn't seem too concerned. She said, "I'll do what has to be done, and anyway, I'll be able to get a new room shortly."

Although Valeri wasn't too keen about living in that little room, her sense of humor and creativity came through later in the semester, when she wrote a short story for an English class. The story went as follows:

*It was a gloomy September day. The clouds began to rumble and roll (or was that my stomach?). Today was the big day - THE BIGGIE. I stumbled out of bed, and a wave of nausea passed over me as I saw the boxes filled with all my prized belongings in the corner. My treasured stuffed Hippos, Beetle Eep Boop Boop and Helium, carefully placed in the box, looked dejected after being removed from their familiar spots on my shelf. "Really," I thought, "an eighteen-year-old 'woman' going away to college, with her prized possessions, stuffed hippos; that's maturity!" Those hippos were precious to me though. I had acquired them as gifts from my friends. I started liking hippos when I was in junior high. I just thought they were kind of cute. Everyone else thought they were ugly, though. My friend Marilyn gave me Helium when I sprained my ankle at camp. He is so cute: psychedelic shades of purple, inquisitive eyes, and a tiny piece of rope that forms a silly smile. I received Beetle Eep Boop Boop when I was in my freshman year in high school. I strolled into school that day, kind of depressed because I was turning fifteen. Wow, old age, huh! I walked up to my locker and found crepe paper strewn all over it and a huge sign saying "Happy Birthday, Val!" I opened my locker and a deluge of balloons poured out; among them was the fat sailor-looking hippo, Beetle Eep Boop Boop, from my friend Marie. I felt so happy those days. Everything was so much fun. Now, my hippos would find a new home and so would I. Maybe none of us would be accepted, I shrugged.*

*I plunked down on my bed, and stared at my room with the exotic bamboo-striped wallpaper. I saw the television, stereo, and the now-empty closet that stretched the length of one wall, and my shelves filled with non-educational books. The room seemed so large and the sandy brown carpeting filled with warmth and serenity. I would spend so much time in here thinking and dreaming. Hours of my leisure would be spent listening to the radio. I was always commanded to turn it down; and watching television, all the shows my Mom recommended I shouldn't watch. Suddenly reality hit me like a slap in the face: today my life would change.*

*"Val, it's time to go!" I jumped at the sound of my mother's crisp voice. I imagined her standing in our foyer, wearing her Calvin Klein skirt and top, freshly polished black boots, jet-black hair in its fluffy style, a pleasant smile on her face, and her eyes swollen with tears.*

*Going away to college had been a touchy subject in my family. We talked constantly about whether I, "the baby" of the family, should go away to U of M and leave the family. It wasn't really as though I was going to leave the family* forever. *But finally, though, that day came - the day my mother dreaded because her youngest daughter was growing up, or so she thought. I chuckled as I glanced at my two hippo-friends. It was the day my father dreaded because it meant being on my own and making my own decisions. I trudged down the stairs and said, "I'm ready," endeavoring to speak over the lump in my throat. As I left, I patted my dog and noticed his droopy tail.*

*Soon the car was loaded, and we were well on our way. It seemed like there was an eternity of silence. The songs on the radio flowed through my mind and each triggered a fond memory. I thought of how my friends and I spent the night before at our favorite neighborhood ice cream store. We used to go there often, probably every night. It was a wonder we didn't turn into blimps. We would act crazy, ordering huge sundaes, and laughing until our sides would ache or until one of us would have to leave the table because the ice cream could not pass the giggles in our throat. We would sing songs over and over. Often the timid, extremely slow waitress, who always forgot my chocolate sprinkles, would threaten to kick us out if we didn't behave. Those times would be gone. Now, I had to act grown-up, like a college student.*

*"I thought of how my Mom cooked my favorite meal of Spinach*

*Pie and Lamb. It was great. I ate so much. I had this overwhelming feeling I wouldn't be eating for eight months. Everyone told me horror stories about dorm food and I'm so picky, I figured I would never eat at school. My Mom's dinner seemed like The Last Supper. Everyone was so solemn. My dad kept attempting to be humorous. My mom kept adding things to the list of gear I had to take to school. I, though, kept shoveling the food in my mouth, partly to get all the nourishment I could get, and partly to avoid the tension in the air.*

*"I thought of how my Dad and I watched the baseball game on TV. I always seemed to have time to root for the teams with my dad. Who knows, though, if I'll even remember which teams need rooting for, like the Tigers who lost six to two.*

*"How could I leave my family and friends? Why would I want to leave my family and friends? Because everyone expected me to go to college. It was normal. Yeah, but whoever said I was normal? Remember, I'm the one with the stuffed hippos in the trunk. I'm the one who got flung in the air on a parachute at orientation. And, I'm the one who rode a tricycle in the eighth-grade talent show and rammed into a brick wall. Normal was not me, I surmised!*

*"Vali, we're here!"*

*"Huh?"*

*I looked up in a daze and saw the herds of pedestrians filing off the curb in front of the approaching cars. Then, I saw it - my new home, Betsy Barbour. We circled the streets over and over without finding a single spot to spare in the rows of multi-colored cars. After a large passage of time, out of frustration my parents chose to leave me off to fend for myself. I stood outside my car door with my luggage and faced Barbour. I wanted to scream and run back to the car and order my father to take me home. I couldn't, though. I felt paralyzed, but I had to take the first step. I had to know why my parents always planted the idea of college in my brain. I knew my life would change, but maybe change was important. Wasn't it? I figured maybe once I was inside my room everything would be all right. I would love the place. I gave one final glance back to where my parents' car was, and saw it drift away. I began to march toward Betsy Barbour, the place that could be the end of me.*

*As I entered the building, I saw the stark, white walls which gave me a sudden shiver. I made my way through the chattering girls and piles of junk in the hall, and went to the main desk.*

*"Yes, what's your name?" the lady said coldly from behind the metal desk.*

*"Valeri Samaras."*

*"Here's your key. Be at the mass meeting tonight," she said mechanically and looked back down at the papers piled on her desk.*

*"Excuse me, where is room 103?" I asked a girl leaning against the wall in the unoccupied hall.*

*"I don't know!" she snapped.*

*I stared at her for a few seconds and then continued walking, destined to find my room by myself. I wandered through the hall to the stairwell. Finally I saw a tiny fire door that said rooms 102 and 103. I entered and there I was standing in a very small aisle with room enough for one person. Thank goodness I was small. I fidgeted with the key and tried to steady my hand as I put the key in the lock. I turned the key first one way, but found that I had to turn it the other way to succeed. I slowly pushed the door open and it slammed against the bed, which was supposedly across the room. I stood, scrutinizing my abode. The door took up half the room; the bed took the other. The contrast from this pale, white room was sharp when I thought of my lively, warm room at home. How could I live, eat, sleep, study, or do everything in this room? I knew, though, that this room was only the beginning. I had yet to face walking into the cafeteria alone or finding my classes in a maze of walkways and rushing cars, of tackling the homework, and grasping the knowledge this college had to offer. I heard my echoing gulp fill the bare room.*

# 13

# A New, Exciting World

VALERI'S life as a university student began the following Monday, when she attended classes for the first time. It was a shocking experience for her to see the thousands of students walking back and forth to their classrooms. Fortunately, Valeri loved crowded places and felt very much at home on campus in a short period of time. It seemed that everywhere she went there were throngs of people, whether it was in classrooms, the streets or the Student Center. She took a liking to this immediately and rationalized: "All these students are doing the same thing I'm doing, trying to further their educations and get a nice job later on in life."

Valeri selected communication arts as her major field of study. The classes in her first year revolved around general education courses. She did have classes in English, and also continued to study French for one more year. She liked the communication field and found it extremely interesting because it dealt with reaching people by way of radio, television, or press - using the media to pass a message onto people. Valeri was intrigued by communications and wanted to learn to become a part of this field. She loved a challenge and felt that by studying communications she could someday establish herself in the media profession.

Valeri fell in love with the campus lifestyle and in her new-found independence. The independent lifestyle of a campus student gave her the opportunity to identify with the adult world that she would enter in the near future. She loved making decisions for herself on a daily basis. Also, she enjoyed her classes and the professors, the city of Ann Arbor, and especially the life at Betsy Barbour Dormitory and the new friends that she made.

Being a night person, Valeri made sure that her classes were in the late morning and early afternoon. This schedule would permit her to sleep until late in the morning, which she loved to do; and, of course, it would assure that she received enough rest from day to day.

Soon, Valeri realized the difference between high school and college, as far as the amount of classroom work. In college, she realized that attending classes fifteen hours a week was only the beginning, because then she would spend many, many, more hours doing the homework required by the instructors. She established an excellent routine and did well in overall planning. Although her days were very busy, she seemed to get all of her work completed on time.

There was always the worry about needing a transfusion and having to take time off from school. But, since she had no Friday classes, Valeri could come back home and go to St. Joseph's Hospital for a transfusion on Friday, rest up on Saturday, and go back to school on Sunday, ready for Monday's classes. This worked out quite nicely.

Because of her anemia she also had a problem with her right knee. The anemia prevented Valeri's bones from forming correctly. As a result, she had a difficult time straightening her leg. As time went on, Val worked around this, even though eventually she wasn't able to straighten her leg completely. She learned to walk quite normally without any aids.

Marietta and I had peace of mind because we had decided to communicate with Valeri by telephone every night. Either she would call us or we would call her. Also, we visited Valeri quite often during the week, as Ann Arbor was only fifty miles from our doorstep and very accessible by Interstate 94. We found it very enjoyable to jump in our car and drive to Ann Arbor after work. During our visits, we would walk around Ann Arbor and shop with Val. Typically, the evening would end by going to a nice restaurant in Ann Arbor and then walking her to the dorm. Marietta and I always had the feeling that Valeri immensely enjoyed our visits. We appreciated spending time with our wonderful Val and listening to her talk about her life.

Valeri fell in love with the University of Michigan and the city of Ann Arbor, with its splendid restaurants and beautiful shopping malls. Most of all, though, she loved the friendly people throughout the city. She always felt it was a perfect environment for a "big-city girl" like herself. Ann Arbor had all the components of a large city: tall campus buildings, major shopping areas, an outstanding university medical center, business and industrial sections, a large residential area for the students, and a large residential section on the outskirts of town.

Being a university town, there was much emphasis on the cultural scene, with a movie theater, the legitimate theater, and art museums. It was an absolutely electrifying community. During the school year, there were an additional thirty-five thousand people in Ann Arbor. Valeri loved being a part of that scene. Her years at the university were a high point in her life.

Marietta and I loved being included, because it gave us an impression of campus life, which we had never quite enjoyed when we attended Wayne State University in Detroit. We loved taking the quick drive to Ann Arbor to visit Valeri. It was common for us to buy her a little gift, like a university sweater or something for her room, before driving home. We often said it was an opportunity for Valeri to really see what the world was like away from home. It gave her an opportunity to become an independent person and to adjust to this world.

The University of Michigan has always enjoyed the reputation of being an outstanding academic institution with an outstanding medical center. It is also an outstanding athletic power, with a football program that has always been among the best in our country. So, it was only natural for Valeri and her friends to become very involved in attending football games and the festivities before and after the games.

A University of Michigan football fan since childhood, I seized the opportunity to attend several football games each year. The first one that Valeri, her friends, and I attended took place at the end of her first week of classes there. I drove to Ann Arbor, picked up Valeri, Sue and a couple of other friends from the dorms, and followed the parade and band by car to the stadium located on the outskirts of Ann Arbor. On the way there we noticed thousands of people lining the streets, hanging out of windows, and sitting on decks by their homes, waving as the band marched by. The girls couldn't help but notice the good time that was being had by all. I could see a glint in Valeri's eye, knowing what she was thinking - that she would love to be a part of this partying scene and planned to do so eventually.

At the football game that afternoon, a player named Anthony Carter touched the ball for the first time on a punt from Northwestern University, and ran sixty-five yards for a touchdown. The second time he touched the ball was on another punt, and he ran that one back for another touchdown - seventy yards. The girls screamed and hollered; they were really excited about both runs. Valeri and her friends enjoyed the whole scenario: the stadium filled to capacity with over one-hundred thousand people; the wild cheering of the crowd; the cheerleaders who would somersault off of a little brick wall every time a touchdown was scored, a somersault for each point accumulated, as the huge crowd counted in unison; the mascots on the field; the excitement of the immediate crowd passing remarks back and forth; the hitting of beach balls, starting at field level and going all the way over and out of the stadium; and the band's performance, at half time and at the game's conclusion. All of this extravaganza was a memorable afternoon for Valeri and her friends. Val told me that she planned to be the team's best fan.

I had the feeling that the girls couldn't wait for me to drive home, so that they could join the party that was being planned at the Betsy Barbour dorm. As I dropped them off and kissed Val good-bye, I said, "See you later. Enjoy yourself, honey."

I attended almost all of the home football games that fall with Valeri. She seemed to enjoy my company. On several occasions that year I would pick up Val at her dorm, drive to a local restaurant and meet my long-time friend Jim Demetry and his son, young Jim, who was also a student at the university and knew Val. We would all have breakfast together and then attend the game. Jim and his son were avid football fans. We enjoyed attending the games together. After a game was over, we would walk to a local restaurant, share our thoughts about the game, and eat dinner. Afterwards, Val and I would bid the Demetrys good-bye, and I would take Valeri back to her dorm, then drive home.

I made a promise to Valeri (at her insistence, of course) that if Michigan should win the Big Ten championship and be selected to go to the Rose Bowl in California on New Year's Day, I would take her to that game. (Michigan was a regular contender at the Rose Bowl during those years.) Since I had always wanted to attend a Rose Bowl game, I also hoped that Michigan would win their league championship; but, unfortunately, they did not. So, we did not attend the Rose Bowl.

Valeri took part in numerous social activities planned by Betsy Barbour's entertainment committee, and in general learned to enjoy dormitory life. In fact, she even raved about the cafeteria food from time to time - especially about the super-duper double chocolate sundaes with whipped cream.

Valeri developed a nice friendship with Susie Soltero, who was from Puerto Rico. Val and Susie had one thing in common: staying up late at night. They had a great time talking into the early hours of the morning about life, school, and other things that girls usually talk about. Susie was also a communications major, and they both joined the staff of the *Michigan Daily*, the university's newspaper. They were special assignment sports reporters.

Mary Beth, a business student from Bay City, was another of Valeri's close friends during that first year. Val's circle of friends increased as the year wore on. She felt that the Betsy Barbour dorm group was almost like a sorority because of the similar college lifestyle of the residents. Valeri never discussed her anemia with her university friends. Consequently, they didn't know that she had a major health problem. When it was time for a transfusion, Valeri would casually tell them, "I have to go home this weekend to take care of some business, and to get back-on-track health-wise. It's nothing major. I'll see you guys on Monday."

Valeri still kept in close contact with Sue Fattore, and she crossed paths with many of her other friends from church and high school. Valeri would often tell Marietta and me that she would see more friends and acquaintances "up at school" than she ever did at home.

Occasionally, Val came home on a weekend just to spend time with family and friends. Although she could easily find a ride home, I would often insist that it was no problem for me to drive to Ann Arbor and pick her up. My ulterior motive was to call on my friend Jim Demetry and set up a meeting at the University of Michigan golf course, one of the best and most challenging in the country. Valeri went along with this most of the time. Jim and I would golf late Friday afternoon, and afterwards I would pick up Valeri at her dorm and then drive home.

It was easy for Valeri to find things to keep herself busy on her weekend visits home. And, since there were so many other friends' sons and daughters returning to the campus, it was fairly easy for Val to secure a ride back to Ann Arbor. When Valeri had a large suitcase of clothes to take back with her, she'd often say, "Dad, let me call Mike Daskas. He gives me curb service." By that she meant that Mike would take her directly to the doorstep of her dorm, carry her suitcase to her room, and make sure she was comfortable before leaving for his own dorm. She gave him the nickname, "Mike the Gentleman."

Campus life always held a deep interest for Valeri during that first year. She enjoyed riding the bus, which carried her around campus to all the various dorms and locations, and also to the new campus near the outskirts of Ann Arbor. She enjoyed seeing all of the activities that were taking place around the university and Ann Arbor. Quickly, Valeri found the activities in which she wanted to participate. Often, she would stroll through the Diag and people-watch. As the focal point of campus, the Diag was conducive to demonstrations and other displays by radical groups within the diversified student body.

Sometimes demonstrations were held near the Student Center, next to Betsy Barbour. Val would walk on the perimeter of the action, read the signs carried by the radicals, and try to determine what point they were trying to make. She would study the behavior of the group. Sometimes she would encourage them, because she felt strongly about their beliefs on that particular issue; and at other times she would look on with disfavor, but not say anything, when she disagreed with the demonstrators. Primarily, she would feel that many of the groups were "radicals without a cause." But she felt the demonstrations were an interesting part of college life.

Val and Susie Soltero received satisfaction as roving sports reporters for the *Michigan Daily* newspaper. Val learned much about the total sports activity program going on at the university. As a freshman roving sports reporter, Valeri's basic assignment was to interview athletes on the track team, and also to follow the activities of the women's track team. This involvement was intriguing to Valeri because it gave her a first-hand opportunity to write about outstanding college sports figures.

Valeri was a very conscientious academic student during her freshman year. There were many times she had to "burn the midnight oil" to complete or catch up on assignments. The academic setting, with outstanding teachers who made interesting presentations, combined with the easy-going atmosphere of the classroom, intrigued Valeri. She appreciated the in-depth knowledge she was acquiring from her classes.

Sue Fattore often said to Val that she was overwhelmed with school and that the pressures of the academic work were getting her down. Sue couldn't understand how Val could take such an easy-going approach to her studies and do so well. Also, it seemed that Valeri was never hindered by or concerned about her illness.

Regardless of what other people thought about Valeri's outwardly casual attitude towards pressures as a student, inwardly she had considerable thoughts and concerns about her school work. There were times during her first year when she would receive a good grade on a test but would still be very upset with the results. After doing poorly on one exam, Valeri wrote in her journal:

> *Well, remember the good, old optimism? It went to pieces the minute I got my media mid-term back. Today was a cruddy day. It was just awful. I don't know what to do. I'm doing so badly. I started out good, too. Oh, well, I'll just have to begin by doing my best.*

This was indicative of her personality when things weren't going exactly right. She ended up with excellent grades during her first year at school.

As the year wound down, Valeri expressed normal feelings of a young lady moving into the adult world. She wrote in her journal:

*Well, as the end of my freshman year slowly draws near, I am totally depressed. I feel so hopeless. I'm tired of not having a boyfriend. I'm tired of flunking classes and constantly feeling discouraged. I want excitement! I want to have someone and something to look forward to, to have someone who loves me. I guess my first year hasn't totally lived up to my expectations. The only one who asked me out was Mark and I blew it with him too. I'm so picky though, I want the American gigolo and nothing less. Oh, well, maybe tomorrow at the last party, I will be with Rock or some other dream-boat for the entire night.*

The summer following Valeri's freshman year at the University of Michigan was a very relaxing one for her. This was by design. Marietta insisted that Valeri take it easy for the summer and prepare for her sophomore year. Valeri found many things to do socially, and she also worked part-time at the Assumption Church Cultural Center, writing and sending out press releases. She also spent time baby-sitting for her sister Debra's two children, Michelle, who was four, and Phillip, who was two. Often she would take them to the Grosse Pointe Woods City Park Pool and the three of them would enjoy the day swimming and lying in the sun. Val and the children developed a very close bond that summer. Somehow the name "Poochie" became Val's nickname. It was originated by Michelle, who refused to call Valeri "auntie," and began to call her "Poochie." Eventually, even Phillip called her that, too. This nickname was a permanent fixture in their relationship. Val loved having them call her "Poochie" and they enjoyed calling her that name. It was amusing to hear Michelle and Phillip say, "Hi, Aunt Poochie!"

In mid-August of that summer, Valeri was introduced to the American Hellenic Educational Progressive Association's (AHEPA), national convention. The AHEPA is an organization for Greek people that boasts over 40,000 members in the United States and around the world. Each year it holds a one-week convention in one of the larger cities in the United States. It happened that the 1980 convention was being held in Washington, D.C., and was attended by about 4,000 people.

Actually, the AHEPA is a male organization, but affiliate clubs are a part of the organization as well, such as the "Daughters of Penelope," "Sons of Pericles," and "Maids of Athens." The convention included business meetings for the various organizations, sporting events for the youth, a golf tournament for men and women, awards banquets, dances, and after-hour social functions. All in all, it offered an interesting and busy week for everyone in attendance. I was honored earlier that year by being selected basketball coach of the National Team which toured Greece and competed against their teams for 21 days. One of the reasons I attended the AHEPA convention was to summarize the National Team's trip to the AHEPA Athletic Committee.

Marietta, Valeri and Val's girlfriend Vasilia, and I drove to Washington, D.C., which was only a ten-hour drive from Detroit. We spent several days sightseeing, and we reminisced about our earlier trip to D.C. in 1965, when I had attended the Counseling Institute at Maryland University. Valeri didn't remember too much about that trip since she was only four years old at the time.

Every day was filled with activities. Marietta would attend social functions, I would go to meetings, and Valeri and Vasilia would shop at the many beautiful stores or go sightseeing. In the afternoons, Valeri and Vasilia always migrated to the swimming pool, where hundreds of young people would socialize, eat snacks, swim, and lie in the sun. And all of us derived much satisfaction from dining at interesting restaurants for our evening meal.

While Marietta and I spent our evenings socializing with our friends, Valeri and Vasilia would venture off to the many social gatherings and after-hour parties. Both girls must have had a great time, because they wouldn't return to the room until four or five o'clock in the morning. Of course, they would sleep until the late hours of the morning before starting their activities for the day.

The convention ended with a large farewell party for the young and old together. It was a marvelous affair. Of course, Valeri and Vasilia went to the after-hours party, and we didn't see them until six o'clock the following morning.

It was time to leave for home. Needless to say, both Valeri and Vasilia slept the entire trip home, except when we stopped to eat lunch and dinner. Both Valeri and Vasilia talked excitedly about attending next year's AHEPA Convention in Toronto.

It took Valeri some time to recuperate from the strenuous AHEPA convention. Time was getting short and her return to Ann Arbor was imminent.

Although Valeri had several transfusions during the summer, she was feeling very well. She was very active and energetic, which was heartening to both Marietta and myself, especially with Val's busy sophomore year about to begin.

## 14

# *Academic Struggles, Social Highs*

EVERYTHING fell into place nicely for Valeri when she returned to the university to begin her sophomore year. She was excited and confident upon her return to the University of Michigan. This time, there was no speculation about what to expect of the university or what her room would be like or if she would make friends. Everything worked out very nicely, with no complications.

Valeri had purchased a loft bed from one of the other students. The loft, a popular type of bed for students at that time, was really an upper bunk attached to the wall with two legs supporting it. A step ladder was attached so she could climb up to the bed. This bed delighted her very much. She would kid and say, "I'm getting up in this world already, Mom and Dad."

The fall semester was enjoyable for all of us, as it had been the previous year. Valeri and I attended the football games. Jim Demetry and I golfed on the challenging golf course, and then we would take young Jim and Val to dinner afterwards.

Unfortunately, the football season didn't go as well as Val and I had wanted. In the back of our minds, we hoped to go to the Rose Bowl this year. But, Michigan lost their final game to Ohio State; so, once again, there was not a trip to Pasadena for the Rose Bowl.

When Valeri came home for the weekend, she was always very conscientious about her homework. At times, Marietta and I felt she worried too much, especially since she would do so well in her classes. It was routine for her to worry about a class until she finally obtained a good grade.

One weekend in the middle of December, she came home and spent two days writing a term paper. When it was time to return to school, Val was informed by Sue Fattore that Steve, Sue's brother, would drive both of them back to campus. Valeri gathered up her books and her completed term paper, and got into Steve's pick-up truck. The three were on their way to the university.

It happened to be a windy day. When they came into Ann Arbor, the wind began blowing the luggage around in the bed of the pick-up truck. Val looked out the window and saw papers flying around on Washtenaw Avenue (one of the main streets in Ann Arbor). She said, "Stop the truck, Steve," which he did. Valeri had realized that it was her term paper blowing all over the street in heavy traffic. "Oh, no!" Valeri screamed. "My term paper! I have to have it done by tomorrow morning!" So the three of them proceeded to recover as many of pages as they could in the blowing wind; a difficult task under the circumstances.

After returning to her room, Valeri was a little upset, but not nearly as upset as Sue and Steve. They worried about what Valeri would do about the paper, since it was due the following day.

Sue telephoned Valeri early the next morning. She asked Valeri what she was going to do about the paper. Valeri replied, "Oh, nothing. I rewrote the paper last night. I stayed up a little later than usual, but I managed to finish it." Sue exclaimed that she didn't know how Val had done it. Val always seemed to have the ability to sit down and put her thoughts on paper so rapidly. Sue wished she had this talent. Needless to say, the incident caused kidding between Sue, Val, and their friends for some time.

During her sophomore year, it seemed that Valeri developed a more realistic view about what the world was like. Perhaps this was because she was living on her own and being independent in many ways. She showed this maturity when she wrote about her feelings of Christmas in her journal:

> Well, it's Christmas Eve and it seems as though the year has passed in one day. It seems as though everyone has forgotten the true meaning of Christmas. I know I forget often enough. I forget to be thankful and to be kind to everyone. I guess Christmas is a nice time of year, but I just feel it is often the same old thing. I wish people would remember why we have Christmas anyway, because Jesus was born, not so we can accumulate the most presents. Who am I to talk! I am an offender myself. Oh well, Merry Christmas!

Later on during the holidays she also wrote:

> I am in such a deep-thinking mood today (great English). I don't know. Much has happened. School had gotten better (not classes, but

*this year I was asked out by two guys and also had two one night stands, which consisted of dancing and a good-night kiss). That's it, but that's the point. That's enough. I get so sick of hearing about all these girls who have sex with their boyfriends. And I get sick of guys who particularly require girls who will go to bed with them on the first date. I mean why? Making love should be something special, not just given freely and without thought. I don't know . . . I feel like an oddball because I think that way.*

When the new semester began in January, Valeri telephoned us one evening and sounded very depressed. Marietta talked to her and, after hanging up, told me how Valeri sounded. Of course, we realized it wasn't abnormal for her to feel depressed, as high and low moods were a part of surviving college life. I picked up the telephone and called Valeri back. "Valeri," I said. "I know you're doing homework and you're concerned and worried about it. But I insist you put down the homework immediately. Even though it's eleven o'clock in the evening, get a couple of your friends and go across the street to Dooley's Bar and have yourselves a good time. Forget the work until tomorrow. Do you understand me?"

I heard a weak "Yes, Dad, okay."

Marietta got on the phone. "You heard what your dad said. I too want you to do that."

A few days later, we went to visit Valeri on the weekend. As we walked into the dorm to pick her up, several girls came up to me and said, "Mr. Samaras, thank you for the great idea you had the other night. Dooley's was fun and a great place to go. It looks like it'll be on our calendar often." What they predicted was true, because Valeri spent more time socializing, especially when pressures from school affected her.

Another time while in a down mood, Valeri wrote in her journal:

*I hate it! I hate this whole place! I hate school. I want to go away. I'm a bitch who is going mentally wazoo!*

Obviously, Val wrote in her journal as a release from the pressures she felt. The girls in Val's dorm would continually say, "She's always laughing. She laughs more than all of us put together." These comments hit home with Marietta and me, because they showed that Valeri, in her constant attempt to be like any other young lady, suffered the ups and downs that the other girls endured. Basically, she was a very happy-go-lucky young woman, who had various problems in her life that she learned to cope with, particularly through the good experience of attending a university. Later in the semester, Valeri wrote in her journal:

*I wish I knew where I was headed or what I'm doing. I think maybe I need a change. Change of schools, change of scenery, change of men. I was looking forward to going to Puerto Rico. Now we probably won't go. Already I feel that Susie is drifting away. She just doesn't come over as much. Now we probably aren't going to visit Puerto Rico with her. Oh well, I guess that's how life is. Things change, people change, seasons change . . .*

Later in the semester, Valeri wrote again about depression and things around her:

*Depression again. You name it, I am depressed. Because of men, I am flunking school, because I never saw the Beatles! It's true. I have never seen the Beatles. I think that's sad. I just get so angry. At myself mostly. All I do is complain, but for some reason, I'm messing up so bad. But I have no reason to complain, I have a wonderful family and great friends. I really am grateful for what I have. I just have to be more appreciative of it. I still wish I could see the Beatles, but now after John's death . . .*

Prior to the end of the semester, Valeri telephoned to tell us that there were a lot of demonstrations at both the Diag and the Student Center. She said that many radical groups were complaining about everything from A to Z. The general opinion of the campus population was that many of the radicals either weren't going to return to Michigan or were doing poorly in school or were frustrated from the school work and wanted to have some sort of release for their energies. Valeri didn't understand why there were so many demonstrations, except that it was a very common occurrence at the University of Michigan, particularly as the school year progressed.

The demonstrations provided Valeri with an in-depth knowledge of human behavior, along with some of the issues that turn people on or off, and why certain types of radical maneuvers are used. The semester finally came to an end. Valeri described her feelings in this manner:

*Well, school is out after my sophomore year, it was fine. How odd, I remember so distinctly, that awful feeling in my stomach when I was going away to U. of M. Now I am half finished . . . I don't know, but so much has happened. I guess in some ways I'm not as naive as I once was and I'm not as sheltered. However, I'm not so sure if that's good or bad. I mean, I've learned so much in these last two years, not only academically (corny), but I'm serious. I've learned about people; however, in a way I feel I've changed some for the better and maybe also some for the worse . . . I take things for granted and often I judge and criticize people. I don't know. Sometimes I feel I'm searching for something, but I am not sure what. I get so apathetic sometimes, and I often take my feelings out on other people. My parents mostly. I take them for granted. Is this part of becoming independent? I love them very much, yet sometimes I really treat them badly.*

*Gosh, my thoughts have drifted. I also wanted to say something about friendship. I made some really good friends in the past two years. Julie, Mary Beth, Stacy and Stella. Next year at school, however, is going to be very odd. Julie has moved to California and I may never see her again and I feel very sad. We used to do crazy things at Dooley's every Wednesday.*

*Mary Beth, I also probably won't see her next year. She's going to be in an apartment with Bonnie. I just feel so bad because I always considered Mary Beth such a good friend.*

*Stacy, although I didn't know her very long, I felt very close to her as though we had been friends forever. She really is a unique person. She's not very conventional, says what's on her mind. That's why she's so interesting. She's just so special. I could talk to her about anything and although she had a different background in some ways, it didn't seem bad. It seemed natural. If she doesn't come back, at least I've made a good friend and I've learned that (this is so confusing to say) she may have different views on things that didn't make her different. I accepted it, and learned not to judge people.*

*Although Stella may seem to be tough on the outside, inside she's a very sensitive, thoughtful person, and I'm glad and happy to have shared so many good times with her.*

*Gosh, all of this may sound rather queer, but I just want it to be known what wonderful friends I have, and we've all had great times. I've learned so much and grown so much from having been friends with them.*

*I don't know. My twentieth birthday is coming up and I guess I'm getting sentimental in my old age.*

When Valeri returned home after the semester ended, she was unpacking her school books and putting them away when she said, "Oh,

Dad and Mom, maybe you'd like to see one of the poems I wrote for an English class." She went on, "It isn't anything outstanding, but it was something I enjoyed doing and it kind of reflects my feelings about school." The poem went as follows:

*BIG TEN SCHOOL*

*Sitting in a classroom, feeling like a fool. Do I really*
*fit in at this **BIG TEN** school?*
*My friends are geniuses; so suave and so cool. Me, I'm*
*just a dummy, at the **BIG TEN** school.*
*Sororities, fraternities; they all belong. Me, I'm just a*
*nobody, wonder what's wrong?*
*I guess I'm an exception to every single rule - the*
*whole philosophy of this **BIG TEN** school.*
*I have nothing to fear. For what else can I do? Just*
*hope that I will graduate by 1992.*

*by Valeri Samaras*

Marietta and I loved that little poem and have read it many times since. It really described for us her feelings at that time.

Her sophomore year was completed and she was to leave Ann Arbor for the summer. This time, returning home to spend the summer was quite a let-down for Valeri. All of the action and excitement in Ann Arbor was interesting to Valeri; coming home and adjusting to a low-key type of life style was a little boring and sometimes depressing.

Again, Marietta and I agreed that it would be better for Valeri if she took the stress out of her life and relaxed during the summer, doing the things that she enjoyed doing. It sounded good and always turned out to be enjoyable, but Valeri often thought that she should be working and doing other kinds of things, instead of only relaxing and doing very little to challenge herself. Being a dynamic person, Valeri liked to feel she was moving ahead in some way or other. She would vent her feelings in her journal:

*Ugh! Depression supreme! I just can't even snap out of it. I don't*
*have anything to say except, ugh!*

*Well . . . maybe I do have something to say! Where am I going?*
*I feel so useless, like I do not serve any purpose. I don't have a job, yet*
*I don't care to work. I don't even know what I can do. I feel totally*
*numb. Like I'm following a strange path and I do not have any idea*
*where it leads. I am just moving without taking action, without it*

*meaning anything. As corny as it sounds, I just don't know what my purpose might be. I don't know if anyone understands. Everyone has answers, but I don't think they know the questions.*

It wasn't long after writing this that Valeri found many things to keep her busy. She and Chris Garkinos renewed their friendship. Chris, Val, and some other friends attended several concerts at Pine Knob during the summer.

Also, Valeri often swam with me in the evenings, after I would finish teaching summer classes at Wayne State University. We had a nice routine. I would do my warm-up and stretching exercises, then jog to the Grosse Pointe Woods swimming pool, which was exactly two-and-one-tenth miles from home. Valeri would change into her bathing suit, wait fifteen minutes, and then drive to the pool. We had it timed perfectly so that we would both arrive at the pool at the same time.

Our swim would include competitive games, like who could kick off under water from the side of the pool and float out the farthest or who could stay afloat the longest, as well as some short distance races. Oh, how she still loved to win! If I would beat her at any of the competitive games, she'd insist that we keep trying until she could win. After the cool swim, Valeri would drive both of us home. We would then eat our evening meal and be on our own for the remainder of the evening. For Valeri, the day was really only beginning, as she would call her friends to find something else to do.

Valeri had deep feelings about wanting to see her family and friends be happy. Apparently she was in such a mood when she wrote the following:

*I really don't know what's bothering me. It just seems things aren't right. It seems like there's so much injustice. I know no one ever said life was fair or life was just; yet, why is there so much hardship and heartache? It seems evil prospers and good flounders. I know that's cynical, but I worry about things like . . . my father, he deserves to get a promotion, but yet no one recognizes it. I know he'd love to be a pro coach. My mom, who longs to be out of teaching. She applied for a principal's job, yet politics ruled and she didn't get the job. Debbie wants a happy marriage and all she gets is a man-boy who doesn't even appreciate her. Nikki wants to get married but can't find anyone because men are so egocentric lately. I just want everyone to be happy and secure. I love life, but I want it to love me back, and love my*

*family and friends, too. I just get upset when I see people I care about,
who deserve so much, getting treated unfairly. There I go talking
about fairness. I guess I want things to be perfect and they never are.
They never can be. I just want the people I care about and love to
have the best of everything.*

At other times Valeri expressed unhappiness at not being in love,
and how it seemed so easy for others to be in love. She wrote:

*I just want to tell the world to go to hell! (Even though it already
has.) I'm just in a feisty mood. I'm tired of seeing couples everywhere
on the street, at the park, at home, on television. I'm sick of television
making everything seem so wonderful and magical and easy. Love is
"easy" and if you lose one lover there's always another one just waiting
to step in. Ha! Ha!*

Valeri usually did her deep thinking late at night or early in the
morning after watching "The Johnny Carson Show," which she loved so
much. It seemed that at that late hour she could relax by writing in her
journal. Later that summer she wrote:

*I feel as though the world is passing me by. Everyone seems to be
progressing, except for me. I'm still twelve it seems. I stay home like
when I was twelve, I'm still small like when I was twelve, my mom
treats me like I'm twelve, I act as if I'm twelve. I know less about
where my future's headed than when I was twelve.*

*Oh, well . . . I don't know what the point of this is, pity
time or self-analysis, summer blues, lack-of-companionship disease, what
. . . but I wish something good would happen soon. something to
surprise and please me! Ha! Ha! Within reason, of course!*

Obviously Valeri was doing some soul-searching during those summer months. She would spend much time in the early morning watching
television, and finally fall asleep around three or four o'clock and sleep
until close to noon. She would take advantage of the quiet early morning
hours to write and to organize the following day.

Marietta and I did not mind the hours that Valeri kept, and they fit
into what Dr. Charbeneau had told us when Valeri was a youngster: that
children suffering from anemia seemed to have more energy in the evening
and were much more active at that time. Additionally, Marietta and I
were generally very active at night and also loved to sleep in during the
mornings, when it was possible.

As the summer began winding down, Valeri had one more big event
to look forward to before returning to the University of Michigan for

her junior year: the AHEPA convention in Toronto, Ontario during the middle of August. Remembering the wonderful time she and Vasilia had in Washington, D.C. the previous year, the two of them made extensive plans to have a good time in Toronto. Since they had both joined the Daughters of Penelope organization, they attended some of their meetings during the convention, but they also found many other things to do and see. As usual, they enjoyed the dances, after-hour parties, and everything that went along with the convention.

During the convention, Marietta and I heard of the AHEPA Cooley's Anemia Foundation. We investigated it and found that Judge Steve S. Scopas was the chairperson of that organization. Judge Scopas had been a criminal court judge in New York city for many years. He and his wife, Clio, had two children who had died from Cooley's Anemia. Their daughter Stephanie died at the age of seventeen and their son, Steve, had died two years prior to this convention at the age of twenty-four. Judge Scopas and Clio had one other child, Pamela, who was healthy and didn't have the anemia. Pamela was the secretary for the organization.

Marietta and I invited Judge Scopas and Clio to breakfast on our final day in Toronto. We asked them many questions about the organization. We told them that Valeri had Cooley's Anemia and discussed how she was progressing. They gave us some excellent insights on what was going on in New York regarding the disease.

Judge Scopas explained that the goals of the AHEPA Cooley's Anemia Foundation were to have youngsters tested to determine if they had the Cooley's Anemia Minor trait, to give monies for research in Thalassemia, and to hold seminars in New York City to bring in doctors and experts to update the committee members on the treatment of Cooley's Anemia victims. He and Clio founded the organization when their youngsters were afflicted with the disease. It was their way of helping other children and their families cope with Cooley's Anemia. In fact, there was a clinic set up at the AHEPA convention for any person wanting to receive a blood test to identify the Cooley's Anemia trait. There were also quite a number of pamphlets available for those who wanted to learn more about the disease.

Our conversation centered on the new treatment that would extract iron from a victim's body, since iron overload is the deadly danger caused by blood transfusions. An overload of iron will eventually destroy the heart, liver, and kidneys, causing the individual to die. Judge Scopas mentioned that Desferal (dysferoxamine) was the drug being used. There was some experimentation done on his son, Steve, injecting the Desferal intramuscularly. Unfortunately, this method was unsuccessful, but through research it had been determined that if Desferal was injected subcutaneously (inserting a needle just under the skin in the stomach or thigh) over a period of eight to twelve hours, considerable more iron could be extracted from the blood recipient. The iron was extracted with the use of a little pump. Although this treatment had been in use for three or four years, it had only been on an experimental basis and only in a very few selected hematology center hospitals in the country. Judge Scopas said that now, it was more available for general use and he strongly suggested that we research the pump and get Valeri started on Desferal as soon as possible.

This wonderful news intrigued Marietta and me very much, because if the iron could be extracted from Valeri's system, her life could be sustained for quite a long period of time.

We thanked Judge Scopas and his wife for all their information, asked that they enroll me as a member of the organization, and also asked to be updated on all the information regarding the disease. I also wanted to be invited to his seminars, so that I could be updated on the research and treatment of Cooley's Anemia. Judge Scopas gave me his telephone number and address, and he urged me to feel free to contact him at any time, under any conditions.

Marietta and I were very excited about the pump. Later, we told Valeri about our meeting with Judge Scopas and Clio, and all about their organization and its goals. Valeri was very happy to hear this. She, too, felt that the pump could help her considerably, if it lowered her iron count.

It must be noted that Marietta, Debbie, Nikki, and I rarely talked about the deteriorating conditions that would occur in Valeri's body with the passing of time. We discussed the danger of the iron overload. Now that there was ongoing research, all of us felt that a treatment was imminent. Tests indicated that Valeri's iron count, although high, was not at a dangerous level - yet. Dr. Charbeneau was purposely giving very limited pints of blood to keep the iron deposit count down. Valeri, on the other hand, was never very inquisitive about the iron overload danger, although in the near future she was to learn a lot more about the disease.

# 15

# Extenuating Circumstances

WHEN classes began at the University of Michigan that fall, Valeri bade good-bye to dorm life and welcomed apartment living. Sue and Val decided to rent an apartment with two other girls, so that they could try apartment-style living. It seemed that at the University of Michigan this was quite a tradition; students would spend the first two years in a dormitory and then either move to a sorority home or into an apartment in their junior year.

Valeri and Sue found an apartment several blocks away from the Diag. The apartment that they leased was on the fourth floor. There was no elevator, which meant that Valeri would have to walk up four flights of stairs to get there. This worried Marietta and me, since we knew it could put some strain on her heart and be overtaxing to her physically. But Valeri insisted that she would be very careful about the number of times she would use the stairs each day. Also, she promised to walk up very slowly and to rest in between landings, if necessary.

The apartment was very nice and spacious, with a large kitchen and living room area, and two bedrooms with two beds in each. Val and Sue felt that if they invited two other girls to live with them they could all share expenses and it would be less costly for them. Sue invited two acquaintances from Cousins dormitory, Julie Jacobowski and "Helen." (I will use the name of "Helen" to prevent any discomfort to the individual.) It was a very compatible group. They all had the same idea in mind: to live comfortably while attending their classes that year.

The arrangements were for Julie and Sue to share one bedroom, while Valeri and Helen shared the other. It was agreed that each girl would be responsible for her own cooking and cleaning, and that they would alternate cleaning the entire apartment. Everything seemed very well planned.

Unfortunately, the previous June, prior to the end of her sophomore year, Valeri had signed a lease to live in the Betsy Barbour dormitory for the fall semester. So, again we were faced with a housing dilemma, only this time we were trying to get out of a lease instead of trying to find a dorm room. We ended up meeting with the Vice President of Housing once more. When he saw us walk in the room he laughed. "Oh, no! Not you three again." After discussing the situation, the Vice President again was very helpful and said that Valeri could break her lease for the room at Betsy Barbour. But, on the way out he warned: "Please, I don't want to see the three of you here anymore. This is it!" We laughed as we thanked him and left.

Another problem we had to resolve was how to help Valeri get back and forth to her classes, which were located a considerable distance from the apartment. The other girls could walk very easily to their classes, but we knew it would be tiring for Valeri to walk so much, especially during the winter months.

Valeri and I set out to find her a used car. We were unsuccessful. Finally, I decided that I would buy a used station wagon and give Valeri her favorite light-brown Pontiac Sunbird to drive. Of course, this meant that Valeri could be independent, which she loved. It also meant I would not travel to Ann Arbor as often.

Having a car made Valeri very happy and made her life easier. Again, the football season started. We went to several games, and Marietta even joined us on several occasions. Football Saturday at the University of Michigan is exciting. That fall we even had a tailgate party behind the stadium before one game, and Marietta and I attended Parents' Day activities prior to another game. It seemed as though the whole world stopped for a great day filled with excellent football.

As happened the previous two years, Michigan's powerful football team was upset by Ohio State. Again, this meant there was not to be a Rose Bowl game for the team, or for Valeri and me that year.

Sue and Val loved apartment living. They spent a great deal of time studying together. Instead of cooking they would go out to dinner almost every evening. They frequented Bill Knapp's and Bimbo's (which was their favorite) or they went to one of the many pizza restaurants in the area. Sue used to kid about the way they would eat the one or two large pizzas they had ordered. They would cut them in little, two-inch pieces and eat until the pizza was finished, while laughing about their accomplishment.

While living together, the four girls learned a great deal about other peoples' habits and idiosyncrasies. Sue laughed about how Valeri stayed up until all hours of the night to do her homework and then slept until her late-morning and early-afternoon classes. Sue marveled at the way Valeri could relax and not worry about classes. Valeri did not do any homework in the evening; rather, she would take naps while watching television, then get up around nine-thirty or ten o'clock and say: "Well, it's time to get up and begin my homework."

Sue knew that Valeri would stay up late into the night and early morning hours, doing her work while munching on candy bars and other goodies. Meanwhile, Sue would go to bed after finishing her homework by ten o'clock.

They were opposites. Sue was the early morning riser; Valeri was late. But they got along very well. The other two girls, Julie and Helen, seemed to be on their own. They kept their own schedules. Valeri made a brief reference in her journal about the apartment arrangement shortly after moving in with Sue and the girls:

> *This year I'm living in an apartment with Sue, Helen, and Julie, girls from Sue's dorm. It's fun. I have a great time. In a way I've become closer to Sue and can understand her better than I did in high school. She gives me encouragement and support, and she even laughs at my jokes.*

One of the highlights of Valeri's first semester in the apartment was when she and Sue planned a gangster party. They wanted to hold an open house for their friends. The boys had to wear wide-brimmed hats and gangster-like suits, while the girls were to wear short dresses. It was to be a costume party. Valeri designed a flyer in the form of a ransom note, which she used to invite their friends and acquaintances. It read something to the effect that "if you're going to be kidnapped, someone's going to have to pay a ransom to get you out of our apartment because you'll be having such a good time at our party." Needless to say, the party was a tremendous success.

That winter was much colder than normal, with much more snow than usual. Valeri always found it very difficult to get around during the winter. She always thought that some day she'd like to move to a warmer climate because of the misery brought on during the cold weather. A combination of the cold, dreary days; heavy clothing, and slipping and sliding around on the snow and ice while driving all affected Valeri's energy level. Consequently, her emotions were influenced. Again, she never showed anything outwardly, but she wrote her private thoughts in her journal:

*I do not know why things really bug me about myself. I'm such a grouch. I'm just in a totally negative mood. I try to snap myself out of it. Or at least I realize my frustration, but I can't do anything about it. First of all, I hate winter. Oh yes, it's pretty, but I hate all of the hassle: a big heavy coat, hats, gloves that I always have to keep track of, and sloshing around almost breaking my neck. Second, I have no social life. The bars are bad up here and I don't seem to fit into any parties.*

*It just seems that I'm always fighting something. Weather, teachers, and everything. I don't know. I think I need a change or at least to reevaluate myself. My attitude. I just hope everyone's patient with me until I do.*

Actually Valeri was off to a very good start in the second semester. When she would come home, she seemed very happy and continued to be excited about apartment living with the girls.

A major concern for Thalassemia or Cooley's Anemia victims is heart problems. The fact is that the heart will deteriorate as a result of the iron overload, and eventually the victim will die. This was an underlying fear that Marietta and I carried throughout the years - that Valeri would have severe heart problems. Up to now, through all the medical examinations that she had (except for a minor heart murmur) Valeri's heart appeared healthy.

Around midnight on a Sunday early in March, a telephone call turned our fears into reality. Valeri told me that her heart was speeding up considerably and beating very fast. She was perspiring and feeling weak. She said her heart would slow down to a normal pace, somewhere around seventy-five beats per minute; then it would speed up to well over 170 beats per minute.

With my background in teaching health classes at Wayne State University, I realized that Valeri was suffering from tachycardia (speeding heart). I became very upset and so did Marietta. I told Valeri to lie down and rest. I would call Dr. Charbeneau to see what he suggested. Dr. Charbeneau told us that Valeri should just sleep quietly that night, and that if she had a recurrence of tachycardia the next morning, we should drive to Ann Arbor, pick her up, and bring her to his office.

When I called Valeri back, she said that her heart had slowed down, and she was feeling somewhat better. I relayed Dr. Charbeneau's message to her, and instructed her to call us immediately should she have any other problems during the night, as I would rush to get her.

It was a Catch-22. I knew that tachycardia can be physical and/or stress-related. I wanted to make sure not to add stress by frightening her, but I did want her to know that if she wasn't feeling well, to call me immediately so I could get her.

Marietta and I spent an uneasy night. It was difficult for us to sleep, worrying about Valeri. The next morning she telephoned us around eleven thirty and said, "Dad, I got up in the morning feeling pretty good, but my heart is starting to speed up again." I told her to lie down again and I would come to pick her up, which I did.

I took her to Dr. Charbeneau's office. When we arrived, her heart was speeding. He examined her and touched the vagus nerve in her neck; and with his finger, pushed his finger against the nerve to squeeze it and the neck muscles. Her heart slowed down. He let her rest for a short time. When he came back to examine Valeri again, her heart was beating normally. Dr. Charbeneau told us that Valeri's heart was actually beating, not fibrillating. He felt she should rest for a couple of days before returning to school. If she had any problem with tachycardia, she was to push on the vagus nerve, and hopefully that would slow her heart down.

Valeri rested at home all day and night. Her heart was beating normally, so we began to feel more at ease. The next morning at six o'clock she knocked at our bedroom door. She said, "Dad, my heart is speeding up again. I'm not feeling well." Dr. Charbeneau had mentioned that if she wasn't feeling well to go directly to the hospital and admit her.

I tried not to alarm Valeri, because the doctor had verified that stress could cause the heart to speed up. "Well, Val," I calmly said, "let's go to the hospital and have the doctors check your heart and get you straightened out, so you can return to school shortly." Valeri agreed. Both Marietta and I drove her to the hospital and had her admitted. They put her in the Cardiac Ward. Her heart continued its rapid beating all morning.

The danger in tachycardia is that an insufficient amount of blood is pumped out of the heart due to the fast beats. Consequently, not enough oxygen gets into the body or to the brain, causing the person to become weak and eventually to pass out. To prevent this in Valeri, she was hooked up to machines that showed the number of heartbeats, the strength of the beats, and the amount of pressure exerted on the arteries (the blood pressure count). These machines were monitored by the nurses, at their station.

Valeri's heart continued at the speeded-up pace throughout the day and early evening. We stayed with her, trying to comfort her, waiting for tests to be completed and analyzed. Tachycardia by itself doesn't destroy the heart or damage it. However, there may be an underlying problem causing the tachycardia that can be serious.

Dr. Charbeneau recommended a heart medicine for Valeri and directed her to rest until the reports from the tests were in. Dr. Rikenberger, the cardiologist, would make recommendations for treatment the next day. We stayed well into the evening before leaving for home. Even though Valeri's heart was speeding most of the time, she seemed comfortable and told us not to worry, and to go home and rest.

The tests found that Valeri needed a transfusion. Her blood count was eight grams, well below the desirable ten to twelve grams. This caused her heart to pump harder to get more oxygen to her body tissues. On the way out of the ward, I looked at the monitor and noted that Valeri's heart was beating around 165 times per minute, which worried me. Marietta said that once they gave her blood, she was sure Valeri would be back to normal.

We returned to the hospital the next day. Dr. Rikenberger had ordered a beta blocker called Propranolol. I would take an occasional walk out to the nurses' desk to check the monitor to see exactly what Valeri's heart was doing. Up to this point her heart was still pumping around 165 times per minute, which was much faster than her usual seventy-five to eighty beats per minute.

That afternoon, we asked Valeri to relate what had happened prior to her tachycardia. She told us that she was very busy in school with a lot of homework, in addition to other activities. Her roommate, Helen, was having some emotional problems. Helen had been talking in circles, out of reality, throughout the night. The next morning Helen left for class. Instead, of going to class, though, Helen wandered around Ann Arbor. She returned to the apartment and again started talking strangely, in a disturbingly psychotic manner. Sue, Julie, and Valeri tried to keep Helen comfortable and calm; which at times she was. Helen went to bed for the evening, but then woke up and started her unrealistic talk. This frightened Valeri. Valeri felt that it would be helpful for Helen to keep calm and try to sleep, which eventually, Helen did do, but not until late the next morning. Valeri explained that this had gone on for several nights. Val could get only limited amounts of sleep, as she worried about Helen. She was completely exhausted.

Finally, Sue called Helen's father, who lived in the area. He came and took Helen to a hospital. That was the night that Val called home, informing us of her heart speed-ups. Marietta and I were very upset and told Valeri that she should have called us the very first day that Helen gave an indication that she wasn't well. Valeri realized now that this would have been wise, but at the time, she and her friends thought it was just a temporary problem for Helen and that it would pass. When it continued for a couple days, they all worried about her and didn't know what to do. Because Helen would tune in and out of reality, they thought that maybe she was going to be okay. Besides, Helen had insisted that they not call her parents.

An hour later I went out to the monitor at the nurses' station to check her heart rate. It was back to a normal beat. I realized that Helen wasn't the only cause for Valeri's heart to speed up, but it undoubtedly had some effect.

Valeri was feeling much better later that evening. When we came back to the hospital the following day she was feeling as good as new. Val wanted us to call Sue to find out what had happened to Helen. She was very concerned.

Dr. Charbeneau came in later that afternoon and told us that Valeri had atrial tachycardia. Her heart tested normally and was functioning quite well. Whatever caused the tachycardia was not found. He felt that her low blood count had helped to bring on the problem. He ordered three pints of blood to take her to a very high gram level. The transfusion took place that night and was completed the following day.

Almost immediately, Valeri showed tremendous improvement. She got out of bed, walked around, and was feeling as strong as ever. I checked the monitor at the nurses' station every hour on the hour and found that her heart was beating at almost a perfect seventy-three to seventy-five beats per minute. I felt much more relaxed. Later that day, the nurse removed the IV's from Valeri's arms and permitted her to walk around, which helped her to regain her strength. Dr. Charbeneau planned to send her home the next day.

That morning, Dr. Charbeneau told us that he was going to put Valeri on a heart medication to help regulate the heart beat and to strengthen her heart muscles. It was called Lanoxin, a derivative of Digitalis, which was the best heart medication available for heart patients. I asked him about the beta blocker and whether she should take that kind of medication. His response was no, since a beta blocker is used for different situations. Dr. Charbeneau indicated that the test results showed that Valeri's heart was still quite strong and that there shouldn't be any immediate problems.

He discharged Valeri and we took her home, planning to follow his directions which were to let her rest that weekend. She could return to school on Monday. Valeri left the hospital on a Friday. By Monday she was feeling quite well, and I drove her to her one o'clock class that afternoon. Later at home, Marietta and I discussed at length what this might mean for Valeri. The .125 milligrams of Lanoxin was considered a very light dose, but she would probably have to take this medication for the remainder of her life.

Meanwhile, Helen had been admitted to a hospital for emotional problems and had to withdraw from school. Unbeknown to us, she had telephoned Valeri in the hospital to see how she was doing and to apologize if she had done anything to cause Valeri's tachycardia. She also sent Valeri a letter, which arrived the day Val returned to school. Val told us about it on the phone that night. She said that Helen sounded pretty normal over the phone, but it was recommended that she stay out of school for the rest of the semester, as finals were fast approaching and would cause too much stress for her. Valeri wrote in her journal:

*So much has happened since I last wrote. My roommate Helen went,
I don't know what you'd call it - she had a nervous breakdown,
probably. It was so sad, so sorry. It's strange to see her empty closet.*

Marietta and I decided that we would offer Valeri an opportunity to go to Florida for five or six days of rest prior to taking her final examinations. It happened that my spring break at Wayne State was coming up, and I felt it would be a good opportunity for her to get away to the warm climate, which she so loved. Valeri could relax, rest, and lie on the beach to get some sun. I called Valeri and made the proposal to her. "What am I going to do about school, though, Dad?" she snapped back. I suggested that she contact her instructors to inform them about her health problems and also to let them know that she planned to go to Florida to rest for a few days. The instructors agreed to her request. Val received her homework assignments, which she would conscientiously complete. Valeri was very excited about the prospect of relaxing in the sun.

I made all the arrangements and drove to Ann Arbor the following Tuesday to pick her up. We would fly to Pompano Beach and stay until late Sunday evening, then fly back. I would drive her back to Ann Arbor in time for her Monday morning classes. After picking her up at the apartment, we drove to the airport and enjoyed an uneventful flight to Florida.

We arrived at the motel about an hour after leaving the airport and checked in. Later that evening, we found a nice restaurant on the outskirts of Fort Lauderdale. As usual, it was wonderful being with Valeri on vacation, as we always had such a nice time together. We made our plans for the next five days, which included me going to a driving range early in the morning for a couple of hours to practice my golf swing. I would return to the motel around noon, about the time that Valeri would be waking up. We would then head for a restaurant to have breakfast, followed by an afternoon of lying on the beach, swimming, and sunbathing. We would then go back to the inn and relax for a while, get cleaned up, and find a nice eating spot for our evening meal. After supper we would drive around and find a place with entertainment and dancing. Finally, we would go back to the hotel cafeteria and have a late snack and then retire for the night.

We spent five wonderful days in Florida, following our game plan for the most part. In the evenings we went to Dooley's, which was a lively spot in Fort Lauderdale; to September's; and to one of the Rocko Discos, which was great. Each night was much the same: I would leave Valeri by herself and wander off and sit, either watching the dancers or television. Val would spend time meeting people, particularly young men; dance and have fun. At the end of the evening I would drive us back to the motel. Each night she met some nice young fellow who would call her the next day, but she wouldn't answer the telephone. Instead Valeri elected to go on to a new adventure the following night. She liked it this way and it was fine by me.

On the flight home I reminisced about the last six days and felt Marietta and I had accomplished our mission. Valeri seemed to have regained her health, and I was quite satisfied with the work I had done on my golf game.

Valeri looked over at me and said, "You know, Dad, I was so happy we were able to attend the Baltimore Orioles - New York Yankee baseball game the other day. You know I'm such a baseball fan and I love Brooks Robinson. With him retiring and all, it gave me a chance to see the new third baseman, Cal Ripken (the rookie who was going to replace Brooks). Boy! He sure does look like a great baseball player, Dad. And, he is so big and strong, and able to hit the ball consistently. His real asset, though, is that he's very handsome! I think he's going to be quite a good baseball player." Her prediction was right. Cal Ripken became a potential Hall of Fame player through the years for the Baltimore Orioles while playing the iron-man role for participating in over two thousand consecutive games.

Soon the airport was in view, and it wasn't long before we landed. We picked up my car and drove to Ann Arbor to take Valeri back to her apartment. When we arrived, she thanked me several times. She seemed so grateful for the trip. Of course I thanked her for being such a wonderful traveling companion. I was elated that she was feeling so much better. With final examinations coming up it was going to be a stressful time for her. She said, "Don't worry Dad. I'll be able to handle them very well." She kissed me on the cheek and said good-bye.

On the way home I was relieved that she was feeling so healthy. But, in the back of my mind I still worried about possible complications from the tachycardia and what was to come later. When I arrived home and talked to Marietta, she reminded me: "Bob, remember our philosophy. Let's enjoy every day and not wear ourselves down by worrying about what the future holds."

Valeri completed her finals and another successful year in school. She bid the girls at her apartment good-bye, and came home for the summer. In her journal she disclosed some of her feelings about her bout with tachycardia:

> Sometimes I become really scared I'm going to die. I know it's morbid and a terrible thought, but I guess ever since I went in the hospital I began to think about that. I don't want to leave this world. I know heaven is supposed to be a better place, but I just figure I haven't contributed enough to the world as yet. I want to still do so much, but I feel I will never have the chance. I'm so happy with my family, so grateful for them, and I'm so happy with my friends and my life. I'm just scared it's all going to be shattered. I trust God, but I'm also frightened of Him in a way. I guess I just can't imagine me in the future, so I think that there's not a place for me in it.

Once again, Valeri never indicated these feelings to us. Instead, she always seemed so happy and well-adjusted. She seemed to know her direction and displayed a powerful desire to move toward her goals.

# 16

# *A Memorable Year*

ONCE again, Marietta and I insisted that Valeri not work during the summer. We felt that she should rest, in preparation for a hard and strenuous senior year at the University of Michigan. Although she objected vehemently, Valeri went along with our wishes and did not work full-time. However, she did work part-time at the Assumption Cultural Center for their administrator, Joan DeRonne. Joan was a highly creative and well-organized administrator, with an excellent background in public relations. Valeri felt that working for Joan would be an enriching experience. And, under Joan's guidance, Valeri learned much about public relations. Her main responsibility was writing press releases for the multiple activities that were offered at the center.

Sue and Valeri had signed up for a sociology class at the University of Michigan, as they both needed additional hours to graduate in June of 1983. They commuted back and forth to Ann Arbor twice a week to attend the class.

Valeri also socialized quite often with her friends. She spent much time talking with Chris Garkinos about the University of Michigan, since he was going to attend that school in September. In fact, Chris rode with Sue and Val on several occasions to Ann Arbor, so that he could walk around the campus and familiarize himself with the university. He was quite excited about attending the school, and Valeri was happy that he would be in Ann Arbor. She took him under her wing and laid the foundation for Chris to get off to a good start at the university. Chris appreciated this.

The summer was flying by. As usual, Valeri wasn't satisfied with her efforts during the summer. She felt that she should have accomplished more, and expressed feelings of guilt in her journal. She wrote:

*Gosh, I feel like a fool. My life is so messed up. I can't find my cash. I've lost twenty dollars. I spent sixty dollars in three days. I have a paper due before I go to Atlanta. I got sloshed last night and made a fool of myself. I haven't written Julie, Stella or Sue. I hardly ever say my prayers anymore. It's as if I just want to bury my head under my pillow and forget it all. Maybe I should start saying my prayers again. I need God on my side.*

It was almost time for the AHEPA convention in Atlanta, Georgia. This year Valeri would attend the AHEPA convention with some girlfriends from Junior G.O.Y.A., as Vasilia couldn't go to Atlanta. Valeri saw many of her old convention pals, and did many fun things. However, this year she also took a big step toward learning more about Cooley's Anemia. She met Judge Scopas and his wife, Clio, at the Cooley's Anemia Committee meeting. Afterwards, Valeri talked to the Judge, and he introduced her to Dr. Joe Graziano (Ph.D.), the medical advisor for the AHEPA Cooley's Anemia Foundation. Dr. Graziano was a teacher at the New York Columbia Presbyterian University Medical School. He was involved in extensive research and study of Cooley's Anemia. Valeri enjoyed talking with Dr. Graziano and gained more insight into the disease.

The most important thing that resulted from Valeri's conversation with Judge Scopas and Dr. Graziano was that she learned about the subcutaneous pump being used for Cooley's Anemia victims. The pump was beginning to show signs of being very helpful in removing iron from their bodies. In fact, Judge Scopas took Valeri by the arm, asked her to sit down, and gave her a long lecture on why she had to insist that her parents get the pump for her to use as soon as possible. He then took her by the hand and led her out to the lobby to join his wife. The three of them went up to Judge Scopas' room and called me on the telephone. Judge Scopas emphatically insisted that I look into getting the pump for Valeri. He said, "Valeri is here with me right now. I've just spoken with her about the importance of the pump and its success. I want you to know that you must make it a priority to find out how and where you can get one for her to begin using, as soon as possible." I promised him that I would look into the matter immediately. I also thanked him for speaking with Valeri and for calling me.

I followed through with my plan to learn more about the pump, the leading treatment for iron chelation - extracting iron from the body through urination - to prevent iron overload. I called Dr. Charbeneau the next day. He said he would look into the matter and get back to me.

Upon her return from the convention, it was time for Valeri to begin serious planning for her senior year at the University of Michigan. She was under strict orders from Marietta and me to secure as much rest as possible in the two weeks prior to returning to school. Her health was generally good, she felt quite strong, and she was looking forward to her senior year. Valeri was patient and followed our advice for those two weeks. When the time arrived for her to leave for school, she was ready and raring to go.

Just prior to leaving, Valeri looked at us and said, "Gosh, Mom and Dad, I cannot believe how fast three years have flown by. Here I am, going into my final year at school. So many things have happened in such a short time. It seems like time is zipping by; yet there's so much for me to accomplish this year, before I can graduate in June. I'm happy that I will complete college this year; but, on the other hand, I'll feel sad when it has all ended."

Marietta replied, "Valeri, have fun your senior year in college because when you graduate in June it will end an era of your life. And, soon after that, you'll begin a new and exciting stage, when you find yourself entering the work force."

As the two of them spoke, I couldn't help but feel very apprehensive about what her senior year might bring. I was certain it would be difficult enough to complete a final year at the University of Michigan without any health problems. Although Valeri was enjoying reasonably good health now, she still had problems to live with continually. There was always the potential for tachycardia to recur or other heart problems to surface. As Val left, she seemed to be in a happy-go-lucky spirit and was not overly concerned about her health.

After she left, I turned to Marietta and said, "The unknown factor is what will take place this year. But, let's go along with the adopted philosophy that we have lived under for so long: to enjoy each day while continuing to be optimistic about the future."

Valeri and Sue Fattore had two new roommates for their senior year: Sue Latimore and Tina Behr. These girls had both attended Grosse Pointe North High School with Sue and Val. Tina was to room with Val, and Sue Latimore with Sue Fattore. That seemed to work out very well. All four were seniors, and were very conscious of putting considerable effort into their studies, to make sure they would graduate with their class in June 1983.

The fall semester began with students on campus being optimistic about the wonderful opportunity for the University of Michigan football team to finally win the Big Ten Championship and head for the Rose Bowl. Spirits were high. The team was undefeated heading into the final game against Ohio State at Ann Arbor. The winner of this game would represent the Big Ten conference at the Rose Bowl on New Year's Day. Valeri was caught up in the excitement and attended each home game along with Sue and Chris. On occasion, I joined her with Jim Demetry and his son. The most enjoyable times came, however, when Chris, Sue and Valeri would attend the traditional bonfires or rallies the night prior to the ball games. Naturally the biggest bonfire, the biggest rally and the most excitement took place the night before the final Ohio State game.

The next day, Val, Jim, Jim Jr., and I all sat together at the game, with Chris, Sue and her brothers sitting nearby. The game turned out to be a very dull contest with Michigan losing by four points in a low-scoring affair. When the final whistle blew and Michigan failed to score the winning touchdown from the ten yard line, Val and I looked at each other. She said, "They did it to us again. No Rose Bowl this year." We worked our way to the football field. As we walked across it, listening to the band play and watching the thousands of disappointed people walking out of the stadium, both Val and I shed some tears.

I said, "You know, Val, it just isn't in the books for us to go to the Rose Bowl during your college days. However, maybe someday in the near future we can work something out and go."

Val was excited to be walking across the football field, because we had never done this before. She remarked, "Gosh, this is what it's like for the football players, to look up and see those thousands of people looking down, screaming and yelling." By the time we left the stadium, she was smiling again. Then she tried to cheer me up with some jokes.

Val and Sue enjoyed their final year residing together. They ate out even more than in the past year, cooking on very rare occasions. They had a great deal of fun going to the medical library to do their studying. They kidded about the old joke: "Let's go down to the medical library to study and meet some doctors." The primary reason for studying there was that the library was located only two blocks from their living quarters. Of course, they didn't mind the fact that they met several young residents and medical students.

Sue and Val had their own comfortable and cozy social group. Sue's boyfriend, Steve Schucker, visited Sue and Val often. Val had her close friend Chris Garkinos, who attended classes at the university and who would stop by often as well. Sue's brothers John and Steve also visited them periodically, primarily to make sure that everything was going along well, especially with Sue. Marietta and I also continued our habit of traveling to Ann Arbor at least once every other week and meeting Val and taking her out to dinner, inviting Sue to join us. Our favorite eating place was the College Inn near Val's apartment.

As the fall semester was drawing to a close and Valeri was preparing to take her finals, a near disaster almost took place with Marietta, Debbie and her two children, Michelle and Phillip. Marietta was driving them to Mt. Clemens late in the afternoon of December 2, 1982. Marietta was driving very carefully in our new Cadillac Seville on I-94 in the right lane. Debbie was sitting in the front seat and Michelle and Phillip were in the back seat, when a drunk driver, speeding along at approximately 75 miles per hour, zig-zagged and smashed into the left side of the car, forcing it to slide sideways and then turn abruptly left, hitting the center median of the expressway. Fortunately, the other drivers on the road saw this drunk driver wildly weaving his way through traffic. They slowed down considerably and were able to stop without smashing into Marietta's car as it sat there with the front end embedded into the dividing wall.

Although this violent crash took less than five seconds, it seemed like an eternity for those inside the car. Of the four, only Marietta was injured seriously. She was bleeding profusely from the mouth and was lying motionless. Debra, who injured her ankle and shoulder, began screaming, "Mom! Mom!" Phillip and Michelle, who had their seat belts on in the back seat, were shaken up, but not injured. Marietta, though conscious, knew that she was badly hurt. She could taste blood and felt tremendous pain on the left side of her face, along with other pain throughout her body. She lay still and was afraid to move, thinking that any movement might cause further damage to her body.

People jumped out of their cars and ran to help the four of them. Fortunately, there was one person, probably a doctor or some other highly-trained medical person, who stayed with and cared for Marietta until the ambulance arrived.

After extensive tests at the hospital, it was discovered that Marietta had suffered crushed facial bones on her left side, including the eye socket bone. Luckily, a little bone had closed off an artery that was bleeding profusely. This probably saved her life. Marietta was taken by ambulance from St. Joseph Hospital in Mt. Clemens to Bon Secours Hospital in Detroit where she could be treated by Dr. Tsangalis, a family friend. Although Dr. Tsangalis wasn't available, Dr. Peter McCabe was; we readily agreed that he would be her attending physician. Marietta was given a shot to enable her to sleep. She was quite comfortable that night and I went home. I realized after calling Nikki to inform her about her mom, that I had to call Valeri too. This was going to be a very difficult task, knowing how close Valeri was with her beloved mother. It had to be done, so finally I made the call.

"Valeri," I began, "something serious has happened to your mother, but she's going to be okay." I then explained the accident to her and could hear her crying on the other end of the line. I told her that the doctor planned to operate the following day and that I would be present, along with Nikki and Debbie. We would inform her immediately after the operation how successful it had been. Valeri screamed, "No way!! I want to be there before, during and after the operation, Dad. Please come up and get me or I can drive home." I told her I would be there early in the morning to pick her up.

The four of us spent the entire morning in the room with Marietta, who was trying to cheer us up. She was in a relatively good mood and was happy that the doctor was going to operate later that day to repair the fractured bones and to replace the eye socket bone with a plastic piece. Around noon the orderly came in and wheeled Marietta to the operating room as Debbie, Nikki and Valeri all talked at once, trying to comfort their mother. The operation took three hours. Soon after, Marietta was back in her room. Dr. McCabe came to the room and told us everything had turned out fine and she would be as beautiful as ever.

We were grateful that everything seemed to be going along well, and that Marietta had suffered no other broken bones or serious injury. The four of us stayed through the evening visiting hours when Marietta finally ordered us: "Hey, you four better get going. Go get some rest. Valeri, I want you to return to school and get ready for your finals. I will call you several times a day and let you know how I'm doing." Valeri gave her mother a big hug and told her how much she loved her. She agreed to go back to school and do as her mother had directed.

Valeri completed her finals and once again received excellent grades. She maintained her 3.5 honor average and was pleased that her classes had been a lot of fun. All that was left until graduation was one more semester. She vowed to have a relaxing and happy Christmas vacation in preparation for the final semester beginning in January. She was also thrilled that her mother had recovered nicely from a serious auto accident.

When the new semester began, Val signed up for an acting class, a requirement for communication majors. Sue also felt this would be a good class to attend as an elective. It would be an easy-going class, and she would certainly do well with Valeri being her tutor. The class was taught by a teacher assistant who told Valeri that she must participate in the warm-up drills or she wouldn't be allowed to stay in the class. Valeri had explained to the instructor that, due to her illness and problems with her heart, she wasn't able to do any strenuous exercising. After discussing her health limitation with her advisor, the advisor talked to the instructor, who allowed Val to stay in the class without participating in any vigorous warm-up exercises, although she had to do some very light ones.

Right after the semester began, Valeri experienced a recurrence of the tachycardia. She called home and announced, "Dad, guess what? I'm having heart speed-ups again and I'm quite worried. I'm not going to come home. I'm going to stay here in school and finish. I'm sure I'll be all right." I told her I was going to call Dr. Charbeneau and follow his suggestions; somehow it would work out, particularly since she probably needed another blood transfusion. The last test showed her red blood count was hovering around nine, which was getting low for her. In fact, maybe that's why the tachycardia began.

That night as Valeri lay there, with her heart beating close to two hundred times a minute, she realized that she might have to go back to the hospital, and the uncertainty as to when she might return to school to finish work on her degree. She wrote in her journal:

*I feel so scared . . . uncertain. I guess it's just finally hitting me that I'm growing older and I may (hopefully) graduate from college soon. I guess that's why I'm so scared. I don't know what to do, or what I'm doing. I know everyone at my age feels this way yet somehow I feel my thoughts go one step further. I guess I just realize my life isn't normal. When I was young, I went to the hospital, yet it was rather in the background. Now it seems to be surfacing more and more. I have been getting blood sooner, my heart speeds, thyroid problems . . . pills. I guess I'm just wondering what I'd do if I ever secured a job. How do I explain? Or if I was ever really serious with any one person. I suppose that's why I've never had a boyfriend. Maybe God knows I wasn't ready. Will I ever be? I mean physically. There are so many questions and problems I have to deal with. I don't know how to. I guess my parents and God will pull me through. (Not necessarily in that order.) If I stop and ponder my problems I will be defeated and will accomplish nothing and it'll be my own fault. Somehow I feel I'm going to get through this. Things have always looked bad in the past, yet they have worked out. I'm trying to be optimistic.*

I called Valeri the next day. Her heart was still speeding, so I imme-diately called Dr. Charbeneau. He again suggested that I take Valeri to the hospital for tests. I drove out to Ann Arbor to pick Valeri up and took her directly to St. Joseph's Hospital in Mt. Clemens. At the hospital she had several heart tests, and because her count was very low, she also received three pints of blood. Dr. Charbeneau's diagnosis was that Valeri's Lanoxin count was dropping down too low to be helpful; consequently, she had to take more Lanoxin (.250) at midnight and at noon. Taking it twice a day would keep the Lanoxin count constantly high in the blood system.

Valeri's heart slowed down again and the tests indicated that it was functioning in a normal range. In fact, her heart seemed to be very strong, which was welcome news for Val and me to hear. I felt so emotionally high to know that her heart appeared to be in what was described as a "normal range," even though it was on the upper edge of that normal range. This meant that basically her heart was still strong, and that she would be all right for an indefinite period of time. It was probably the best news we could have received. It gave Val and me a different outlook on her prognosis.

When we told Marietta the good news, she was extremely elated. Val stayed home that night and I drove her back to school the following day. However, I was still quite worried because her heart was still beating at a rate of about 150 times a minute, which was considered tachycardia.

I dropped Valeri off at her apartment and went back home. Later that evening I called to find out her heart rate. The news was good: her heart was back to her normal seventy-five to eighty beats per minute. She excitedly said, "Dad, you won't believe the impetus that caused my heart to go back to its normal beat. I drove Sue to drama class and when it was over we walked back to the car. When I tried to enter on the driver's side, I banged my head against the door. I was stunned for a couple of seconds and then, all of a sudden, I realized there was something different taking place. I yelled, 'Hey, Sue! My heart slowed down. It's beating normally.'" Val and I enjoyed a hearty laugh, and so did Marietta when I told her.

I called Valeri again that evening to see how she was doing. She was not in the apartment, so I assumed that she was out having a good time and that things were all right. She called us after midnight to let us know that she was feeling much better and getting ready to get some genuine rest.

Val came home two weeks later on a Sunday to attend the Super Bowl party Marietta and I had planned for our friends. It was a great party and our house was crowded, reminding me of the days at the University of Michigan stadium when one could hardly move around during one of their football contests. Young people were there - friends of Val, Debbie, and Nikki - as well as Marietta's and my friends. A good time was had by all. Valeri wrote a little about that Super Bowl Sunday in her journal:

*Super Bowl Sunday: I just want to say this was a fun night. I'm finally at the age when I'm not "little Val." I think Nikki's boyfriend, Abe, is sharp. Also, we went out with Lydia and Jim. They were hysterical. I want to thank them for being so nice. Abe's brother, Mitch . . . he never treats me like a little girl. Oh, well, life is fun.*

People were suddenly recognizing that she was growing up to be quite a young lady, instead of "little Val," which pleased her.

The semester was flying by. There were so many things that had to be done in preparation for graduation: taking graduation pictures, getting a cap and gown, and meeting with the seniors. It was all very exciting. Valeri also included more excitement in her social life with Sue and other friends. They figured that this was their last semester and they were going to renew old acquaintances, visit their favorite eateries, bars, and clubs, as well as have several house parties in their apartment. All in all, time was growing short and finals were rapidly approaching.

Sue woke up one morning and announced, "Val, we have to finish our paper for drama class."

"Oh, no problem!" Val answered. "I've got mine all planned out. How are you doing on yours?"

"I really haven't started, Val." Sue was an excellent student in the business field, but she knew very little about communications, particularly drama. "Val, you know that our agreement was that you would carry me through this class, and if you were ever to take a business class, I would do the carrying," Sue replied.

Valeri laughed. "Don't worry, Sue. Everything's in the bag. We'll get our term papers done, we'll get our A's, and we'll both be happy."

A couple of hours later both term papers were completed. Sue looked at Val and asked, "How did you ever learn to do so much work in such a short time and do such a quality job?"

Valeri just laughed and said, "Really, that's not too fast. That's about normal time." Sue always laughed about the incident when she would tell the story, because Valeri ended up getting an "A" for the course and Sue only got a "B-." Sue would always say: "The big-time business student could hardly get through a drama class, even with the help of her friend."

Soon finals were completed and plans were set for graduation day. Valeri had informed us earlier that Lee Iacocca, the Chairman of the Board of Chrysler Corporation, was going to be the speaker at graduation. Marietta and I both admired him and we were looking forward to hearing him speak. In fact, Marietta joked and said, "I always had a crush on that man. I hope I don't swoon or jump out of my seat."

The morning of graduation was filled with clouds and rain. Valeri and Sue were racing to load up their car with final remnants from their first-floor apartment, as the landlord had warned everyone to be out of the apartment by the time graduation ceremonies were ended. Valeri was taking him at his word. She announced, "We've got to get everything out of here." They loaded Valeri's car up with so many things that there was barely room for them to fit inside. The car looked like a woman's huge purse, filled so full that nothing else would fit in. Then they drove to Crisler Arena to meet their group in preparation for the graduation ceremony.

Marietta, Debbie, Nikki, Valeri's grandmother Ianthie (Marietta's mother), and I drove to Ann Arbor to attend the ceremony. The several thousand graduation tickets were limited strictly to close family members for all students. When we drove up to the arena, it was our good fortune to find a parking place immediately outside one of the doors. It was pouring rain outside. We entered the arena, found our seats, and waited anxiously to see the June 1983 graduates walk into the arena.

It was extremely exciting to watch the graduates march in. When we spotted Valeri, both Marietta and I began to cry. I had coached for many, many years in several sports and knew the thrill and excitement of winning, but nothing could top the feeling I had the moment I saw Valeri take her place for this event. I was overwhelmed with emotion and looked over to see Marietta expressing a similar reaction. We held and squeezed each other's hands and Marietta asked: "Can you believe this, Bob? Our Valeri is in that audience waiting to receive her B.A. degree from the University of Michigan. With all the odds that were against her at birth and over the years, and knowing the pain she endures continuously - for her to be able to go through all the necessary requirements to get to this point - I think she is great!" We both began crying again.

Since this was the first time I had attended a graduation ceremony at the University of Michigan, I didn't know much about their traditions. I soon found out what they were. After the opening prayer, there were several short speeches made by staff members and the president of the university. Finally, the president of the university introduced Mr. Iacocca, who began to step forward very confidently and aggressively towards the microphone. As Lee Iacocca was being introduced, I noticed that many students were pulling something from underneath their graduation gowns. A moment later I realized what it was: champagne. The graduates were popping the corks towards the stage as Mr. Iacocca rose to make his presentation. I expected that the students would discontinue the cork-popping tirade once Mr. Iacocca began to speak. To my surprise, even more corks went flying towards the stage. I wondered how Mr. Iacocca would react. I received my answer very shortly, when he began smiling, then laughed and actually paid little attention to the students' actions. I realized that this, too, was a tradition.

Lee Iacocca began talking in a confident voice and impressed the audience immediately with his speaking ability and grace. The theme of his speech was: "There's a world out there and there's a place for all of you, but you have to earn your way. You will be battling odds often, but it's an exciting and interesting life, and it'll be a very marvelous life. It will take drive, determination, and commitment if you are going to make it."

The audience often cheered and even gave several standing ovations. He gave examples of some of the difficulties that were taking place in the outside world - difficulties that would effect all people on this earth, especially regarding future employment. He also suggested solutions for these problems. As Mr. Iacocca's speech progressed, so did the cork-popping. Corks were hitting the stage all around him. From time to time he would make a humorous remark and smile, then continue his speech. He was absolutely marvelous in his delivery and content, and worked up to this final climax: "There is a world for you students. Students, start your engines."

This final comment brought the graduates and the rest of the audience to their feet, cheering and clapping for several minutes while he waved and returned to his seat next to the university president. Marietta looked at me and repeated: "Students, start your engines. What a wonderful comment to make to this group."

Immediately following Mr. Iacocca's speech, the president then asked the deans to introduce the graduates from their colleges. Soon it was time for the dean of Liberal Arts and Sciences to introduce the graduates from his school, which included Valeri and Sue. The dean made a brief speech and then asked the students to stand. When they did, Marietta, Debbie, Nikki, Valeri's grandmother, and I stood up and cheered and clapped with much emotion and feeling. We could see Valeri standing, and we realized that she, too, was one of the cork-poppers. We also noticed that she had a very big smile on her face.

A short while later the ceremonies finished and the graduates began leaving the arena. We rushed down to the area where we were scheduled to meet Valeri. Upon seeing her, we hugged and kissed her. We were so thrilled and happy! There she was, so excited, laughing and talking a mile-a-minute with all of us. We congratulated Sue and we greeted her family. All of us stood there as the two girls ran to the other graduates, shaking hands, and hugging so many of their friends.

Finally Sue and Valeri finished their good-byes and we drove to Weber's. Both families had agreed earlier to go to Weber's Restaurant, a very popular and distinguished eatery near the university, following the graduation ceremony. After we had finished our celebration meal, it was time to leave for home. We hugged and kissed Val, and told her to be careful driving home.

When Val arrived home, we sat around with her sisters and reminisced about what had gone on that day, particularly the dynamic speech by Lee Iacocca. Finally, Val looked at us and said, "You know, this means that I must begin job hunting."

"Don't worry about that, Valeri," Marietta replied. "We insist that you relax for a while. We are going to have your graduation party this Sunday at Dimitri's of Southfield. Then we're going to take the trip to Europe that is being offered through our Assumption Cultural Center."

Valeri's eyes lit up and she replied, "I forgot about that with all the excitement. Boy! That sure is something to look forward to - a graduation party and *then* a trip to Europe."

I agreed with her. "I'm looking forward to it, Valeri. I know one thing, you're going to have to use your French to help us enjoy Paris when we're there."

She laughed. "Dad, I've been waiting to see Paris again, and I want to show Mom and you how beautiful Paris is." Then she quietly added, "I do have some phone calls to make. I plan to meet some of my friends and go out for a little while. I might be in a little late, but I will sleep until late morning, as you know." Marietta and I looked at each other, acknowledging that this was a wonderful day in our lives, one we would probably never match for a long time.

A graduation party honoring Valeri was held the Sunday after the graduation ceremonies. Marietta, Debra, and Nikki sent invitations to over one hundred people. The guest list included Valeri's closest friends, college acquaintances, relatives, and family friends. The gala event was to be held at Dimitri's of Southfield. I had made arrangements with Dimitri, who, along with his wife, Naomi, and sons Paul and Nick, were friends of our family. The restaurant, a very fine establishment with an excellent reputation, catered parties. The affair was to be held in the main dining room and would include their famous Sunday brunch. The brunch was well-known because of the variety of hors d'oeuvres, entrees, salads, and desserts. I knew that Dimitri, his two sons, and the manager, Lou Bricolas, would give a special touch to add to the quality of the party.

Valeri wore her cap and gown that day. Debbie, Nikki, and Marietta printed out several signs congratulating her on her graduation. Dimitri put lovely flowers on each table. It was a very cozy and attractive atmosphere.

As the guests arrived they were ushered into the dining room by Lou Bricolas. Upon seeing Valeri, the guests would run over to hug and kiss her. You could hear much laughter and happy conversation. The thing I noticed most was Valeri's happy, infectious laugh above the noise of the crowd.

We were pleasantly surprised when Dr. Rothman arrived with his daughter. (Dr. Rothman's wife, Reggie, had passed away two years earlier.) Dr. Rothman, now almost eighty years old, walked up to Valeri, hugged and kissed her, and smiled. He commented on how wonderful it was to be invited, and how happy he was to see her. After all the guests had arrived, I realized that there was one person missing: Dr. Charbeneau. Although he didn't attend the party, he did send a lovely gift for Valeri. There was a great deal of laughter during the cocktail hour. It was thrilling to see the guests pouring out their affection and love for Valeri. The buffet dinner that followed was second to none, as we had expected. From the opening invocation by Father Kavadas, to the toast on Valeri's behalf, until the final dessert was eaten, a happy episode in our lives unfolded before us. Watching Valeri's expressions and seeing the happy glow on her face was so heartening to Marietta and me. Immediately following our meal I stood up to make a couple of comments about Valeri. I thanked the guests for attending this wonderful occasion. I said, "You know, at the graduation ceremonies, Valeri was listening to Lee Iacocca speak. I was watching the corks from champagne bottles shower him while he spoke. Following the ceremonies, we went to find Valeri in the graduates' reception lounge. I couldn't find our tiny Val at first, but as I looked and looked, there she was, with her cap and gown, and a big smile. (At this point I became very sentimental, choking up with emotion. Tears came to my eyes. I quickly recaptured my poise and continued.) There she was, holding a corkless bottle of champagne in her hands, yelling at the top of her voice: 'Hey Mom and Dad! Here I am!'"

Dr. Rothman stood up. "I would like to say something, if I could, please."

"We would very much welcome your comments, Dr. Rothman," I responded.

He turned to the crowd and said, "You know, this is one party I knew I had to attend. This lovely young lady has done so much in her life, under such trying and difficult circumstances with her health problem. We in the medical field didn't know if she would live past two years of age, and we felt that she would certainly be fortunate to survive her teenage years, and even then barely move around and exist. Here she is, a graduate of the University of Michigan. I am so very proud of her. Furthermore, I am so proud that I was invited to see wonderful Val." He then, in true Dr. Rothman style, said: "I do have a joke or two to tell." He then proceeded to make the guests laugh for the next several minutes.

Marietta jumped up and added: "You know me. I have to put in my two cents' worth. I would like to say something, too. We are so proud of Valeri for working so hard to get her degree. We just love her so very much. Val, Debra, Nikki, Bob, and I want to thank all of you for coming to help celebrate this occasion. We love all of you for making this such a wonderful day."

Suddenly, one of the guests yelled out, "Speech, Valeri! Speech!" The rest of the guests joined in: "We want a speech!"

Valeri got up and seemed embarrassed, but with a big smile she said, "Gosh, I was afraid you wouldn't ask," which brought a roar from the guests. When they had quieted down, she said in a very serious tone, "I'm so very, very happy to have had the opportunity to attend the University of Michigan, to have this wonderful party, and to have all of you wonderful people come here to honor me. I love all of you and will remember this all of my life. Thank you so very, very much." Then she sat down.

Soon the guests filtered out and the only people left were our family and Dr. Rothman and his daughter. He came over to Valeri, who was standing next to us. He hugged her and kissed her on the cheek and said, "Congratulations, Valeri, and good luck in finding a job. Keep up your wonderful work."

She thanked him and replied, "I really appreciate you coming to my party, Dr. Rothman, and I love you for it." He turned and walked away. That was the last time we saw Dr. Rothman alive, as he passed away two months later after a bout with cancer.

We thanked Dimitri and his family for the wonderful meal, accommodations, and his personal touches that made it such a satisfying party. Our family and Valeri left the restaurant with a feeling of exhilaration.

After arriving home, Valeri proceeded to open up her many gifts and envelopes with money. She was overwhelmed with the generosity of our guests and began to cry softly as she told us, "It's so wonderful that people did this for me." She then thanked Marietta, her sisters, and me by hugging and kissing us. Suddenly she looked at us with that lovely, happy glow in her eyes and said, "Hey Mom and Dad, our European trip is coming up very soon. We're going to see all those great places over in Europe - sure is something to look forward to!" Then she turned and retreated to her room to start the network of telephone calls to her girl-friends to make plans to go out and have a happy celebration that evening.

The trip to Europe was planned through our Assumption Cultural Center Travel Program. We felt this trip would be a wonderful summer adventure for Marietta, Valeri, and me. All of us loved traveling and the thought of visiting European countries. I was disappointed that Debbie and Nikki couldn't go on this trip. They both looked so sad. Debbie spoke up and lamented, "Oh, well, here's another one that we're going to miss."

Nikki chimed in, "But when you gotta work, you gotta work. And, if you have a family, you have a family. We'll get there sometime. I know you three will have a good time."

Marietta looked at me and announced: "Oh, no! I'd better get started on our packing; travel time is coming up soon."

# 17

# *Beautiful Europe*

IT WAS Marietta's idea to present the trip to Valeri as a gift for working so hard to graduate from the University of Michigan. I felt it was a wonderful idea. Marietta and I were just as thrilled as Valeri to be going to that famous part of the world. It was something Marietta and I had dreamed about for many years, and this was a great opportunity to make it a reality for us and for Valeri.

The first thing Val did immediately after graduation was to visit St. Joseph's Hospital for a blood transfusion. We hoped the transfusion would raise Val's blood count up to fourteen, one of the highest levels that she had ever had in her life. This would give her more energy to endure the hardships of traveling for thirty-two days. Dr. Charbeneau had recommended this as a way to keep Valeri at a high red blood cell count whenever we were away from home for a long period of time. Everything went fine with the transfusion and Val was soon home, getting ready to leave for the trip, which was scheduled for two days later.

The tour included flying to New York, with a five-hour lay over there, before flying to Heathrow Airport in London. We would stay in London for three days, and then go to Paris via Calais, France. Once we arrived in Calais, we would board a bus, which was to be our mode of transportation for the remainder of the trip. The tour package included the bus transportation, and breakfast and dinner at all of the stops.

Our personal plans called for us to leave the tour at Madrid on the last day, fly to Athens, and take a plane to the Isle of Rhodes. We would stay in Rhodes for eight days; then we would return to Athens for three days before flying to London, and later, home. We would travel a total of thirty-two days, instead of the twenty-three included in the regular tour.

Valeri's Grandmother Ianthie paid for Valeri's flights from Madrid to Athens to Rhodes and back to Athens. Grandmother Ianthie had sold some properties in Greece, and in addition to paying for Valeri's air fare, she also paid for her daughter Mary Backos, her daughter Toni, Toni's daughter, Andrea, and herself to join us for eight days in Rhodes.

All in all, Marietta, Valeri and I were anticipating this exciting trip, especially the climax of spending time in Greece with Valeri. Valeri had always wanted to visit Greece, as she had heard so much about the country from Marietta and me after our trips there.

It was June 21st. We were packed and left to meet the other members of the group at the Assumption Cultural Center, where Joan DeRonne, the center's administrator, was holding a reception for the travelers and their families. The group consisted of thirty-two women and six men. Six of the women were young ladies and there was one young man. The rest of the travelers were middle-aged folks and older, including the ninety-two-year-old Mrs. Stinson.

At the reception everyone had many laughs. There was much hugging, kissing, and well-wishing by all. Then, it was noon, time to board the bus for Detroit Metropolitan Airport to meet our flight.

The flight to New York was uneventful. The lay over was a little long, but soon we were en route to London. Val seemed to be taking it all in stride and was extremely excited to be heading for Europe. I was always a little apprehensive when I thought about Valeri. I wanted to make sure that she would get her rest and give herself the opportunity to be very active while avoiding any health problems. I was particularly concerned that the strain of travel might be difficult and cause tachycardia.

Valeri was consistently happy-go-lucky and you could hear her infectious laugh constantly. It was obvious that her only thoughts were to enjoy the trip with Marietta, me, and her new-found friends. She had her favorite camera along, ready to claim her status as a good amateur photographer. She had brought along many roles of film and intended to take endless pictures throughout the countries we were to visit.

The flight over the Atlantic Ocean during the night seemed to pass very quickly. Although I didn't sleep much, Marietta and Val certainly did. When morning arrived, Valeri looked out the window and saw England, our destination. "Hey Dad, look. We're flying over London now on our way to Amsterdam where we will land, only to take another plane back to London. That seems like a waste of time, doesn't it?" The reason for this was that KLM Airline was based in Amsterdam, and the plane had to make a stop there before going on to its final destination, which was London.

A short while later we landed in Amsterdam and then flew to London. We landed at Heathrow Airport where there was considerable commotion and movement of people. The action was exciting. We boarded a bus that was reserved for our group and went near downtown London to the Barston Hotel, where our group was to stay.

We were to meet our group guide, a young woman from Yugoslavia, at the Barston Hotel. She would accompany us throughout our tour in Europe. It so happened that the regular guide had a family emergency and couldn't join us, so the touring company sent this woman as a substitute. This change in guides proved to be a little unfortunate for our group as the substitute wasn't that knowledgeable about Europe, and some of her idiosyncrasies were very aggravating to the group. But, the switch didn't make that much difference or prevent us from having a good time.

After the orientation lecture and final instructions, Valeri, Marietta, and I went to our room. We quickly changed, ran out to a cab, and headed for the shopping district. Even though we were very tired, Marietta and Valeri, the two famous shoppers, wanted to go to Herrods Department Store, which is internationally-known.

Fran Georgeson and Tess Gakis, two of Marietta's friends, went along to Herrods with us. Herrods proved to be a huge department store, much like many of the large department stores in the United States. We began touring some of the women's departments, particularly the clothing ones. Gradually, we worked our way up to the second floor where there were some very exclusive tea lounges. Valeri and I told Marietta that we were not in the mood for tea, since we were very sleepy and tired. We urged Fran, Tess, and her to go ahead and enjoy themselves for awhile. Valeri and I would sit down on the comfortable couches in the exclusive furnishings department, which was next to the tea lounge.

As Val and I sat and talked, the next thing we knew, both of us had fallen asleep. Here we were, taking a nap in this exclusive department! Interestingly enough, no one made any comment about our choice of a nap-site. In fact, when we awoke, one of the young men said pleasantly: "I hope you two enjoyed the comforts of our lovely furniture," as he smiled and walked away.

We got a big kick out of his comment and joked: "Boy, we came all the way to England just to sleep on this lavish furniture!"

Marietta and her friends joined us shortly and we spent considerable time going through many of the other shops that afternoon. While shopping, Valeri and Marietta both bought Gucci purses, which they were to cherish for many years. Later that evening, back at the hotel, we had a wonderfully delicious English chicken meal.

The next two days of sightseeing proved to be very exciting. Valeri was fascinated by the fancy long, sleek, black taxi cabs and the double-deck buses and the bobbies (policemen) who stood in the middle of the street directing autos in the heavy traffic. We witnessed the changing of the guard at the Queen's castle, and had a snack in a pub underneath the London Bridge on the Thames River, where Valeri and Marietta enjoyed the beer. Trafalgar Square, the center of London, interested Valeri a great deal, with all the people-watching that was available. Piccadilly Circus was extremely interesting, with the thousands of people and many stores. Westminster Abbey Cathedral was a marvelous adventure for all of us. And when we visited St. Paul's Cathedral, the second-largest cathedral in all of Europe, it was breathtaking to get up in some of the high places and realize what a wonderful structure this was. An interesting point to note was that during World War II when Hitler's planes were bombing London night after night, St. Paul's Cathedral was not damaged in any way. Valeri laughed when she visited 10 Downing Street and remarked: "Gosh, I think a job working in this financial center wouldn't be too bad for me."

We left London two days later and went to the small town of Canterbury, where we saw the wonderful Canterbury Cathedral. From there, we were taken by bus to see the White Cliffs of Dover. Then, we boarded a ferry to cross the English Channel to Calais, France. It was a two-hour trip across the channel, and we enjoyed the beautiful view along the way.

In Calais, the driver of the tour bus was a middle-aged Spaniard. "*Venga, venga!*" he announced. "Let's go. We're ready to drive to Paris where we're going to stay for the next three days." The guide elected to take the back roads into Paris rather than the expressway, feeling that it would give us a good view of the small towns in France. After enduring a long, slow ride and a severe thunderstorm, we arrived in Paris about midnight.

After checking into the hotel, our guide informed us that, unfortunately, we had missed the supper hour. Marietta became very upset and told the guide that it was her responsibility to find a place for us to eat. After several minutes of arguing back and forth, the guide finally suggested that the best thing to do would be for us to find a restaurant, pay for our own food, and she would reimburse us the next day.

Valeri, Marietta, and I stopped at the front desk and asked the clerk for suggestions as to where we might secure a meal. The clerk gave us the name and location of a restaurant, but as we left the desk, Valeri began crying. Marietta and I asked her, "What's the matter, honey?"

She looked at us and replied, "You know, ever since that wonderful trip to Paris during my junior year in high school, I've wanted you and Dad to see this beautiful, lovely, wonderful city, and everything is turning out backwards. It just upsets me that you two aren't happy and that we're not seeing the beauty of the city."

"Sweetheart," Marietta quickly assured her, "don't worry about it. We'll feel much better after we eat, sleep and get up in the morning to begin our tour."

"Valeri," I added, "I know we're going to see the beauty of Paris. Please don't feel this way. Let's just enjoy ourselves this evening. I know everything you told us about Paris is true. We will love Paris."

During the next two days, Marietta and I realized what Valeri had meant when she'd told us about the "beauties of Paris," and why Paris is called a city of culture, light, beauty, and charm. There were no skyscrapers in Paris, and everything looked bright, light, and cheerful. The sights were beautiful everywhere we went. Valeri was so excited when we visited the Eiffel Tower; it was a breathtaking scene for both Marietta and me as we stood in the park alongside the tower and looked up to see this wonder of the world. The Arc de Triomphe, the center of Paris, with twelve major avenues originating in that square, was another delight. We crossed the Seine River to get to the Notre Dame Cathedral. It was such a large and outstanding landmark that we spent considerable time walking throughout and around the cathedral. Unfortunately, there were too many people waiting to get up to the top of Notre Dame, so we didn't have a chance to go there, but we did walk up and down many of the other walkways.

Of course, Valeri was snapping pictures of Marietta and me everywhere we went. We almost had to force her to let us take one with her in it. The museums in Paris were outstanding; the Louvre is a world classic. At the Louvre we saw the statue of Venus de Milo, which has thrilled so many people over the centuries. The climax was when we saw the original Mona Lisa portrait. It was encased in a thick safe, covered with a glass front, and it was well-lighted.

We also saw the Rue Rogue and Montmartre artists in the park, on a hill near our hotel. This was the place where many artists brought their photographs and paintings to exhibit and sell to the thousands of tourists who visited the area.

Valeri spent the last night in Paris with several young friends who were on the tour, taking the subway to downtown Paris to see the beautiful lights that illuminated the city. Marietta and I spent that night in the Montmartre area.

After breakfast the next morning, prior to boarding the bus for Brussels, we hugged Valeri. "Valeri, everything you said about this city is exactly right," we told her. "It's lovely and beautiful. There's one thing we'd like to do in life and that's to come back and visit it again. Hopefully all three of us will be able to do that together." As the bus left Paris, Marietta had tears in her eyes, thinking about what a beautiful city Paris was.

Several hours later our bus arrived in Brussels, the capital of Belgium. We spent that evening sitting in the Market Place Public Square, which is one of the most interesting in all of Europe. Brussels is known for its lace, curtains, and furniture production. All were very visible in that square, as we wandered in and out of the stores before having supper in one of the lavish restaurants.

After dinner, we wandered back to the square and prepared to watch the colored lights that would be turned on. It was fun to sit and mingle with the other people in the square, and to talk with members of our tour group while we sipped refreshing drinks - me with my Coca Cola, and Marietta and Val with their beers. We enjoyed the pleasant evening weather and waited for the flashing colored light exhibit to begin. When it did, the exhibit lasted for half an hour. Multicolored lights moved up and down the huge buildings surrounding the square.

Later, as we sat in the hotel lobby, the three of us talked about the magnificent sights we had seen so far on our trip. Valeri kidded me about my early-morning jogging and the dangerous European drivers. She was referring to my plan to jog two or three miles, two out of every three mornings during our trip. Since traffic was limited in the morning, I would jog in the street. Val had a point: it could be dangerous jogging in the streets, as drivers in Europe seemed more careless than American drivers.

Next on the itinerary was Amsterdam and The Netherlands. The city of Amsterdam was extremely interesting, with its many cathedrals and miles of canals. Much of the travel there was done by boats on the canals. The center of commerce and finance in The Netherlands, Amsterdam has a worldwide reputation of being an outstanding cultural city. Also known for its progressiveness, Amsterdam appeared to have more than its share of young hippies wandering in and out of stores or sitting in the parks along the canals. As with America's hippies, the traditional beard and old or ragged clothing seemed to be common among Amsterdam's hippies. The highlight of our stay in Amsterdam was a boat ride through the canals, with the guide pointing out many famous homes and landmarks.

The itinerary for the next morning was for our group to visit The Hague, the proclaimed financial center of Europe. However, the guide, who Valeri had nicknamed Hulda (Hulda was a tough woman in a movie that Valeri had seen recently), decided to change the plan on her own by asking the group whether they wanted to see The Hague or have another miniature review of Amsterdam. The group almost unanimously voted to see the miniature Amsterdam display. Marietta objected vehemently, and I supported her. We wanted to see The Hague; besides, it wasn't fair to change the itinerary. We felt the guide should follow the itinerary completely and not ask people to vote for changes. Consequently, and much to our dismay, we did not visit The Hague.

After leaving Amsterdam, our next stop was Cologne, Germany - and then on to Frankfort, where we were to stay that evening. The stop in Cologne was interesting. Our bus driver drove slowly through the busy streets, permitting us to enjoy the sights of that city. He then parked at the train center, which was a huge depot. Next to the depot was a beautiful and tremendously large Gothic cathedral known as "Hymn in Stone." We spent about two hours looking through the cathedral and learning about its history.

At the train depot we saw thousands of people boarding dozens of different trains. At lunchtime, we noticed that many people were patronizing Quickie Sausage Shops, so the three of us decided we would try one of the delicious-looking sausage sandwiches. We entered a little sausage shop, bought some sandwiches, and took them out to the front lawn of the depot where there were benches, sat down, and began to eat. Without a doubt the sausage sandwiches were probably the best we ever ate. They were delicious and plump. We even joked about taking a few dozen pounds of the sausages back home with us.

To accompany their sausage sandwiches, Valeri and Marietta ordered a dark German beer. They had decided to taste the beers of all the different European countries we visited, and to rate which one they thought was best.

Soon we heard "Hulda" calling for us to hurry and board the bus as we had a scheduled boat ride down the Rhine River shortly. The group quickly climbed onto the bus, and we headed toward the outskirts of Frankfort to a little boat dock, where we boarded a large ferry and began our trip down the Rhine. The view was magnificent. We saw marvelously exotic castles on both sides of the river.

Following the ride down the Rhine, we re-boarded the bus and were on our way to Lucerne, Switzerland. This part of the trip captured our interest because of the Alps. It was overwhelming to see these tremendously high mountains. Our driver gave us a thrill by electing to drive up one side to the top of a mountain and then driving down the other side, rather than going through the underpass as we did later. The view from the top was absolutely wonderful.

Valeri ran up from her seat in the back and said: "Mom and Dad, look at this! I feel like we're on top of the world! It's beautiful!" I expected Valeri to be a little leery as we drove up the mountain, but she had just the opposite reaction. As in the past, I realized that Valeri was a daredevil in many ways. To her the altitude was exhilarating; to Marietta and me it was a little frightening. We were somewhat apprehensive about looking over the side of the road and seeing nothing but space.

Upon arriving in Lucerne, we began to experience Switzerland. Lucerne was a large and lovely city surrounded by mountains, with a big, old tower near its center. The streets were crowded with people, as were the banks along the river. It seemed that they didn't work but instead just sat along the banks and looked at the water, appreciating the fresh air.

The next day we toured the downtown area and found that the Bucherer Watch Company, which was internationally known and also sold Rolex watches, was an interesting place to visit. The Bucherer store was a watch-shopper's delight. It had every kind of clock and watch imaginable. We spent considerable time looking around at all the marvelous time pieces. The three of us bought Bucherer watches to wear and take home as souvenirs.

That night Valeri experienced her first try at casino gambling. The casino was along the river winding through Lucerne. It was fun, although not too profitable. This made Valeri comment that she preferred discos over casinos.

Later that evening, Valeri and some of the other young travelers visited a disco where they danced until late, late, late (Valeri time)!

Early the next morning we boarded the bus to Innsbruck, Austria. The journey would take all morning and a good part of the afternoon. The view of the mountains was spectacular. We could look up and see the many peaks, trees, shrubbery, and other types of greenery. It was a fantastic view; and at times, we could barely see the sky. By now, we were in the middle of the Alps. After arriving in Innsbruck, the bus driver took us through the main part of the city, before taking us to the top of the smaller mountain where our hotel was located.

Innsbruck was the site of the 1976 Winter Olympics. From our hotel room we could see the ski slopes where the competitions had been held. The view from our hotel room was absolutely exhilarating; we could see the central part of the city as well as the mountains that surrounded the entire area.

After supper Valeri remarked, "Well, we youngsters are going to take the ski lift ride to the top of the big mountain." The ride was over a mile and a half from the ground level, several thousand feet higher than where we were located.

I looked up and saw the cables leading to the top and said, "Valeri, are you sure you want to go up there?"

"Of course, Dad. Come on. You and Mom are invited to come along."

I took one look and saw the cable forty feet off the ground leading to the mountain top and replied, "No thanks. I elect to watch from here." I thought to myself, "There goes that daredevil again."

She left with two of the other young people to purchase a lift ticket at the depot, only to return a few minutes later. I asked them what happened. Valeri replied disappointedly, "They're closed, Dad. It's getting too dark and the lift will not go up now." Then she perked up and continued, "But, we can take the track car down the side of the mountain to the town below and walk around for awhile if you'd like."

I looked at the track car in the mountains. "Oh, no," I said, "that looks pretty high to me too."

"Come on, Dad," Valeri answered. "Get Mom and let's go. No ifs, ands or buts." So we asked if anyone else wanted to go along, and several agreed to accompany us. We boarded a track car and made the steep descent to the town below. After walking around a section of the city, we walked along the park lake and got back on the track car, went back up the mountain to our hotel, and spent the rest of the evening socializing with the others.

Early the next morning we got on our bus and headed for Venice, Italy. Along the way we stopped in a lovely little country called Liechtenstein. The country is just slightly larger than the city itself; very quaint and pretty. Liechtenstein had stores of all different shapes and sizes, and was a true tourist paradise, especially with its open-air restaurants. Marietta and I noticed Valeri with her camera, walking around and looking at some of the other tour buses that were parked in the big, special lot. "What are you looking for, Valeri?" we asked.

"Oh, nothing," she answered. "I'm just looking at the people coming from the bus lot." Then we saw her suddenly perk up and say, "Oh, what a sight!" When we looked across the street, there was a handsome young man that Val had seen in one or two of the other tourist spots along the way. "I want to get a picture of that guy, Mom," Valeri said. She ran across the street and waited for the man to cross the street. Determined to get a better picture of him, Valeri stepped into the street when traffic was delayed by a crowd of people trying to cross the street. She was trying to avoid having him notice her.

When the crowd had crossed the street and the cars began moving again, I warned, "Val, you're going to get run over. You'd better be careful." The three of us laughed.

Shortly after, Valeri came running across to where Marietta and I were and exclaimed, "I got it! I got it! I know it's going to be a beautiful picture!"

Soon it was time to board the bus and be off to Venice. When we arrived in Venice the bus parked in an area close to the river-bus station. We planned to take the river-bus to St. Mark's Square and spend the day and part of the evening there, before returning to the bus for the drive to a hotel. We boarded the canal-bus, as they called it, which made stops on the different smaller islands, and of course at the main island of St. Mark's Square. When we arrived at St. Mark's Square, we were amazed at what we saw. The enormous St. Mark's Cathedral was lavish and beautiful inside, with all kinds of traditional statues and other ornaments. The chandeliers were like those of most cathedrals - fantastic and amazing to see. The square itself was surrounded with big buildings, of which the cathedral was the largest. There were several streets leading away from the square, lined with restaurants and shops of all kinds; again, a tourist's delight. As the evening progressed, St. Mark's Square's lights shown brightly, giving the impression that it was daylight. It was an outstanding sight to behold.

"Hey, Mom and Dad," Valeri announced, "some of the kids are going for a gondola ride. I think I'll go too. Do you want to come along?"

"No thanks, Valeri," I answered.

"Not me," Marietta added, "but you go ahead and have a good time." So Valeri and her friends took a gondola ride, returning later to tell us about the beautiful view from the big canal. They said the music and singing by the accordion player on the boat fit in just beautifully.

Valeri was very happy. None of us could believe that we were sitting in Venice, enjoying refreshments and looking at the beautiful facade of St. Mark's Cathedral.

Later that evening when Marietta and I were ready to retire, Valeri, as usual, was just beginning to come to life and wanted to find something else to do. It happened that a disco dance was being held in the hotel and would start shortly before midnight. Valeri convinced some of her friends to attend with her.

When we arose the next morning, Valeri was still sleeping soundly, and she didn't wake up until about ten o'clock. She was very tired, and she described her evening as "different." When we asked her what had happened, she replied, "Oh, the disco was great, but later on, about three in the morning, the stage crew for Rod Stewart, a well-known rock star, came into the ballroom and began preparing the room for a concert Rod Stewart would be giving the following night. We introduced ourselves to some of the stage hands and began conversing with them. Then, after their job was completed, we ended up having some beer with them, dancing and talking until six o'clock in the morning. We enjoyed ourselves and enjoyed their company." Valeri would smile and laugh every time she mentioned something about the stage hands.

The highway to Rome was not especially busy. The roads that we travelled on throughout Europe were mostly expressways in outstanding condition. As the bus approached Rome, we noticed the well-organized vineyards on the mountain slopes and the picturesque flatlands; both were beautiful.

As our bus drove through Rome's streets toward our hotel, Valeri said to us, "This is truly a marvelous, historic city, Mom and Dad. It's known as the "Eternal City" because of its ability to survive wars, famine, revolutions, and all kinds of destructive forces. It's truly a city worth visiting. I'm so happy for this wonderful opportunity to see the sights here. I'm sure it will serve as another great history lesson for me."

We spent the next three days visiting many memorable historical sites: Vatican City where the Pope lives in the Vatican Palace; St. Peter's Cathedral, the largest cathedral in the world with a dome that was designed by Michelangelo, the great artist; the Sistine Chapel, which included some of Michelangelo's greatest works; the Forum, which is the heart of ancient Rome and the focus of stories about the ancient Roman Empire; the Coliseum, where Christians were forced to battle the lions; and the Arch of Constantine, which was built in 311 A.D. and is one of the most famous of the many arches in Italy. Valeri and Marietta also visited the catacombs and found them extremely interesting, although very morbid, frightening, and claustrophobic.

Rome has many fountains throughout the city commemorating people or eras in history. The fountain we found really interesting was Trevi Fountain, which had a tradition that if you threw three coins in the fountain, you would return someday. As Valeri, Marietta, and I threw three coins in Trevi Fountain we had tears in our eyes. "God willing, someday we will return and see this beautiful, ancient city again," Valeri said.

It happened that we were in Rome on the Fourth of July. As we spent time in one of the squares, we were astonished to hear the Italians singing songs. It was like a big party, people laughing and hugging each other. We found out later that it was somewhat of a tradition for the Italians to honor the United States. We felt very emotional while taking part in this scene. Probably one of the most humorous remarks Valeri made on the trip was in Rome. She said, "You know, Mom and Dad, we got the idea of pizza from Italy, but we actually make better pizza in the United States than they do here."

The next morning we were back on the bus, heading for Florence. We would spend several hours viewing Florence, then spend the night there before traveling to Pisa. Florence also impressed us with its beautiful churches, art galleries, palaces, and museums. It was a city that rose to prominence during the Renaissance. In one of the museums the most impressive statue of all was Michelangelo's David. Valeri stood under the statue, looked up, and said, "Hey Mom and Dad, this is my main man!" She laughed heartily. When we visited the church where Michelangelo was buried, all of us were quite solemn. Val read the inscription as tears ran down our cheeks, thinking about what a great contribution he made to the world of art.

During the late evening, we took a local bus to the hilltop - a small mountain just outside of Florence. The hilltop offered a spectacular view looking down at the city of Florence, which was illuminated by thousands and thousands of lights. The lights were so bright we could actually pick out famous historical landmarks.

The next morning, it was a short bus trip to Pisa. The most outstanding tourist attraction there, naturally, was the Leaning Tower which was built centuries ago. The Tower leans seventeen degrees off center. After walking around the first level, Val wanted to take the stairway in the middle of the Tower to the top. I felt that the five-floor climb would be too strenuous for her, so I suggested that she visit the souvenir shop with her mother while I go to the top; which is what we did. As we later sat in the park that surrounded the Leaning Tower, Val said with tears in her eyes, "I just can't believe we're in Italy looking at the leaning Tower of Pisa."

The next day we visited the principality of Monaco. There we saw gambling casinos, the playgrounds of the rich; and we viewed the docks that were crowded with yachts of tremendous size. The beautiful water and mountain views were overwhelming.

Later, our group moved on to Nice, France, a beautiful Mediterranean city. It was definitely a tourist haven, with its huge hotels along the ocean, sandy beaches, and beautiful shopping areas.

Marietta and Val's visit to Cannes the next day was especially interesting to Valeri, as Cannes was the city of the Movie Festival. The international tradition of viewing and evaluating films impressed Valeri, who always found films and television intriguing. She was also highly impressed with the beautiful flower gardens throughout Cannes.

We were now coming to the final phase of the tour, which was to visit three cities in Spain: Valencia, Barcelona, and Madrid. Our first stop was the famous cathedral of Barcelona, a most imposing sight, especially in the early evening when the lights were turned on, displaying the beautiful statues.

When we visited the cathedrals, it was our tradition to light a candle and say a prayer in each one. The main emphasis for Marietta and I was to pray for family health and that a cure for Thalassemia would soon be discovered - a cure that would help so many people throughout the world.

We visited the shipping docks to see a replica of the 15th Century caravel which Christopher Columbus sailed when he discovered America. It was supposed to typify the structure of the three ships Columbus had in his entourage: the *Santa Maria*, the *Pinta*, and the *Nina*. We spent much time walking through the vessel, trying to imagine what it had been like sailing across the ocean and spending so much time at sea.

The most impressive landmark in Valencia was its large seaport, considered to be the second largest in Europe. With such wonderful ports on the Mediterranean Sea, it was no wonder that the Spanish sailors were so outstanding through the centuries.

That afternoon, we headed for Madrid, the final destination of the tour. Two thousand feet above sea level, Madrid boasts impressive skyscrapers and busy shopping areas. The key entertainment was bullfighting. Although we didn't have time to see a bullfight, many of the natives described what a bullfight was like, and it sounded extremely gory.

In the evening there were many places of entertainment, including chorus-line dancers in a theater, beautiful night clubs, and fine dining establishments. Madrid also had several outstanding disco dance halls. For one last fling, Valeri and her five young friends decided to go to one.

Naturally, they stayed out until the early morning hours. From what Val said later, they had a marvelous time enjoying the wonderful Spanish music. Valeri found Madrid to be an exciting city.

The tour came to an end, and the group was scheduled to fly back to Amsterdam to return home to Detroit. Our plans were to fly to Athens and then on to the Isle of Rhodes.

It took us most of the next day to reach Rhodes, arriving there in the very early evening. The Isle of Rhodes is three hundred miles from Athens and only fifteen miles from Turkey. Rhodes was part of Greece through the centuries, except when Turkey dominated Rhodes for a fifty-year period, until 1912, when the Italians captured the island. During the thirty-five years the Italians controlled Rhodes, they devoted themselves to building and rebuilding many parts of the island. It was reclaimed by Greece again in 1947 after World War II. Rhodes is surrounded by the Aegean Sea on one side and the Mediterranean Sea on the other, with beaches lining both seas for miles and miles. Historians believe that the Colossus of Rhodes, one of the Seven Wonders of the world, stood at the gateway of the port of Rhodes.

Marietta's mother, Ianthie, and father, Nick, were both born on Rhodes in the village of Afantou. They remained there until they married and then immigrated to America. Since their relatives still reside in Afantou, we decided to visit the island.

Valeri was absolutely exhilarated with the thought of seeing the country from where her mother's family had migrated. She was always very proud to be of Greek descent. Valeri had read extensively about Greece and Rhodes and the old Grecian empire, and couldn't wait to begin seeing the sights.

Although Valeri couldn't speak Greek fluently, she did understand the language and could hold a conversation to some degree. She said that one of the things she would like to do, now that she had finished college, was to study the Greek language and learn to speak Greek.

We stayed in the city of Rhodes the first night, then joined Valeri's Grandmother Ianthie, Aunt Mary, Aunt Toni and cousin Andrea as we had planned. They were renting several rooms just outside of Afantou. We planned to walk into Afantou each day and visit our relatives, eat lunch at the square, and then have the evening meal somewhere along the way to the city of Rhodes, 18 kilometers away, or the town of Falirakion, three kilometers away. We spent a marvelous week in Rhodes.

In addition to seeing our relatives, another highlight of our stay was visiting the city of Lindos, fifty kilometers south of Afantou. It is located high in the mountains, where the ancient Greeks used to protect the island against invaders who tried to enter from the eastern end. At Lindos, Valeri rode a donkey up the mountain and just couldn't stop laughing. She thought that it was a most wonderful ride and more fun than she had had in a long time. The view was breathtaking from the ruins at the top, where the monarchs had lived and where the soldiers had defended the island.

Valeri swam every day with her cousin Andrea. The ninety-five degree heat and continuous sunlight was ideal for spending time at the beach. Probably the most fun they had together was using the snorkel sets they had bought in a local town. With their snorkels resembling submarine periscopes, Val and Andrea would swim underwater and explore. It was fun to watch them.

The week came to a rapid end. Valeri, Marietta, and I bid our relatives a sad good-bye and left by plane for Athens early the following day. We only had three days remaining in our trip.

Once we arrived in Athens we stayed at the Poisidine Hotel along the Mediterranean seashore. Our room was on the eighteenth floor and had a beautiful view of the sea. Valeri was extremely excited about the view and the landmarks we visited over the next three days. She fell in love with the Acropolis and the Parthenon. Another landmark that she loved was Mount Lekivicos in the center of Athens, with the Church of St. George built at the very top of it. From this site one could view the entire city and the surrounding area, including the Acropolis, the Parthenon, the Mediterranean Sea, the Olympic and International Airports, and many other famous sites.

The seaport of Piraeus, where the movie *Never On Sunday* had been filmed several years earlier, was also very interesting to Valeri. Of course she loved Constitution Square and the King's Palace, where soldiers marched back and forth in high-stepping military fashion day and night.

After three wonderful days of sightseeing, mingling with people, and eating our favorite foods in wonderful restaurants, it was time to return home. We woke up very early on the day we were leaving in order to arrive at the airport for our scheduled 9:00 a.m. flight. Lying in bed we could hear airplanes taking off overhead, traffic on the main highway, boats sounding their horns, and a rooster crowing. All three of us began to laugh hysterically as Val announced, "This is great! This is Athens! All kinds of city action and yet we can hear a rooster crowing!" W h e n we finally arrived at the airport and realized we were leaving Greece to go home, all of us became tearful. Val remarked, "I sure would love to come back and visit this wonderful country of our ancestors again and stay much longer."

The flight home was on schedule and fast. It felt like we had just taken off from Athens when we landed in New York, even though the trip took a total of nine hours. During the flight I noticed Valeri was relaxed and slept much of the time. She loved flying and knew how to both entertain herself and how to rest during the flight.

Immediately after landing at La Guardia we had to take a bus to Kennedy Airport, several miles away, to catch our flight to Detroit. I noticed that the sky was getting very cloudy and dark. I turned to Marietta and said, "You know, it looks like it might rain shortly." And rain it did. Immediately after we arrived at Kennedy Airport, a tremendous storm hit the city. In fact, lightning struck the airport, and all the lights went out for a short while. It was really scary, seeing so much rain and lightning, not to mention having the experience of lightning striking the airport. But Valeri took it all in stride, sitting in one of the chairs that had a television attached, watching her favorite programs.

After about three hours we boarded our plane, only to sit for another two hours while Val took a good nap. Finally, the plane took off and we arrived in Detroit an hour later. The first thing Valeri did when we got home was to give Marietta and me a wonderful hug. She cried and cried. "Thank you so much for taking me on such a wonderful, wonderful trip, Mom and Dad," she said. We cried too.

# 18

# *The Pump*

THE next morning at breakfast Valeri described the trip to her sisters. "There was so much to see and do, and to learn about European life! It was exhilarating, educational, and just plain marvelous," she exclaimed. Valeri also expressed her gratitude to us again for making that wonderful excursion possible for her.

"Hey, Val," Marietta reminded, "don't forget we experienced the trip too, so it was nice for us."

Val told her sisters: "I hope in the near future that you two will also have an opportunity to travel through Europe."

After breakfast, Valeri began calling her friends. For the next two weeks the phone jumped off the hook as they would call her back and talk for hours about her experiences and what had gone on while she was away. They were all anxious to see pictures of Val's trip.

Valeri made a wonderful scrapbook with all the pictures she had taken. The book was set up in chronological order, beginning with our meeting at the Assumption Church and ending with our return home. The album described almost all of our experiences beautifully, especially with the clever and descriptive comments she wrote below the pictures. Val's excellent sense of humor was evident throughout.

A short while later Valeri announced to us that the fun and games had ended and that it was time for her to get serious about going out and trying to find employment. She was getting a little itchy about being inactive and decided it was time to complete a résumé and start looking for a job via the newspapers and by word-of-mouth from friends. She also planned to contact many advertising companies and local television and radio stations. She was very enthusiastic about starting a career in communications.

Meanwhile, I was completing my compilation of medical information on Thalassemia that I had started a couple of months earlier, when

Valeri was having her problems with tachycardia. At that time, I made the decision to research extensively what was being done about Cooley's Anemia and the status of treatments throughout the United States and anywhere in the world. I felt that it was time for me to pick the brains of any doctor or medical researcher who might know more about the disease.

Currently, Valeri seemed to be in good health, in spite of occasional bouts with tachycardia. It was my feeling that if anything could be done to retain her present health status, we should know about it. The only way I could do this was to contact medical people myself, since our doctors were busy and didn't seem to have time to do any research. My medical inquiries by phone included contacting the following people:

· Dr. Patricia Giordina of Cornell University Hospital, Transfusion Lab and Hematology Oncology Lab. I had been in contact with that hospital for years, and she was currently the person in charge. Dr. Giordina was working clinically with approximately one hundred patients, and it seemed to me that she should know more than anybody in the country about treating patients and anything concerning new discoveries.

· Dr. Robert Grady, a researcher at that same hospital, who was doing extensive work in researching iron chelation with a new drug, Desferal.

· Dr. Joe Graziano of Columbia Presbyterian Hospital in New York City, who was doing extensive research on all facets of the disease and its treatments. Dr. Graziano was also the special consultant to our AHEPA Cooley's Anemia Foundation. He was later to become a very good friend and was very helpful throughout the years.

· Dr. George Honig of Chicago Children's Memorial Hospital in Chicago, Illinois who was the director of the hematology department and was responsible for treating nearly twenty Thalassemia patients through the years.

· There were also two doctors I contacted at the Hematology Clinic at Children's Hospital in Detroit. The first was Dr. Sharada Sarniec, who was involved with the transfusing of sickle cell anemia patients and Cooley's Anemia patients. (There were only five or six Cooley's Anemia patients at Children's Hospital.) The other was Dr. Jeanne Lusher, the director of the Hematology Clinic. She had an excellent background in the disease, and in hematology in general. Dr. Lusher had become the director a few years earlier and was pleasantly surprised to hear that I remembered meeting her with Dr. Zuelzer when Valeri was only eight months old. She was pleased to hear that Val was doing so well.

· My final efforts centered on my friend, Dr. Nick Papadopoulos, who worked for the National Institute of Health as a medical researcher. He sent me the latest information on Cooley's Anemia, including treatments that were available at the National Institute of Health. This organization, of course, contains the most recent information on all diseases in our country.

After making contact with these medical professionals I felt updated on the disease itself, as well as more informed on the latest treatments available. My goal was to make sure that Valeri had the advantage of all research and experiments going on in this country regarding Cooley's Anemia. The information I received pointed to the following conclusions:

1. Modern medicine had extended the average life span of Thalassemia victims to eighteen years. There was not much done for the victims, except treating symptoms that they contracted along the way and keeping the patients as healthy as possible.

2. A victim would have many complications, but the major problem that usually caused death was heart failure - so the heart should be kept as stable as possible and the patient should be kept under the constant observation of a cardiologist.

3. Sugar diabetes could still be a major problem for patients who were living longer.

4. Gall bladder problems also occurred with older patients.

5. Contrary to earlier reports, Vitamin E did not offer much help to Cooley's Anemia victims.

6. The red blood cell count should be kept at a very high level, as victims seemed to function much better and to enjoy a higher quality of life.

7. Iron deposits and limited chelation was still a major problem.

8. The infusion pump was the most important discovery in treating Cooley's Anemia. There was much research in progress to evaluate to what degree the pump was being successful in chelating the iron from the victim's system. The early indications were that the infusion of Desferal to chelate the iron from a victim's body showed very successful possibilities and trends. Each doctor I spoke with and the materials I read emphasized the fact that all Cooley's Anemia victims should be using the pump. In actuality, it was the only hope that Cooley's Anemia victims had of attaining a longer life span. The assumption was that if the iron count could be held down to about one thousand grams, close to normal for any person, the victim would sustain a quality of health

that he had currently. The transfusions might have some adverse effects, but basically the iron removal would be the most important factor and the pump seemed to raise optimism for those in the medical profession who were concerned with Cooley's Anemia.

9.  A patient receiving a blood transfusion should also receive Desferal simultaneously by way of an IV in the other arm.

10. Each patient should have a thorough physical examination and a complete evaluation at least once a year.

The information I collected brought me up-to-date on what was going on in the world of Cooley's Anemia. I contacted Dr. Charbeneau and had a brief conference with him. He agreed again that Valeri should be on the pump, and he said that he would contact the doctors in the Hematology Department to determine what information they had. The reports from the Hematology Department at St. Joseph's Hospital also indicated that Valeri should get a pump as soon as possible.

So, I phoned the Glassrock Medical Supplies Company and spoke with a company representative about Valeri receiving a pump. I was told that the pump was very experimental in Cooley's Anemia, and probably would not be covered by our medical health insurance, but the representative would definitely write a letter to our insurance company to request that Valeri be covered for the use of a pump, as the pump and medication were extremely expensive.

I conveyed this information to both Marietta and Valeri. Val was a little skeptical about inserting a needle into herself five or six nights a week and keeping the needle in place while she slept for eight or nine hours. But, she was willing to try it if we thought it would be helpful. Marietta told Val that using the pump to chelate the iron out of her system could help her remain healthy, and help avoid many of the other related symptoms. This seemed to satisfy Valeri.

*19*

# Life After College

WITH all of the activities of the past few months behind her, Valeri very enthusiastically began making plans to obtain a job in communications. She completed her resume, emphasizing her background in script writing, program planning, production organization, stage props, and program organization and planning. Her resume also noted her ability to speak in front of cameras and her background in radio. Valeri sent her resume to the local newspapers, television stations, and advertising companies. Unfortunately, this was a bad year for job seekers since the job market was declining due to the current recession.

Communications had always a been a very difficult field to enter; and to make matters worse, most available positions in the field demanded several years of experience. The most practical way to get started in communications was for a person to get a job at a small town radio station. Of course, Valeri declined to move to a small town because of her health. She elected to stay home, near her family, where she could get our support when necessary, and also get her transfusions at St. Joseph's Hospital, where she was familiar with all the medical personnel. As adventuresome as Valeri was, she felt it much wiser to stay in our area.

One other factor compounded Valeri's difficulties in finding a job - each application requested information concerning the applicant's health. Valeri always pondered over the question. Should she tell them about her anemia or not? It was a dilemma for her because if she didn't inform them, her employer would eventually find out, and she felt she would probably be fired. If she did tell them, then she probably wouldn't be hired. Valeri felt the morally correct thing to do was to list her anemia and write a brief paragraph about her treatments, and also that she could function very well. Her transfusions took place on weekends, so she wouldn't have to miss work.

She hoped that the law protecting the handicapped from discrimination would help her. Perhaps employers might even wish to hire a person who was considered handicapped, since the law encouraged employers to hire handicapped persons. Unfortunately, most of the employers seemed to avoid hiring a person with a medical problem. As Valeri had done so often in the past, she was battling the odds. Again, she attacked the adverse situation with optimism and enthusiasm. She was determined to find employment, regardless of her health.

Letters responding to Valeri's application all had the same familiar words: "We are not hiring at this time." "We are searching for an experienced person for the open position." "Your background doesn't fit the position available." "The position for which you've applied has been filled recently." "Thank you for applying. We will keep your application on file for future consideration." Valeri did receive two or three interviews, but she was not hired.

Sue Fattore, who worked for an advertising company, informed Val about an opening and suggested that Val apply. Valeri was interviewed, but when it came to the choice between Valeri and one other candidate, the other received the position. This process went on for several months. Although very frustrated, Val at times seemed to almost laugh about the idea that she was turned down, and made fun about the way the letters were written. Then she would say, "Well, I'll just have to keep scanning the paper and keep trying." On one particularly frustrating night, she wrote in her journal:

> *This may be one of the low points of my life. All is well with my family, and I have graduated. Yet I feel so unsettled. I am awake every night until four - wide awake with a million thoughts in my head: worries, doubts, dreams of all I want - but frustration to no end about how to get it. I can't even con myself into sleeping. I awake in the morning and never feel rested, but worn out instead, like I was struggling all night. I want romance, love, money, cars, clothes, a jock, fun travel, my family to always be happy and together, world peace, a cure for anemia and a cure for cancer . . . Ugh, sleep.*

Being a late sleeper myself, I would often go into Valeri's room and sit. We would have philosophical conversations. One night the topic turned to families and marriage. She spoke in a very interesting and sincere manner. "You know, Dad, I know my limitations in life. I know that I can never have my own baby and I've accepted this fact. I also know that my life could be in jeopardy at any time or I might live for a long period of time. I remember seeing the Marcus Welby TV movie on

Cooley's Anemia a couple of years ago, and that gave me greater insight into the prognosis for a Cooley's Anemia victim. I know Mom and you never discuss in depth the fact that my condition could worsen and I could die in the near future; rather, you have always been encouraging. And, from what Mom and you say, I have the potential to go on for many years. I could always adopt a child or children and I feel that it's worth going after . . . a life where I'll have a mate and a family. I get so anxious to get started in life because I feel there's so much that I should or must do. Honestly, I will be patient and will keep trying to find a job, and I will enjoy life as I go along."

I then reminded Valeri about the philosophy that I had been teaching my college students in my Individual Health class. It revolved around the fact that there are two predominant desires that young adults have. One is to find an occupation or a profession that they enjoy through life, and the other is to find someone to love and establish a family together. I told her to keep pursuing these goals and to keep dreaming about these two things. I also told her that she had the right idea about receiving satisfaction along the way. That's what my philosophy was for all of the athletes participating on our teams - to smell the roses along the way.

Valeri agreed. "Don't worry," she said. "I will have fun along the way, you know that." She seemed very relaxed as I left the room.

Valeri did have fun along the way, with her new acquaintance, René, the younger sister of Chris Garkinos. The two of them, along with Chris, Sue, and some of her other friends, would hit the hot spots in town quite often. Val's sister Nikki, who was familiar with the real fun places in the Metropolitan area, would send Valeri off on a weekly venture to seek out fun and laughter.

A big event that was fast approaching was Nikki's wedding in October to Abe Rahaim, a young man whom she had met two years earlier. The wedding took place at the Assumption Church with Father Kavadas presiding. The reception was held at the King's Mill Restaurant, which was owned by our friend Ernie Backos.

It was a beautiful church wedding, with Nikki adorned in a lovely gown. Again, it was a thrill for us to see Valeri walk down the aisle as the maid of honor, looking as lovely as a young bride herself. I was also extremely thrilled to escort Nikki down the aisle and present her to her groom, Abe. As I stood there watching the ceremony, I said to Marietta, "Well, that's two of our daughters married. I hope and pray that some time in the future I'll be able to escort Valeri down the aisle, too."

Needless to say, the reception was enjoyable. Afterwards, we bid good-bye to Abe and Nikki as they left for their honeymoon. Valeri looked at us and said, "You know, I'm going to feel lonesome at home without either one of my sisters there."

"Don't worry, Val," Marietta reassured her. "It won't be too long before we have a big wedding and reception for you. Then you'll leave us two old fogies all alone to fend for ourselves."

Later that year, another big event took place - the marriage of our goddaughter Tina Harrison. At the wedding and reception Valeri once again bumped into her godsister and friend Rena Skuras. They had grown somewhat distant over recent years, while Valeri was away at the University of Michigan and Rena was finishing cosmetology school. They spent most of the time at the reception exchanging news of the past several years. Near the end of the evening, Rena said, "Hey, Val, I saw a real nice deal about a trip to Hawaii."

Valeri looked astonished, and repeated: "Hawaii! I've always wanted to go there, Rena. Please find out more about the trip and let me know so we can go together." A couple of days later, Rena notified Valeri about the details and their plans were made. The trip to Hawaii was scheduled for the following April.

Rena and Valeri immediately re-established a very intimate friendship. It became common for them to talk to each other on the phone at two o'clock in the morning, as both of them enjoyed staying up late, and they also went out often together.

Although many wonderful events took place in 1983, one of even greater importance would happen in January 1984. The news came via a phone call from a representative of Glassrock Medical Supplies Company who informed me that chelating iron from a patient's body by way of a subcutaneous pump was no longer considered experimental. Instead, the insurance company felt that iron chelation was proven to be successful enough that they would pay expenses for patients to own a pump, and that the company would pay for the needed medication.

This meant that Valeri would have a pump to use every night to inject Desferal to chelate iron from her body! She could get rid of the overload of iron that was forming in her system. It offered real hope that she could retain her present health for many years. We were elated with this news. The representative, a nurse, said that she would bring the pump over in three days to demonstrate how to use it.

When the representative brought the pump over to our home, she also brought along some syringes, tubing, needles, and medication. The pump, as described by Valeri was "kind of cute." It was six inches long by two inches wide. The Glassrock representative explained that when Val received blood, she would also receive 250 milligrams of iron with each pint. The body cannot get rid of the iron that it receives from foreign blood. Valeri, who received approximately forty pints of blood a year, would receive approximately eight grams (eight thousand milligrams) of iron a year. If the iron was permitted to accumulate in her body, it would not be long before organ deterioration occurred. The representative explained that Dr. Charbeneau had prescribed two thousand milligrams of Desferal five times a week, which was enough to eliminate all of the iron in the blood given to Valeri for a month, plus several hundred more milligrams of iron. This meant that over a period of time Valeri would be getting rid of iron that was stored in her body, plus the new iron acquired from a transfusion.

The representative demonstrated how the syringe should be filled with medication, mixed with sterile water, and then put onto the pump. Val would insert the needle subcutaneously, that is, it wouldn't go deep into the muscle, but rather just under the skin. It would then be taped in place and the pump turned on, emptying the contents of the syringe over a period of eight to ten hours as Valeri slept. The Desferal would then pick up iron from her body and the following day Val would dispel the iron through urination.

Valeri asked many questions, such as: "Where can I inject it? Will it cause irritations? Can I overdose on it and create other problems?"

The representative answered, "You should move the spot of injection around, from the abdominal area to the hip area, and it shouldn't cause any complications to the skin. There is little chance of overdosing in any way from Desferal." She smiled at Val. "Well, you're on your own, kid. Just remember one thing: this is extremely vital for you to maintain good health."

Valeri gave her a smile and said, "Thank you very much," and then stared at the pump and said, "Oh, boy!"

The representative then mixed the medication and put the needle into Val, taped it in place, and turned on the pump. She looked at it with its little flashing red light indicating that it was working. Then she told us that if we had any other questions to please feel free to call, and she left.

For the next few days there was much apprehension in our household, worrying about putting the pump on correctly, mixing the medication properly, and injecting the needle without causing Valeri too much pain. However, after a few days, everything seemed to be working out in textbook style. Val decided that she could insert the pump needle herself, along with mixing the medication, and if necessary I would prepare the medication for her on occasion. Although Valeri was skeptical about using the pump continuously, she did agree with us that it was a vital necessity in retaining her health.

We had hoped and prayed for this breakthrough in chelation therapy, since a cure wasn't imminent. The supposition was that if the chelation worked over a period of time, Valeri's iron count, which was about four thousand at this point, would drop considerably and be closer to a normal range. We also asked Dr. Charbeneau to use Desferal by way of an IV on Valeri during her transfusions, which meant a tube of Desferal in one arm and a transfusion tube in the other. Our hopes were that the pump would keep Val in good enough health through the years that, should a cure be discovered, she would be well enough to take advantage of it. If one's health deteriorated too extensively, nothing would be of any assistance.

One night while lying in bed watching television and seeing the little red light blinking on her pump, Valeri wrote some pleasant things in her journal about favorites:

*Rocky, Mom and Dad, soaps, Taxi, basketball,*
*Johnny Carson, Debbie, Nikki, Michelle, Phillip, baseball,*
*Tigers, splendor in the grass, Vasilia, Wolverine, Chris,*
*sports, Schatzie, Lynn, Sue, hot fudge cream puffs, and*
*hippos.*

All these had a special meaning for her and she loved listing her favorites in her journal occasionally. She felt it was a way of reminding herself of all the nice things in her life.

Soon it was April and time for Valeri and Rena to head for Hawaii. Valeri had saved money she had earned working for Terry Alfonsi, a high school classmate who managed a family-owned Sir Speedy franchise. Valeri had put it away for a "rainy day," which meant a trip.

The day arrived. I drove them to the airport and they disappeared between the doors. I was so happy thinking that two close friends were about to embark on a new adventure. As they walked toward the gate to board the airplane, they noticed three girls in hula skirts dancing to Hawaiian music being played by a band. Rena and Val started laughing. "Oh, boy!" Val remarked, "I bet the airline stewardesses will wear hula skirts and all!" Once they boarded the plane, they noticed that the stewardesses *did* wear the hula skirts. They laughed at that.

Upon arriving in Hawaii they took a bus to their hotel. When they were shown to their room, Valeri looked around and announced, "This room has a view of another part of the outside of the hotel and no beach. This is not for us, Rena."

Rena just said, "Oh, Val, we probably won't be in the room much, so don't worry about it."

"I didn't come all the way to Hawaii to look at some windows," Val replied. So she got on the phone and complained to the assistant manager and presto! Fifteen minutes later they found themselves in the most gorgeous room with the most beautiful and fascinating view you could imagine. The skyline, water, beach, and the swimming pools below were magnificent.

Rena laughed and commented, "You know, Val, you're just like your mom. You get things done. Just like when things go wrong when you're in the hospital. My mom is kind of laid back and doesn't say too much. I'm like her. I think we should just call ourselves Marietta and Ann." They both roared. Rena looked out the window and said, "Look at that beautiful view! It feels like we're in heaven on a dream trip."

They spent eight marvelous days in Hawaii swimming, sunbathing, drinking margaritas, going out to the night clubs, and of all things, watching the Detroit Tigers play on television.

One day they decided that they would try smoking cigarettes. They felt that it was time for young ladies who were sophisticated to learn how to smoke. They went down to the lobby, and each of them bought a pack. They went back to their room, pulled out a cigarette, lit it, and after several minutes of coughing, making faces, and feeling that it was almost time to regurgitate, they looked at each other and agreed: "This smoking is sophistication? It's awful." They laughed as they threw the cigarettes away. That was it for cigarette smoking.

They spent the last few days dating two young tourists they met. It happened that Valeri was watching the baseball game in a hotel bar when one of them came up and talked to her about baseball. He was astonished at how much she knew about the game. One thing led to another, and soon they were dating each night and having a lot of fun.

When it came time to leave Hawaii, Rena suggested that they stay for another week. They could wire home for money and enjoy one more week of this heavenly living. At first, Valeri agreed, but after awhile said, "Well, since we've got all the plans in place, Rena, let's get back. I'm scheduled to resume working at Sir Speedy."

Reluctantly, they both boarded the plane and took off from beautiful Hawaii. They sat there, staring into space, when Rena mused, "You know, I think we got really good sun tans. All that lying on the beach gave us great tans!" Except for when they were eating, they slept all the way home.

In Detroit, Chris Garkinos was waiting at the airport. "Why don't the two of you have a sun tan?" he teased.

Both Rena and Val looked at each other and exclaimed "Oh, no! Don't tell me it doesn't show!" When Chris dropped Rena off, Valeri got out of the car, and they hugged each other and cried as they kissed each other on the cheek. They thanked each other and said, "Boy, this was the greatest time I had on any vacation."

Valeri returned to her job at Sir Speedy Printing, which included responsibilities in client relations, copy preparation and layout, and maintaining client files. She learned all about the machines that were used, gave them little names, and enjoyed tinkering with them. Terry, her brother Tony, and his fiancée, Ellen-Juif, all struck up a congenial friendship with Val. They had a wonderful time working together, and time would fly by. A good thing about this particular job, which was just temporary as Val was still attempting to get into communications, was that it was less than a mile from home.

Now that Valeri was working, it was time for her to buy a car. Her desire was to own a convertible, but there were few of them available. One could be ordered, although that would take time before the car was even delivered to the dealer. We went to a Dodge dealer who had several convertibles on his lot. We walked out to look at them and Valeri called out: "Dad, there's my car!" It was a beautiful brown Dodge 600 convertible, with leather seats, AM/FM stereo radio and a tape deck, white-wall tires, and a light brown top. She immediately fell in love with this car and said, "Dad, that's for me." Valeri took the car home two days later. She was absolutely thrilled with her new "automachine" as she called it. It was very exciting for her to load up the car with her girlfriends, put the top down, turn the radio on full blast, and cruise around. It seemed that this car was just built for Valeri. It was a part of her life from that time on.

During the 1984 summer the Detroit Tigers were red hot. They won thirty-five of their first forty ball games and were contenders for the American League pennant. Valeri and I attended several games that year. She loved every minute of every game. Her favorites on the team were Alan Trammel, Lou Whittaker, Kirk Gibson, Lance Parrish, and, of course, team manager Sparky Anderson. Actually, she adored all the members of the team and thought they were the greatest ever. She would listen to the games on the radio or watch them on TV almost every day; living every pitch, every hit, every out, and all of the ups and downs with them. It was a dream season for her and the Tigers. Eventually the Tigers won the pennant and the World Series. She spent a great deal of time celebrating with her friends.

In June 1984 Vasilia was married at our Assumption Church. Just prior to Vasilia's marriage, Val wrote on some of the things she was going to miss. They were:

> Our man-hating conversations, our man-loving conversations, watching porno flicks, your psychic powers, my friend, pal and confidante, your encouraging words, your cheering me up always, a most honorable woman, our nightly three-hour phone calls that if anyone taped we would be arrested for, reminiscing, speaking foreign languages that no one understands. Shirley [they called each other Laverne and Shirley]. Your advice, Doctor! Our shared passion for hot fudge cream puffs and men.

Again Father Kavadas presided over the ceremonies, and again, Valeri was maid of honor. Vasilia was a very beautiful and radiant bride. As Valeri walked down the aisle, again both Marietta and I had tears in our eyes as we dreamed of the day I would have the honor and thrill of walking Valeri down the aisle.

Shawn stood up in the wedding with Valeri. They had become quite close for a while, dating on a regular basis. He wanted to get serious, and he invited Valeri to meet his parents up north. But Valeri had other plans and decided it would be better if they broke off their steady dating, since she wasn't ready to make any kind of a serious commitment.

A little later that year, Valeri's sister Debbie came back home to live with the family. Debbie and her husband, Joe, divorced. They had a mutual agreement to take care of their children, Michelle and Phillip, who would stay primarily with Joe and his new wife, but would also stay two to three days a week with Debbie in our home. It was a sad time in all of our lives, because Debbie had so enjoyed her marriage. But things just didn't work out.

Valeri found it enjoyable having her niece and nephew around. She spent a lot of time taking them to the local swimming pool and other places, and she loved it when they called her "Poochie." Val had a wonderful way with the two youngsters and they loved her very much. Debbie was able to return to work as a waitress and assistant manager at one of the Big Boy restaurants near home.

Val was quite helpful to Debbie as she was overcoming her depression from the divorce. It was humorous to hear Valeri try to entice Debbie into going out at night with Rena, Valeri, and their other friends. Debbie wasn't ready to do that yet. "But when I'm ready, I know you'll take good care of me, Valeri," Debbie often kidded.

*Sammy, Debbie, Val, and Nikki enjoying the backyard pool on a sunny day. 1967.*

*Mom, Valeri, Nikki, Debbie, and Dad. 1982.*

*Right:*
Starting up the mountain! Isle of Rhodes, Greece. 1983.

*Bottom Left:*
A dream come true – Paris, France with the high school French club. 1978.

*Bottom Right:*
Monaco: Money, Men, and Cars! 1983.

*Facing Page:*
*Top:*
Christmas gathering. All of the cousins. 1984.
*Bottom:*
Graduation from Grosse Pointe North High School. 1979.

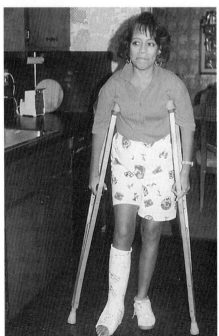

*Above:* Valeri and Rena spent eight glorious days in Hawaii. April 1984.

*Left:* During the 1986 Annual AHEPA Convention, held in Miami Beach, Florida, Valeri parasailed for the first time. Rough landing!

*This is life: beer, music and sun! Valeri relaxes in Miami, Florida. 1985.*

*The chorus line! Best friends: Julie, Sue, Jill, Val, and Lynn. 1984.*

*Wow! University of Michigan Commencement. April 30, 1983.*

*Right:*
*New York! Her city! 1984.*

*Below:*
*"29" and going strong. 1990.*

*Right:*
*Val and*
*Chris...*
*They shared*
*everything.*
*Chinese*
*restaurant.*
*1985.*

*Bottom:*
*Finally ...*
*a student*
*teacher.*
*Grosse Pointe*
*North High*
*School. 1986.*

# 20

# *Two Major Decisions*

S HORTLY after Val began working at Sir Speedy Printing, she made two major decisions. The first was to give up trying to gain employment in the communications field; instead she would attend Wayne State University on a part-time basis to pursue a teaching certificate. She gave this idea considerable thought. The primary reason for this decision was that she enjoyed traveling, and if she became a teacher, she would have lots of time to travel during the holidays and summer months. Additionally, Valeri enjoyed children and felt teaching would be very gratifying; and although the school day was very rigorous, the hours were limited compared to an eight- or nine-hour job. Finally, there were more opportunities for employment for a person like herself in the teaching field.

Valeri's first step was to contact Ms. Toni Nicholas, a family friend, who was in charge of the Records Department for graduate students in the College of Education at Wayne State University. Toni invited Val to her office to evaluate Val's records and to inform her of the graduate-level classes that would be necessary for Valeri to complete to become a certified teacher. Toni proved to be of tremendous help in preparing a schedule for Val to follow for the next two years. First, Val had to take several courses in English, since that was to be her major, followed by educational techniques and methods courses, and finally the student teaching contact for one full semester. Val planned to receive a secondary school certification in English for grades nine through twelve. This would qualify her to teach any classes in an English department of a junior or senior high school. Toni explained that Valeri would have to take about thirty hours of class work in order to be ready to complete her student contact for certification. Val was very happy and pleased with all of Toni's assistance. She resolved to start school in September.

The second decision emanated from discussions with her sister Nikki, who worked as a pharmaceutical representative for Stewart Pharmaceutical Company. Nikki had developed a slight thyroid condition shortly after returning from her honeymoon, and she was being treated by an endocrinologist. Nikki felt this endocrinologist was a very conscientious and knowledgeable doctor. During one of her visits, Nikki and her doctor discussed Valeri's anemia and the fact that Valeri had never had a menstrual period. (Of course, this meant that Val could not have children.) The doctor was rather encouraging in his comments regarding the possibility for Valeri to begin menstruating.

When Nikki talked to Valeri about this, Val decided to visit the endocrinologist and see if it was feasible for her to take medication for her to develop a little more physically and to begin menstrual periods, which might lead to the capability of becoming pregnant. Valeri often felt that she looked so much younger than her nearly twenty-three years and thought perhaps she could be helped by seeing the endocrinologist. She was always being kidded about looking like a teenager, which wasn't all bad, but she wanted to have a more mature physical appearance.

Valeri scheduled an appointment to see the endocrinologist the following week. He gave her a thorough examination, including several different tests. Then he sent Valeri to see a female hematologist on his staff. Under the hematologist's guidance, Val underwent several more tests and then spent quite a bit of time discussing Cooley's Anemia with her. The conversation was distressing to Val, as the doctor said that there was no way that Valeri had Cooley's Anemia Major - otherwise Val would have been dead a long time ago. The hematologist felt that people with Cooley's Anemia Major couldn't survive more than eighteen or nineteen years, and Val was too healthy to be a Cooley's Anemia victim. Valeri stated that she was getting transfusions every month because of the anemia. The doctor still insisted: "Regardless, there's just no way that you have the major. Instead, you probably have the intermediate, which is a very mild case of the anemia." It seemed that no matter what Valeri said, the doctor disputed it. After a while, Valeri quit making comments.

When Valeri told Marietta and me about her visit with the hematologist, we became very upset. We were especially disturbed by the comment that she kept repeating, that Valeri would have been dead a long time ago if she had the major anemia. I decided to telephone the doctor the next day to speak to her. When I did, she told me the same thing: "Valeri just doesn't have the major anemia because she just wouldn't live this long." I spent some time talking with her, and I told her that she shouldn't make comments about a topic she knew very little about. I also suggested that if she wanted Valeri's records for further study, she could contact Dr. Charbeneau. Our conversation came to a halt shortly. I had the feeling that the doctor didn't believe Val was getting the transfusions as often as she had said. Whatever happened, she never met with Val again.

A couple of weeks later Valeri went in for an appointment with the endocrinologist to have an analysis of all her tests. The doctor was very helpful in explaining exactly where Valeri was in her physical development. He felt that she was normal, and with the aid of estrogen pills, she could begin having menstrual periods. He prescribed two drugs that contained estrogen: Premarin and Pravera. He felt that the birth control pills would start her menstrual cycle. Valeri told us about her conference and was anxious to get started on the birth control pills.

I was very skeptical about the whole situation, so I called Dr. Patricia Giordina at Cornell University Hospital in New York, as I often had before when there was a major decision regarding Valeri's condition or treatments. Dr. Giordina explained that some of the young girls took both of the medications and had periods. It appeared that some were capable of becoming pregnant. Dr. Giordina said it was impossible to know much about Valeri's condition unless she were to go to New York and be examined by her. However, it seemed as though the endocrinologist was right in his recommendation and that Valeri would eventually have periods. She said, "It's Valeri's life, and whatever she wants to try, she must try." Her final words were, "Let the chips fall where they may."

I informed Val about my conversation with Dr. Giordina. She was happy to know that other girls were taking the pills and that the medication did not appear to endanger them in any way. So she began to take the Premarin and Pravera. One month later, Valeri returned to see the endocrinologist. She told him that she was having different feelings internally, to which he commented that it sounded as though things were progressing well. He asked to see Valeri if and when she had her first period.

The big event took place about a month later, when Valeri began a menstrual period. Even though there wasn't much bleeding, it was an actual period. When asked about the discomfort she felt, she replied with a laugh: "Now I know what I've been missing all these years." After being examined by the endocrinologist, he informed her that everything seemed to be going along quite normally, and that he would like to see her in about six months, unless there were other complications.

This was an exciting time in Valeri's life - to think she was quite normal and had periods like other girls. It made her feel very feminine and womanly. We could notice the difference in her attitude.

It was much too early to know if Valeri could become pregnant, as she would have to take the pills for a long time before this question was answered. The next time she went in for a transfusion we had a long discussion with Dr. Charbeneau about the effects of her period and any foreseeable problems. He said he didn't think there would be any. He thought that Dr. Giordina seemed to be accurate in her assessment. Of course, we would have to observe Valeri very carefully.

Valeri found much pleasure in post-college life. She took several trips, her beloved Detroit Tigers won the World Series, she had fun working for Sir Speedy, and she began taking classes at Wayne State University. Even the task of inserting the needle into herself and setting the pump to work five nights a week was no problem. In fact, one night she said, "Dad, the pump isn't so bad after all. If I was ever confronted by a burglar, I could hit him over the head with this thing!"

Socially, Val had a nice mixture of friends. René, Kim and Dino Stathis, David Petrouleas, Alex Kocovis, Steve Gust, Alex Mellos, and others were ready to go bar hopping or to shows or wherever to have a good time on the spur of the moment. Sometimes Valeri would join Sue Fattore and her boyfriend, Steve Schucker, for social events. And, Rena was ready to do anything Val had in mind. It seemed that there was always something to do socially, especially dances with the singles youth group at our church cultural center.

Valeri was a conscientious churchgoer and loved her religion. She also enjoyed taking part in the affairs at the cultural center and city-wide events with the Orthodox Youth Associations. All in all, 1984 was another fine year in Val's life.

While working at Sir Speedy, Valeri also became involved as a part-time volunteer at Grosse Pointe Cable. She was a crew member of a movie evaluation talk show and was responsible for staging and script writing. This assignment lasted for four months. Valeri enjoyed it immensely, since it was what she had been trained for at the University of Michigan.

In June 1985 Valeri decided to leave Sir Speedy and take a new job with a company called Creative Services, owned by Angie Bournias, a family friend. This small public relations firm handled advertising accounts for Crowley Department Stores, and the Ford Motor Company, as well as other local accounts. Angie hired Valeri to write press releases and to learn the business of public relations. It was a wonderful move for Valeri and she enjoyed the job tremendously.

Even with full-time work, Valeri found time to continue her travels. She went to Tucson, Arizona with Rena, who was now a flight attendant. They stayed with Rena's brother Billy, who was a lifelong friend. He went out west to seek employment. Billy treated Rena and Valeri like queens the entire ten days of their visit. They visited the Grand Canyon and many other fine sights. They had a wonderful time. Unfortunately, Billy was to fall victim to alcohol later on in life, which saddened Valeri.

Also on the travel calendar that year was a trip to Washington, D.C. Rena was to be stationed there a couple of days in-between flights and invited Val to stay with her for free at the hotel. Valeri jumped at this opportunity and went to D.C. with Rena. While in Washington, Rena and Valeri were walking down a street and wanted to have their picture taken beside one of the large buildings. Valeri noticed a homeless person wandering nearby who had stopped about fifty feet away, sat down, and began watching the two of them. As Rena asked a passing stranger to take a picture of them, Valeri said, "Wait a minute, Rena." She walked over to the homeless person and asked, "Sir, could you please do us a favor and come over and take your picture with us, please?"

The man looked at her in amazement and asked, "Do what?"

Valeri grabbed his hand and said, "Come on, I'll show you. Come with me." He got up and followed Valeri over to where Rena was standing with the stranger. Valeri said, "I want one of you to take a picture of, Rena, our friend here, and me."

The man looked at her sheepishly and began patting his hair down with his hand. He said, "Wait a minute. I don't know if I should do this."

"Nonsense," Valeri answered. "We'd be honored if you did this for us." So he stood there with Rena and Valeri with their arms around his shoulders and smiled as the other person took the picture of them. He thanked Valeri very much and said he appreciated her kind gesture. She took him by the hand and said, "Thank you for helping us by taking part in this picture." He smiled and slowly walked away.

Rena said, "I know that made his day, Val. He was smiling for the first time." Val and Rena enjoyed Washington D.C. immensely.

Valeri once again attended the AHEPA convention, this time with René and some other friends. That summer the convention was held in Boston, Massachusetts. One of the highlights of this trip was when Valeri went to Fenway Park to watch a night baseball game. She felt the much-heralded tradition of that ball park and was excited to see the Red Sox play.

Later that year, during the basketball season, Valeri, René, Dino, Kim Stathis, and several other friends, along with Mrs. Mellos, mother of Alex Mellos, one of the basketball players, traveled with the junior men's team to cheer them on when they competed in tournaments in Chicago, Indiana, and several other places near Detroit. They enjoyed watching the team, as they were excellent players and also very good friends. Alex Kolovis, Alex Mellos, George Belalas, Dave Petrouleas, Steve Gust, Dino Stoukas, and the Caruso twins comprised the junior men's team. Val and her friends knew the young ball players from the time they were in the junior GOYA together and had developed a very fine friendship.

At the games Valeri and her friends could be found cheering wildly. Val would often get up and start screaming at the referees, "Open your eyes, ref. You're missing a good ball game!"

On occasion Valeri traveled to Chicago to watch Assumption's senior men's basketball team play. This team was powerful enough to win two or three of the prestigious national Greek basketball tournaments each year. Valeri and her friends would often watch them play, and they were very proud of the team's successes.

One night, one of Valeri's friends asked Valeri why she liked to travel so much. "Wouldn't it be fun just staying closer to home more often?" she asked. Valeri must have given some thought to her friend's question, because in her journal she wrote:

> *Why is it I travel? Because I love it! I love the entire feeling despite my complaints. I love having new experiences. I love eating at new restaurants . . . sightseeing, people watching. I feel like I'm getting an education that no book can teach. I feel so relaxed as if nothing is wrong . . . Kind of like everything has stopped . . . so I can enjoy myself . . . even though quarrels occur . . . we get lost . . .the hotel may not be the best . . . nobody can agree on what to do next . . . nothing can compare to walking the historic streets of Washington, D.C. . . . enjoying New York's night life . . . breathing the balmy Boston breeze . . . . . partaking in Artesian pastries . . . just experience life!!! It's great! I love all the excitement and the vigor. (Love is my favorite word!)*

These strong feelings explained why Valeri was ready to travel at the drop of a hat. It seemed like her bags were always packed, ready for her to go on to a new adventure.

That summer Valeri spent much time visiting Nikki, who lived in Bloomfield Township near a small lake with her husband, Abe. They had purchased a twenty-foot motor boat and spent many evenings and weekends cruising on the lake in the boat. When Valeri visited, Abe would often take the boat out and all of them would go tubing. Tubing involved attaching a rope from the boat to a huge inner tube. A person would get on the inner tube and be pulled around by the boat. The person driving the boat would speed and make quick and abrupt turns, causing the tube to go flying in a big arc, often tipping over and throwing the person into the water. That was one of Valeri's favorite ways to spend an afternoon. Nikki also had several backyard parties at her home and would often invite family members to attend them. These parties were always enjoyable for Val, because she loved being together with her family.

In September 1985, Nikki gave birth to her daughter, Alexandra. It was an exciting moment for all of us, especially for Valeri, who had grown very close to Nikki in the last three years. Valeri would drive out to see Nikki and help her take care of Alex during the first two months after her birth. This was easy for Valeri to do, because she worked near Nikki's home. Val enjoyed bathing Alex and attending to her needs. She often thought it would be wonderful to one day have the privilege of doing this for her own child.

A new semester began at Wayne State. Valeri decided to take an extra class so that she might earn her teaching certificate in less than two years. She loved the activity around the University Student Center, where thousands of students were doing their thing. She especially liked the television room on the second floor, where she could watch TV with the other students and relax while waiting for her class to begin.

This semester, Valeri was enrolled in two English classes and loved them both immensely, as they involved creative writing, a favorite of Valeri's. The overall academic atmosphere was positively superior, according to Val.

No matter how busy Val was, she always kept in close contact with Chris Garkinos, who was now a senior at the University of Michigan. It was common for Val to talk to Chris on the telephone after midnight. He would bring her up-to-date on what was going on in his life, and she would reciprocate. Occasionally, she visited him at the university and he would come home periodically. While reflecting on their friendship, she wrote in her journal:

*I just talked to Chris. He cracks me up. We talked about childhood, life and camp. He's so cool, . . . smart and sensitive. Sometimes I think it would be so easy to fall in love with him. I can picture us sometimes getting married with all of our friends and family looking on happily. I don't know, Chris and I get along well. He makes me laugh and understands me. I don't know how I could ever let him know. I'd be afraid of course. I'm always afraid. I wouldn't want to burden him because I don't know how normal my life will ever be. I never let guys get too close to me because I might have to deal with that ??? situation. I don't know where I stand . . . could I have kids? We're friends first and always. It's great to have a male who's just a buddy. And I don't want other people to ruin it because they don't understand. I believe men and women can be friends and can gain so much from that type of relationship.*

Nineteen eighty-five flew by rapidly by for Valeri. It was already Christmas; a season that Val especially loved because of the family gatherings. Each year the family would have one big party late on Christmas day. The party would be rotated to a different family on an annual basis. After the celebration in our home that year, Valeri wrote in her journal:

*Sue, Rena, and Chris came by. That was nice. Bridgette came by with a gift - a cushion pillow with a desk top and a Miami Vice calendar. She's such a sweetheart. I went to church. This morning I felt great. My parents bought me this leopard print outfit and I looked good, I thought. Or anyway I felt good for a change. I was so happy I went to church and thanked God for everything I have. Now it's all over and the leftovers are in the 'fridge and I feel sad. I'm scared because another Christmas is going by. Another year of my life. And I have yet to accomplish something significant in my life.*

Occasionally, Valeri would express her guilt feelings to Marietta and me. When she talked that way to us, we would tell her that we loved her very much and ask her to be patient, as she was doing just what she should be doing at this point in her life. Later that week, Valeri wrote:

*December 29, 1985. Christmas is over . . . already. My least favorite holiday is approaching. New Year's Eve without someone special. Today I stayed in my pajamas all day and watched TV for twelve hours. Yep . . . I saw the movie that reminds me of my mother . . .* Terms of Endearment. *When her mother runs down the hall to the nurses station and screams at the nurses - God was that a familiar sight! . . . I think how hard it must be for my parents to have done this with me for twenty-five years. All the pain they went through with me. I always forget, and at times I treat them so badly. I don't know why. I wondered if they had known about me before whether they would have ever had me. It's strange how some people would not have wanted the responsibility, but not my parents. They've been great.*

Valeri always expressed deep appreciation to us and showed much love and affection. She let us know that she was very, very grateful.

That New Year's Eve Valeri, René and the gang had a great time at a local hall party, and then they ended up in Greektown, their favorite hangout, until seven o'clock in the morning.

On New Year's Day it was a tradition to have a party to celebrate Valeri's name day, as January 1 was the name day honoring St. Vasilios (which in English interpretation is the name William or Bill or Valeri). The party was always held at our home. We would invite close friends and relatives. Although tired from celebrating the night before, Valeri always loved this holiday in her honor. Later that night, when all the guests had left and Val was in her room, she wrote in her journal:

*Favorites for 1985: Mom and Dad, Rena, Sue, René, Chris, Lynn, Nikki, Debbie, Michelle, Phillip, Alexandra, Margaritas, Vodkas, Toni, chocolate milk, grilled cheese, Therpoeta, Spanakopita, English Beat, driving with my top down, Madonna, Don Johnson and Jeff Bridges.*

In February 1986 my mother, Demetrula Samaras, passed away. She had been quite ill for several months and died at the age of 86. Since her middle son, Peter, had died many years ago of Cooley's Anemia, Grandma Samaras developed a protective and loving relationship with Valeri. She often reminded Marietta and me to make sure that Valeri was getting proper care and rest, and especially not to pressure Val into trying to do too many things. Grandma Samaras felt that Valeri should lead more of a life of leisure, as she knew too well the devastating effects of the disease.

My mother was a very religious person. Whenever Valeri would be ill or would go in for a transfusion, her grandmother would go to church to pray for Valeri. Valeri appreciated her grandmother's concern and enjoyed a close relationship with her, often visiting her grandmother at the condominium where she lived following the death of her husband. Valeri cherished the thoughtful gifts that her grandmother showered upon her. It was a very sad time for Valeri when her Grandmother Samaras passed away.

Val was very busy with her hectic schedule at Creative Services, attending classes at Wayne State University, and enduring the physical rigors of receiving monthly transfusions. Additionally, Valeri maintained her active social life, as her friends meant so much to her. Meanwhile, the estrogen pills that Valeri was taking seemed to be working. According to her doctor, she had developed secondary sexual traits and was having a regular period each month.

Marietta and I felt that Valeri should see the doctor more often than his prescribed six-month check ups. When we mentioned this to Val, she would say, "Oh, Mom and Dad, he knows what he's doing; everything is going along nicely."

Valeri put much effort into her studies at Wayne State, particularly the English classes, which gave her a more refined insight into methods and techniques for teaching this material to high school students. Her love for writing helped her obtain superior grades in all of her classes. The "A's" were rolling in at a rapid pace as the semesters rolled on.

Valeri found it interesting to write about some of the events that took place in her life, and she wrote many such articles for some of her English courses. One article that was well-liked by the teacher involved a song written by an outstanding musician and singer, Billy Joel. The song was entitled "The Stranger."

> *We all have a face*
> *That we hide away forever*
> *And we take them out and show them to ourselves*
> *When everyone is gone*
> *Some are sad and some are steel*
> *Some are milk and some are leather*
> *They're the faces of the stranger*
> *But we love to try them on.*

Valeri's personal reactions to these words were the following:

> *These words often flow through my brain. I feel like they are a part of me - like they're talking about me. I find that sometimes I hide my true feelings or act one way for some people and act differently towards others. I can be very outgoing at times, put on my "show-off" face and try to entertain people or I can be very quiet if I'm unsure of the people I'm with or I can be a spokesperson if the situation calls for it, if I feel strongly about something. I think I get that from my mom. She's a fighter . . . but only for justice - she's very perceptive.*

*At other times I'll keep everything inside . . .*

*There's a lot of me (schizophrenic that I am) that no one ever sees. They're built on hopes, dreams, fantasies of how I long to be or even how I think I am. People, even my close friends, who see many of my faces, can never see these. They are deep within myself. I think that if I let out or tell people about them they'll expect too much of me or won't take me seriously. So I try to write about them or spend hours lying awake thinking about them . . . I believe "The Stranger" to be one of the most significant songs to me . . . It strikes me as a hard-hitting, insightful revelation.*

Her teacher felt this was an excellent description of some of the inner feelings people have and commended her for that brief paper.

In an English class taught by Dr. James Boyer, Valeri stated that she felt it was an honor to be a student of such an outstanding professor. Dr. Boyer gave her some unique ideas on how to write in descriptive terms, and what he called cinematic approach and scientific terms. She really appreciated these because they gave her such an enriched background in writing. An example of Valeri's work for Dr. Boyer is the following description of the whole hospital/transfusion scenario, involving mostly the people.

*The place is a stark white, perfectly square hospital room. Nothing but a crucifix disturbs the monotonous white walls. Dingy aqua curtains hang sloppily from dulled chrome bars above the four beds. One set has hooks missing, which causes the curtain to fall uneasily. There is one narrow slit of a window which allows only the darkness of the downpour outside to be seen. This produces a gloomy shadow that streams through the glass, as well as random glimmers of a sharp light searing the sky, while an endless splatter of water glides down the pane.*

*There are two high, straight-backed cushion chairs made of hard, dirty, beige vinyl pushed neatly against the wall. There is also a wooden chair, obviously not meant for long visits because its bolts protrude on the backrest of the chair. A floor lamp stands ominously in one corner - the kind which shines blindly - and its neck bends and twists to any angle for inspections.*

*Four patients fill the half-raised beds. One bed holds a very old woman mumbling in her sleep, entwined in a barrage of metal bars, ropes and bandages. Her two legs held by traction remain perfectly still while the lady continuously murmurs on. There are flowers of blue, pink, and vast amounts of green cluttering her nightstand. Cards hang plentifully along the thick, sturdy supportive bars.*

*A middle-aged woman occupies the bed directly across from the napping old woman. This woman rests on her side, endlessly inhaling a cigarette to the butt, stomping it out and lighting another. Noises of clapping and screaming come from the small rented television which extends from a long arm attached to the wall. Her daily twelve o'clock ritual of watching "Family Feud" is not disturbed by the irregular surroundings. An orange and beige plastic tray sits on her stand with half-eaten green Jello, traces of macaroni and cheese, untouched tomato soup, and an empty matching orange cup, all waiting to be picked up and removed from view.*

*Next to the bed, a thirty-ish blonde woman visitor stands, shouting futilely at a sleeping and obviously hard-of-hearing older woman in the next bed. The patient only stirs slightly. The blonde pauses for a moment, sticks her hand in the pockets of her pale green shorts, and then begins shouting once again.*

*Amidst the lady sleep-talking, the lady chain-smoking, the lady shouting, and the lady not hearing, is a much younger twenty-year-old girl sitting up very alertly. She is enthusiastically eating a grilled cheese sandwich. She rather proudly and systematically dips a corner of the sandwich into the tomato soup, bites the moistened part, chews, and sips her chocolate milk out of the brown and white carton with a Flexi-straw. The pale girl continues to indulge in chocolate chip cookies and Jello, despite the mangled tubing implanted in both hands. Two IV's simultaneously pour liquids into her body. In one hand, a large bag of clear liquid endeavors to empty its contents. In the other hand, a scarlet-hued solution slowly drips from a small pint-size bag supplying the essential life liquid into the girl's anemic system. At bedside, a dark-haired woman, the girl's mother, sits nonchalantly reading a newspaper, as if nothing is out of the ordinary.*

Dr. Boyer commended her for what he called an excellent descriptive article.

Valeri was hooked. She completely fell in love with the idea of teaching youngsters in junior high and high school how to write. She was extremely enthused about finishing her class work, doing her student teaching, and completing her pursuit of a teaching certificate. In fact,

Valeri was so excited that she elected to finish her class work during the spring and summer semesters, which would allow her to begin student teaching in September of that year. This meant that she would have to attend school several times a week throughout the spring and summer.

I felt that perhaps Valeri was pushing herself too much, both physically and mentally, and that it would be best for her to quit her job at Creative Services so that she could concentrate all her energy on her courses at Wayne State. She objected vehemently to my suggestion. I told her that in my judgment she would be better off not working a full eight-hour schedule on top of pursuing her education. Since her job with Creative Services was very enjoyable, especially the social life that came with meeting friends for lunch, Valeri chose not to quit.

# 21

# New Health Problems

I T SEEMED that the pressures of work, school, and social life caught up with Valeri late in May 1986, after the spring semester had just begun. She was feeling nauseous and did not have an appetite. This was out-of-character for her, as Valeri could eat a variety of foods at almost any time of the day or night.

She began having vomiting spells in the morning, but then would feel a little better in the evening. Although we assumed it was just a virus, we had Dr. Charbeneau examine her. He also felt it was just a virus, and he advised us to wait and see what happened in a day or two.

It so happened that Valeri's godsister Diane Kastran, daughter of John and Dolly Kastran, was getting married that Sunday. Our family was invited to the wedding, which promised to be a gala affair. Val didn't feel much better on Sunday, as we left home to attend the wedding ceremony.

The wedding reception was held at the Lochmoor Country Club near our home in Grosse Pointe Woods. I noticed Valeri was still not feeling too well, but that she was making an effort to eat. Needless to say, Marietta and I were very worried and kept watching her as she sat with the young people at a different table than us. Shortly after the meal, Valeri came over to us and told us she felt nauseous and was going to go home. This was unusual for her, as Valeri loved the Greek line dancing that would follow, along with all the wedding traditions that would take place involving the bride and groom. A short while later I drove her home so she could rest and be comfortable. She insisted that I go back to the reception.

When Marietta and I returned home from the wedding reception late that night, we discovered that Valeri had been vomiting again and was feeling very ill. Early the next morning we called Dr. Charbeneau. He told us to take her to the hospital and he would meet us there.

We followed his directive and helped Valeri settle into one of the rooms. Her condition seemed to get worse. She could not put anything in her stomach, including water; as soon as she swallowed, she would regurgitate. She also had a high temperature.

Over the next three days Valeri underwent many tests. Although all of the tests proved to be normal, she still had a high temperature and was unable to eat. Meanwhile, she was losing weight, as she often did whenever stricken with an illness. This meant that Valeri was also getting very weak. She could hardly get out of bed and move around.

After five days in the hospital and an entire battery of tests, Valeri was finally able to eat and keep food in her stomach. When the test results were in a few days later, Dr. Charbeneau was still unsure of what Valeri's trouble had been, although he thought it might have been another hepatitis attack. She seemed to be feeling a little better.

I decided to call Dr. Giordina at the New York Cornell University Hospital to ask her what she thought might be wrong with Valeri, and whether some of her patients in New York had similar types of problems. She indicated that Dr. Charbeneau and the staff at St. Joseph's were on the right track in the tests they had prescribed, and more than likely it was another attack of hepatitis.

By the seventh day Valeri was feeling much better and was anxious to get out of bed and resume her normal life. Dr. Charbeneau gave her a physical in the morning and said that he felt she was bouncing back quite nicely. It was all right for her to go home, but she must take it easy and eat only light meals for several days. Dr. Charbeneau indicated that it seemed like a different type of hepatitis other than the A or B type, but hepatitis, nevertheless. There was some type of irritation or infection in the liver, but the liver, being sturdy, would heal. She would have to help the healing process by watching her diet and getting a great deal of rest.

After this scare we took Valeri and left for home, happy to see that she seemed to be in good condition, including her heart. As usual, heart problems worried us the most, since with Thalassemia patients it was the heart that caused fatal problems. Tests indicated that Val's heart was still functioning within a normal range, and that it was still strong and a normal size. This made Marietta and me feel much better.

There was one thing that did bother me. I asked Dr. Charbeneau to explain why, on occasion, Valeri's right carotid artery in her neck moved in and out as her heart beat. He told me not to worry, it was only a reflex action of the artery to the beating of the heart. This bothered me because it was the same reflex action that took place in my mother when she had heart problems near the end of her life. In Valeri's case, this reflex action would take place for a short time, and then subside.

Valeri finally followed our wishes and left her job at Creative Services. She told Angie that she was going to concentrate on her school work and wanted to have a more restful summer in preparation for the fall semester. Angie agreed that this was probably a good idea, especially since Valeri would expend a lot of energy during her student teaching in the fall.

Valeri continued to work hard in her classes at Wayne State. She also relaxed by going on a couple of trips "to keep life from becoming too monotonous." One trip was to New York City with René. They had a wonderful time seeing the sights and dancing until the early morning hours at the Gas Light, a popular night spot.

The last night they were there, Valeri and René met the group of people with whom they had been socializing. As they walked toward the dance floor, a young, big, strong man who weighed at least 220 pounds ran over to Valeri, picked her up, and gave her a big squeeze, saying: "Hey, Tiny, how ya' doin?"

Valeri heard a crack and thought to herself, "Oh no, my ribs have just been broken." She said nothing to the burly, handsome monster, but laughed and kidded around with the group as though nothing had happened. Meanwhile, she was in pain all evening.

Upon arriving home the next night, Val told us what had happened and we thought maybe her ribs were broken, because she did have excessive pain when she breathed. Fortunately, after taking her to the Emergency Room, x-rays showed that she had some severe bruises, but no fractures. The doctor told her to take it easy for a few days and leave the wrapping on for a week, until her bruised ribs felt better. As expected, this experience was the focus of many jokes for the next couple of weeks.

Again, Val worked at Assumption's annual three-day festival in early August. She worked ten hours each day, at different refreshment stands, performing different duties.

Then it was time to head for the AHEPA national convention. This year it was being held in Miami Beach, Florida. This trip would be different, as Val's sister Debbie, who was still living with us, decided to attend the convention, along with their aunt Toni and her daughter, Andrea. Several of Val's friends, including René, were also planning to attend. However, Debbie, Toni, and Andrea would have to leave Miami

Beach a day-and-a-half early, as they had to return to work. Val and René could stay two days longer.

At the convention, Valeri saw many of the conventioneers parasailing over the Atlantic Ocean behind the luxurious Fontainbleu Hotel. She indicated to Debra that she definitely wanted to go parasailing this year. "You'd better not go," Debbie warned, "it looks too dangerous!" Valeri said no more about it until the day Debbie was leaving. Debbie looked at Val and said, "I know what you're thinking. You're thinking that when I leave, you are going to parasail, right?"

"Oh, no," Valeri answered. "I probably won't go; but, who knows?"

As Debbie left the room for the airport, she warned one final time: "Valeri: Don't you dare go parasailing. You hear me?"

"Okay, okay, big sister. I won't."

But Debbie's intuition told her that Valeri would parasail. It was Val who went on the highest roller coasters and the most dangerous rides at Cedar Point in Sandusky, Ohio; and at Disney World in Orlando and Disneyland in Los Angeles. Valeri was a daredevil, she loved challenges, regardless of what her physical health was like.

Later that afternoon after Debbie, Toni and Andrea had left, Valeri went to the beach and decided to go parasailing. She was the only one in her group that decided to try this wonderful venture. After receiving instructions on how to take off and float along behind the boat, the instructor told her that landing could be very difficult, so she should be very careful when she landed. Two young men would be there to catch her and to prevent her from getting hurt. Valeri was hooked up to the rope that was tied to the boat. The boat would drive along the beach, picking up speed, until the big parasail would take her up in the air. The boat would drive around for approximately half an hour on the ocean, as Valeri floated along.

Up in the air, Valeri loved every second of the flight. Eventually, it was time to come down and land. The boat had overshot its mark slightly, and the young men who were supposed to catch Valeri were not in position as she was about to touch the ground. She hit the beach, fell, and rolled over. She heard a crack in her right ankle. Not wanting to show any pain, she got up quickly, and announced, "I'm fine," when they asked how she was doing. But, finally she admitted, "No, I'm not. My right leg is very sore." They put an ice pack on her leg, and René and a couple of friends carried her back to the room.

Although her leg was very painful and swollen, Valeri refused to see a doctor that night. The next day when they got to the airport, René had to help Val as she limped onto the airplane. Upon landing in Detroit, René ordered a wheelchair for Val, and she wheeled Val through the airport and to her car. This irked Val, as she didn't want to look like a sissy. When Val came home that night, Marietta and I were out, but Debbie was home to greet her. When René helped Val limp into the house, Debbie looked at her and said. "Oh, no. I knew it! You went parasailing, didn't you?"

"Yes, I did . . . But it was fun! Debbie, you'll never believe how beautiful it was, sailing high over the ocean!" Valeri's eyes were shining.

Debbie took one look at the swollen leg and ordered, "Let's go up to St. Joseph's and have it examined," which they did. The x-rays showed that there was a crack in one of the bones in her ankle joint.

The next day I took Valeri to Dr. Fairmouth, an orthopedic surgeon, who put a cast on Valeri's leg up to her knee. He really wanted to put a full cast up to her hip, but agreed to keep it to the knee if Valeri would be careful.

Val was quite worried as to whether or not she would be permitted to student teach with a cast. Her godfather, John Kastran, the principal of the high school, informed her that she could teach with a cast provided she could maneuver easily and there were no other complications. Luckily, the shorter cast would permit her to student teach.

Her classes ended at Wayne State the following week. Once again, she received straight A's in her two classes, which meant she was eligible to assume the student teaching assignment at Grosse Pointe North High School. For two weeks Val did as Dr. Fairmouth had directed: she rested, she didn't move around too much, and consequently, she was feeling quite good.

As the end of summer vacation rapidly approached, Valeri stayed up several nights doing her favorite thing: watching "David Letterman" and other favorite programs after one o'clock in the morning. She expressed many times how she loved her room, which included her telephone, television, four-tier radio and stereo, souvenirs, favorite hippo dolls, music tapes and records, very comfortable bed, and all of the wonderful clothes in her closet. Valeri absolutely adored being in her room, both day and night. It happened that she was in a sentimental mood one morning as she wrote the following in her journal:

> *Thanks for my mom, my nurse, doctor and lawyer. And Dad, my buddy. Nikki my eating partner and sister Deb. Also for Michelle and Phillip, my niece and nephew, they're so cute. I am very grateful and appreciative for the wonderful things I have. I may not say it*

*often, or ever, but nothing means more to me than my family and I love them greatly. They are so patient with me and never treat me like a fragile object. They're always supportive, and I love them for it. Even if I never find one man to love or show my love with, I will always know the meaning of love, because I see it in my parents and it is also given through them to me. That's the most precious treasure in the world.*

The following night she wrote once again about some of her favorite things. The idea to have this list was planted in her mind by "The David Letterman Show:"

### Fun Times
*Boston, Toronto, Chicago, Atlanta, Vero Beach,*
*Los Angeles, Beverly Hills, Europe, Arizona, Paris,*
*Washington, Miami, Chicago again, Hollywood,*
*Florida, Hawaii, New York and Paris.*

The stage was set for Valeri to begin her student teaching. She had a blood transfusion which brought her red blood cell count up to 13 grams, which was the usual procedure before Valeri took on a major task. The higher the blood count, the more energy and strength she had. Val was very pleased with her assignment at Grosse Pointe North. She was assigned to the English department head, Mr. Robert Reimer, as her cooperating adviser. He was an outstanding educator, a marvelous individual, and a super cooperative adviser. She had known him a short time prior to the assignment and had heard he was the best. The school was only about a mile from home, making it easy for her to drive back and forth.

The big day arrived when Valeri was to begin her student teaching. She was excited as she clumped her way through the halls with her leg cast. She had access to an elevator, which made it easier for her to maneuver throughout the three floors of the school. As with all opening days, this one was very exciting. She had an opportunity to meet the teachers at the meeting before the students arrived. The staff and new teachers were introduced first. All in all, it was a marvelous and happy beginning for Valeri.

Her assignment was to observe classes for a week and then to take an active teaching assistant role. By the third week she would continue in an assistant role, in addition to having her own class to teach. She would be there for the entire school day. Grosse Pointe North offered an outstanding English program, including classes in English literature, creative writing, writing workshop, debate, and American literature.

Val enjoyed her first week tremendously. She loved everything about the entire school program and couldn't wait to begin work each morning.

Of course, the problem she did have was trying to get sufficient rest due to her unorthodox sleeping schedule. It didn't take long before Valeri established a routine of retiring earlier, and also taking naps after coming home each afternoon.

It seemed that each day brought her new ideas. Valeri enjoyed working with the students, and they kidded her about the cast on her leg. Several of them signed the cast, as did some teachers and other staff members. She particularly liked spending time tutoring and counseling individuals and small groups of students after classes. Observing teachers in different classes and using varied teaching methods and techniques was interesting and informative for Valeri.

Soon it was time to teach her own classes: creative writing and the writing workshop. She spent a great deal of time planning for these classes at home and at school under the direction of Mr. Reimer. He evaluated Valeri's progress every day and offered suggestions and ideas, giving her support whenever necessary.

As the end of September and the fourth week of classes drew near, I noticed that Val was beginning to run out of energy. Although she would soon need another transfusion, it was out of the ordinary for Val to be so run-down, even with a low red blood cell count.

At this time, Val was also busy preparing for Sue Fattore's wedding to Steve Schucker, which was scheduled for October 4th. Val was to be the maid of honor and she was busy shopping for her dress, having fittings, and attending the parties associated with the wedding. Val made a supreme effort to get proper rest during this demanding time.

We often talked during the evenings about teaching and the progress of Val's classes. She expounded on some creative ideas. Marietta suggested and offered to construct a bulletin board for Val's English Writing Workshop, which pleased Val. Marietta made one that night. It was loaded with creative ideas that they had devised together. Marietta provided the cut-outs and Val got the pictures and charts, and the bulletin board turned out very well. Valeri took the material to school. Although it took a couple of days, it was finally displayed in one of the showcases near the English office. It received excellent reviews from teachers and students.

Sue's wedding was quickly approaching and the preparations were almost complete, except for the bachelorette party that Valeri was to sponsor, and the rehearsal dinner on the eve of the wedding. It was a thrill for Val to have been selected as Sue's maid of honor. With the help of Lynn Ekstrom and two other of Sue's bridesmaids, she enthusiastically planned Sue's bachelorette party. It was a gala event held at the Kingsley Inn, an exclusive restaurant in Birmingham. The room was decorated very nicely and included condoms blown up as balloons, among other silly things. The event ended in the early morning hours, and Val, Sue, and a couple of the other girls stayed overnight at the Kingsley Inn. According to Sue, it was a party to be remembered.

Val enjoyed herself at the rehearsal dinner. She had always shared a nice relationship with Sue's family, especially with Sue's three brothers John (the best man with whom she was to stand up), Steve, and Jimmy.

The wedding took place the following day at five o'clock in the evening at the Star-of-the-Sea Church in Grosse Pointe Woods. Marietta, Nikki, Debra, and I enjoyed the ceremony immensely, especially as the girls marched down the aisle. When our Valeri walked down the aisle in her beautiful ivory and lace dress with her lovely smile, Marietta and I both began to cry. Once again I thought: "Someday my little sweetheart and I will walk down the aisle as a bride and father. We would have such a wonderful wedding ceremony for her."

The reception was held at our favorite wedding hangout, The Gourmet House. Everyone had a lovely time and everything ran smooth as silk, with Sue being an absolutely adorable bride. One reason so many guests enjoyed themselves was that most of the young people present had attended high school and college together. It was like a reunion. When the reception ended, Sue and Val hugged each other and cried and cried. Finally, Steve, the groom, insisted: "Let's go, honey. It's time to go on our honeymoon to the Cayman Islands and on our Caribbean cruise." Valeri gave Steve and Sue one more hug and kiss "for the road." The happy couple was soon off to begin their new life together.

Marietta and I both embraced Valeri and told her, "It was a wonderful wedding, Valeri. You did a commendable job and some day we're going to celebrate yours the same way. Believe me, you ain't seen nothing until you see your wedding!"

# 22

# *Tragedy Strikes*

V ALERI was very tired upon returning to her student teaching the Monday following Sue's wedding. She seemed very lethargic in the morning, and after school, she told Marietta that she needed a blood transfusion. Her last report had showed her count was running down rather rapidly.

Marietta called Dr. Charbeneau and set up an appointment for a transfusion on the following Saturday. The routine at this time was one that had been used for the past several years: the day before a scheduled transfusion, Valeri would go to the hospital for an examination and blood test, then return home. The following day she would return to the hospital for the transfusion. It gave the Hematology Department time to cross-match the blood and prepare it properly for the transfusion.

Valeri's right leg was still sore, as the cast had only been removed two weeks prior to the wedding. On Tuesday Valeri seemed to have a bit more energy. She got up early in the morning and left for school with much enthusiasm. After school that evening, Valeri, Marietta, and I were talking in the family room when Val told us, "You know, a strange thing happened at school today. I suddenly became blind in my right eye for about ten minutes. It was a little scary and I just kind of sat there and waited and it cleared up."

When she heard this, Marietta became very upset and announced: "I will call Dr. John Kane, your ophthalmologist, and make an appointment for you as soon as possible." When she called Dr. Kane, he wasn't available, but his receptionist made an appointment for the following day.

Meanwhile, I asked Valeri if it was the type of blindness she would experience during one of her seldom-occurring migraine headaches.

She agreed, "Yeah, it was kind of like that, Dad." I let the matter go, not giving it much thought. I expected that the ophthalmologist would check her out completely. That evening Valeri attended an open house for parents at the school. When she returned, she was feeling quite good. She told us that one of the parents had offered her a job writing press releases for his company and would contact her in the near future. This would be a part-time job along with her student teaching. Writing press releases was right up her alley, and she loved doing it.

Wednesday, October 8th, promised to be another busy day for Val. After school, she was going with Debbie and Nikki for a dress fitting for Debra's upcoming wedding to a nice young man, Brian Dittmer, the following February. Val was going to be the maid of honor and Nikki would be a bridesmaid.

That afternoon about two o'clock, Valeri had a free period and went to the English lab to work on a computer. Merrie Gay Ayrault, a staff member in charge of the lab, was also in the lab. As they conversed occasionally, Merrie Gay noticed how busy Valeri was. "Valeri," she commented, "you seem to be working very hard on that computer. Why don't you rest for a few minutes?"

"I'm doing fine," Val answered.

A few minutes later, Merrie Gay looked over and saw Valeri with her head down on the desk next to the computer. She went over to Valeri. "Are you okay Valeri?" There was no response.

Finally, Valeri raised her head, looked at Merrie Gay, mumbled something, then put her head down. Merrie Gay asked again, "Valeri, can you hear me? Are you okay?"

Receiving no further response from Valeri, Merrie Gay quickly called the principal, Dr. John Kastran, and the school nurse, Lorna Vroom. They rushed into the room and tried to awaken Valeri, who would only mumble unintelligibly. Lorna took Valeri's blood pressure; it was extremely low, something like 80 over 40. She told Dr. Kastran to call 911, which he did immediately. While waiting for the ambulance to arrive, Valeri remained incoherent.

Dr. Kastran called Marietta at Roosevelt School in East Detroit, where she taught. He asked her to come as soon as possible. Marietta asked Principal Steve Lapicola if he would drive her to the school, as she was too anxious and frightened to drive. He agreed. By the time they got to Grosse Pointe North, the ambulance had already taken Val to St. John Hospital.

Dr. Kastran also called me at Wayne State University, but I was not in my office. I was downtown at the Renaissance Center, cashing a check at the bank, as I usually did on payday. Upon returning to the office, my secretary told me that something had happened to one of my daughters and I was to call Dr. Kastran. I telephoned Dr. Kastran's office and was told that Valeri wasn't coherent and that I should drive to the hospital immediately. My thoughts were that Valeri had had a heart attack and was near death.

Meanwhile, Valeri was taken to the Emergency Room where, as luck would have it, Dr. George James Kouskoulas, a friend of ours, was the attending resident. He recognized Valeri and by the time Marietta had arrived, he had everything organized. Valeri was hooked up to a heart monitor and two IV's. Dr. Kouskoulas had called for a neurologist, a hematologist, and the attending physician to quickly come to the room to examine her. The receptionist wouldn't permit Marietta to go through the Emergency Room door. Marietta announced: "I am going in there to see my daughter and I don't care who tries to stop me!"

Fortunately, Dr. Kouskoulas emerged from the room at that moment and saw Marietta. "Come with me quickly," he directed, and Marietta went into the room. She saw Valeri hooked up to several machines. Valeri was experiencing some muscle spasms and occasionally a convulsion. She appeared to be unconscious. Marietta walked up to her, crying.

Valeri looked at her and said, "Mom, Mom, what's happening?" - and fell into an unconscious state again.

Meanwhile, I was on my way to St. John. There was heavy traffic, but I got there fast. I ran into the room and demanded, "What happened?"

"Bob, they think she's had a stroke," Marietta answered.

"A stroke? I can't believe that." I moved quickly to the bed where Valeri was lying. "Valeri, Valeri! It's your dad, honey. It's your dad."

She opened her eyes, mumbled something like, "Hi, Dad," and then fell asleep. Meanwhile, the doctors continued examining her. Valeri would wake up for a few minutes at a time and then slip back into unconsciousness.

I told Marietta I was going to call Dr. Giordina in New York to see if she had ideas as to what might be taking place. I went to the lobby and placed the call to the Cornell University Center. Dr. Giordina was always my ace in the hole whenever anything went wrong. Clinically, she and her colleagues knew more about treating Mediterranean Anemia than any of the other doctors in the country.

Luckily, Dr. Giordina was there. I explained what had occurred. She thought that Val might be having some sort of a sugar attack. "It is not characteristic for Cooley's Anemia patients to have strokes," she said. The only case she'd ever heard of was several years ago when a nine-year-old boy had a stroke and died the following day, but the circumstances were different. She told me, "If Valeri's doctor wants to talk to me, please tell him I will be very happy to converse with him."

I returned to the room and found Dr. Sparks, a hematologist and oncologist, examining Valeri. When he finished, I mentioned my conversation with Dr. Giordina. I told him he could call and speak with her, since she had offered her assistance. He looked at me strangely and said, "Thank you, but the doctors at St. John know what to do with patients. We know how to examine, test and diagnose their problems, and also how to treat them. We don't need to call anyone out of state." I kept quiet and only listened to what he had to say.

He asked Marietta if Valeri was on any kind of medication. Marietta answered affirmatively, telling him about the Lanoxin, DHT, and also the estrogen pills, Premarin and Pravera.

Dr. Sparks looked at Marietta and said, "Oh, you're kidding? Estrogen! Oh, boy, get her off those damned pills immediately. We suspect that Valeri had a stroke. And," he explained, "it could be from the estrogen pills. It happens quite often that women - especially young women - on estrogen have strokes."

We sat with Valeri for quite some time after Dr. Sparks left; then I went to the lobby to call Debbie and Nikki. They were still waiting at home for Valeri, to go to the dress-fitting. They were shocked and upset to hear the news and came to the hospital immediately.

I also called a good friend of mine, Dr. Raymond Bauer, a neurologist and a former instructor of medical students at Wayne State University. I called him for moral support, and because he could give us so much information that other doctors wouldn't. Unfortunately, Dr. Bauer wasn't home. I left a message with one of his children to let him know what had happened and that we were at St. John Hospital Emergency Room.

Dr. Kouskoulas would periodically come into the room and bring us up to date on what was happening. He said that the machines indicated Valeri was stabilized. Now it was time to start testing and have a neurologist examine her and to verify whether or not she did have a stroke.

Dr. Kouskoulas was very supportive during this difficult time. He answered our questions and was very optimistic, giving us somewhat of a morale boost. Meanwhile, I would wander over to the heart monitor to check on Valeri's heart function. It appeared to be quite normal, with ninety beats a minute, and her blood pressure had gone to 100 over 60, an encouraging sign.

As Valeri lay there, she was still having spasms and an occasional convulsion. We were too upset to think of anything other than to have her stabilized and to save her life. We would worry about the problem and how to treat it later.

Soon Nikki, Debbie, and Debbie's fiancé, Brian arrived at the hospital. They sat in the waiting room, anxious to see us. Several other relatives also arrived when they heard what had happened. Debra and Nikki were able to spend a few minutes with Val. She recognized them, but would again fall into unconsciousness.

The neurologist came in and examined Valeri. He stuck little pins in her leg, and did other similar tests to find out if she had any feeling on her right side. After his examination, I asked him what he thought. "It looks like she has had a stroke," he replied. I told him what Dr. Giordina had said earlier about Cooley's Anemia victims not having strokes. He said that when he had lived in Greece, he had heard of Cooley's Anemia patients having strokes. He reiterated that at this point it appeared as though Valeri had a stroke.

Several hours later, Valeri was still in the Emergency Room. Marietta and I were getting impatient from waiting to have her transferred to a regular hospital room and bed. Marietta went to the main desk and asked the receptionist when Valeri could go to a hospital room. "You have to understand that St. John is a very large hospital and has a huge Emergency Room, with dozens of patients being brought in continuously every hour," she replied. "It's going to take some time to get things organized before we can get her transferred to a room."

"I don't care about the dozens of patients," Marietta responded. "I feel sorry for them, but I am only interested in my daughter, who apparently has suffered a stroke and seems very uncomfortable in the Emergency Room. Please try to arrange for a room immediately." Another two hours passed, and Marietta was getting even more impatient. She reverted to her usual role when things weren't progressing properly or that procrastination was excessive. She went back to the desk and said, "Young lady, I want Valeri sent to a regular hospital room **now**! No ifs, ands or buts. If you can't do it, maybe your boss or the director of the hospital can, but I want her in a room, fast."

"Well, I'll see what I can do," replied the receptionist. "I will make a supreme effort to get her a room." A short while later, seven hours after Valeri's admission to emergency, the receptionist told us that Valeri was being moved to a bed in a hospital room.

The orderly came in and moved Val by cart. He wheeled her to an elevator as we followed, then up to a room on the third floor. After Valeri was put in her bed and made comfortable, she continued with the same behavior: she would wake up on occasion, look at us, try to mumble some words, and then would fall asleep again. The nurses in the ward were very attentive. One came in almost every other minute to check on Valeri.

By now, it was near midnight. A nurse came into the room and told Marietta, Val's sisters, and me, "All of you can go home."

Marietta said, "Debra and Nikki, you two can go home, but your dad and I are staying here all night with Valeri. There is no way we're going to leave here tonight." I agreed.

Val opened her eyes and seemed to know what was happening when her mother explained, "Valeri, we're staying with you all night, honey. You're going to be all right. Try to get some rest. We'll be right here the entire time."

I added, "Valeri, you had a little problem and you're going to be okay, honey. Just try to get some rest. They're going to do some tests tomorrow and decide how to treat you so you'll get better." She seemed to understand what we were saying, but couldn't communicate very well. Then she closed her eyes and fell asleep.

Marietta and I sat in two lounge chairs next to Valeri's bed. We talked through much of the night. We observed that Val would wake up and look to see us, then close her eyes and fall asleep again. She was still suffering from the muscle spasms.

The next morning the nurse's aide gave Valeri a sponge bath. Valeri seemed to be opening her eyes more often. She looked around the room and stared at us constantly. She tried to talk, but could only mumble. She often held out her hand to Marietta or me for us to hold. This seemed to give her confidence and helped calm her.

It wasn't long before a lab technician entered the room and took some blood from Valeri. She was then taken to the x-ray room.

It was almost lunchtime. Dr. Bauer arrived. He checked Valeri's charts and explained what a stroke was all about. Having Dr. Bauer present was a blessing, as he knew so many of the doctors on staff at St. John Hospital. Some of the doctors would occasionally peek into Val's room to see how she was progressing.

Shortly after Dr. Bauer left, Debbie and Nikki came to visit Val. Marietta and I went into the lounge near the elevators to relàx. Marietta looked up and saw a statue of the Virgin Mary and suddenly cried out: "Why? Why are you doing this to our Valeri? She's had so many problems, so much illness in her life - and now this is the worst thing of all. Why do you do this? Please show her some mercy! She's such a wonderful girl." Then she started to cry. "I don't know why I'm so upset with the Virgin Mary, but I just can't help it," she said.

I held Marietta in my arms and comforted her. "Don't worry, honey. God understands. This is a very difficult time."

We began talking about other things, and Marietta said, "I wonder what this means? Will Val ever be able to walk again? Will she remember her education and the information she learned at college? I wonder what it means?"

I answered, "The only thing I can say is that the doctors mentioned that the stroke happened while she was young. Therefore, she has a much better chance of a complete recovery."

We spent the rest of the day sitting by Valeri's bed, holding her hand and talking to her. We encouraged her to talk, but she had little success in communicating. Valeri tried to eat a small amount of jello but couldn't. She obviously wasn't hungry, and since she was being fed intravenously, there was no concern about her inability to eat.

After all the visitors left in the late evening, we sat quietly with Valeri. I thought to myself, "The doctor said that she definitely had a stroke and that her right side was crippled. She's having a difficult time talking, but they feel that she understands what people are saying to her."

Valeri was sleeping again when Marietta and I were sitting across the room, whispering about what had been happening over the last thirty-six hours. I said to Marietta, "I just can't believe something like this has happened. Our lovely, exuberant, intelligent, bright, brown-eyed, curly-haired, beautiful daughter who was doing so well in all aspects of life and developing a nice career for herself suddenly has something like this happen to her."

Marietta answered, "We don't know what is going to happen with her now."

"Yes, life has been so hard and now it's so uncertain. We just don't know what's going to happen. It will be a miracle if she returns to normal, considering her condition before this point."

"You're right, Bob," said Marietta. "It would be a miracle." We told Val that we were going home for the night, but that we'd be back early in the morning. She nodded her head and mumbled something like, "Okay, go, Mom and Dad." We left the hospital around midnight.

We called the hospital twice during the night to make sure everything was progressing properly. The next day the results from some of the tests began arriving. Dr. Puzios, an internist who had studied under Dr. Bauer several years ago, was assigned as Val's doctor in charge. He came in to talk to us. He explained to us that Valeri had definitely suffered a stroke and that she was crippled on the right side of her body. He felt she would recuperate nicely, but everything depended on whether or not she could move her right arm and leg within a period of a week. Any arm or leg movement within that time meant that the extremity could be re-trained to function through physical therapy.

Valeri seemed much more alert that day. She ate some of the food given her - mostly jello and liquids - and she sat up periodically. Meanwhile, she was being treated with a steroid to prevent any further clotting of blood in her body.

Visitors began coming in at all hours. We permitted two in her room at a time. This seemed to keep Valeri more alert. Although she could not talk much, her eyes were wide open. She seemed to understand what people were saying to her.

After the visitors went home that evening, we sat with her, as she seemed to comprehend some of the things we discussed and she was attempting to speak. Finally, she said: "I would like a chocolate sundae with sprinkles from Friendly's." We were astonished that she could recite a complete sentence.

I jumped up and announced, "I'll be back shortly with a sundae, sweetheart." I ran to my car, drove to the Friendly's Ice Cream Parlor, ordered a nice, big chocolate sundae with sprinkles, raced back to the hospital, and took the sundae to her bedside. Her eyes lit up, as she sat up and devoured it in a matter of minutes. It sure made Marietta and me feel good to see her respond in that manner to the sundae.

For the next hour or so she would doze off and then wake up and attempt to speak to us. Just before we left for home, Valeri opened her eyes wide, looked at us, and quietly asked, "What happened?"

"Valeri, you had a problem with a blood clot in the brain," Marietta said. "The doctors are going to have it dissolved and you're going to get well again."

Valeri began crying a more painful cry than anyone could ever imagine. We began crying with her. The three of us sat there crying, almost hysterically. After a few minutes, Valeri stopped, and we did too. She looked up and in a very clear voice, said: "That's enough, Mom and Dad. Whatever happened, happened. Let's go on from here."

That was the same comment she had made as a youngster, when she said: "Mom, I'll stop crying, if you stop crying." She wanted us to stop sympathizing with what had happened and to take steps to move ahead. She gave us a smile and then fell asleep.

We kept thinking about what she had said as we left for home. "Let's go from here." Of course we called the hospital at least twice that night and asked how she was progressing. The nurses on the floor told us that everything was going along quite nicely and urged us to get some rest ourselves.

A computerized tomography test (CT scan) was taken again the following day with the hope of determining exactly what had happened. A short while later Dr. Puzios explained that Valeri had a thrombosis, or clot, in the left cerebral artery in the basal ganglia area. He further explained that a clot in the brain stops blood from reaching certain other parts of the brain, causing destruction of the cells in that area. He said, "There are enough cells left in that part of the brain for her to recover from the stroke, but there will be a considerable amount of therapy necessary."

We asked if Valeri would regain her memory. He said he wasn't sure about that yet. As on previous days, several doctors, residents, a psychologist, and a speech and physical therapist came into Valeri's room and gave her more tests.

Meanwhile, Dr. Bauer would come in every day and talk with us extensively about her treatment and what the doctors were planning. Later that evening, Dr. Sparks came in to talk with us. He said that Valeri's blood count was extremely low - below nine - and that he recommended four pints of blood in order to give her the strength to endure the coming weeks.

After the transfusion, Valeri had a much better day. Her appetite improved and she was more responsive to people. The next day we saw her early in the morning. She was sitting up, eating, and smiling. I looked to see if she had any movement in her right hand or leg. Her right arm was moving, which was a good sign - but her right leg was not.

A speech therapist entered the room and asked us to join her in the lobby so she could explain to us what the test results showed. Once in the lobby, she explained that Valeri was taking in and comprehending information as usual, but she couldn't verbalize the information properly. There had apparently been some damage to that part of her brain, and this was causing the problem. We asked whether Valeri would retain the knowledge that she had acquired through the years. "Frankly, I don't know," the therapist answered. "It's too early to tell, but she is young and I suspect she's going to come a long way."

By the fifth day in the hospital following her stroke, Valeri was sitting up more frequently and responding more to her visitors. However, she still slurred and mixed her words. We noticed that when we were alone with her, she actually understood almost everything we said and knew what she wanted to do or say, but that when she talked, she would use the wrong vocabulary to describe whatever it was she wanted. In other words, she would say: "I want the chair," when she actually meant: "Put my pillow behind my head." This was happening continuously.

Marietta and I took that as a step in the right direction. Valeri was speaking and knew what she wanted to say, but just wasn't using the proper words. With hope, it was just a matter of time until she would begin using the correct words.

Late that afternoon a social worker came in to say that plans were being made to discharge Valeri in two days. She wanted to know where we wanted to send her for rehabilitation. "You know, she can't go home yet. She needs considerable rehabilitation. She'll need physical, occupational, and speech therapy." The social worker suggested Harper Hospital as the best rehabilitation institute in the area. We thought about that for a minute.

Harper was an inner-city hospital near Wayne State Medical School, and it was only five minutes away from my office at Wayne State. This meant I could visit Valeri often during the day, when Marietta was working. Marietta worried some about the hospital's inner-city location, but Dr. Bauer told her what a wonderful institution Harper was, and about the fine medical staff and care that Valeri would receive. He spoke from personal experience.

Dr. Puzios came in a short while after the social worker left and told us: "Bob and Marietta, you realize that Valeri moved two toes and her leg today. This is the first good sign that she will have potential rehabilitative ability in her leg. Valeri will be able to walk again." Upon hearing this great news, Marietta and I looked at each other and began crying.

The next day we gave the social worker permission to have Valeri transferred to Harper Hospital's Rehabilitation Institute. She said the transfer would take place the following day, October 15th.

When Dr. Bauer came in, we told him that Valeri was scheduled to be moved to Harper tomorrow. He felt that it was premature for her to be moved, since she was still experiencing headaches and was weak. He recommended that Valeri stay at St. John for three or four more days. Unfortunately, regulations at the hospital dictated that she had to be released.

We explained to Valeri that she was going to Harper Rehabilitation Institute to begin physical, occupational, and speech therapy. We told her she would stay there for a few weeks, after which time she'd be feeling like her old self again and would be ready to come home. Valeri just looked at us, smiled, and said, "I hope so."

Early the next morning when we arrived at the hospital, Dr. Puzios was there to greet us. He ordered an ambulance to take Valeri to the Rehab Center at Harper Hospital. He predicted that Valeri would come a long way and feel much better in a short period of time. He wished us good luck, and warmly said good-bye to Val.

Dr. Kouskoulas had seen us a little earlier that morning, and he also came in to wish us well at Harper. He was positive that Valeri was going to be doing very well very soon. We asked him who would be her primary doctor, as our Dr. Charbeneau was at a different hospital. He replied that it would probably be Dr. Sparks, since he worked out of Harper.

Soon, the social worker told us that the ambulance was ready to take Val to the Rehab Institute. Valeri seemed a little lethargic and very apprehensive about what was going to happen to her at this new hospital. I told her not to worry and that her mom would go with her in the ambulance. I would follow in my car, and she would be situated there in a short time. Within a day or two, the rehabilitation center would begin to help her regain her strength and mobility. We told her that she would regain the use of her right leg, as she had already moved it. After I informed her of her high blood count, Valeri agreed that the four pints of blood seemed to be helping her considerably.

# 23

# A Hard Road

THE Harper Hospital Rehabilitation Center was located in the medical center near downtown Detroit. It included the Wayne State University Medical School, the city hospital, Children's Hospital, and the Harper Hospital complex, including Grace Hospital and several other clinics. It was an overwhelming situation, but Valeri was fortunate in being accustomed to big cities and having people around her all the time. We were sure she would have very little trouble adjusting. In fact, Marietta might have more trouble than Val in this new situation.

The actual rehabilitation building was being refurbished, so Valeri was given a room on the sixth floor in a regular hospital wing which overlooked the institute. That wing was used temporarily for stroke patients. Her room was a pleasant one. Her roommate, an African-American woman who was well over seventy years old, was also a stroke victim. The woman's daughter, a very pleasant person, would visit her mother often, as would the rest of her family.

Valeri was assigned the bed near the window, with a television set up high against the wall facing her. She had a remote control by her bed. Of course, this was very good for Valeri, as she loved watching her soap operas and was very interested in the baseball World Series which was being played between the Boston Red Sox and the New York Mets.

A few minutes after Valeri had settled in her bed, a gentleman with a beard entered the room and came over to talk to us. He said his name was Dr. Lamb and that he was the director of the Rehabilitation Institute. He told us that the doctor in charge would be a young African-American female named Dr. Rice. We later found out that Dr. Rice (a fine doctor) was suffering from Sickle Cell Anemia herself, and it was a wonder that she had been able to complete medical school and become a doctor. (Sickle Cell Anemia is a serious blood disease most common among African Americans. The red blood cells change their form to look like little sickles and congregate in the joints. This is very painful for the victim. However, with the proper treatment, Sickle Cell victims have the potential to live almost a full lifetime.)

Dr. Lamb explained the services of the rehabilitation center to us. We looked down at Valeri, lying there almost helpless, while we listened to Dr. Lamb speak. He reviewed the program and the various therapies that patients receive every day. On Thursdays patients and their families would go to the main hospital dining room to eat supper with other patients and their families. And, if a patient had to stay at the Rehab Center for more than a month, the patient would be given a weekend pass to go home at least once. He said it was discovered that patients seemed to recover much faster if they had contact with home at least once or twice during their stay in the hospital.

Then, with a serious expression on his face, Dr. Lamb looked down at Valeri and said: "You know, I'm a little worried about you. You look like you're somewhat of a weakling and that maybe you're going to quit on us. This worries me. It's going to be a hard grind trying to regain your health, and I don't know if you're up to the task." I thought to myself that this was a hell of a lousy locker room pep speech by the doctor. She looked at him with hollow eyes and didn't say anything.

I just couldn't hold back. "Wait a minute, Dr. Lamb. You don't know my daughter Valeri. After what she's gone through all her life and the way she bounces back, she's going to make you eat those words. She's a fighter all the way and she will fight to regain her health here, too. I don't think any of us appreciated your remarks. They were inappropriate."

He just looked at me and said very sternly, "We'll see," and walked out of the room. I followed him.

"I think I know what you're trying to do. I think you're trying to give her a little boost. But I don't think she needs it, Dr. Lamb. I think she's going to prove that she's a very fine fighter."

"Well, I hope you're right," he replied, "but I worry about her."

He requested a meeting with Marietta and me the next day, to give us all the program details and to answer any questions we might have. He was leaving for a two-week vacation the next afternoon, and his assistant would be in charge until he returned.

I went back to the room, held Valeri's hand, and reassured her, "Valeri, he doesn't know you, honey. You just hang in there and we'll work together. I know you will get well again."

Marietta hugged and kissed her. "We know what you can do, Valeri," she said. "Let's make him eat those words." We stayed quite late that evening, then left to go home when Valeri fell asleep.

Early the next morning, immediately after we arrived at the hospital, Dr. Bauer entered the room and greeted all of us. He said, "Valeri, I know that in a few weeks you will be able to do many things that you did before, and then you will be going home. You'll again be a healthy young lady." Valeri gave him her little smile. Then he said, "Come on, Bob and Marietta. I want to show you around the hospital. Perhaps I can make Marietta feel a little more at ease." He did this because Marietta was a little disturbed with the whole hospital scene.

He took us around and introduced us to many of the people on that floor, and on the second floor, where recovering heart and other stroke victims were housed. I told him what Dr. Lamb had said, and he told us to forget it, as we all knew what Valeri could do. He felt confident that she was going to bounce back pretty well. "They're going to start the therapies very shortly," he informed us, "and Valeri's going to have to work very, very hard. She will be tired, but she'll also be getting much rest. I think you'll see her improving every day."

In the meeting with Dr. Lamb and Dr. Rice, the whole routine was once again explained to us. Dr. Lamb said that he felt if everything went well, Val would do what other patients did when they were released from the hospital: she would hug her therapists and they'd cry together. He said, "You'll see, when it comes time for Valeri to go home."

Over the next few days, several things took place. I was able to visit Val every day between my classes at Wayne State. She was able to verbalize somewhat more, although her comments were brief. She was very happy that the New York Mets, her favorite team next to the Tigers, were playing good baseball and were tied with the Red Sox in the World Series. The final game was to be played the following night.

The routine of the various tests and the visits of doctors, residents, and medical students was repeated again, as at St. John. Valeri didn't have much spare time, as there was always something to be done. A brace was made for her leg to help her become more mobile once she would be able to begin walking. Soon she was told it was time to begin her therapy. Her mode of transportation to the different therapy rooms was by wheelchair. She was getting a bit more accustomed to climbing out of bed and sitting in the wheelchair, ready to be moved around. She liked the idea of getting out of bed.

The occupational therapy was designed to help Valeri learn how to take care of herself: comb her hair, wash and shower, get dressed, and other life-adjustment necessities. The physical therapy was to exercise the right side of her body, as well as the left, to develop her strength and to regain the lost mobility in her arms and legs. The speech therapy was to test her strengths in comprehension and verbalization, followed by work to improve her weakened areas. There was also recreational therapy, where she played different games and participated in activities, but the other three were the vital therapies.

Valeri was quite excited; these therapies were the beginning of her comeback to a normal life. It was disappointing for Val to discover in physical therapy that she lacked strength in her right hand and leg, as well as her overall body musculature. In occupational therapy she easily picked up the grooming and personal skills. In speech therapy, Valeri was disappointed because, though her comprehension was good, she couldn't express herself very well. The speech therapist told Val that she had a long road to travel before she reached the peak she had been at prior to the stroke.

After the first day of therapy, Valeri could hardly move. She was very, very tired and wanted to sleep most of the afternoon and evening, even when she received visitors. I was extremely worried about her heart, thinking that the strain of the therapies might be excessive and could create other cardiac problems. The cardiology report showed that her heart, slightly enlarged, showed signs of the tachycardia, but should be strong enough to permit her to sustain all of the therapies without any major problems. All other tests indicated that, physically, she was bouncing back nicely.

The question was: What caused the stroke? It could have been the estrogen pills. It also might have been caused by her heart skipping from time to time, which caused a clot to form in her heart and then moved to her brain. But the underlying question that kept bothering me was why it should happen to Valeri, when victims of Mediterranean Anemia didn't usually have strokes. It was interesting that three young ladies under thirty years of age in that ward who had had strokes had two characteristics in common: they smoked and they had been taking estrogen pills. Of course, Valeri had never smoked, but she was on the estrogen until her stroke.

The other theory was that Valeri had what were called "sticky platelets." This meant that the platelet cells were more numerous in her body than in the average person, allowing blood clots to form more easily. This theory was never proven completely in medicine, but it was one that the cardiologist who examined Valeri believed to be true.

I was asked to bring Valeri's Desferal pump to the hospital because Dr. Sparks wanted her to go back on Desferal to chelate iron from her body.

Dr. Bauer asked Dr. Tranchida of the Hematology Department to stop in and see Valeri if he had time. Although he was very busy, Dr. Tranchida took time to see her and to talk to her. He was cut out of the same mold as Dr. Bauer: a wonderful person who was very attentive and conscientious about examining Valeri to see what was happening. He made recommendations for her treatment.

Dr. Bauer was also wonderfully conscientious with patients. He truly loved medicine and wanted to retain his contact with the hospital. He visited the hospital daily to serve as a consultant, since technically he was on a medical leave. There were many nights when I called Dr. Bauer at his home, as either Marietta or I, or both of us, would be having anxiety attacks, worrying about what was happening with Valeri, what would take place, and what the future held for her. He would come to the phone and spend as much time as needed to calm us down and reassure us that everything that could be done was being done, and that Valeri had a good prognosis, in his estimation.

The Rehabilitation Institute routine was set. Valeri would attend each of the therapies daily. I would visit her between my classes whenever possible. Marietta would work on occasion, but she would come in with me and spend the remainder of the afternoon and evening with Valeri. Val's friends would stop in during the day and evening to see her. Many friends and family members would come, and we would wheel Valeri into the lobby where the ten or fifteen visitors would be waiting. We'd all talk and have fun.

Two of the people who visited Valeri to make sure that everything was going well were Michelle Venettis and Florence Kartsonas. Michelle worked at the hospital in the rehab department and would visit Val every day. She would perk Valeri up and encourage her by relating events that were taking place at the hospital. Florence, who worked at Harper Hospital as a secretary, would stop in almost every day to see Val, too. These impromptu visits by Florence and Michelle were really appreciated.

Also, Rena, Val's godsister, visited Val almost daily. Rena would help Val with her speech and verbalization, while they both watched soap operas together by the hour. This was also a good morale-booster for Val.

Sue Schucker returned from her honeymoon. She was totally stunned. When she first saw Val, she cried hysterically. As she hugged Val, Sue kept repeating: "You're going to be okay, Val, we know that. You have been through rough times before. We will help you get better." Later, Sue told us that she was shocked to see Val in her crippled state, but that she was confident that Val would recover.

After about the third week of therapy, Valeri was wheeled to the support bar that helped her when she attempted to stand and to walk. It was going to be her first all-out attempt at walking. She stood there for a few seconds, while the therapist stood by and watched. Valeri began to take steps. After she had taken several, someone behind her said, "Valeri, you're walking! You beautiful gal! You're walking!" She turned to see Dr. Bauer. He ran up, hugged her and began to cry. "I'm so happy, Valeri. This is just great," he told her, and then she began to cry, too. This touched her very deeply to see Dr. Bauer so happy and emotional when she was able to take her first steps. He assured her, "You'll be walking plenty very soon. We won't be able to hold you down."

Val continued to receive gifts, flowers, and cards, which included comments about her Mets winning the World Series. She would show us a card indicating that the person who sent it knew that she loved the Mets.

One evening her friends Kim and Dino Stathis and René Garkinos came to visit her. They wheeled Valeri out to the lounge, where they could talk and have a good time. When they wheeled Valeri back to her room, she attempted to get out of the wheelchair and into bed by herself, forgetting that she could not use her right leg or arm very well. As a result, she fell and hit her head against the wall. Three nurses rushed into the room. As Valeri lay crying, they kept asking her: "Are you hurt? Are you hurt?" Her pride was hurt more than her body, although she did have a small bump on her head. Her guests were very upset and realized what it meant to have a stroke. Once Valeri climbed onto the bed, she laughed about the incident.

Val received a boost quite often from her good friend Chris Garkinos, who had graduated from the University of Michigan earlier in the year and obtained a job in San Francisco working with the Clorox Company. He would call her frequently and joke with her. He mentioned to Val that he wanted her to hurry up and get well so she could visit him in San Francisco. He wanted to show her a good time. Val began talking about visiting San Francisco. Marietta said, "Don't worry, you're going to go soon."

I picked Val up at the hospital on a Saturday morning and she came home with her wheelchair and brace for a weekend furlough. She stayed home, slept in her bed Saturday night, and then returned to the hospital late Sunday evening. As Dr. Lamb had said, this seemed to give patients a good morale boost. She was able to slowly climb the seven steps of our quad-level home to her room. She walked in her doorway, looked at the closet that was open and wailed: "My clothes! My clothes!" and began to cry. She didn't like showing us any sad emotion for fear it might upset us. She stopped crying almost instantly, but we could tell the terrible emotional pain that she was experiencing.

Near the end of her stay at the Harper Rehabilitation Institute, Dr. Lamb, who had returned from his vacation, came into the room to speak to Valeri, Marietta, and me. He said that he wanted Valeri to be present at an educational seminar for residents and interns the next day to answer questions regarding her Cooley's Anemia and her stroke, along with any other medical questions the students might ask. Valeri consented to attend the seminar. After Dr. Lamb left, she had second thoughts. "I don't know. Do you think I should do it?" she asked.

"Of course," we answered. "You'll do very well." Apparently she was a little embarrassed about the crippled condition of her leg and arm. She felt that perhaps her general appearance wouldn't be as pleasant to view as she would like, but she went ahead with the seminar.

The day after she participated, Dr. Lamb stopped in to thank her. "You've come a long way and I really appreciate you attending the seminar. The students thought you were a wonderful, courageous young lady and were so happy that they had the opportunity to meet you."

The post-supper time was always a happy and active one for Valeri because Debbie and her fiancé, Brian, as well as Nikki and her husband, Abe were there almost every evening. Marietta's family visited quite often also, as well as Val's friends from the University of Michigan and her high school classmates. Others who came were members of the teaching staff from Grosse Pointe North High School, and her godfather John Kastran with his new wife, Connie. Dolly Kastran, Valeri's godmother, also visited several times with her new husband, George Diain. (John and Dolly Kastran had divorced several years prior to Valeri's stroke.) All in all, Valeri loved this social gathering and seemed to respond positively, both physically and emotionally.

After four weeks it was time to leave the Rehabilitation Institute and return home. The evaluation of Valeri's condition at this time showed that she could continue to improve physically by being at home and attending therapy sessions as an out-patient at nearby St. John Hospital or at Bon Secours Hospital's therapy center. Although she had to use a cane, she could walk quite well. Since Valeri would tire easily, sometimes she needed to be pushed around in her wheelchair. Her speech capabilities were returning rapidly, although she still experienced some slurring. Her communication skills were almost normal. Her arm had gained strength, but her fingers were folded in such a position that she couldn't straighten them. Consequently, Valeri was unable to write with her right hand. However, she was learning that skill with her left hand.

Val was very excited about her overall improvement, particularly in the last two weeks. The cardiologist report indicated that Valeri's heart was still quite strong, though it was suggested that she take an aspirin a day as a blood thinner in order to avoid any kind of clotting in her system caused by the potential "sticky platelet" condition.

I drove to Harper Hospital on Saturday, November 6th, only two days short of a month from the day of Valeri's stroke. I picked her up, along with her wheelchair and some of the flowers that she wanted, and headed for home. (She had donated most of the other flowers to the hospital to give to other patients who might enjoy them.)

Debbie and Nikki had put up a sign on the front porch that read: "Welcome Home, Valeri!" Several people were there, including Sue and Rena. Many of her other friends had planned to attend a little get-to-gether on the following day. As I drove into our driveway and opened the garage door with the automatic opener, Valeri saw her car. "My car! My car! My little convertible!" she exclaimed and began to cry. Once in the house, we helped Valeri walk down the stairway into the family room. Our quad-level home was turning out to be a disadvantage because of the seven steps leading from the family room to the main floor, and another seven up to the bedrooms. The stairs were difficult for Valeri at this time.

We stayed in the family room, and Valeri joked around with her friends. Later, some of our friends stopped in to see Valeri, also. It was heart-warming to know that our Valeri was back home again, and that she was beginning to recover.

The next day when Valeri got up, we helped her walk down to the first floor. We planned to take her by wheelchair to the family room so that she could watch her favorite soaps. Marietta and I were trying to decide how best to lift the wheelchair down the stairs and into the family room. I was trying to use the suggestion from her therapist, which was that I take the feet-end of the wheelchair with Marietta maneuvering the top. It would be safer for Valeri that way, but Marietta argued that it would be better in reverse, and that I should hold the top.

Marietta won the argument and we began going down the stairs. We were within three steps of the bottom when Marietta couldn't hold the legs of the wheelchair any longer and, as a result, the chair began going down the stairs. Valeri came flying out of the chair, landed on the carpeted floor, and rolled over once. We were very frightened and thought: "Oh, no! She didn't go through all that therapy to have *this* happen!"

Valeri looked up at us and began laughing. "Forget the wheelchair," she said. "I'm going to try to walk. My life's in *real* danger with *you* two wheeling me around!" We all laughed, and were grateful that she wasn't seriously hurt. We used the wheelchair minimally in the family room, and Valeri learned to sit on the stairs and to navigate up one step at a time. Soon, she could walk quite well with her cane and brace. It wasn't too long before she was walking up and down the stairs very slowly - a positive sign that strength was returning to her right leg.

All of her therapy sessions were set up at St. John Hospital's Therapy Department near our home. Usually Marietta or I would drive her to and from the sessions. On occasion, when Debbie wasn't working, she would drive Valeri. The physical and speech therapies were helping Val tremendously. She did not need to go to the occupational therapy, as she had done very well in personal adjustments. However, speech therapy was still necessary.

Valeri came home one day and said that her speech therapist had said that Valeri had the knowledge, speech ability, and communication skills of a fifth grader. Marietta and I jumped in the car, while Valeri stayed with Debra, and raced back to St. John. Marietta went into the speech department and told the department head that she didn't want that therapist working with Valeri anymore. Although the director of the program agreed immediately to assign a new therapist, she also suggested that perhaps we were over-reacting.

Marietta replied: "Anyone that tells Val at this time that she's like a fifth grader and probably won't improve is not going to work with my daughter." It was a good move because the new therapist was marvelous. The other therapist did send a letter of apology, stating that if she had done anything wrong, she was sorry.

Valeri was under the medical care of Dr. Sparks and his associate, Dr. Kindle. Both hematologists worked out of Bon Secours and St. John Hospital, where we felt Val would be treated best. We had already telephoned Dr. Charbeneau and explained that Val was changing doctors and hospitals. This was best, as she needed a hematologist to care for her. Another reason for changing hospitals was that St. John was less than four miles from our home, rather than the twenty-mile drive to St. Joseph's in Mt. Clemens. Dr. Charbeneau agreed, and also suggested that we should feel free to call on him at any time if necessary. He then told us to wish Valeri the best of luck.

Valeri had a consultation with Dr. Sparks, which we attended with her. He was very knowledgeable and seemed to understand Valeri's condition reasonably well. He said that he would make arrangements for Val to receive her transfusions at St. John, but he would not visit her during the transfusion as he didn't feel it was necessary. Also, he felt that we should let Valeri be more independent and that she should make decisions for herself instead of Marietta and me making them for her. We never felt we made decisions without consulting Valeri, but this was his opinion. He also wanted to see Valeri within two weeks to see how she was progressing so we could make some plans for the future in helping her recover from her stroke and alleviate her anemia.

Both Dr. Sparks and Dr. Kindle were extremely busy oncologists and hematologists. They treated many very ill patients and lived with death every day. To them, Valeri was only another person with a very serious problem. Marietta and I felt it might be better if we could find a doctor who didn't have so many critically ill patients. Unfortunately, we didn't know whom else to turn to. Besides, we were well aware that both doctors were very knowledgeable and well-respected by their peers. This was going to be a new adventure for all of us, after twenty-five years with Dr. Charbeneau. But we were willing to give it a try.

# 24

# *Overcoming Roadblocks*

ONE evening Valeri began to talk about her experiences while she was a patient at the Harper Hospital Rehabilitation Center. She described the horrible feeling of being paralyzed on one side of her body and of being so helpless when she first entered the center, the feeling of personal accomplishment when she was first able to maneuver around by herself and was able to walk with the help of a cane, and the wonderful treatment she received from so many caring nurses and other medical people there.

Valeri also recalled the prediction made by Dr. Bauer that she would see a vast improvement in her condition in a short period of time, and the prediction by Dr. Lamb that upon her release from the center, she would probably cry and hug the therapists who worked with her. "That's exactly what happened," Valeri said. "I hugged everyone who worked so extensively with me during those four weeks. I couldn't help myself. I was so appreciative that they helped get me back on my feet and regain my maneuverability and speech. And, they probably cried because they saw me progress due to their efforts. I remember they told me that the improvement I made during the first two or three months following my stroke was what I would retain for the rest of my life, so it was up to me to work hard with the therapists at St. John Hospital."

Valeri had progressed a long way from the time she had the stroke, when she was almost totally paralyzed on the right side of her body and unable to speak. By the time she was released from Harper Hospital Rehabilitation Center, she had recaptured much mobility and was beginning to speak very well, she had regained much of the strength on her right side and was able to walk by using a cane for assistance and her leg brace to prevent her foot from flopping. Although Valeri had a rough time expressing herself over a long period of time, she could speak in short sentences, and after resting for a moment, continue speaking. Her abilities to communicate were coming back quickly.

Valeri would tire quite rapidly. However, after a few moments of rest, she would get up and begin walking again. Her right hand was functioning well, though her fingers remained curled. She could not straighten them without assistance.

Valeri could do routine things, like shower and get up and down the stairs; but again, these were difficult tasks and she would tire quickly. She was able to dress herself and whatever else was necessary for daily living; and fortunately, she could read as well as ever.

On occasion, just getting up and walking to the bathroom to brush her teeth tired her. Her heart was actually functioning quite well, although she did have heart skips from time to time. Sometimes I would see the artery in her neck moving in and out, indicating her heart was not beating as it should or was skipping again.

Valeri still used the pump with Desferal five nights a week, to continue chelating the iron out of her circulatory system. Initially, I had to insert the needle, but eventually she was able to do this on her own again. As with her other basic needs, she insisted on doing this herself, even though it could be quite time-consuming for her.

Valeri still had the same sleeping habits she had prior to her stroke. She liked to stay up late at night and sleep late in the morning. She said it was difficult for her to fall asleep early, even if she tried. So, instead, she watched the "David Letterman Show" and late-night movies until she fell asleep. We also put a little bell at her bedside that she could ring in case she needed anything. Valeri never did use the bell during her recuperation period, characteristically electing to handle things herself.

Watching Valeri trying to regain her mobility, strength, and verbal abilities indicated how difficult it was for people who have a stroke and part of their brain damaged to work to a point to where they can function well. Fortunately, Valeri was young and able to improve quickly. Emotionally, she was on a roller coaster for some time. She was up more than down. She worked toward living a more normal life very well, because she had such a strong desire to do so.

Soon Valeri was back to making many phone calls, having friends visit, and going out with them. Her sister Debbie, who still lived with us, was a considerable help. She drove Valeri around to her friends' homes the first few weeks, and she would often take Val to local restaurants, particularly Big Boy's where she worked, and treat her to either a snack or a meal. This helped Valeri's morale tremendously. During this time she contacted all her friends, brought them up-to-date on her progress, and kept up with the news in their lives.

As I watched Valeri progress, I couldn't help but feel how terrible a thing it was when she had the debilitating stroke. Valeri was relentless in her efforts to recover, using up so much energy to get back to a point where she could function on a normal basis. It was extremely difficult for me to see a person I loved suffering from a major disease, then experience a catastrophic health set-back that knocked her off her feet and forced her to use all her ability and energy to attempt to bounce back physically and emotionally. I loved and respected Valeri enormously for being so courageous, once again, and for fighting so very hard to regain her status and style in life.

About a week after arriving home, a dear family friend, Gus Kocovis passed away. Mr. Kocovis served as an integral part of our Greek community, particularly in our church. Due to back problems, he had been unable to walk for several years prior to his death. Mr. Kocovis, his wife Sophie, son Alex, and daughters Eva and Cynthia were good family friends, too. Alex (who Val always felt was a Tom Cruise look-alike) was one of her favorite basketball players on our church team. Alex and Val used to have some great conversations. She would laugh heartily when he displayed his wonderful sense of humor. Valeri insisted on paying her respects to his wife and children, so I drove Marietta and Valeri to the funeral home. When we arrived, Valeri, struggling to walk with her cane, entered the funeral home. Upon seeing Mr. Kocovis' children, she hugged them and cried, "I just had to come to see your dad." His children expressed their gratefulness to Val, as they knew how difficult it was for her to get around.

The next several weeks were very difficult. Valeri spent a great portion of her time going to the St. John therapy center for treatment. Each of the two sessions lasted an hour, and she attended them three or four days every week. Again, Debbie drove Valeri to the sessions when Marietta and I could not.

Valeri worked diligently with her therapists, who were very understanding and helpful. Marietta, Debbie, and I experienced a big boost in seeing a picture of Valeri with her speech therapist in the St. John's Allied Health Handbook, which was to be distributed for publicity purposes. In the photo Val was sitting next to the therapist, and Val had the biggest smile on her face. This was the Valeri we knew and loved so much, with her glowing smile. Needless to say, Valeri was thrilled to have her picture in the handbook.

Following her stroke, a new arrangement for medical treatment was established for Valeri. Now, she was under the care of Dr. Sparks and his partner, Dr. Kindle: both hematologists. As an adult, it was imperative that she be under the constant care of a blood specialist. Valeri now needed transfusions every four or five weeks. The established procedure included taking a blood test at Dr. Sparks' office. If her blood count was low, a nurse would call either Bon Secours or St. John Hospital and schedule a transfusion. Unfortunately, sometimes this would take several days, whereas previously Valeri could go into the hospital for a blood test and then get her transfusion the next day. Also, if the nurse drawing the blood at Dr. Sparks' office decided that Valeri didn't need a transfusion, then the nurse would not schedule the transfusion. In the past, Valeri would help make the decision of when she should go to the hospital based on how she felt.

Eventually, Valeri was able to drive her car short distances. One day she had an appointment at Dr. Sparks' office to have a blood test. Valeri decided to drive that day and left for the appointment around noon. At 1:00 p.m., when Marietta returned home from teaching, Valeri was still not home. A few minutes later, Val walked in and sat down. She was completely exhausted and began to cry. "Mom," she said, "I went to Dr. Sparks' office and sat there for almost three-and-a-half hours waiting for my appointment. The receptionist said that the doctors were extremely busy and told me to wait, which I decided to do."

Marietta immediately telephoned the receptionist and asked to talk to the person in charge of the reception room. When the head nurse answered the phone, Marietta told her that she thought it was irresponsible on the part of the staff to allow Valeri, a patient recovering from a stroke, to sit in a waiting room for three-and-a-half hours before seeing the doctor. Someone was at fault and Marietta wanted to know who. Marietta also warned that the situation better not happen again or there was going to be trouble.

The head nurse replied: "Well, you know we are very busy here. This is an oncology office too and there are many, many patients, and that's just how it is."

Marietta again warned, "It had better not happen again."

We knew that both Dr. Sparks and Dr. Kindle had many patients suffering from cancer and other fatal diseases. They were extremely busy, and it was not unusual for their staff to see people who were dying come in for appointments. What the staff member meant was that Valeri just couldn't be treated any differently than anyone else who had a serious disease. The head nurse did say that they would do whatever they could to the best of their ability.

This response was not acceptable to us. While we felt that every patient should receive the best care, Valeri was our main concern and it was imperative that she receive the special attention necessary for her to survive. I was sure that all of Dr. Sparks' patients felt this way.

Except on rare occasions when Valeri was sent to Bon Secours Hospital for a transfusion, she was sent to St. John to receive the treatment. The transfusion routine at St. John Hospital was somewhat different than at St. Joseph's in Mt. Clemens, where Valeri was usually in a private room. At St. John Hospital transfusions were given in an outpatient ward, which meant there were many patients in the same room. In the beginning, Valeri felt there was too much action taking place around her, but after a brief acclimation period, she enjoyed the outpatient ward and liked watching the activity going on around her.

The nurses in the ward were outstanding. They were some of the finest nurses who ever treated Val. Any time she went in for a transfusion and was cared for by Teresa, Marianne and Jeanine, Val knew that she was going to have efficient and special care. Valeri also knew that these three nurses could find an open vein almost one hundred percent of the time, which was not a consistent ability with many of the other nurses she had met over the years.

Valeri's care in this ward was excellent. The only unfortunate part about her treatment was that neither Dr. Sparks nor Dr. Kindle would ever visit her to make sure that everything was progressing well. It was their practice to have the patient visit them at their office within the next couple days. Even without visits by the doctors, Valeri felt very comfortable with the treatment and care by the nurses in that ward.

After a transfusion and just prior to the Christmas holidays, Valeri went to see Dr. Sparks. He had asked for a consultation with Valeri and me. As Valeri and I sat in his big office, looking at him, he told Valeri, "There are a couple of things I want to discuss. First of all, you are an adult and we're going to have to treat you as an adult. You will be responsible for your own treatment, not your mother or your father. The second thing is, you have so much iron in your system at this time that I feel we should try to do something to chelate it out in a very aggressive manner. If you were to try to board an airplane and get past the checking station, you would probably be turned back because the metal in you would set off the alarm!" Valeri laughed. "Seriously, though," he continued, "I have a plan on how we can get the iron out of your system."

"Dr. Sparks," I interjected, "would you consider calling Dr. Pat Giordina in New York to find out how they chelate their Thalassemia patients?" My thinking was that they treat so many anemia patients, they must have some idea of what would be the best aggressive method to use.

Dr. Sparks looked at me and very sternly replied, "We chelate cancer patients all the time. We know how to chelate iron out of a person's system and we intend to use our own methods. Believe me, this method will work as well as any used anywhere in the world."

He told us that he felt Valeri should have a Mediport put into the left side of her chest. A Mediport is a small outlet plug, with a tube that connects to a vein leading to her heart. This would enable Valeri to receive a transfusion by way of a needle into the Mediport, and would make it somewhat easier than sticking needles into her arm. It was a safe method that was being used extensively throughout the country at that time. He said that, after the holidays, the Mediport would be inserted by minor surgery. Dr. Sparks wanted to use his pump (a several-pound gadget), have his nurse insert the needle into the Mediport, and let Valeri carry the pump for six straight days, both day and night. He felt that this would get rid of much of the iron faster than Valeri's little pump.

Valeri and I felt that the doctor was giving worthwhile advice, as he did say that he believed Valeri could get her iron count down to a normal level within a year to eighteen months. Whatever health condition she was in at that time she might retain indefinitely. We went home and told Marietta. All of us were extremely happy. This is what we had hoped for: a method to help Valeri survive for many years to come.

We spent the wonderful holidays together with our family, relatives, and friends. It was a very happy Christmas season, as Valeri was recovering so well from her stroke. We were also hopeful at the prospect of seeing light at the end of the tunnel, by chelating such an extensive amount of iron from Valeri's system.

During the vacation, Marietta said to Valeri, "I think you should have two goals in mind. The first one is to visit Chris in San Francisco in January, since he keeps inviting you out to see him; and the second is to plan to go back to student teaching during the winter semester, which will begin some time in late February."

Valeri agreed. "I like your first idea, Mom, to visit Chris for a week or so in January; but, I think the second idea is too premature."

"That's what we're shooting for," Marietta retorted. "That's what I want you to do and that's what you should do." So Valeri just smiled, knowing it was difficult to debate a question when Marietta had made up her mind.

Valeri was walking much better now, and she was much stronger. However, she was still not close to her pre-stroke condition. After the holidays, Valeri went immediately into the hospital and had a Mediport inserted in the left side of her chest. The operation was successful and didn't seem to affect her very much. The area on her chest healed rapidly.

A week later, Marietta announced: "Valeri, you're heading for San Francisco in a couple of days."

"Okay, Mom and Dad," Valeri agreed. "I'm going to give it a try."

Valeri would fly to San Francisco with Nikki and her husband, Abe. They would all be together for the first day, then Nikki and Abe would leave for a trip through Southern California, and Valeri would stay with Chris for ten days.

The big day arrived. As I drove Valeri to the airport, she wasn't very talkative. We did have some conversation, to the extent that I encouraged her to get around as much as she could, but cautioned her to get the rest she needed. I also told Valeri to enjoy each day, as San Francisco was a wonderful city. (After her stroke, it was common for Valeri to be very quiet from time to time, choosing to listen to people talk, rather than taking a great part in the conversation, as she had in the past.)

I walked with her into the terminal and we found Nikki and Abe. As we sat, waiting for the plane, I couldn't believe how Valeri had perked up. She seemed to be her old self again. She began talking, laughing, and kidding around. This was very heart-warming for me, as it seemed that the old Val was back. It occurred to me that when Valeri was with her own group, she seemed to be a different person and that the old Val was returning. I kissed Nikki and Val good-bye, told them to have a good trip, and told Val to telephone Marietta and me each day to let us know how life was progressing.

As I walked out of the airport, I turned around to see Valeri laughing and making gestures with her hands and arms while talking to Nikki and Abe. This made me feel good and I realized that she would get along well in San Francisco.

Valeri had a wonderful visit with Chris. As usual, he was a marvelous person to be around and a wonderful host. He showed her many of the sights in San Francisco and the Bay Area. They visited the Golden Gate Bridge, Fishermen's Wharf, and the picturesque town of Sausalito. They took a ride through some of the mountains and visited the ocean, which Valeri always loved. It was an invigorating vacation for Val. She always said Chris was the greatest, and once again he proved that he was. He could make her laugh, make her feel comfortable, and make her feel happy, and he did for ten days - which were probably better than any therapy she could receive. Valeri became confident that she could live a relatively normal life again.

It was time to depart San Francisco and return home. Valeri hugged and kissed Chris, and wished him well on his job. She thanked him over and over again for showing her such a wonderful time. The trip did wonders for Valeri's recovery.

After Val's return home, Marietta realized that perhaps she was asking too much of Valeri to continue her student teaching in February. Finally, Marietta listened to my advice and that of the doctor, and changed her mind. "It may be too soon for Valeri to try to tackle tasks that big at this time, but in reality she should gear up to go back to student teaching in September." The plan was set. Valeri would continue rehabilitating; relaxing; and enjoying her soaps, movies, and friends for the next few months - then return to student teaching in the fall to receive her certification.

In February, Debbie was to marry her fiancé, Brian Dittmer, a young man she had met while working at Big Boy's. They both decided they wanted to try marriage for a second time. The wedding day arrived and the ceremony took place at the Assumption Church, with Father Kavadas presiding. Unlike Debbie's first wedding where four hundred people had been invited, this time there were only one hundred and fifty guests. As usual, all of the girls looked lovely, and Debbie was a beautiful bride again. Marietta and I were proud of Valeri as she walked down the aisle without a limp. Her lovely gown brought out her beauty again, as in past weddings. Once again, the thought ran through my mind that one of these days it would be Valeri's turn to be a bride.

The reception at Vintage Hall, was marvelous. I was thrilled that Valeri danced so much. Near the end of the evening, she sat down next to Marietta and me and said, "You know, it's been a wonderful wedding. I'm so thrilled that Debbie and Brian have gotten married because they're such wonderful people. I just know they're both going to be very happy. On top of that," she added, "I want to baptize their first child, whenever that takes place." All of us laughed. A short time later, we sent Debbie and Brian off on their honeymoon. As we sat there talking with other guests, Valeri turned to us and confided, "You know, I'm gonna miss my buddy Debbie. She's been a wonderful companion, especially in the last few months after my stroke. I'm extremely happy for her. She's a wonderful sister."

Val was now back in her traveling mode. In the early spring, she and René Garkinos, Chris' sister, decided to take a trip to Acapulco. They were both in the mood to appreciate warm weather after a hard, cold winter. In Acapulco, they took in the sights, did their social thing, swam every day, and developed good tans.

Valeri still had some walking and climbing problems and sometimes it was difficult for her to get into the swimming pool. She would get irritated with René when she offered to help Val up and down the ladder. As René said, "Valeri's very stubborn and refused any kind of assistance, unless it was an emergency." The two friends enjoyed themselves immensely and had many stories to tell when they returned from their vacation.

It wasn't long before Valeri and René took a trip to Chicago. Once again, they did their thing: sightseeing, socializing, and shopping. They enjoyed each other's company; René was a good traveling companion for Valeri during that time. It seemed that, as soon as they'd return from one trip, they already had plans to go on another.

Val also enjoyed visiting René at home, joking around with her father and mother. One day, Valeri drove into their driveway and bumped into the garage door by stepping on the accelerator instead of the brake. There was some damage done to the garage door, and Valeri was very upset. René's father came out, looked at the garage door, and began to laugh. He said, "Just another woman driver. As long as you're okay, don't worry about a thing." That little bump was there to stay permanently, as he said it would remind the family of Valeri. Valeri laughed at that.

Although Valeri's general health was quite good at this time, the chelation system set up by Dr. Sparks wasn't working too well. Valeri tried carrying around the heavy, noisy pump a couple of times, and found too many problems. Each treatment almost immobilized her for six days. Also, the inconvenience of trying to get one of Dr. Sparks' nurses to insert the needle was aggravating. They had problems inserting the needle into the Mediport, and made Valeri feel as if she was stealing time away from other patients by requesting that a nurse insert it. Additionally, I discovered that Val was only receiving approximately eighteen thousand milligrams of Desferal for six 24-hour periods by way of Dr. Sparks' pump, whereas I had been injecting forty thousand milligrams of it via her little pump five nights per week.

We asked for a consultation with Dr. Sparks to discuss the chelation method he was using. As usual, whenever we tried to make an appointment to see him, the answer was that it was going to take a couple of days because he was very busy. On top of that, one receptionist was always very obstinate and at times, just plain rude.

Finally, we were able to see Dr. Sparks to discuss the chelation method he had prescribed. He said it was foolproof and worked on all of his other patients. Of course I could not dispute his claim, but I did refute his argument to the extent that his patients were not Cooley's Anemia victims and that there had to be a different method used in other parts of the country to chelate Cooley's Anemia patients. I asked him once more if he would please call Dr. Giordina in New York. She would welcome his call, as she had mentioned to me in several conversations after Valeri's stroke. He looked me straight in the eye and again sternly stated: "I'm sorry, this is the only method I use. Take it or leave it."

Valeri was unhappy with Dr. Sparks' method. She looked at me and said, "Dad, I would rather not have that method used on me. How about if we just use my pump extensively? Would that help?"

Dr. Sparks looked at us and said, "It will help, naturally. It won't take out as much iron, but it will help." He concluded the appointment by saying, "I'm sorry that you won't use my method, but I will not call anywhere else, because I know this is a very successful way of chelating iron."

I wasn't at all pleased with the meeting. After having contacted people throughout the country for many years, I felt that Dr. Sparks should call the doctors in New York to inquire about what they were doing for Thalassemia patients. Maybe there were other kinds of pumps being used. Of course, I appreciated the fact that he was a very busy person, but I was terribly concerned about Valeri's health.

Also, I was unhappy with the rude treatment Valeri received from one of his receptionists. At times the receptionist was actually belittling to Valeri. Val didn't let it bother her too much, but it bothered Marietta and me when the receptionist treated Valeri that way. Another thing that was frustrating was that we were accustomed to more personalized service from Dr. Charbeneau, who would always call us back or ask us to come to his office immediately, so that he could see Valeri and answer our questions. This privilege was not equally available with either Dr. Sparks or Dr. Kindle.

I knew that both Dr. Sparks and Dr. Kindle were excellent doctors; therefore, I was willing to overlook some of the idiosyncrasies of his staff to keep Valeri as their patient, but I did wonder if perhaps a change of doctors was imminent. Most importantly, I worried about whether or not Valeri was getting enough iron removed from her system with her own pump. However, I didn't know what other steps to take.

Meanwhile, Valeri continued to socialize with Sue, her godsister Rena, and also with Lynn and René. Late at night she would often call Chris or he would call her. They would talk until well into the morning.

In August, the AHEPA convention was going to be held in New Orleans, Louisiana. Val knew that Marietta and I were planning to attend, but Valeri wanted to go with her own peer group, so she made plans. The group consisted of nine people, including: René, Kim Stathis, Kim's brother Dino, John Latinos, and Dolly Panagos. They were going to rent a suite, with the guys sleeping in one room, and the girls in the other. They were going to live it up for one week in New Orleans.

Our trip to the convention was another great adventure. As usual, Marietta and I played in the golf tournament and attended various social functions. I attended several meetings, including the Cooley's Anemia Foundation meeting directed by Judge Scopas and his wife, Clio. Marietta went shopping with her friends, and in the late evenings we would talk with our group in the lobby until early morning, discussing daily events and plans for the following day.

Meanwhile, Valeri and her friends participated in all kinds of activities: boating, sightseeing, and attending dances and after-hour parties. It was one great, hectic, wild, fun week for all of us. By now Valeri was once more becoming active physically and better able to keep up with the rest of the group. Her speech was much improved. In fact, even with her slight limp and her curled fingers, one would hardly know that she had ever had a stroke.

We saw her on the last day prior to flying home, and she announced: "Well, Mom and Dad, the fun times are going to end tonight. When I get back, I will have to make some plans to return to student teaching in a couple of weeks." Then she went off to another party.

Val would always retain her position as the life of the party. Others would fall asleep, but she would continue to celebrate and enjoy herself. This is probably one reason many of her friends didn't realize the severity of her disease. Val could outlast them and continue until long after they were fatigued, seeming to be as refreshed at five in the morning as at one. This always astonished her friends.

It was the day after Labor Day and a pre-semester meeting was scheduled for the returning teachers and faculty of Grosse Pointe North High

School. At this meeting the faculty are welcomed back and plans are made for the opening of school one or two days later. Valeri, who attended the meeting, was sitting quietly near the back of the room, when Dr. Kastran, the principal, said, "I do want to welcome back our young student teacher, who wants to complete her assignment after having a health problem last year. Valeri, sweetheart, would you please stand?" When she stood, the teachers gave her a standing ovation, which made Valeri feel very welcome.

After the meeting, many teachers came to talk to her. They asked how she was progressing, welcomed her back, and told her that if they could be of help in any way to please call on them. Valeri was made to feel very much at home.

Bob Reimer, the English department head, continued as Val's supervising teacher. He was thrilled to see her back and anxious to help her begin her assignments. Val would have the same classes that she had the year before. Mr. Reimer was extremely encouraging to Valeri during a special session in his office afterwards. He asked her to keep him informed daily regarding her classes and offered his help at any time. He wanted her to succeed and to receive her certification. He also wanted Valeri to regain and retain the wonderful creativity she had shown in the past for establishing plans for her students.

Later in the day, Dr. Kastran came into Mr. Reimer's office, where Val was preparing some assignments for her student teaching. He said, "Valeri, I want you to be co-editor of the Grosse Pointe North school yearbook, along with John Monahan. I want John and you to work together to produce a great yearbook, which I know both of you are capable of." Thrilled by this opportunity, Val thanked Dr. Kastran. She was well-acquainted with John Monahan and called him later that day. They soon developed a good working relationship as school yearbook editors.

Mr. Reimer was a real gem. His outstanding guidance helped Valeri in developing lesson plans. He evaluated her performances, suggested ways Valeri could improve herself as an all-around teacher, helped her to understand the methods and techniques of disciplining and motivating the students, and also suggested how to teach various materials and how to get the most from the students. To Valeri, he was the perfect supervising teacher and also a very fine friend.

Marietta and I also assisted Val in some of her class preparations. We would do some typing for her, as well as share our ideas about teaching and all of its components. In fact, on occasion we would help Val practice some of her future lectures by pretending to be her students.

It was difficult for Valeri to student teach on a full-time basis. She would come home immediately after school to plan her assignments, take naps, and go to bed early. She did everything she could to feel refreshed for the following day. The long hours were tiring for Valeri. It was strenuous for her to do so much talking and explaining to the students. Communicating with large groups was especially hard on her. However, when it came to small groups and individuals, Valeri excelled.

As the semester progressed, she was getting better and better, and finally her assigned time to teach was over. At the end, Valeri had regained much of her teaching ability and was doing an excellent job, according to Mr. Reimer. He noticed a tremendous growth in her capabilities during the time that she student taught. He was elated that Valeri was able to complete her assignment.

Meanwhile, Val was busy working on the school yearbook with John. They came up with an outstanding theme that year, and they divided the responsibilities. They worked together beautifully. All of the preparations for the book went smoothly and deadlines were met with no problems.

Then one day, Valeri asked to talk to Marietta and me. Her tone was very serious as she said, "Now that I'm feeling so much better, and I've finished my student teaching, I want to begin looking for a full-time teaching position. I love working on the school yearbook with John, and I'll keep that as a part-time project, but I want to think in terms of going after a full-time job. I plan to begin by talking to Toni Nicholas at Wayne State. She can direct me to the person in charge of teacher placements throughout the entire area. Then, I will follow through by sending out letters and my resume. I want to go after a job for next year." She had a determined look on her face, which we were to see so often.

I thought to myself: "If Val's going after a job, she's going to go after it very hard." I just hoped that the situation would work out so that she'd have an opportunity to find one, as there was very little hiring of teachers anywhere in our metropolitan area at that time.

In February 1988, John Monahan, Valeri, and their small staff of student yearbook workers completed their work on the yearbook and sent it to the publishing company. Valeri and John celebrated with the student staff by having a pizza party. They were elated that the task was completed on time. The only thing left now was to distribute the books when they arrived in June.

There were quite a number of social events about to take place in 1988. Debbie and Brian had a baby boy and named him Brian. Valeri was very much in love with her nephew, especially since Debbie had consented (as promised) to have Valeri baptize little Brian. The baptism was to take place in July of that year.

Another major event was the marriage of Rena to Mark Venettis on Memorial Day weekend. Rena and Mark had been dating for over a year, and she had relinquished her flight attendant job.

Meanwhile, Valeri was having some sporadic difficulties with viral infections. As usual, whenever she called Dr. Sparks' office it was very difficult to get an appointment. So, one day when Valeri had a virus infection I telephoned Dr. Sparks' office and asked the receptionist if I could talk to the doctor. In a rude tone of voice, she refused to let me speak with him or to give us an appointment. Instead, she gave me to the head nurse, who told me to look into Valeri's throat with a flashlight to see if she had white spots. If there were white spots, Val had strep throat, and only then would she make an appointment to have Val see Dr. Sparks. A couple of days later I asked Dr. Sparks for a meeting because we were not happy with his staff. Although we respected him, we found it very difficult to get an appointment to see him.

At our meeting, Dr. Sparks said that never before had anyone complained about his staff. We told him that in twenty-five years we'd never complained about anybody's staff, either. We explained that the rudeness and belligerence on the part of a couple of his people, especially one of the receptionists, was uncalled for and upsetting. He promised to try to straighten out the situation. So, we agreed to try to develop a better relationship with his staff and to retain him as our doctor.

As I left the office, I had to speak with the receptionist about the bill; she was her usual rude self. I thought to myself, "This isn't going to go on much longer. These people have to remember that the reason they have a job is because they have patients, and Valeri happens to be a patient."

Unfortunately, our relationship between Dr. Sparks' staff and us did not improve, so we decided to ask Dr. Sparks to refer Valeri to another doctor. We felt that perhaps an internist would be more accessible to Valeri.

Dr. Sparks was very cooperative and recommended Dr. Bill Carion, a young doctor who worked out of the hospital's medical center. Since Dr. Carion was closer to Valeri's age, Dr. Sparks thought that he might better relate to and communicate with Valeri, and that perhaps it would be a beneficial change for her. We thanked him for the referral and made an appointment to meet Dr. Carion.

When Valeri and I met with Dr. Carion, he seemed to be a fine young man, and very enthusiastic about helping Valeri. He even asked me to make a list of doctors in New York whom he could contact should Valeri have any unusual problems. Val took a liking to Dr. Carion, and she seemed to communicate with him quite well. Although he was busy, Dr. Carion always tried to make time to see her. He would almost always contact us within a short period of time when we left a message for him. He also said that he would try to visit Val during her transfusions.

We made another appointment with Dr. Carion so that he could see how Val was doing after her latest transfusion, and so that he could give her a more extensive physical examination to evaluate her general health. When Valeri was called into the examining room, I went with her, as this was a practice I had followed for years.

When Dr. Carion entered the room, he greeted us and began the physical exam. Immediately after finishing, he asked Valeri how she was feeling overall. She responded, "Fine, except I feel sluggish at times."

Somehow he got on the topic of Cooley's Anemia. He looked at Val and said, "You've already outlived your life expectancy by several years; so, whatever you're getting now is a bonus. Youngsters who have Cooley's Anemia don't ordinarily live that long."

I was stunned by his comments, and I knew that Valeri was too. I quickly said, "Dr. Carion, we understand that Valeri has lived for a long time; however, I have spoken with doctors from around the country who have patients that are living into their thirties, and are doing well. That's what we want for Valeri and that's what we expect you to help us to strive toward." He quickly caught himself and apparently realized what he had said. He then said that he didn't mean it to sound that way. He agreed that the goal was to keep Valeri healthy. We would work together, and he would do all that he could to help us achieve this. Val and I felt better.

Valeri enjoyed having Dr. Carion as her doctor because she could speak with him about all kinds of problems, and he was very receptive. He was also humorous, informative, and caring. She felt that a nice patient-doctor relationship was beginning. His office staff was pleasant and easy to work with, which pleased us all.

One night when Valeri was watching "The David Letterman Show," I couldn't sleep, so I went into her room. She turned the sound down and we began talking. We philosophized about different things that had taken place. She seemed relaxed and noted, "You know, Dad, there's been a lot of rough spots through the years, especially this past year with my stroke and related problems. It's funny, but when I was little I always thought that by the time I was thirty years old I would have a husband, and maybe a couple of adopted children, and everything would be going nicely in life. Here I am, close to thirty and nothing has really been settled." There was a sad tone in her voice and she was staring at the floor. Suddenly, she looked into my eyes and said, "Yeah, I really was very optimistic and thought things would fall into place nicely for me."

"You know Valeri, you still have about three years until you reach thirty, and a lot can happen in three years," I said. "I'm betting that if we just keep you healthy and you keep enjoying life and continue with what you're doing, things are going to fall into place, and you can still achieve your childhood dreams."

She looked at me, smiled, and hugged me. "Thanks, Dad. I appreciate what you're saying and I'm really going to try for it. I hope and pray that sometime in the near future things will start falling into place. Thank you so much."

We watched the rest of the show together before I said goodnight and went back to my bedroom and lay in bed nearly asleep. I thought about what Valeri had said. I felt that she had a wonderful philosophy and, God willing, some day she would live to see her dreams come true.

# 25

# Weddings Can Be Dangerous

ONE cold, late-spring evening, as Marietta, Valeri, and I sat in our comfortable family room watching TV, with the fireplace glowing, Valeri began to talk about her post-stroke era. She often referred to times as either pre- or post-stroke. She said, "In the pre-stroke era, things were quite exciting. I did many things with my friends. We were in our early twenties and we did things characteristic of that age group. It seems as though in the post-stroke era there are so many exciting activities taking place, but that my friends and I have a more mature attitude. We're not only looking for a good time and trying to forget the world, but rather we're looking for experiences that bring stability into our lives. We are looking for knowledge that will lead us toward a family, an occupation, and the ability to afford the good things, such as new automobiles and homes. It's all in our attitudes. That's where we are at this time."

She continued, "There are so many exciting things going on: marriages, children being born, baptisms, and all kinds of social events sponsored by our church. Also, many trips are being planned, my job hunting, and my job with the Grosse Pointe North yearbook - it seems like there's always so much to do, so many places to go and so many people to see."

Valeri observed that our family was quite large and was continuing to increase in number. There were so many activities going on with our total family and relatives, along with her friends and their families. In addition, there were the social events through other Greek Orthodox churches and activities in the Detroit area that were being planned. "How about the sporting events I love?" Valeri added. I still like my Michigan football games, my Detroit Tigers and Detroit Piston NBA games. Boy, I'm just having a very exciting life, Mom and Dad. I have so many things to accomplish. Days are just flying by!"

We spent a considerable amount of time that evening talking about the social aspects of our lives that were unfolding. We focused on Rena's upcoming wedding with Mark Venettis on Memorial Day weekend. Val said, "It's hard to believe how fast the years have flown by. Here we are, ready to attend my wonderful godsister's wedding in a very short time."

Val reviewed the plans that were being finalized in preparation for the wedding in three weeks. She talked about all the nice things that were scheduled to happen at the wedding and reception. "The sky's the limit as far as having fun that night," Val announced. "We're going to send Rena and Mark off on their honeymoon in fantastic style."

The three weeks flew by, and it was time for Rena and Mark to get married. Val woke up early that morning and went over to Rena's home, with her maid of honor dress in hand. She and all the bridesmaids planned to dress at Rena's home. She also helped Rena put on her wedding gown and make-up. All the girls looked beautiful and were ready to go. Suddenly everyone began crying. Val and Rena just sobbed and hugged each other, and talked about what a wonderful day was about to take place.

As the guests arrived in preparation for the wedding at our Assumption Church, Rena, Valeri and the girls were very nervous, releasing their tensions with much giggling and laughter. It was time for the wedding to commence. The bridesmaids and ring bearers walked down the aisle, as is the tradition. Valeri preceded Rena. Once again, Val looked lovely in her peach, tea-length dress. She didn't wear her brace, but rather wore a regular shoe with a ribbon tied around that shoe - an ingenious design by Marietta to have Valeri walk down the aisle without the shoe slipping off her right foot. Rena followed Val and was a very beautiful bride.

Father Kavadas and Father Makrinos presided at the wedding. My job was to be the cameraman. I was using my video camera to take pictures of the entire wedding as a gift for Rena and Mark, even though I was an amateur photographer.

At the reception at the Gourmet House, all of the guests were in congenial spirits. I was very proud of our god-daughter Rena, remembering what a wonderful friend she had been to Valeri, Debbie, and Nikki through the years.

It happened that Chris Garkinos, Valeri's wonderful friend, was in town for the wedding. In the late evening, Valeri, Chris, Mark, Johnny Kalyvas, René, and some of the other kids got together and began having a chug-a-lug contest while laughing and kidding about all the happenings at the wedding. It was nearing midnight and the reception had another hour to go before it was over.

I went to the rest room and on the way back stopped at the bar to get a Diet Coke. As I looked up, I saw a crowd on the other side of the dance hall. Then, I saw René running around and suddenly realized that she was looking for me. When she saw me, she exclaimed, "Come on, something has happened to Valeri!"

I ran over to the other side of the dance floor and saw Valeri lying down, with our friend Maggie Veras, who was a nurse, kneeling beside Valeri and talking to her. The first thing that crossed my mind was, of course, what I feared the most, that Val's heart had given out. I felt maybe she had had some type of heart failure or heart attack. "What's going on, Maggie?" I asked.

"Well," Maggie answered, "Valeri was dancing with Billy Skuras (Rena's brother) and just as she started moving around quite actively, she collapsed."

As Maggie said that, Val looked at me and said, "Dad, something happened to my leg. It just went from under me and I couldn't help it. Good thing Billy caught me or I would have hit the floor very hard and been hurt seriously." Upon examination by Maggie, we found that what happened was that Valeri had been so active during the evening without her brace, her leg had just given out and she couldn't stand anymore. I quickly took Valeri's pulse and asked her how she was feeling otherwise. Needless to say, Valeri had had several drinks during the evening, and she was a little sluggish, but she answered, "I feel okay otherwise, but my leg feels very painful in the area near my groin and hip."

At this moment the manager of the Gourmet House, who had called a 911 ambulance to the scene, ushered the medical technicians to where Val was lying. Maggie explained to the technicians that Valeri had collapsed because her leg had given out on her. One of them said "I think it would be best if we took her to the hospital. We'll carry her out on a stretcher."

Valeri declined, saying: "Oh, no. I'm going to walk out. I'm ruining Rena's wedding." Then she began to cry and repeated, "I'm ruining Rena's wedding!"

Rena and Mark consoled Valeri as they stood nearby. They told her that she hadn't ruined anything and that the reception was almost over anyway. They said she'd be okay and to do what the medical people wanted her to do. Rena hugged and kissed Val and said, "Thank you for everything, honey. You've been absolutely wonderful and I'm sure you're going to be okay. Mark and I are going to see you at St. John Hospital immediately after this is over in about an hour."

This seemed to make Valeri feel somewhat better and she waved at Rena and Mark and threw them a kiss as she was being carried out to the ambulance. Marietta was quite upset and announced: "I'm going with Valeri in the ambulance. Bob, drive our car over to St. John's Emergency Room where I will be waiting."

Several of our friends volunteered to go to the hospital with me in my car, but I felt it wasn't necessary. Debbie and Nikki were both crying and insisted, "Dad, we're going to come to the hospital too. We'll meet you there." Debbie went with Brian and Nikki went with Abe.

I followed the ambulance to St. John and met Marietta there. Together we walked behind the stretcher. Valeri was in pain but seemed to be feeling quite well by now and doing a lot of giggling, probably due to the effects of the alcohol. A few minutes later, Chris and René Garkinos arrived. Val was taken into one of the Emergency Rooms to wait for x-rays and other tests. The policy at St. John was to allow only the parents to visit the patient for a few minutes every fifteen or twenty minutes, if they wished. One parent could stay with the patient at all times. So Marietta and I took turns going in to see Valeri. Nikki and Debbie took turns going in, too, after they arrived at the hospital. Chris and René did get a chance to see her for a few minutes while Marietta and I were in the waiting room with Debbie and Nikki. Later, somehow all of us were in the same area to see Valeri. She was comfortable because they had given her a shot for the pain in her leg, and she was still laughing and giggling with Chris, René, Debbie, and Nikki.

We received a phone call from Rena who said that she wanted to come to the hospital, but Nikki told her to stay at the reception. So she stayed with Mark. Rena was very upset, wondering what was happening to Valeri. Nikki explained that Val was having a series of tests and x-rays taken to see if there were any broken bones, and that Valeri was in a pretty good mood and joking around with everyone in the room. The doctor on call said that Valeri would be asked to stay all night, and the results of the test would be given to us the following morning.

Before going to her room in the hospital, Valeri began to cry. "I ruined Rena's wedding, Mom and Dad."

Marietta scolded her. "No you didn't. Rena said that if you said anything like that again she will become very upset. She just wants you to get well and to be on your feet and moving around by the time they get back from their honeymoon in two weeks."

A few minutes later Valeri was taken to her hospital room. Marietta and I went up to see her before she fell asleep. Debbie, Nikki, René, and Chris came along. Chris hugged her and said, "Valeri, I'll be going back to work tomorrow, but I'm going to give you a call every night until I feel that you're okay."

This pleased Valeri very much and she thanked Chris. She gave him a kiss and said, "I'll wait to hear from you." As it was 3:30 a.m., all of us went home to get some sleep before returning to the hospital.

Early the next morning we went to the hospital to see what the doctor had found through the x-rays and tests. Dr. Zurawski, a fine orthopedic surgeon who took care of our family in times of need for his services, was Valeri's attending physician. He greeted us later and said, "Don't worry, Bob and Marietta. There's no fracture. It appears that Valeri tore some tendons and ligaments in her hip and groin area. This is going to be very painful for a while. She won't be able to walk very much, if at all, for at least two weeks. When she does begin walking, she's going to have to use a crutch, then a cane, and then she'll be able to maneuver on her own in about three weeks. Everything else seems fine, so I will let her go home. But, please take care of her. Make sure that she takes her medication and don't let her move around too much."

The most memorable thing about getting Valeri home and up to her bedroom was the tremendous pain that she experienced every time we moved her body either up, down or sideways. Marietta and I carried her very carefully, but she still felt pain along the way. Any abnormal type of movement created much pain for Val. We made her as comfortable as possible, by putting extra pillows along the headboard of her bed, so she could sit up whenever she wanted. As long as Val was taking pain pills, she could maneuver some. She looked at us and said, "Wow. I guess I should have kept my brace on or at least put it on after the wedding was over, Mom. The doctor said that the reason I tore the ligaments and tendons was because I walked without the brace for such a long time. My leg became tired and that's when the tears took place."

We looked at each other and Marietta agreed, "Yes, I know. I guess I was really encouraging you not to use it, but we know now, Valeri, that it is a precautionary aid and that you should use it most of the time. Whenever you do not have your brace on, you should have it nearby so that when your leg begins to tire, you can put it on."

"Yep, I guess so," Val said. "I learned the hard way, didn't I?" She then looked around her room and commented, "You know, I love this room so much." She certainly enjoyed our family room and the house as a whole, but that bedroom to her was the "in" place to be. When she opened up her venetian blinds, the lovely sunshine would come through during most of the day. Yes, she loved her room and enjoyed spending many hours there.

"I love my convertible car, too," she said. "Those two things have made me very happy for such a long time. I love driving that car around with that top down. It's what I call really living!"

Then she proceeded to tell us that it was time for her to watch a couple of her favorite programs on television and we were excused to do as we wished for the remainder of the afternoon and evening, at which we laughed and commented: "We get the point, Val."

For the next three weeks, just as Dr. Zurawski had predicted, life was very difficult for Valeri. Whenever we tried to move her, she experienced tremendous pain in her right leg. I tried to carry her around most of the time by myself so that she wouldn't have excessive movement, but even that caused pain to her injured area. After a couple of weeks she began standing up and announced: "This is it! I'm going to start moving again. I have to get back to business, which is going out and having some fun times. Remember, I'm getting ready to take another trip to San Francisco. Chris called several times and he's waiting for me to visit him and it's just about that time." The first few days, Valeri had to use a crutch, but finally she graduated to the cane.

One morning she told us, "If I move slowly enough, I can move without a cane." And that's just what she did. From then on she was back on her feet.

# 26

# A New Source

A COUPLE of weeks after Val was on her feet again, I received a phone call from my friend Nick Cheolas. A former college roommate of Nick's son Steve, Dippo Maboobani, had telephoned Steve from Hong Kong. Dippo's son, who was two years old, had recently been diagnosed as having Thalassemia Major. Steve had told Dippo about Valeri, and that despite having Cooley's Anemia, Valeri had gotten along fairly well through the years. As a concerned father, Dippo wanted to get in contact with me to discuss the disease, its prognosis, and what we had done to help Valeri stay healthy. Of course, I said, "Hey, Nick! Great! Tell Steve that I would be happy to talk with Dippo any time."

The next evening around eleven o'clock I received a phone call from Dippo. He introduced himself and explained that he was of Indian descent from Sri Lanka, an island located immediately south of India. He said his father owned an export shipping company in Hong Kong, where they currently resided. He then proceeded to tell me about his young son. Both he and his wife were very confused as to what they should do and what to expect. We talked for over an hour. I informed him about our belief that Valeri should lead as normal a life as possible, what problems he could expect from Thalassemia, the different treatments that Valeri underwent, and about the pump that she was using, along with other pertinent information. I also gave him names of people in the United States who were involved medically with Thalassemia. I told him I would send him all the names of the doctors with whom I had been in contact. Then I gave the good news. I said, "Dippo, this is the 'Golden Era' for Thalassemia victims. The doctors know what they're doing at this point in treating the disease properly. They are chelating iron from patients at a young age, so their bodies will be normal as the years progress. Although dangerous, there are bone marrow transplants available, and there are some positive genetic advances on the way." I emphasized very strongly that progress was being made for Thalassemia victims and that I thought his son had an outstanding prognosis. Dippo thanked me and said he would keep in contact with me over the next few weeks to let me know exactly what was happening.

Dippo did just that. He called several times over a period of three to four weeks. He kept me abreast of what was being done for his son at the hospital in Hong Kong. He said that he and his wife were starting to accept the fact that their son had Thalassemia, and that he felt that I was correct in saying that this was the Golden Era for Thalassemia victims, although he was very skeptical about what medical treatment he should pursue for his son. Since he had the opportunity to travel to various parts of the world on business, Dippo was planning to visit doctors in Italy, England, and other countries where extensive research on Thalassemia was in progress. He planned to follow up on the leads I had given him, since there were many new ideas and data available on the disease. We both agreed that if we heard anything new happening anywhere regarding Thalassemia, we would contact the other immediately.

Because of the twelve-hour time difference between Hong Kong and Detroit, Dippo would call me at eleven o'clock in the morning, when he was in his office. He did not want his wife to hear our discussions as she was very worried about their son, and became upset easily. The friendship with Dippo became very valuable to me.

During one of his business trips, Dippo visited Dr. Bernadette Modell in England, who was well known for her extensive work in Thalassemia. Although she had written several books on the disease, for some reason she wasn't very popular in the United States. I decided to telephone Dr. Modell to find out what she knew about Cooley's Anemia. Perhaps she could tell me something I had not heard from the doctors in the United States. Most of the information she gave me was much the same; however, she did recommend that I call Dr. Beatrice Wonke in London, who had outstanding results in treating older victims.

I telephoned Dr. Wonke several times during the next week before I was finally able to reach her at the Whittington Hospital in London. Dr. Wonke, a hematologist, was doing extensive, aggressive therapy with Desferal to chelate iron from the patient's body. In fact, after our conversation, I decided to take Valeri to London to visit Dr. Wonke, for the purpose of evaluating Valeri's condition and for Dr. Wonke to recommend a treatment. Unfortunately, Dr. Wonke informed me that she would be gone for several weeks on vacation. She suggested I bring Valeri to London later in the fall, at which time she would give Valeri a procedure to follow for extensive chelation of iron. Dr. Wonke emphasized that Valeri should undergo a very aggressive therapy to chelate the iron as soon as possible, while she was still quite strong.

I thought about Dr. Sparks who, two years earlier, had refused to consider different ways to chelate iron from Valeri's body. Losing two years was vital in Valeri's hope for sustained life.

Marietta, Valeri, and I discussed taking Valeri to England later that fall. We came to the conclusion that maybe it would be better to work through Dr. Carion at St. John Hospital. We could inform him of what was being done in England by Dr. Wonke. Perhaps he could guide Valeri through an aggressive therapy procedure.

Actually and truthfully, the three of us felt that Valeri was still doing quite nicely, and perhaps chelation with her pump was sufficient, along with the Desferal given to her simultaneously during transfusions. We feared that upsetting the current procedure with excessive amounts of Desferal, without the strict care of a doctor knowledgeable in Thalassemia, could be more harmful than helpful. Val said she would be willing to try an aggressive procedure, even use a bigger pump, provided the doctor was extremely knowledgeable. The pump that Dr. Wonke recommended would be used by Valeri day and night continuously for weeks on end.

We were caught in a dilemma. Should we do this and maybe upset Val's current status or should we not do it and perhaps cause worse problems for Valeri in the near future? Dr. Carion suggested that we stay with the current procedure. He felt that we should at least learn more about how to use the new pump and its possible effects before we actually tried a project that aggressive. Perhaps we opted for a way out: Valeri wasn't too happy about having a pump on day and night for weeks and weeks.

We decided not to try aggressive chelating at this time. Before deciding what to do, I couldn't help thinking back on what I was told by Dr. Grady from New York's Cornell University Center. He had said: "There are some patients who are living past the age of thirty with Thalassemia on the pump and some patients who are not on the pump." My feeling was that Valeri's pump was sufficient.

I also spoke with Dr. Joe Graziano, a medical school professor at Columbia University Presbyterian Hospital, who said that in his research, there was not any significant help for older Thalassemia victims when they used aggressive chelation methods or the pump that Valeri was using. On that basis, we decided to continue with Valeri's regular small pump five nights a week, until we found out more information concerning the new pumps and the new aggressive therapy that was being used in other parts of the world.

My plan was to work with Dippo and to do extra research by calling doctors around the United States to see if there was anything newer or better in chelation therapy than Valeri's five-day-a-week pump. Also, Dippo was going to fly more often to other places in the world and would contact more doctors. Every time he found out something new concerning Thalassemia, he would call me and give me the information. Between Dippo's information and my own research, I felt that in a short time we would have a research-proven therapy that could be very helpful to Valeri; we were aware that her heart was beginning to weaken. We didn't know just what would happen, nor how long she would remain in her current health status. Still, our conclusion was that since she was feeling good, her pump was working well enough to help her retain the quality of health she needed to enjoy life at this time and hopefully for an indefinite period of time. There was a nice feeling about the fact that Dippo had given me considerable encouragement to begin a crusade to really follow up on aggressive chelation.

The question Marietta and I always asked ourselves was: "What more could we do to help Valeri remain in reasonably good health indefinitely, if this was possible?"

# 27

# *Busy and Happy Again*

VALERI'S friends and sisters were having babies. The next phase was the baptizing of these children. In our Greek Orthodox religion, a child's baptism is a very major event. Baptizing a child and becoming its godparent is an honor for any individual. The godparents of a child have two major functions in the life of that child. The first is to serve as surrogate parents should anything happen to the biological parents. The second is to encourage the parents to help the child develop a substantial religious background.

Valeri was about to take part in this phase by baptizing Debbie's son, Brian Robert, along with her cousin Nick Backos. She and Nick were going to become Brian's godmother and godfather. The event was set to take place in July 1988, when Brian was seven months old.

Brian Robert was a very cute baby, with lovely long, curly blond hair, blue eyes, and very light peach-colored skin. He was a friendly and lovable infant who was extremely attached to Valeri almost since birth.

The important event took place late on a Sunday afternoon at our Assumption Church, with Father Kavadas presiding. Debbie and Brian invited over fifty family members and friends to attend the baptism. In the Greek Orthodox tradition, a baptism is an event for only one child, rather than for several children as in some religions. The service takes approximately forty-five minutes to perform. As usual, I was the designated photographer, since I had the audiovisual equipment. This was always an enjoyment for me.

The baptism service consists of several different stages. During the first stage, the baby is held by a godparent at the back of the church, while the priest denounces Satan. Then he asks God to help accept the child into heaven, at which time the baby is brought to the front to the baptismal fountain. Then after prayers are read, the baby is undressed, and the priest immerses the baby into the water of the baptismal fountain three times, followed by the two godparents putting oil on the baby's body. A grandparent and a godparent then take the baby into a back room where they dress him in his new clothes. After he is dressed, he is brought back to the fountain, and the priest offers prayers, asking that the child be formally accepted into the religion. This is followed by the baby giving something to God, which in this case is a few strands of hair from his head, which is cut by the priest. Then the baby takes holy communion - a spoonful of wine from the holy cup. After the communion, the priest announces that the baby has been accepted into the Orthodox religion. He requests that the people come up, touch the baby, and congratulate the parents and godparents.

Soon the beautiful service was over, and everyone congratulated Debbie, Brian Sr., Nick, and Val. Brian Robert did very well during the baptism, and actually seemed to enjoy the part where people came up and touched him. After the celebration ended, all were invited to our home to attend a party for Brian Robert.

It was a wonderful reception. Everyone was in a festive mood. Val was very proud of this event. There was to be a loving and intimate relationship between her and Brian Robert.

Valeri looked forward to the end of summer, because the 1988 Summer Olympics were about to take place in Seoul, Korea. She had developed a tremendous interest in the Olympics in 1984. Valeri was an ardent follower of most of the events. She watched the live competitions, and also the taped telecasts of events that she had missed. She became very excited whenever athletes from the United States would win a medal in any event.

For ten days, all that Marietta heard Valeri and I talk about were the Olympics, and the winners in track and field, and all of the other events. Even Marietta became quite involved by the time the events had ended. When the ten days were over, Valeri remarked: "Boy! I can't wait for the '92 Olympics!" They were scheduled for Barcelona, Spain. She asked, "Remember when we were in Barcelona during our trip in 1983? Maybe it might be possible for me to fly there and watch them!"

Both Marietta and I agreed. "Gee, that would be great, Val. It would be even better if you would take us along with you!" We all laughed. In the back of my mind, though, I thought perhaps Val *could* attend the 1992 event.

In September 1988, Valeri returned to Grosse Pointe North to be the co-sponsor of the yearbook with John Monahan. They had formed a fine team the year before and planned a repeat performance. Val had an idea for the book to be produced with a movie studio theme. Each part would be introduced and include the various segments referring to a movie studio. The names of movies would fit in with the particular sections of the book. For example, the Table of Contents was printed on a replica of a film strip. On the other side were the names of many movies representing contents of that segment. For example, the first segment was titled "Fast Times at Grosse Pointe North, 1989, Spell Binder Picture."

John loved Val's theme, since he also enjoyed movies. He knew Valeri had a great knowledge of movies, actors, actresses, and the TV industry, which would be an invaluable resource during the production. Valeri, John, and the students who remained to see the yearbook completed were very proud of the book. It was truly a masterpiece.

Late that fall, Valeri was able to visit Chris in San Francisco again. She spent ten happy and eventful days with him. He took her to many special sites, including Napa Valley, one of the more picturesque sights to see in that part of California. Besides visiting other places around San Francisco and eating in several good restaurants, they also took a two-day trip to Reno, Nevada to see the beautiful scenery. When Val returned home, she was happy and felt very good. She seemed to be overcoming the terrible affects of the stroke she had suffered two years earlier.

The winter months were always very hard on Valeri. Physically, she would tire more quickly and need transfusions more often than during the warmer weather. Emotionally, she was so much happier when it was warm. The one thing that helped her tolerate the dreary, cold winter months was the Detroit Pistons basketball team. She had learned to love basketball by watching me coach, and she applied this love for the game to the Detroit Pistons, who in the 1988-1989 season were challengers for the National Basketball Association (NBA) Championship.

Valeri would watch many games on TV, listen to them on the radio, and read about them in the newspaper. I would also take her to the Silverdome to watch some of the games during the year. Jack McCloskey, the Pistons' General Manager, was a friend of mine from my college coaching days. I also met Chuck Daly through Matt Dobek, who was one of my advisees at Wayne State. Matt also was the sports information director for the Detroit Spirits, a team which I had helped coach in the early 1980s.

Valeri simply adored the players on the team. To her, Isiah Thomas was a great basketball player. Despite his relatively small stature, Isiah

could do so many things for both the offense and defense, and he was
such a fine leader for the Pistons. Valeri thought that Joe Dumars was a
great shooter. When he would attempt a basket, she would shout: "Joe,
Joe, Joe Duuumars!" When Vinnie Johnson got free to shoot, she would
shout: "Go get 'em, Vinnie, go get 'em!" And she would say: "Oh, that
player fouled him again. That basket was good, and he should be shooting free throws!" Val felt that Bill Laimbeer was probably one of the
most humorous athletes she knew. He always had an innocent look on
his face as he knocked opponents over and bumped into players coming
to the basket. She loved the way he would innocently hold his hands out
to the referee and say, "Foul on *me?*" Then Bill would stand over twenty
feet from the basket and begin making baskets like they were going out
of style. She loved the way Dennis Rodman worked so hard blocking
shots, running up and down the court and doing all the hard work,
including playing sound defense at all times. She loved Rick Mahorn,
who, with Bill Laimbeer, helped the team establish the "Bad Boys" name.
She liked the way James Edwards, the center, would spin around and
shoot a jump shot over the smaller opponents. She would chant, "Spin,
spin. Hit, Jim, hit." And John Salley was a favorite because of his personality and his love for the media, along with his great sense of humor,
and of course, some nice playing as the sixth man on the team.

"Dad, they're not really bad boys in the true sense. They're 'bad
boys' in that they're rough, tough, and very good!" That was her interpretation of the Pistons.

Val, being very style-minded, enjoyed looking at the clothes that Chuck
Daly wore. He was known for his fashionable attire, one of the best-
dressed coaches in the NBA. All in all, she was constantly excited about
the way the Pistons were playing that year. It was routine for her to go
up to her room to watch the game, and then to come running downstairs to the family room and ask: "What do you think, Dad? Are they
going to win?" Then she would sit with me and watch the remainder of
the game. If the Pistons won, she would call her friends to set up a
meeting place where they could go and talk about the game and grab a
little snack. One of their favorite hangouts was Telly's Place, a fine family restaurant in the early evening, and a nice place for young people to
congregate and listen to a favorite piano player as the evening wore on.

This season the Pistons did what Valeri expected them to do: win
the opening round of the play-offs by beating the Chicago Bulls and
their star Michael Jordan, whom Valeri disliked, as he created too many

problems for her beloved Pistons. "I can't *stand* that Michael Jordan, Dad. I know you think he's a great ballplayer, and maybe I respect him, but I still can't stand him."

The final play-offs found the Detroit Pistons playing against the Los Angeles Lakers. Each game the Pistons won was an exciting event for Valeri, and a tragedy when they lost. In the end, the Detroit Pistons won the 1988-1989 NBA championship. Finally she could relax. All in all, it was a very exciting season of basketball for Valeri, and it made her life so happy and exciting.

Naturally Valeri and her friends had to go out and celebrate after the championship game was won by the Pistons. They celebrated for two days. Anytime anyone talked about her Pistons or looked at the picture of the Pistons in her room, she would smile and say: "My guys!"

In January 1989 Marietta told Valeri that it would be nice if Valeri expanded her social life by doing some volunteer work at St. John Hospital. Marietta explained, "It's logical, since you're there so often you know what the hospital is all about. You should give a little time helping people. You will be very sympathetic with the patients and you'll understand how they feel. Plus, you will meet and make new friends while doing a good service."

Valeri agreed it was a good idea. She went to the hospital to see Jeannie Sowcrant, who was the coordinator of the volunteer program, and Christine Kokowski, the assistant coordinator. After meeting with them, she came home that evening and said, "Gee, they're such wonderful people. I'm going to train for several hours and then I'll be given an assignment. There's so much amiability being passed on in that department. I will be very happy to be a part of it."

Following her training, Christine Kokowski gave Valeri the assignment to volunteer her time on two different days each week, for a minimum of two hours each day. That was the only requirement. Val was to interview women in the Pediatrics Ward who had just had babies. She was a patient-representative, responsible for talking to the patients on their first day in the hospital, asking them how they were being treated, and if there was anything that they needed. She would keep a record of their comments and help any mother in need. On the second day, Valeri's assignment was selling snacks from the gift cart, which was a big wagon pushed by another person, while Val went into the patients' rooms to ask if anyone wanted to buy something from the cart. Snacks included candy bars, ice cream and juices, and also small gifts. The wagon would be pushed around between lunch and supper, at which time Valeri and her friend would offer the snacks and gifts to the patients on each floor of the hospital.

Valeri took great pride in her volunteer work. She loved the jacket she bought that had "St. John Volunteer" lettered on a pocket. She enjoyed working with Jeannie, Christine, and the other volunteers affiliated with her assignment.

When Valeri visited the Pediatrics Ward on one of her first days as a volunteer, she met her long-time friend Sue Schucker, who had just given birth to her baby girl, Christina. Valeri hugged and kissed Sue. Val was thrilled for Sue and spent much time visiting her over the next two days. Christina was a lovely little baby.

Valeri felt that both assignments were interesting. On the one hand, it was wonderful being around the new mothers who were excited about having a newborn baby. Seeing the infants was exciting for her. The whole ward gave her an emotional lift. The gift cart was interesting because patients would kid around with her and vice versa. They seemed to enjoy the snacks very much. All in all, she really loved her assignments, and she was very happy doing volunteer work. She made many new friends at the hospital. The two days Val volunteered seemed to fly by for her.

Later in the year, Christine informed Valeri that she was nominated to attend a dinner put on by an organization called "Honor for Helping Patients." Valeri had been nominated on the basis of the excellent work she did volunteering. She was to have lunch with other nominees from throughout the city. Val commented, "I don't know if I deserve something like this. There are so many outstanding people who are volunteer workers at the hospital." But Chris told Valeri that in her opinion, Val had done a commendable job and therefore she was to attend with her and Jeannie. When they got to the banquet, Valeri met some nice people. It was quite an honor for her.

Valeri was able to express her feelings about volunteering in the hospital when she was featured in "Pointer of Interest" in the *Grosse Pointe News*, an outstanding newspaper distributed throughout the five Grosse Pointes. "Pointer of Interest" was a weekly article written by Peggy O'Connor Andrzejczyk, assistant editor-feature editor for the newspaper. Valeri was recommended for this award by either Christine or Jeannie at St. John Hospital.

Peggy interviewed Valeri and then wrote an exceptional article about how difficult it was to come back from a stroke, and also about her volunteer assignments at St. John Hospital. Included in the article were her interests, education, and plans for the future. A picture of Valeri standing with "Get Well" balloons and her gift cards accompanied the article. She had a big smile on her face. The caption read: "Valeri Samaras spends Saturday mornings pushing the gift cart around St. John Hospital and Medical Center as part of her duties as a volunteer." She felt quite honored to receive the recognition in the newspaper. The article about Valeri included the following copy:

*"I'm fully recovered from the stroke now. I just write left-handed, which I learned to do back in the second grade when I broke my arm. It's not a big deal," she says.*

*At first, though, Samaras remembers that she would cry and ask God why she had to suffer. "Then I realized that a lot of other people had it worse than I did and I guess it made me stronger. I know one thing: it made me appreciate the value of visits in the hospital by family and friends," which is why Samaras decided to return to St. John Hospital and Medical Center in February, this time as a volunteer.*

*"I know that when I was in the hospital, all of these people - nurses, doctors, therapists, my family and friends - helped me get through things. I know that I never would have made it without them. Now I want to give some of that back.*

*I volunteer because I think that it's a great opportunity to help someone besides myself. I didn't care too much about things like that when I was younger, but I do now. Plus, I know how important it is when you're a patient to have someone to talk to. Heck, even if all the person wants to do is complain, I'd like to think that I've at least been of assistance to give them a sounding board."*

*Samaras blushes a little when a visitor remarks about her dedication to volunteering. "My first response to volunteering in a hospital was, 'Oh, it'll be a bunch of little old ladies.'" Samaras says, "But it's not. It's a lot of people. Different kinds of people who are so friendly and helpful. And really, volunteering is fun. We laugh a lot here. It's kind of a neat thing when you can help people and enjoy yourself too. I like working with the kids best."*

*She would like to remain a hospital volunteer, even if full-time working hours make that difficult for the petite Grosse Pointe Woods resident. "I really do like the time I spend volunteering. Even if I*

*get a full-time job, I'll probably end up volunteering on Saturdays.*
*I think I'm just meant to be here."*

Valeri deeply appreciated the nice article written by Peggy. She felt privileged to be recommended for the honor by one of her supervisors. Many phone calls came to her congratulating her on the article and her comments. Of course, some of her girlfriends teased her, but she was pleased at the opportunity to receive that kind of recognition in the newspaper that served our large community.

The interesting point that Marietta, Val's relatives, closest friends, and I noted was that Valeri never mentioned being a Thalassemia victim in the newspaper article. She just put that aside and didn't acknowledge the fact that she had the disease. Her only comment to Marietta and me about that was, "Oh, well, people don't want to hear all about my problems. They just wanted to hear about some of the interesting things in my life."

Marietta and I just stared at each other and shrugged: "Well, that's our Val. She just doesn't want to burden others with her problems."

Shortly after the article came out, I was to receive some recognition myself. I made an abrupt decision to retire from full-time teaching at Wayne State University. Originally I had planned to teach for at least another eight to ten years, but I felt that there were other things that I found interesting and perhaps this was a good time to free myself from full-time responsibilities.

A project I had in mind for retirement was one I had discussed with Valeri about a year earlier. I wanted to write a book about Thalassemia, Valeri, some of her experiences, and some research that was going on medically that could be helpful to other victims with the disease. Val was interested in being a part of the project. We talked about it casually from time to time, but I felt perhaps it would be the proper time to start doing some serious planning. I was getting more involved in learning about what was currently available in the world of medicine for Thalassemia victims.

Our social committee in the Division of Health and Physical Education had planned a party for my retirement at Mario's, a restaurant near the university on Third Avenue. I expressed to Marietta and the members of the committee that my desire would be to have a small, intimate party made up mostly of the faculty and staff members in our division, my immediate family, and intimate friends. At first, Marietta wanted to have a party inviting several hundred people, but then she changed her mind and went along with my wishes.

It was a wonderful event, including about fifty to sixty people. Fun was had by all. Several of my close associates and friends stood up and threw some wonderful digs at me. Finally, I had the podium and was able to speak my piece about them. I was then showered with several fine gifts, including a Pistons jacket, which was popular attire for people in our area.

I felt very honored to have a party on my behalf, but the most exciting thing for me was that Marietta, Debbie and Nikki and their families, and Valeri were all there with me. I was very emotional thinking that all three of my daughters were able to see me retire. There were times that I wasn't quite sure what would happen with Valeri, but there she was, enjoying the food, guests, jokes and all.

On our way home from the party, Valeri said, "Thank you Dad, for the nice Pistons jacket you are about to give me!"

We laughed. "Valeri, if you so wish, it is yours," I offered.

"Of course I so wish, Dad. I graciously accept your contribution. Thank you, thank you, thank you!" She wore that jacket often in the following months. It made me feel very good to see how much she loved wearing that Pistons jacket.

# 28

# A Happy Life, Regardless of Health

IT DIDN'T take long for me to adjust my priorities from working as a teaching professor at the university to concentrating on my golf game. (Actually, Marietta and I had been golf addicts for some years.) I was on the golf course finishing a round one day when I walked into the Pro Shop. Jack Clark, our fine golf pro, said, "Mr. Samaras, there's a message from your wife Marietta. She wants you to go straight to St. John Hospital when you leave the golf course. She took Valeri there for an examination. It's not an emergency, so don't get too upset, but she would like you to go there directly."

I thanked Jack for the message and jumped in my car. Regardless of what Marietta had said about it not being an emergency, many serious thoughts went through my head. Any time we had to take Valeri to the Emergency Room, it was something quite urgent. I felt it was time to worry. I thought about how the artery in Valeri's neck had been protruding and contracting more often in recent weeks, which meant she was having heart problems or arrhythmias. Valeri would never acknowledge this, only saying, "Oh, my heart's just skipping a little bit, but I'm okay."

Upon arriving at the hospital, I walked briskly into the emergency waiting room where Marietta was sitting in the corner. I approached her and asked what had happened. She looked at me and began crying. "The doctors think that maybe Valeri is having another stroke." This comment almost knocked my feet from under me.

"Another stroke? What happened? What are her symptoms?"

"She was having numbness on the right side of her body," Marietta explained, "but it didn't seem to be a tremendous amount of numbness, Bob. Val said that it felt a little different than it did the last time and that she just didn't feel comfortable with the numbness." I knew that if Valeri had said it was just a "little numbness," that it was more than that. She wouldn't come to the Emergency Room at St. John Hospital unless it was something that she thought was serious.

Their Emergency Room was always extremely busy, as it served a large portion of the east side of Detroit and the eastern suburbs. This meant that it would be a three- to five-hour wait before Valeri would receive tests and whatever else had to be done. She appreciated the outstanding medical people at the hospital, but she wasn't too keen about spending the hours lying there on a cot waiting for a diagnosis. She also had some very upsetting memories of the Emergency Room from her stroke. So, I felt that if Valeri had requested to come in for an examination, she was worried.

I asked Marietta if I could go in and visit with Valeri. She replied, "I'm sure you can, but you'll have to get permission." Fortunately, our good friend Mario was on duty. He was a patient representative and supervisor in the Emergency Room.

When Mario saw me in the waiting room, he came over to us and said, "I'm sorry to hear about Valeri, but we're doing all we can to check her out." I asked him if I could please see her. He said, "Of course! Come on, follow me."

We went into a room where there were many beds and cots in the multi-complex, and we walked down the hall. I saw Valeri in one of the rooms. I looked at her and asked, "Sweetheart, what's going on? What's happening? How are you doing?"

As she had answered so many times before, with a smile on her face, she replied, "Oh, I'm fine. Don't worry, Dad. I just had this tingling and numbness on the right side of my body again. I thought it would be wise to come to the hospital and get it checked out. Incidentally, I don't have any numbness now. I'm feeling okay."

This certainly sounded good to me, but I was still somewhat skeptical, so I just told her quietly, "We'll be out in the waiting room. Mario and I will let you rest for a while and Mom and I will keep coming in periodically. You know Mario's on duty and he'll take good care of us."

She looked at me, smiled, and said, "I know, Dad. He always does."

After several hours of testing, the doctor called us into the Emergency Room and told us he felt Valeri was okay, but he was a little concerned because of her Thalassemia. He thought she should be admitted into the hospital for a day or two for further tests and observation. He glanced at Valeri as he said that.

She smiled and said, "Oh, well, what are we going to do?" So we set out to have her admitted. By the time that process was completed, Valeri was feeling very good. In fact, she felt so good she joked, "Dad, I think I'll put on my shoes and we'll run to the car and get out of here and go home!"

But we agreed to follow the doctor's orders and let her stay for a day or two for observation and further tests. Up to this point, all tests indicated that she was doing fine.

Marietta and I went home and returned the next morning to find Valeri feeling very well. She said she had been walking around the room and that everything was okay with her. Later that afternoon, we talked to Dr. Carion when he visited Val. He said that it seemed that Valeri was fine. The Emergency Room doctor suspected a Trans Ischemic Attack (TIA). He explained a TIA is a very minor, temporary blockage of a blood vessel in the brain. Usually a TIA tends to clear up by itself. He cautioned: "It's a warning that a patient should be watched and some action must be taken to prevent a major clot in the brain in the near future." He further explained that generally these attacks usually don't last very long and Val should be fine; but he wanted her to stay another day or two for a CT scan and for further observation.

The following day we saw Dr. Benvenuto, who was on duty instead of Dr. Carion. Dr. Benvenuto told us it appeared Valeri was doing quite well, and was rather healthy, but the thing that bothered the doctors was that they didn't know where the slight clot had originated or even if it had been a Trans Ischemic Attack. He felt it would be wise if they administered one or two more tests to find if the clot had come from her heart as a result of excessive skipping or if it had been located elsewhere in her body and later had moved to her brain. He then suggested a test to see if there was any other clotting in the heart area. If there wasn't, then Valeri could go home later that day.

We thanked him and sat back, patiently waiting for Valeri to receive the final test. Following that test, which proved negative, Val was allowed to go home. The only recommendation was that she take an aspirin each day to keep her blood thinner to prevent future clots from forming.

I thought about the report by the cardiologist at Harper Hospital following her stroke three years earlier, when he said that Valeri may have sticky platelets, which meant that from time to time she would have some clotting occur. Dr. Benvenuto did not feel it was sticky platelets, but perhaps just an errant clot caused by arrhythmia that had left the heart and happened to move into the brain. "Fortunately," he said, "everything seems fine and Valeri should be healthy."

Once at home, I couldn't help thinking how scary it was to live with the possibility that Valeri might have another stroke. She had suffered so much through her life, and she had worked so hard to overcome the damage from her terrible stroke, that it just didn't seem fair that there was the potential for Valeri to experience another stroke as a result of her arrhythmias. But, we vowed to follow the doctor's orders and to make sure she took an aspirin each day. We hoped that this would keep Valeri in good condition.

Whenever Valeri underwent a crisis, Marietta and I would feel the effects of the tension from the stress. We never complained; instead, we found activities to help release our tension and permit us to relax. We did this by being very active: playing golf and bridge, working as volunteers for our church, and enjoying family gatherings. Being extroverts, we were able to release a lot of our tension and to cope quite well.

I happened to read an article one day that stated that tension can overwhelm a person, and is probably most significant between four and six o'clock in the morning. It seemed that whenever Valeri had problems, I would awaken between those two hours and feel the pressure. My way to combat this was to get up and do something that was interesting, to take my mind off what was bothering me. Usually this worked.

Honestly, though, no matter what Marietta and I did, we could always feel an internal tension. We learned to cope with it and live with it, but there were times that it was almost unbearable. Often when we retired at night, we would feel very tense. Then, we would hear Valeri in her room, talking and laughing on the telephone. This was a signal to us that everything was fine. We could relax and fall asleep. Valeri's laughter was telling us: "Everything is okay. Don't worry. Go to sleep."

The TIA scare made us all the more determined to find out about the current happenings with Thalassemia locally, nationally, and internationally, to see if there was something new that might help Val. I extracted my notes from previous years, including all of the information concerning doctors and hospitals throughout the country, and began doing a study to see exactly what was available or what I might have overlooked.

It also happened that Dippo called me from Hong Kong to inform me about some of the doctors that he had spoken to around the world. Unfortunately, it still seemed that there was not any significant change in the treatments. However, one thing that drew my interest was Dippo's recommendation that I should confer more extensively with people who were using different methods of aggressive chelation of iron from Thalassemia victims.

I decided to speak to the people at Binson's Medical Supplies in Centerline, Michigan, concerning various types of pumps that were available. A nurse indicated to me that there were several pumps that might be appropriate for Val. I also spoke again to Dr. Grady in New York City about oral chelation and the LI drug with which he was experimenting. He informed me that the experiment was in its infancy, and he didn't know if and when the oral medication would be available. He suggested that I contact the Thalassemia Action Group (T.A.G.) in New York City and keep in contact with their medical personnel to stay abreast of the latest medical actions. I contacted T.A.G., and a representative told me he'd send me a newsletter from time to time. He confirmed that the New York information concerning Thalassemia was current, and he felt that aggressive chelation was very promising.

It happened that Marietta and I had planned a trip to Athens, Greece in June 1989. We would travel with eight other couples to Athens and charter a boat for one week. We would sail to several of the Greek islands, return to Athens for three days, then fly to London for three more days before coming home.

I felt our stay in London would be a great time for me to visit with Dr. Wonke. After all, she presumably was more knowledgeable about chelating older patients than anybody in the world. Valeri and I hadn't had a chance to visit her during the past year, so I would make every effort to contact Dr. Wonke while in London. I was looking forward to discussing the possibility of taking Valeri there so Dr. Wonke could examine her and recommend a chelation regimen for Valeri.

I telephoned Dr. Wonke and made an appointment to see her when I was in London. She seemed very enthusiastic and expressed an interest in meeting me. She promised to spend some time discussing what could be done for Val.

Our trip to Athens and the Greek islands was unusually magnificent, and we had an exciting, wonderful time. Upon arriving in London, my first priority was to call a cab and travel the several miles to the Whittington Hospital, where Dr. Wonke was on the staff. I went to her office and was told by the receptionist that she wasn't in at that time, but would return shortly. I waited over two-and-a-half hours, and Dr. Wonke never showed up for our appointment. It was a big disappointment for me, as I really wanted to discuss Thalassemia and all the intricacies of the disease with her.

I returned to the hotel by cab, and sadly informed Marietta that I never met with Dr. Wonke. She was disappointed as well. I worried, as Valeri was also going to be disappointed that I hadn't conferred with Dr. Wonke in person.

I had called Valeri twice during our trip, as we constantly wondered how she was doing. Each time I called, Valeri said: "Hey Dad, I'm great! Hope you guys keep having a good time. See you later. Make sure you visit Dr. Wonke. Gotta go!"

I was awakened early the next morning by the phone ringing. When I picked up the receiver, I found it was Dr. Wonke. She quickly apologized for having missed our appointment, explaining that she had had an emergency to deal with. She felt badly that we hadn't been able to get together, but asked: "What are some of the things you'd like to talk about?" I began asking her questions concerning the chelation methods she was using. She did talk some about the method, but actually gave me very limited information. The brief phone conversation didn't accomplish what a personal conference would have. She suggested that when we returned to the states I talk to Val's doctor about securing a larger pump and having her on the pump twenty-four hours each day. Her last advice was: "Stay on the pump until the iron count is down to twelve hundred or so," and she suggested that if there was a doctor anywhere in the United States who knew more about chelating, to fly Valeri to him and then let him put her on the aggressive regimen. Finally, she offered that if I so wished, I could bring Valeri back to her and she would personally take care of her.

The following day we boarded the airplane for the flight home. Although our stay in London was extremely interesting, with so many sights to see and places to visit, I felt a void - as the conference with Dr. Wonke had never materialized.

After arriving home, I spent much time looking into the idea of the new pump and searching for a doctor who might be able to begin the regimen for Valeri. I also called Dr. Carion and asked if he could meet with us. Maybe it was time we used a more aggressive treatment to chelate the iron from Valeri's body.

Val, incidentally, wasn't too happy with the idea of wearing a pump twenty-four hours a day. For her, there were too many uncertainties surrounding aggressive chelation, and she was not anxious about taking on such a new project. Valeri wanted more information from a doctor who could authenticate this new medical technique. Would it actually be effective in chelating the iron from her system?

In conferring with Dr. Carion, we again decided the best thing for Valeri would be to stay with her small pump, and to increase the dosage of Desferal from five days to six days. He would closely monitor her to see if the increased dosage chelated iron more extensively or not. If not, we would once again consider switching to the larger pump.

It was late August and Grosse Pointe North High School was about to begin another school year. Valeri received a telephone call from John Monahan, who said, "Valeri, I want to apologize, but I won't be able to work with you on the yearbook this year. I have some new teaching assignments added to my schedule, so I won't have the extra time to work on a project such as the school yearbook." Needless to say, Valeri was disappointed that John wasn't going to be able to work with her that year. He was a knowledgeable worker and they had made a good team.

Val took stock of the situation and vowed: "You know what? I'll do the yearbook. I'll work hard to make it one of the best ever." The more she thought about the assignment, the more confident she felt that she could do a good job by herself. Dr. Kastran also offered Val the opportunity to teach the debate class, which she accepted. Unfortunately, the debate class was canceled as not enough students signed up for the course.

Valeri set her sights on working hard on the yearbook and fulfilling the obligation of upholding the tradition of excellence, as she had in the past. Valeri called an organizational meeting. Once again, over thirty students attended the meeting and all of them expressed an interest in working on the project. Val smiled to herself as she knew that in a short time, when the students realized the responsibility and work that was involved, many of them would lose interest and drop off of the staff. Valeri called daily meetings for some time, to establish the foundation for the yearbook. After several meetings, she noted that only a dozen students remained; however, they were a good group and anxious to begin with their assignments.

Valeri introduced the theme for the 1990 yearbook. It was to be "Seize the Day," the slogan cited by actor Robin Williams in the movie *The Dead Poets' Society*. This statement had made a tremendous impression on Valeri. She felt she could use that quote and accompany it with a picture of the four Marines who were planting our flag into the ground on Iwo Jima during World War II. Her plan was to depict four students posting the flag, instead of the actual photo of the Marines. The students thought it was a marvelous idea, which pleased Valeri.

"Seize the Day," she said to Marietta and me. "I love the idea. I loved that part of the movie. It's quite a dynamic quote to me. I think we humans should 'seize the day' and make the most of it."

Valeri and her staff began working diligently on the yearbook. Val would attend school several days a week, after two o'clock in the afternoon, and stay until seven or eight in the evening. She enjoyed the school setting as much as she had in the past. The office workers, teachers, and department head Bob Reimer gave her wonderful cooperation.

One of the secretaries on staff, Linda Schade, saw Marietta and me at a Gowanie Golf Club function. She said, "We love having Valeri come around every day because she's like a fashion model. She's always wearing something cool and attractive. She's an absolute doll. And, with her infectious laugh, she builds enthusiasm during the latter part of the school day." Her comments made Marietta and me feel very good, knowing that Valeri was so well appreciated at the school by her co-workers.

With the school year well on its way and the yearbook progressing nicely, Marietta and I felt that Valeri was putting too much emphasis on work and not enough on play. We thought she might need more exercise to keep her mind off the hard mental work she was doing at the high school. Valeri came up with an idea. "Mom and Dad, I have a suggestion. Since you are concerned that I should exercise more, why don't I join Vic Tanny?" Vic Tanny was a health spa in our neighborhood. With the cold weather just around the corner, we agreed that it might be a very good idea for all of us. Then we could go together, to enjoy the benefits of an exercise program.

Marietta answered, "That's a great idea, Valeri. We can all join." Val thought this would be much fun, exercising some evenings with her parents, at other times on her own, and yet other times with her friends. The next day, we enrolled on the special family plan.

Although Valeri enjoyed sports and liked being active physically (she did a considerable amount of swimming), she couldn't take part in the most strenuous activities. It was difficult for her to run or move fast over long periods of time. Basically, Val had to be very careful not to aggravate her heart condition. Therefore, joining Vic Tanny was a good choice on her part, as she could exercise within her capabilities and still take part in a total exercising program.

We would go to Vic Tanny's at least once or twice a week in the evenings. I would go through my regular exercise of running two to three miles, and then work out on the weights. Meanwhile, Valeri and Marietta would work on the weights and then take part in water aerobics. Val loved the water, and so did Marietta. They would get into the pool with an instructor and would go through the exercise movements to music with the rest of the class.

There was one piece of exercise equipment that Valeri very much enjoyed, one that I always had to warn her about not doing too vigorously. That was the rowing machine. She loved to set the visual monitor for three minutes. The monitor would display her boat's movements in relation to another boat to see if she could match speed and distance during a specific period of time. It was a very vigorous exercise, but she loved doing it. I suggested that she not use it at all, as it was too strenuous for her heart. But she would say, "Oh, Dad, this is so much fun! I just love it! I love to beat that other boat!" After our workout, we would enjoy some refreshments at the club, and then go home in a happy mood, ready to watch our favorite TV programs.

Another happy occasion for Valeri was serving as a "starter" for the Men's Assumption League (MAL) Golf Tournament in early September. It was a fun tournament that had been initiated by John Kastran, John Kopotas, Jim and Dino Skuras, and me approximately thirty years earlier. The idea was to bring the guys together for an enjoyable and inexpensive tournament that any one of us might win, as compared to some of the other "classy" tournaments which attracted the better golfers. The tournament was held at the Maple Lanes Golf Course in Warren, Michigan and attracted over a hundred golfers. It would begin early in the morning and last until late in the evening.

Valeri and René were the starters for the tournament this year. It was always difficult to find someone to act as starters, organizing the players and sending them off at their assigned times, taking pictures of each group, and to collecting the fees. When Val and René finished their starting chores, they were to bring the money to me; I would be somewhere on the golf course. We were very fortunate that they offered their services, as it seemed all the male friends we had were playing in the tournament, while most of their wives elected to play golf at other courses on that day.

When all their work was done and the money collected, Valeri and René took a golf cart and set out to find me in order to give me the total number of men playing and the money they had collected. When they found me on the fifteenth hole, Valeri jumped out of the cart and announced, "Gosh, Dad, that was so much fun! I love doing this. It was great! Everything worked out very well. René took pictures of all the guys and wrote down their names. We told the chef how many people were playing. Everything is taken care of and here is the money." Both Valeri and René were smiling.

Valeri had such a good time that she would serve as starter again the following year with her sister Nikki. One day I asked Valeri what she enjoyed about serving as a starter for the M.A.L. She replied, "Dad, they're the nicest and most fun guys a person could meet. I love being around them."

With winter ready to begin, another big event was starting to unfold in Valeri's life. Her godsister and loving friend, Rena, was expecting to give birth to her baby in early March. It happened that Mark, Rena's husband, was working as a sales representative for a paint removal company. His job took him out of town quite often. Rena would be very lonesome when Mark would leave town, so Valeri would go over to her home and spend many evenings there. On occasion, Val would stay overnight to keep Rena company. It made Rena feel very comfortable.

One evening, as Rena was lying on the bed getting ready to go to sleep, she said, "Oh, look Val, the baby is moving!" It was the first time that Rena had noticed the movements of the baby.

Valeri quickly put her hand on Rena's stomach and felt it. She looked at Rena and exclaimed, "Rena, we're going to have a baby!" Both of them hugged each other and cried, "It's really happening."

Rena looked at Val and told her, "Valeri, I want you to be the godmother of my baby." There were tears in Valeri's eyes. "Thank you, Rena. I think that is a wonderful honor. It fits in perfectly, considering our long and loving friendship." They both cried a little longer and then went to sleep.

Valeri told us about the incident the following day. She was thrilled and honored to be selected as the godmother for Rena and Mark's first child.

Valeri was quite content during the winter of 1990. She was very busy working on Grosse Pointe North High School's yearbook; Rena was expecting her baby in a few short months; and there were many family functions, such as birthdays and holiday celebrations. Valeri's social life always centered around her family: her sisters' families, her grandmother Ianthie, Aunt Toni and her daughter Andrea, as well as her cousins. Also important to Val were Steve and Sue Schucker and their daughter Christine, with whom she would visit almost each week; and, of course, Rena, whom she would see several times a week.

Val also began developing new friendships with several other single girls from our church. She had much in common with these young ladies, and they all enjoyed spending time together at the various social functions. This new circle of friends included: Harriet Stoukas, who was very active in our church's Philoptochos Organization, a group of women dedicated to helping needy children throughout the world; Roula Tsaparalis, a CPA; Barbara Saros, a real estate and financial planning businesswoman; Angie Rothis, Val's friend from the University of Michigan; Georgia Katsaros; Jill Haley, a high school classmate who was currently working and living in Hillsdale, Michigan; and others. Val enjoyed her new group of friends.

Of course, Chris Garkinos would call her weekly from San Francisco to keep her updated on what was happening in that part of the country. Valeri also kept in touch with the young basketball players from our church, both at church and by watching them play their games during the basketball season. All in all, Valeri was very happy with her social life.

The yearbook was progressing nicely, but it had become very difficult for Valeri - as once again, the yearbook staff had dwindled to only five or six faithful workers. The Christmas holidays had come and gone. The New Year was well under way, and Valeri's primary concern was to meet the early February deadline. The book materials had to be completed at that time if it was to be printed and sent back to the school for distribution in early June. She spent many grueling hours with her five or six students, striving to meet that deadline. Marietta and I even helped out a few times when some typing or name corrections had to be made, or if work was needed on the index. Val and her crew finished the night before the deadline. All of the materials were set for the yearbook company. She gave a deep sigh of relief and announced: "It's all done, Mom and Dad. I can't wait to see it in book form in June."

"We can't wait either, sweetheart," Marietta replied. "We're sure it's going to be an outstanding yearbook."

With the pressures of that project off her shoulders, it seemed that Valeri was in a complete state of relaxation and appeared to be quite happy. She assumed a laid-back attitude, and she enjoyed her volunteer work at the hospital and her social life. She was sleeping more soundly and seemed much more at ease in everything she accomplished. The next big event would be the birth of Rena's baby, which was due in a month.

But, as had happened so often before, when everything was moving along smoothly for Valeri, another health problem appeared. It was a Friday morning in February. Marietta and I had Joanne, our cleaning woman for several years, come to our home every other Friday morning. Marietta found it very difficult to keep up with the household chores, in addition to her teaching responsibilities. So, having the additional help relieved her of these tasks. Joanne did wonders around our home and was a most enjoyable person. Whenever Joanne would show up to clean the house on Friday mornings, Marietta, Val, and I would go out for breakfast and do other things that would keep us out of Joanne's way until she had completed her work.

This Friday morning we went to the Big Boy Restaurant to eat breakfast, as well as to see our daughter Debbie, who was working there. After we had eaten, Marietta and Valeri decided they wanted to shop at Dayton-Hudson's at the Eastland Center. I was agreeable with the plan, because while they shopped, I would stroll around the mall to look at things that interested me.

So we went to the mall. Upon entering Hudson's, Marietta directed: "We'll meet at the Eight Mile door where we always meet in forty-five minutes to one hour." With that in mind, Val and Marietta went their way and I went mine.

When I returned some forty-five minutes later, I saw Valeri sitting in a chair with Marietta next to her looking worried. "What happened?" I asked.

"Oh, nothing, Dad."

But Marietta explained, "Valeri suddenly became light-headed and felt she was going to faint, so she sat down for awhile until she felt a little better. I think we'd better take her to see Dr. Carion." I agreed.

Valeri, although claiming to be feeling very good, consented. "Okay, I'll go to see the doctor to make you two feel better."

On the way to see Dr. Carion, I thought to myself: "What does this mean? Another TIA? Or is it something to do with her heart?" At the doctor's office, we explained to the receptionist what had happened. She told us that Dr. Carion was going on a skiing trip, but that Dr. Benvenuto was there. Since he knew all about Valeri, he could check her out.

Marietta and I waited in the reception room while Valeri went in to see Dr. Benvenuto. He ran some tests, the first of which was an electrocardiogram to find out how her heart was functioning. I had noticed in the last couple of days that the little artery in Val's neck visibly expanded and contracted to each heart beat. I knew this meant that her heart was skipping excessively. That didn't necessarily mean that it was something serious.

After the tests were completed, Val came out to the reception room and told us, "Mom and Dad, Dr. Benvenuto said that the electrocardiogram results are fine and that I can go home. If there are any recurrences or I have any other symptoms, I should go to the Emergency Room."

Dr. Benvenuto came out to talk to us briefly. "Valeri's all right, but let's watch her for a few days." He also told us he was ordering a Holter Monitor for her. The Holter Monitor was a machine in a small plastic case about the size of a small tape recorder which, when attached to a patient, would monitor the heart beat for twenty-four hours. This would give a good overall reading on how her heart was functioning. He took Valeri back into his office, connected the monitor, and placed it in the case, which he strapped around Valeri's waist.

Soon Valeri came out again and said: "I'm all set to go home with my new little friend."

Valeri was supposed to resume her normal activities, as the monitor would record her heart beat for the twenty-four hour period. She followed the doctor's directions. She went out to supper with us, drove her car around, visited friends, and went out for the evening. The next day we took her back to see Dr. Benvenuto. He removed the monitor and said he'd call us concerning the results the following day. By now, Valeri was feeling like her old self.

The next day the test results came in. Dr. Benvenuto called to discuss them with us. "As you know," he began, "Valeri's heart is somewhat different than a normal heart. It appears that it was beating regularly and was functioning about the same as before. I don't know why she experienced the dizziness and I don't think it was anything like a TIA, but watch her for the next several days and make sure that no other symptoms appear. If they do, take her immediately to emergency."

With this new and scary incident, Marietta and I began worrying again. "Is she all right?" We wondered. "Is the monitor accurate? What does this all mean?" Dr. Benvenuto seemed to be a little concerned when he had spoken to us.

After a few days our worries subsided, as Val seemed to be acting much like her old self and was doing very well again. She had a transfusion shortly after that, and this made her feel very good. (Even when Val said she felt very good, she still had various pains and her heart would skip from time to time; she just didn't pay too much attention to either and carried on in her usual style.)

Valeri was most concerned about the approaching birth of Rena's baby. Although Rena's doctor had told her that she would probably have a normal delivery, he had some concerns that Rena might encounter some difficulty. This would necessitate that he perform a Caesarean section. This upset Rena, since she had never had any physical problems in her life.

Valeri spent much time talking to Rena on the phone and visiting her. She tried to encourage Rena about the upcoming delivery, which was scheduled to take place shortly. At least Rena was happy in one sense, because her husband, Mark, had quit the job that kept him traveling often and had a new job which allowed him to be at home with Rena.

After several days, Rena's doctor told her that if she didn't deliver the baby within three more days, she would have to go into the hospital for a Caesarean section. Three days later, Rena went to Bon Secours, as the baby obviously was not going to be born through the natural process. Val went to the hospital to spend time with her the evening before the surgery, which was scheduled for the next morning. Val assured Rena that she would be there before Rena went into the operating room, and that she also would stay through the day after the operation. This made Rena very happy. She said she wanted Valeri there along with Mark and Rena's mother, Ann.

The next morning Valeri went to the hospital as she had promised. Rena hugged her mother, Valeri, and Mark. "I'm off! See you shortly with my new baby!" A short time later the doctor came into the waiting room and announced to Mark that Rena had a baby girl. He said Rena was doing well, as was their beautiful baby.

All three wanted to see both Rena and the baby. He said the baby would be brought to the nursery in a short time, and that Rena was still in the recovery room. No one could visit her at that time.

Soon a nurse came and said, "Hey, you three, come on over and see the beautiful baby girl!" So they went to the nursery and peeked in the window. There was this lovely little baby with a head full of dark hair. She looked much like the Skuras family, and much like Rena. Valeri kidded Mark: "Sorry, Mark, but you can tell that's Rena's baby." Then she laughed and added, "You know, she does sort of look like you, too!"

Finally, Rena was brought back to her room. She, her mother and Valeri were happy and talking all at once as Mark watched. They would talk and cry and then laugh; it was a very happy scene. I arrived at the hospital a short time later to visit Rena and the baby. I was also worried about Val, as I knew that she hadn't been feeling up to par the day before and earlier that morning. Although Val didn't say anything, I could see the artery in her neck moving in and out, which indicated that her heart was skipping to quite a degree, and she probably wasn't feeling well.

Rena announced: "My baby's name is Andrea. I would love to see Andrea with Val and my mom."

Val told her, "You don't have to go and see her. A nurse will bring Andrea to your room shortly, and then you and everyone else can hold her." Rena seemed very happy with the arrangement. In a little while the baby was brought into the room and everybody took turns holding her. Rena was so happy. Valeri, Rena and her mother all looked at little Andrea and were extremely elated.

Soon it was time for us to go. I walked Val to her car. "Valeri, you're not feeling very well are you?"

"Oh, Dad, I wish you would get off my back. I'm feeling fine. I'm only a little tired, but I'm going to be fine."

"Well, you go ahead and I'll drive behind you, as I'm going home, too."

"Please don't worry about me so much. That disturbs me more than anything else. I have been here since early this morning and am a little tired, but I'm still feeling fine. I promise you, Dad, I will be very careful driving home."

Nonetheless, I repeated, "I will drive behind you anyway as I am going that way. Don't worry Val. I'm just being a parent. Please forgive me for that."

Valeri laughed. "I know, Dad. I understand."

Valeri spent many hours the following week visiting Rena, taking care of the baby, and helping Rena with other duties. The doctor had ordered Rena to stay in the hospital for a week to give her time to recuperate from the surgery. She would need this time to regain her strength.

Valeri, Rena, and Andrea got along very well during the next seven days. Rena remarked, "Remember, Val, the night you said `we're gonna have a baby'? It happened, and I'm very happy." Mark was totally elated, too, and he would come in several times each day to see Rena and his little Andrea. He seemed to be more and more happy each time he saw his lovely little daughter.

Valeri noticed that Rena was depressed from time to time. She mentioned this to Marietta and me. "Do you think it's normal for her to be so depressed at times, Mom and Dad?"

Marietta answered, "Yes, it's post-birth blues, a condition which often occurs in young mothers, Valeri." Val seemed very much concerned.

Rena's brother Billy visited her, and he was happy to see his little niece, Val told us. Rena's father Jim was in Florida working at this time and would call every night to see how Rena and the baby were progressing.

After Rena went home following her hospital stay, she began having some depression problems. When Marietta and I visited her at home, she confided to us that she couldn't get over the depression that she had concerning the operation. The real happiness, however, was her lovely little baby, but she just couldn't help herself. She said she was grateful that her mom was there to help her, and also that Valeri would talk to her often by telephone, and was always visiting and listened to her talk about her depression.

Rena's doctor told her that she would be fine soon and not to become too concerned about the depression. Instead, Rena should continue to take care of Andrea. In the next few weeks, Val continued to help Rena with the baby and listened to Rena, talking to her and encouraging her. It was a difficult several weeks for Rena, Mark, Ann, and Valeri too. Rena did seem to be very depressed. It was difficult for her to overcome these feelings. Gradually, though, her depression subsided, and she began to take control of her life once again. The support Rena received from her family and friends was truly helpful for her during this difficult time. Rena repeated on many occasions that it had meant so much to have Valeri there with her most of the day for so many weeks, helping her with housework and caring for the baby. She expressed her gratitude often. She said, "Valeri was like a second mother to Andrea. She almost got to know Valeri better than she did me."

Valeri was pleased about the wonderful relationship she had developed with Andrea. She loved her so much and loved helping care for her. Val couldn't wait for the baptism, which was to take place in a few months. (Children are not baptized in our religion until they are several months old, as opposed to many other religions that dictate parents baptize their children very soon after birth.)

Marietta and I still worried about Valeri, as she just didn't seem to be feeling as well as she had in the past. We wondered whether this was something that could be very serious or whether it would pass quickly. Valeri's happy attitude, as usual, made us feel better. However, our concerns remained.

# 29

# *More Happy Events*

I WAS quite concerned with Valeri's arrhythmia. It seemed to me she was having more difficulties than in the past. I suggested that the next time she scheduled her six-week check-up with Dr. Carion that she have another electrocardiogram. She did, and after the test, Dr. Carion concluded that her heart was as before: in fairly good condition. She seemed to be doing quite well and should not be too concerned about the arrhythmia. He suggested that she not get too excited about anything, and that she obtain sufficient rest.

Val followed Dr. Carion's suggestion and made sure she got plenty of rest. One of the things she did to help herself relax was to request a copy of chronological scriptures that should be read daily from the Bible from Father Kavadas. After Father Kavadas gave her the requested passages, I suggested that she also buy a personal Bible. After purchasing a beautiful Bible, Val told me, "Dad, I'm going to read the Bible every night. I feel this would be a good way for me to learn more about religion and spiritual life. Also, when I read the Bible, I find it to be very relaxing and satisfying." She followed through with her plan, and every night before turning out her light to go to sleep, she read the passages that were suggested for the day. Often, I would go to her room where we would sit and discuss the passages that she had read.

Over the next few months several exciting events occurred for Valeri. She did her best to remember that Dr. Carion had cautioned her about becoming excessively anxious and stressed. The first of these events involved the Detroit Pistons pursuing another National Basketball Association Championship. As an ardent fan, she still enjoyed the routine ups and downs of the season. After winning the regular season title, the Pistons prepared for the play-offs. Although Val only attended one or two games with me this year, she watched most of them on TV, either at home or out with her friends. As the play-offs were about to begin, Valeri asked, "Dad, I want my boys to win their second NBA title in two years. I think they can do it, do you?" She always seemed to value my opinion about the team's ability. It made me feel good that she had such high regard and respect for my coaching experience, knowledge, and predictions. I would answer truthfully, of course. In my estimation, the Pistons were going to win the NBA championship again, because they were an outstanding team. She responded, "Of course they are, Dad. I know my boys Isiah, Dumars, Rodman, Laimbeer, Edwards, and Salley are going to come through."

The play-offs started, and again Valeri watched almost every minute of every game. As usual, she would start watching the game in her room, and then not too far into the contest, she would come running downstairs to continue watching it with me in the family room. "Did you see that call, Dad? Those refs are giving us a hard time! I don't know, it just seems like the boys are not functioning well tonight. What do you think?"

The way I analyzed the team for the year was that the players were highly skilled and excellent shooters. They played well as a result of good team chemistry. I was very positive and kept telling her, "Valeri, they're going to win. They might get kicked around a bit once in a while, but they're going to win it all!"

The Pistons did win the first series easily, but the second series of play-offs was a little tougher, as they played their old adversary, the Chicago Bulls. Val chanted her familiar war cry: "Boy I hate that Michael 'Air' Jordan, Dad. I respect his abilities, but I just hate what he tries to do to my Pistons."

"Don't worry, honey," I would reassure her, "the Pistons are going to overcome Michael and his team. They are just too good for the Chicago Bulls."

Sometimes she would ask, "What kind of defense are they using now, Dad? How are they going to stop Michael Jordan *this* time? What are they going to do now that we are in the late stages of the game with only a couple points difference?"

"Don't worry, Val, Chuck Daly's got the answer. He'll come up with something. They'll stop the Bulls cold and win this game."

If a game would end in victory for her team, she and I would jump in the car and race to Friendly's Ice Cream Parlor. Val would have a double chocolate sundae with sprinkles, her favorite dessert. "Boy, was that a great game! My team really came through, didn't they, Dad?"

The final game that the Pistons won for the NBA championship against the Western Division champion Portland, was a close one. I could hear Valeri up in her room during the first half, yelling: "Yes!!" every time the Pistons made a good play and would score. When she finally came down in the last half, so we could finish watching the game together, I noticed that light in her eye when the Pistons held the ball and the clock ran out, ending the game. Her Pistons were once again the NBA Champions! She was so proud of the team and very happy. She said, "Dad, no sundae tonight. I'm going out with my friends to really celebrate; and, probably tomorrow and the next two days, because our boys have brought home another championship." It was a gratifying feeling for me, an old basketball coach, that the Pistons had won another title and could make my Valeri so happy.

In early June the yearbooks arrived at the high school to be distributed to the students. Valeri brought a copy home and showed it to Marietta and me, and to her sisters. It was an outstanding yearbook. I marveled that its theme "Seize the Day" tied in beautifully with the picture of the four high school students posting the American flag next to the Grosse Pointe North High School sign. The theme and pictures were inspiring. I experienced many happy emotions as I paged through it.

Another feature that we found unique was that in the section of individual student photos by class, large action photos of students were added for variety. This layout design made each page more interesting. Each picture emphasized the theme "Seize the Day." Also, clever captions were inserted under the pictures. Marietta and I just loved looking through that book and were so proud that Valeri and her staff had produced such a fine product. Val was proud of the book too, especially since the administrators, teachers, and students liked it so much.

Chris Garkinos had a surprise for Valeri; he had purchased two tickets to see Madonna in concert, and he wanted Val to accompany him. She was really excited about the trip to San Francisco and appreciated Chris' thoughtfulness. Although not an ardent fan of Madonna's, Val respected the positive things that Madonna had accomplished through the years, and he thought Madonna was a great performer.

It would be a thrill for Val to see Madonna in person, especially her latest extravaganza that would premier in San Francisco. Val enthusiastically raced to the travel agency to buy her airplane tickets and flew out to see Chris a week later.

They attended Madonna's performance, and Valeri called us later that night. She was so ecstatic about "the greatest performance I've ever seen," as she described it. She told us that the choreography for the dancing was outstanding, the costumes spectacular, and the cast, unbeatable. She had a marvelous time in San Francisco with Chris and came home extremely happy.

Overall, Valeri's health remained quite good during the summer, with one exception: when she attended Susie Katsonis' high school graduation party at our church. After eating, Val complained of a severe headache and asked if I would please take her home, which was only five minutes away. When we arrived home, she noted: "You know, Dad, I had a severe headache, much like this one, when I had my stroke. My vision became blurry. I am afraid that maybe something similar is about to happen."

I helped her up to her room, made her comfortable, and said, "I'm going to stay with you, Valeri. If you don't feel better shortly, we'll go to the hospital." Her stomach was also upset.

A short while later, Valeri felt better. "I'm feeling very good now, Dad," she said. Whatever it was, it had passed.

Of course, we watched Valeri for the next couple of days, and called Dr. Carion. He gave us his stock answer: "If there is any kind of change, take her to the hospital Emergency Room immediately."

That summer, several of Valeri's friends were planning a trip to Greece; Valeri never felt like going. Instead she chose to take a trip to Chicago with her new friends: Harriet Stoukas, Roula Tsaparalis, Georgia Katsaros, and Barbara Saros. Val enjoyed travelling with them very much, and even went to Toronto with them later in the year.

Valeri confided to me that although she loved Greece and had a deep passion to visit there again, her first priority was to save money to visit Australia the following year. She'd been extremely interested in the "down-under" country and had been wanting to visit there for several years.

Another fun excursion was to Cedar Point Amusement Park in Sandusky, Ohio, with Debbie, Brian and their children. Debbie still couldn't believe how Valeri tried every exciting, frightening ride available. Valeri walked everywhere with them, never indicating that she was tired. Even when others were ready to sit down and rest, Val continued looking for more rides.

The baptism of Rena's baby, Andrea, was fast approaching. Val and Johnny Kalyvas were going to be the godparents. Rena and Val talked over the telephone almost every evening, planning the event. Rena was feeling well now, and she was extremely excited to have Johnny and Val baptize little Andrea. Val spent several days shopping for the traditional white gown and accessories that Andrea would wear after the baptism.

She also bought Andrea a little gold cross necklace, and with the impending cold weather, a snowsuit, as well.

The baptism took place at Assumption Church, again with Father Kavadas presiding. Father Makrinos assisted. As usual, I was the designated photographer. The baptism service was beautiful. John and Val took turns holding Andrea. After Father baptized Andrea by immersing her in the baptismal tub, Valeri and Marietta took Andrea to the back room to dress her in preparation for the final prayers.

After the service, a dinner was held at the King's Mill Restaurant. Needless to say, everything was first class. Enthusiastic conversations took place among the guests. I noticed the happiness that exuded from Valeri's face each time she picked up the baby, especially when people would refer to her as "godmother." Now Valeri had one of each: a godson, Brian, and a goddaughter, Andrea.

When Valeri recounted that day later, it was as one of the happiest that she could remember in a long time. Only one thing marred her memory. "Dad, I feel bad that Bill, Rena's brother, didn't come to the baptism." (Bill was an alcoholic and had also been taking drugs at that time.) "You know, Billy has always been a good friend of mine. I love him and I think he's a wonderful person, but he's had some severe problems in recent months. It's probably best that he didn't show up, but it's unfortunate that he's gotten himself into such a condition. I wish there was some way I could help him, Dad. I know Rena and Mark have been encouraging him to go through rehabilitation, but he's just not responding at this time. He missed a wonderful occasion, and we all feel badly that he wasn't here to enjoy it." I could tell it really bothered her, as Billy had always been so good to her. Val cherished the memory of the great time that she and Rena had in Arizona with him a couple of short years before.

In spite of the happy affairs that had been going on during the year, there was one underlying cause for unhappiness: Nikki was going to separate from her husband, Abe. Nikki and her five-year-old daughter, Alexandra, would live with Marietta, Valeri, and me. Valeri had spent many, many happy times visiting Nikki and Abe at their home in Bloomfield Hills, riding on their little motor boat and tubing on the water. Unfortunately, after eight years of marriage, Abe had made some bad financial decisions. Abe decided that he should try to get a job in California with a friend, to see if he could begin repaying some of the numerous debts he had incurred. Nikki and Abe decided that it would be best if they separated, and for Nikki to file for divorce in the near future. Nikki was brokenhearted. She enjoyed her marriage for the most part, but realized that their financial status was impossible to resolve. Abe was a nice person, a good husband and father, but it was difficult for Nikki to think of living on the edge of financial disaster year in and year out.

Valeri made the decision to leave her position as school yearbook sponsor at Grosse Pointe North High School. We felt it was a good decision. It would have been another difficult year for Val, trying to supervise the staff while they prepared the book.

Nikki returned home to live indefinitely. She was back working in the medical field as a service representative for nursing homes in our state. Her job was challenging, and she earned an excellent salary. By living with us she could get back on her feet financially. Valeri planned to take care of Alex during the week: getting Alex ready for school and watching her afterwards, until Nikki arrived home from work. If Nikki was on the road, Val would be completely responsible for Alex until she returned. Nikki planned to pay Val to care for Alex. As Alex was five, she was getting ready to begin kindergarten at the Ferry School, the same school that Valeri had attended for one year.

Valeri gave Nikki her beautiful bedroom set, so that she and Alex could sleep in the same room. Val took an older bed that was in another bedroom. Nikki and Alex settled into our home.

Alex, a beautiful and intelligent child, was very upset that her daddy had left town. To make matters even worse, her mother planned to work every day and leave her. In fact, the first day Nikki had to leave for work, Alex got up and began to cry and scream. Valeri ran down from her bedroom as Alex shouted: "Somebody hug me!" which Valeri did.

She hugged and kissed her, calming her down. Valeri reassured Alex: "Your Mom will be back soon. Don't worry. Aunt Valeri's going to take good care of you. You just tell me what you want. I'll be with you all day." This quieted Alex and allowed Nikki to go to work in peace that day.

Alex began school the following week. She was included in the afternoon schedule, which meant that Val drove her to school at 12:30 p.m. and picked her up from school at 3:15 p.m. You could immediately tell that Alex and Val were setting up a very comfortable relationship.

Like many five-year-olds, Alex could be rambunctious and very stubborn. But Valeri had a firm, motherly way about her, and she could get Alex to do the things she wanted her to do very well, even if both would argue from time to time. It was amusing to listen to them argue about getting ready for school. But Valeri always convinced Alex to attend school on time.

It wasn't long before the two of them had a great routine in the morning. They would sleep in, maybe watch TV for a short time, then, after eating a small breakfast, Valeri would drive Alex to the local McDonald's, where they would each eat a children's Happy Meal. Val would then drop Alex off at school, and get her at 3:15 p.m. The next stop was 31 Flavors Ice Cream Parlor, which was owned by Penny, a family friend. They would have their malted milks or sundaes, and then come home and watch TV. Often Val would take Alex shopping, and then they'd come home to wait for Nikki to return from work. By then it was supper time.

Val and Andrea were developing a close bond. There was a great deal of love expressed both ways. Often in the afternoon and evening they would play games, work on projects together, and in general do things that a mother and daughter would normally do. They loved each other's company. It was a happy role for Valeri, too, as she was being so helpful to Nikki, who appreciated it immensely. Often when Valeri would drive to drop or pick up Alex, she would spend time talking to many of the other young mothers involved in the same chauffeuring activity. Valeri was developing some deep friendships with them, as well. The relationship gave Nikki peace of mind that she could go to work and not worry about Alex, as she knew that with Val in charge, everything would be fine.

Occasionally I would help Val take care of Alexandra, by acting as the driver if there were things that Val had to do. Val was still interested in pursuing a full-time job, but at this time she told me: "I'm just going to let that go temporarily."

For Alex, this arrangement was great fun. Not only did she have her mother, grandmother, and grandfather, she also had her wonderful Aunt Valeri to take care of her when mom was gone.

At times it was rather amusing when both Nikki and Valeri were home with Alex, for she would try to play one against the other. If her mom wouldn't let her do what she wanted, she would go to Valeri and pout: "Aunt Valeri, Mom won't let me do that," or vice versa. But of course, Nikki and Valeri were wise to her ploy, and didn't allow her to play that game very often. A most important and key factor in this relationship was the love Alex was receiving from both her mother and from her Aunt Valeri.

There were times in the evening when Nikki and Valeri would go out socially. In fact, if Marietta and I were busy, Nikki, Val, and Alex would eat out together quite often. Occasionally if we were available to take care of Alex, Val and Nikki would go to eat at a local restaurant or to a popular night spot to enjoy an evening out. They seemed to agree on so many things and had many enjoyable discussions about life in general. They found many things to occupy their time. Shopping together with Alex was commonplace for them.

Alex enjoyed riding in Valeri's convertible. Often on their way home from school she would say: "Let's put the top down on your car, Aunt Valeri!" and they'd go riding down the expressway, playing the radio loudly. It was exciting for both of them. They'd often end the fun with a visit to see Rena and Andrea, or Debbie and Brian.

As usual, Valeri always seemed to find a way to turn a bad situation into a happy one. In this case, she was bringing happiness into little Alexandra's life, at a time when she was so unhappy about the divorce of her mother and father, and her father's departure from the state.

Val was planning a trip to New York City for several days with her friends, Harriet and Roula. She had visited New York several times, and she thought going with these girls would be lots of fun. They began planning their trip to "The Big Apple." Even with her life so hectic and fast, Val still spent time in the late evenings doing the things she had in the past, such as watching David Letterman, reading her Bible, and watching other programs until she fell asleep.

# 30

# *Problems Appear*

ONE evening, while watching television with Alexandra and me, Valeri looked up and announced: "Dad, do you realize that in two days it will be Halloween? Of course it's a fun time for children and I always have enjoyed passing out candy, but there's another significant thing about that last day in October. It will mean that I've gotten through October this year without any major health problems." Valeri had previously noted that, for some reason, many of her crises had taken place in either May or October. So we laughed and vowed: "Let's keep our fingers crossed and hope that everything goes well for these next two days."

When I came home the afternoon of October 31st, Valeri was sitting in the family room looking worried. "What's wrong, honey?"

"You won't believe it, Dad. I don't think I've made it through October without being sick. While I was working at my volunteer assignment at the hospital, I suddenly began getting dizzy whenever I stood up or walked. I thought it would pass, but as I continued to work, it became worse. I managed to finish my assignment and went down to see Jeannie, my supervisor. I explained what was happening and she immediately began to worry. She said, 'Valeri, I'd be glad to drive you home. Christine can drive your car home for you.' I told her that wouldn't be necessary, as I felt all right when I was sitting. I only felt dizzy when I got up or began to move around; and besides, we don't live that far away and I should be fine. So I drove home."

I asked Val how she felt at that moment. "Not bad, Dad, but again, when I get up, I feel very dizzy."

I took her pulse, which indicated the usual skipped beats. It was fast and unsteady. "Val, rather than calling Dr. Carion, when your mom comes home we'll go to the Emergency Room. Remember the last time you had a similar problem, Dr. Benvenuto told you to go to emergency and call him from there."

"Tonight's Halloween," Val lamented. "I was looking forward to helping Alexandra go out trick-or-treating in the neighborhood."

"I know, Val," I sympathized, "but we'd better do first things first." Alex looked at us with a concerned look on her face, but she somewhat understood the gravity of the situation, and said nothing.

Valeri looked at me in mock anticipation and said, "Oh, boy, here goes another four hours in the Emergency Room. I guess what has to be done, has to be done, so as soon as Mom comes home, we'll go."

Marietta arrived a short time later. We explained to her what had happened. When Nikki came home from work, Marietta, Val, and I headed for the hospital. As usual, I was very apprehensive about this symptom. Could it be another TIA? Was it her heart? Or was it just a virus infection? I just couldn't help worrying. When I glanced over at Val quietly sitting between us, she looked very concerned, too.

Once Valeri was checked into emergency, she was taken into one of the rooms and the testing began. Blood tests, an x-ray, and an electrocardiogram - all were administered over a short period of time. When we were allowed in the room to see how she was, Val said, "I have a really fine resident doctor, Mom. His name is Dr. John Barletta. He's just a wonderful person, and so attentive! He's almost making this stay here in emergency a pleasure rather than a serious problem."

A few minutes later, Dr. Barletta entered the room and introduced himself. He was a young resident completing his work at St. John Hospital, in preparation to leave for Florida, where he was going to study ophthalmology. Personable and warm, he was genuinely concerned about Val's condition. He allowed us to stay in her room to keep her company while waiting for the test results. A short while later, he came back into the room and said, "Although we don't have all of the results, I did call Dr. Carion. He wants Valeri admitted to the hospital to have several more tests taken over the next couple of days."

Val looked dejected, but agreed: "I guess we'd better follow the doctor's orders, Mom."

Dr. Barletta continued, "I'll make arrangements to get her a room as soon as possible. I do have several other patients I must look after first, but I'll try to expedite the admitting process."

After he left, I went to the nurses' station and asked if I could please speak to Dr. Barletta. I was worried and wanted to ask his opinion concerning Valeri's condition. He quickly came to see me at the desk. He said that Dr. Carion and he were concerned that perhaps Val had had another TIA. They didn't like the idea that her condition wasn't changing and that she would become dizzy whenever she tried to stand up. He said they would know much more after the other tests were completed.

Valeri was admitted that evening. When she was comfortable in her room, Dr. Barletta visited us and talked with Valeri again. He encouraged her: "Keep your chin up, Val. I'm sure everything's going to be satisfactory."

She lamented, "But I didn't have a chance to go out on Halloween night with my little niece or my godchildren."

"Gosh, I'm sorry about that, but we're going to get you well and you'll have other Halloweens that you can go with them."

As he left, Valeri remarked, "Gosh, he sure gives the ideal impression of a dynamic doctor. I think he's just great."

Val underwent several tests for her cardiovascular system over the next two days. She was then given a cardiac test called the ECHO Profile Test. The following morning, Dr. Carion came in and told us, "We thought that Valeri might have had a TIA, and we're still not sure if she did or not, but she's definitely having some problems with her heart. She's only putting out thirty percent of her potential blood output with every heartbeat, and it should be at least sixty percent. So, we're going to move her to the Cardiac Ward under the care of Dr. Graham, a cardiologist. We plan to take steps to increase her heart output and help her get over this particular problem."

"Is this something that Val can overcome without too many complications?" I asked.

"Oh, yes. Once she gets to the Cardiac Ward, the doctors there will really get her back on her feet in a short time. Basically, her heart is still quite strong."

After the doctor left, Valeri commented: "This room up here has been nice. It's a big room. I have it all to myself, and all my friends have found it very comfortable visiting me here. I wonder what it'll be like in cardiology?"

Just as she finished talking, Alex and Nikki entered the room. Alex ran over to Val and hugged her, saying, "I miss you, Aunt Valeri! Hurry up and get out of this hospital!"

"Don't worry, honey. I'm going to be in good condition very soon. Don't you *dare* worry." Val was always concerned that her hospital visits might upset Alex and put an additional emotional strain on her.

That evening Val was transferred to the Cardiac Ward. At St. John the ward is one of the most modernly-equipped in our metropolitan area. Their medical staff is considered to be among the best. The nurse responsible for Valeri set up an IV and all the necessary machines, including the one that monitors the heartbeat and relays it to a screen at the nurses' station. A nurse was always on duty to keep continuous track of all the patients. This reminded me of the time Val was at St. Joseph's Hospital following her tachycardia problem, when she was attending the University of Michigan years before. I walked out to the station and looked at the monitor. I saw that Valeri's heartbeats were excessive, and the lines were very uneven, not following any positive pattern.

Valeri was examined later by Dr. Graham. He was a very outgoing man, who spent many hours in the Cardiac Ward. He explained to us that after Valeri had received some medication and had rested for a couple of days, she should respond nicely and everything would turn out fine for her.

Valeri was under intense surveillance. Dr. Graham would visit her at least twice a day, Dr. Carion would make daily visits, and Dr. Barletta would visit her twice a day as well. Dr. Barletta would explain to Valeri what was happening, and how she was going to be helped by the medication she was receiving. He also suggested that she get out of bed and try to walk several times a day, even though she was feeling a little light-headed. He felt that she should retain strength and flexibility in her muscles, so she wouldn't be too weak when they were ready to release her from the hospital.

Every time I visited her, we would take a walk down the hall. The first day or two she seemed very shaky, and she would hold onto my arm. But after a few days in the Cardiac Ward, Valeri would say, "Come on, Dad. Let's take a walk," and she would walk along very normally. This was an encouraging sign for all of us.

During her hospital stay, Valeri contracted an eye infection. We asked the nurse to please call Dr. Barletta, and when she did, he was there within ten minutes. He examined her, gave her medication, pinched her cheek and chided her: "Hey, kiddo, let's get well so we can send you home. You understand?"

Val looked at him. "Yes, I do. Thank you. I'm going to try very hard."

After eleven days in the hospital, Valeri was feeling much, much better. All the tests were completed and Dr. Carion indicated to us during a conference that Valeri would be put on Coumadin, a blood thinner to prevent clotting in the arteries in her heart and brain. He also explained that Dr. Graham had been experimenting with the level of Coumadin to prescribe for safe therapy, and he wanted Val to have a blood test in a week to check the Coumadin level. Too high a level would thin the blood too much, which could cause hemorrhaging. If the level was too low, clotting could result. He sat with Valeri several minutes and explained that, in his opinion, she was back to her normal health and she could leave the hospital the next day. He emphasized that Valeri should ease up on her late nights and partying for awhile. They both laughed at his suggestion. He waved good-bye and left the room.

Later that day she was released from the hospital and had a chance to say good-bye to Dr. Barletta. On the way home she reflected, "Mom and Dad, he is the perfect example of the modern doctor . . . and he's very good-looking, too!" We laughed. "He's going to make a very wonderful doctor after he finishes all his schooling. When he becomes an ophthalmologist, I certainly will be one of his first patients!"

Valeri didn't need a transfusion while in the hospital. She was scheduled to go in for her blood test in two weeks. Her appointment with Dr. Carion the following week indicated that the level of Coumadin in her blood was perfect. He felt that with her heart medication, Lanoxin, plus the other medication she was taking, her condition would remain stabilized and she should regain her health. Valeri admitted that she was feeling relatively good, but tired. This weariness would probably be alleviated when she received her transfusion in two weeks.

The next day Marietta came home with a big package under her arm from Jacobson's Department Store. She walked downstairs, where Valeri was helping Alexandra with her reading. "Look what I have for you, Val." Val opened the box and held up a beautiful white coat.

"I know winter is very hard on you," Marietta said, smiling, "especially when you wear your heavy coats. You tire more quickly by carrying the extra weight. This was going to be your Christmas present, but instead, I'm giving it to you early. This is the beautiful light wool, white coat that you liked so much when we walked through Jacobson's before you entered the hospital."

Valeri jumped up, and hugged and kissed her mother. "Thanks, Mom! You're always so great and so, so considerate. I love you very much!"

Alex said, "Gee, I wish I had a nice white coat, too."

Valeri laughed. "Don't worry, you'll have plenty of white coats before long!"

The week of Thanksgiving Valeri went in for her transfusion. As usual, she received wonderful care by one of her favorite nurses, Marianne

Thomas. During the transfusion, Valeri's temperature began to rise. It returned to normal after one pint of blood was administered, so Valeri was given the second pint. (Usually she would receive three pints every transfusion.) Near the end of the second pint, her temperature rose again very rapidly, to well over one hundred degrees. The nurse called the doctor, and was told to stop the transfusion. Two pints of blood was sufficient. The transfusion was stopped and Valeri's temperature returned to normal. Both Marietta and I were very concerned about this situation. Marietta's theory was that the new filter being used, instead of the old system of washing the blood, was the reason, but the doctor disagreed. We took Valeri home after her temperature returned to normal. While somewhat tired, she was feeling much better than she had prior to receiving the transfusion.

A few days later Valeri was feeling much improved and looking forward to Thanksgiving. She never talked much about her difficulties to any of her friends or relatives. Her feeling was: "Never complain, never explain. Don't mention problems and then you don't have to go into long explanations."

We had Thanksgiving dinner at home. Val made her famous cheese pita. Our dinner guests included our family, my mother-in-law Ianthie, sister-in-law Toni and her daughter Andrea. The rest of Marietta's family came for dessert later that evening, along with Rena, Mark, and baby Andrea. Sue and Steve stopped by for a while, with their small daughter Cristina. Jill, who was in town for the holiday, called and stopped by for a while, as well. She told Valeri that she was returning to Detroit early in 1991 to work. She was anxious to come back so they could do many things together, which pleased Valeri. Valeri also talked to Chris on the phone that night to wish him a Happy Thanksgiving.

Over forty guests had visited throughout the day. Val told her mom, after all the guests had left, that it was a very wonderful Thanksgiving Day. "We gorged ourselves with food like little piggies, but it was fun!"

The following week, Valeri had a temperature of 103 and was feeling very weary. She had severe pains in her lower abdominal area, which she guessed indicated a urinary tract infection. When she called Dr. Carion the next day for an appointment, he was not available. Dr. Schwartz, one of the other doctors in that office, suggested that she go to emergency because of the high fever. So, it was back to the Emergency Room with Val for three or four hours of testing and waiting for the diagnosis. The tests indicated that she had a serious virus infection.

The resident doctor on duty telephoned Dr. Carion, and was told to admit Valeri to the hospital. The Emergency Room doctor suspected that it was a possible kidney infection and definitely a lower urinary tract infection. Also, in view of her slightly jaundiced condition, he felt that she might be infected with the hepatitis virus also.

The next day Dr. Carion ordered several follow-up tests in the three areas that the Emergency Room doctors had suggested. Valeri was also put on antibiotics by way of an IV. After several days it was found that Valeri did have a very serious urinary tract infection and a slight kidney infection, but no hepatitis. By now, she was feeling much better and her temperature was back to normal.

A point we brought up with Dr. Carion, when he came to sign the release papers for Valeri, was that we felt perhaps it was time for us to talk with a hematologist and seriously consider a very aggressive chelating therapy. Dr. Carion agreed this would be a good idea, and that we should do this as soon as possible. He suggested a hematologist from Ford Hospital, a friend of his from medical school. He told us he would contact this doctor and ask him to accept Valeri as a patient. Our agreement was that within the next week we would definitely decide what to do about aggressive chelation and find out whether Dr. Carion's hematologist colleague would see Valeri.

When Valeri arrived home the following Sunday, we went to church. After the service I was talking with Dr. Spiro Pappas, a church member and Val's gynecologist. I explained to him what we were planning to do for Valeri. "Isn't it ironic?" he mused. "I want you to meet my friend who is here this morning, Dr. Steven Tapazoglou, a young hematologist and oncologist from Greece. I have sponsored him to come to our country to teach at Wayne State University's Medical School, and also to begin his own practice in both hematology and oncology here in the Detroit area."

Dr. Pappas excused himself and went to find Dr. Tapazoglou on the other side of our church hall. He came back shortly with him. He introduced Dr. Tapazoglou to Marietta, Valeri, and me. Dr. Pappas continued, "My friend is a hematologist. He knows a lot about Cooley's Anemia and its complications."

Dr. Tapazoglou was a kind, soft-spoken person. "I would like to work with you and help with Valeri's aggressive chelation," he told us. He suggested that I make an appointment for Valeri to see him sometime that week.

The following day we made an appointment to see him the upcoming Thursday afternoon. When Val and I arrived for the appointment, Dr. Tapazoglou greeted us cordially: "Come in, Val. I'm going to do some testing. I will take a history of your problems, then follow through from there."

While waiting for Valeri in another room, I pulled out a sheet with several names of the doctors from New York who were involved with Cooley's Anemia whom I had contacted in the past. I also had listed their telephone numbers and a comment regarding my contact with each. I would give this list to Dr. Tapazoglou. He could call any of these doctors and discuss Valeri's case with them for possible treatment.

After the testing was done, Val and I had a consultation with the doctor. He said he would be glad to take Valeri as a patient and do whatever had to be done to give her aggressive chelation. We thanked him for all his help and said we would discuss it at home with Marietta and decide what to do. On our way out, he offered, "If there's anything that you need, please feel free to call me immediately, day or night."

When Valeri, Marietta, and I talked about our consultation with Dr. Tapazoglou, Valeri mentioned that he wanted to know if she had ever had an HIV test. "That's all I need, HIV," she said. There was some frightening news about people who had contracted this virus through transfusions. Family and friends had often asked if Valeri had had an HIV test. Of course, our answer was the same as what the doctors had told us: that we need not worry, because with all the blood testing Valeri had received through the years, it was evident that she did not carry the HIV virus. It was also explained that it was unlikely for a Cooley's Anemia youngster to contract HIV, since only red blood cells are received. HIV is associated with the white blood cells.

"Valeri and Cooley's Anemia youngsters do not receive white blood cells. They receive strictly red blood cells, so the HIV virus is not a threat," I reminded Val and Marietta.

"With all the blood testing that was done years before Valeri received transfusions," reflected Marietta, "I'm positive that the doctors know she never had the HIV virus. It was never indicated at any time." Marietta and I felt comfortable with this.

We decided to wait until after the Christmas holidays before giving serious thought to Dr. Tapazoglou's offer to begin aggressive chelation therapy. He suggested that we keep giving Val the Desferal by way of her little pump and ask Dr. Carion whether she should add a seventh day of chelation to her schedule. We all agreed to add the seventh day, and to take up the issue again after the first of the year.

As Christmas approached, Val became even more involved with her family and friends, especially with Alex. Alex was elated to have Valeri healthy again, and was glad to be going to McDonald's, 31 Flavors, and shopping with Val. Meanwhile, Val was enjoying relationships with the mothers who would wait to pick up their children from kindergarten after school. They'd have their own social gatherings every day. One of the mothers, Ellen Alfonsi, had worked with Val at Sir Speedy several years earlier. She mentioned to Val one day that she was still working part-time there, and said: "Terry and Tony would love to have you come and work one day a week. Saturday would be fine, if it fit your schedule. They still miss you after all this time! We always had so much fun together." Val said, "Maybe I'll take you up on that. Thanks for the offer."

This Christmas was very special, since Alex and Nikki were living with us. They would go shopping with Valeri for Christmas gifts and help with other holiday preparations. When the big day arrived, we arose early and opened our presents. It was a happy time. Alex's enthusiasm was contagious and made us all feel young again. It was good to see her so happy. Once again, we had Christmas dinner at our home with the immediate family. In keeping with tradition, Valeri's friends visited in the evening, and other relatives joined us for dessert and fruit. It was a wonderful Christmas day.

Since all of us were on vacation between Christmas and New Year's Day, we had a great deal of fun being together. Each night Valeri rented a movie video, and Nikki, Marietta, and I would sit down and enjoy it with her. One evening when Nikki and Alex were away visiting Debra, Val asked us to watch a "wonderful film" starring Bette Midler. It was entitled *Beaches*. "No thanks, Val. I've seen Bette Midler before and I'm not impressed with her acting," I answered.

"Dad, I've seen this movie several times before and I know you and Mom will absolutely love it," coaxed Valeri. Since I had other plans for the evening, I still declined, but Marietta agreed to watch the film.

Marietta found it to be an interesting story. It was about a successful career singer, played by Bette Midler, who had a very close friend with a husband and a daughter. This friend was inspirational to the singer, who had no family of her own, and helped her become a more family-oriented person. The friend became ill, and eventually died. This part of the movie was very sad; both Marietta and Valeri cried. In the last scene of the movie, Bette Midler sings the song "Wind Beneath My Wings."

This is a very beautiful song, about the friend whom she thought of as her "hero" because of all the happiness she'd brought into her lonely life. When the song ended, Valeri sobbed to her mother, "Mom, this song is about you. It is exactly you."

Marietta began to cry and answered, "No Valeri, not really. It's really about *you*." They hugged each other and continued crying.

Valeri insisted, "No, Mom, it *is* about you. *You* are my hero. You have given me the opportunity to have a happy life. You have encouraged me to do things. You have always supported me. Mom, that song is about *you*. You are my inspiration, Mom and *you* are the "wind beneath my wings." They cried for several minutes.

When I finally came down into the family room and saw them, I asked, "What's going on with you two?"

Valeri answered, "Nothing, Dad, it was just a sad movie. You know how us women are."

New Year's Eve arrived. Val and Nikki decided to attend Mary Penz's house party together. There would be many people that Valeri knew at the party, including Rena and Mark. Nikki and Val both enjoyed it. After it was all over and everyone had welcomed in 1991, it was time for Val and Nikki to come home. Usually Val would observe: "Hey, it's only three o'clock. Let's go to Greektown!" But this year she just said to Nikki, "I think I'll just be content to go home and take it easy for the rest of the night."

On New Year's Day, Valeri's name day, we were to have our traditional celebration - which Valeri loved because her closest friends and family usually attended this happy and gala event. Valeri had prepared some of her famous lasagna. After a scrumptious meal, the men watched the University of Michigan football team play in the Rose Bowl, and the women socialized by sharing news about their children and grandchildren. The little ones, Alex, Brian, and Andrea, were walking around playing, laughing, screaming, and having a jolly old time.

After all the guests had left, Val hugged us and thanked us for a super name-day party. "It is almost unbelievable that each year the party gets better and better." One person Val missed at the party was Chris Garkinos, who had come home for the holidays but was unable to attend the get-together. He had, however, visited Valeri earlier in the week.

The next day, Valeri was experiencing some pain on the left side of her chest, around the Mediport. I telephoned Dr. Carion's office and was instructed to call his Partridge Medical Center office on Garfield Road in Clinton Township, some twenty miles from our home. I made an appointment for Valeri to see him within the hour. Val and I drove to the center, and on the way she spoke happily of the fun she'd had over the holidays, particularly at her party the day before.

Dr. Carion examined Val's left chest area and took her temperature. He concluded that she had a viral infection. Although the area around the Mediport was sensitive, he felt that there was no infection present. He gave us a prescription for an antibiotic, feeling that the medication should protect Valeri while she was fighting the infection, and she should be better in a few days.

Unfortunately, this did not happen. Valeri's temperature continued to rise and the pain did not subside. We called Dr. Carion's office two days later and he suggested we go to emergency and have Valeri's Mediport checked more thoroughly. When Valeri heard the doctor's suggestion, her reaction was: "Oh, no! Not four-and-a-half hours in emergency again! But, I guess I'd better do it if I want to get rid of this pain."

Once again, we were off to the Emergency Room at St. John Hospital. The routine procedures took place: admission, testing, waiting, and being examined by one doctor after another. While waiting for the test results, Val said, "I can understand the Emergency Room being so busy here, Dad, because it is a very large hospital. It does service the entire east side of Detroit. However, it's very hard at times just lying here, waiting to see what the outcome will be."

I held her hand and agreed. "I know it's difficult waiting and wondering, Val. You should be commended for your patience."

The reports indicated that Val did indeed have a serious Mediport infection. The attending physician felt she should be admitted and that the Mediport should be removed. He phoned Dr. Carion and gave him the message. Dr. Carion then instructed her to be admitted and he would follow-up the next day. Val was admitted and taken to a room approximately an hour later.

The following day Dr. Carion said he talked to Dr. Hawasli, the surgeon who had inserted the Mediport into Valeri a couple years before. Dr. Hawasli examined her later that day and decided to operate the following morning. After he left, Val looked at us and remarked, "Well, here goes another one of those 'little operations.' But, if this helps my chest heal, it will be worthwhile."

The next morning Val was taken to the operating room. Marietta and I waited in her room. Several hours later she was brought back to her bed. She slept for awhile, and when she awoke, she told us some startling news. "You know what? Dr. Hawasli did not remove the Mediport. I was put on the operating table by the nurses. He checked my chest area and said he would not remove it because it is too valuable to me and still very functional."

Marietta and I looked at each other in astonishment. "What does he plan to do?" Val told us Dr. Hawasli would come to see us in a while to explain why he did not operate and what his plan was for her treatment.

About an hour later, Dr. Hawasli came into the room and greeted us. "I know it's a surprise that I didn't remove the Mediport, but I felt that Valeri would need this because of the number of times she has to be infused for transfusions. The Mediport seems to be very functional, so I decided not to operate. Instead, I will treat her with a very powerful antibiotic for the next seven to ten days."

I glanced at Valeri as he said this, and noted her sad expression, and the tears on her cheeks. "Gosh," she lamented, "do I have to stay in this bed for another week to ten days? Isn't there another way?"

Dr. Hawasli shook his head and said, "No, I'm sorry, Valeri, but the antibiotics are the best treatment at this time, and administering it through the IV with you lying in bed for the most part is the best way."

It seemed like a very slow process, as each day Valeri would receive the antibiotic by IV injection, with no other treatment taking place. She was feeling quite well, and wanted to say: "Let's get out of here. I'm feeling okay." But, she was still feeling pain and there was still some swelling.

During the day, Val would watch TV with friends who were visiting. She enjoyed talking with her roommate, an elderly black woman who was having heart problems. The lady's husband would take three buses to get to the hospital to visit her. Val found the couple to be good company, and both seemed more concerned about Valeri than about the woman's own heart condition.

After about her fourth day in the hospital, I greeted Val with something new to think about: "Val, you remember we talked about writing a book together on Thalassemia and some of the things you have suffered through the years, and about some of the new and exciting things Thalassemia patients are looking forward to. Maybe it's time to get serious. Let's make an outline about what we want to write." This announcement seemed to perk her up, and we sat there for over two hours discussing ideas for the contents of the book. We had talked about it before but had never become involved with its planning. For the next two days we outlined what the chapters should include to interest anyone reading such a book. It was a very rough outline, but it included some of the experiences a Thalassemia victim would undergo, and it described events that Valeri encountered that had contributed to the quality of her life.

Dr. Hawasli came into her room one day and announced: "I think the infection is under control now. Valeri is not experiencing any pain. It's time for her to go home." He said that she should spend one more night in the hospital and that we could come tomorrow to get her.

When I went to the hospital the following morning, I took two little bottles of Holy Water with me. (Holy Water is to be given to a person who is in need during an illness. I received it from our priest, Father Kavadas, the previous day. At the conclusion of the special service called Ayismos, the presiding priest of the special liturgy blesses the water to be consumed by people who are ill.) I gave one bottle to Valeri's roommate and explained to her the background of the Holy Water. She and her husband expressed deep appreciation for the gift.

She told me that she was feeling much better herself and would probably be going home in a few days, too. Then she turned to me and said, "That little daughter of yours is the most wonderful person I have met in a long time. She was such great company! I certainly am going to pray for her to get strong again."

Val acknowledged her kind words. "Thank you so much. You've been wonderful and I'm going to pray for you too."

"I want you to call me in a couple of weeks and let me know how you're getting along," she told Valeri.

Val replied, "I certainly will." And she did call her.

Once at home, Val was busy making phone calls and other plans to resume her life. She said in anticipation, "Boy, I really have a big 'social catch-up' to do to make up for the last nine days."

I was pleased by her enthusiasm, but cautioned: "Valeri, I know you're going to be active, but I've been busy the last few days, too. I've been trying to make plans to get you ready for some very aggressive chelation to get the iron out of your system. I'm quite concerned and feel it's time to get started. I went to Binson's Medical Services, where we get your syringes, and I talked to a representative. I explained your need for a much larger pump to chelate more iron out of your system. She showed me several pictures of the various pumps. I found one I thought would be the most beneficial to you. Of course, you would have to use it often, maybe even day and night on occasion. How often you would use it and how much Desferal you put in your system would be up to Dr.

Carion or Dr. Tapazoglou. I told the representative that I would get back to her shortly. She advised me to contact my medical insurance company and find out how such a pump would be paid for, and she would begin making provisions to secure one."

Valeri thought for a moment, and answered, "That sounds like a real ordeal, keeping it on by the hour, but I think you're right. We probably should begin using it very soon, Dad." I told her I would call Dr. Carion and explain to him what I had found out. Valeri said, "I know I'm going to put on my little pump, get going again, and hope that it is correcting the problem for me, at least for the present."

"We should contact Dr. Tapazoglou and bring him in on your case with Dr. Carion," I continued. "I think the two of them working together would make an effective team and be quite helpful to you. Meanwhile, I'll call Dr. Peomelli in New York for advice and to inform him that Dr. Tapazoglou will probably be calling him in the near future."

"Okay, Dad," Valeri repeated, "it all sounds very good. You go ahead. But how about if I use my pump for a little while longer? You know you're planning a trip to Florida in a couple of weeks to visit George and Jeannie Kordas, and then I'm going there with Rena and Andrea to visit Rena's parents. Two weeks after that, Nikki, Alex, and I plan to go to Orlando for five days. Remember, I'm going to take care of Alex while Nikki works at the doctors' convention at the Orlando Hilton Hotel. Probably it would be best for you to make all the preparations and I will use the new pump immediately after that, when I have more time, since I won't be travelling much until I go to Los Angeles to visit Chris for my birthday in May."

"Okay," I agreed. Did you get your ticket for L.A. yet?"

"No, Dad," she answered, "not yet. I have time for that." I thought this was unusual, since normally she would have purchased the ticket several weeks in advance to take advantage of discounted air fares. I thought to myself, perhaps the rates would be less expensive in the spring than winter, when there was a greater demand for people wanting to enjoy the California sun.

It was heartening to see Valeri returning to a sound routine and feeling much better. The thing that concerned us was the transfusion she would need in a few weeks. Val went back to her routine of visiting Rena on Mondays, seeing Sue later in the week, and going out with Roula and Harriet on Thursday evenings to enjoy the music and laughter at Telly's Place.

Val would still go to Vic Tanny's for an occasional workout. Sometimes she swam, but generally she would work with the weights, walk, or do other light exercise. Of course, she still liked to end her regimen with a three-minute rowing contest with the computerized rower. As usual, she'd try to avoid telling me about the rowing machine because she knew how I felt about it.

In the evenings Val continued with her TV watching, telephone conversations with friends, and Bible reading. The routine was interrupted somewhat due to the military activities taking place in the Persian Gulf. She was very upset about the Gulf War, which had begun a week earlier. After watching the news coverage of events taking place there, she'd come down to the family room and give her opinion: "Gosh, it's just terrible that this war is taking place. So many people will be killed and injured." She was sympathetic toward our combat troops who were risking their lives in Operation Desert Storm. On a positive note, she declared: "I do like this news correspondent, Arthur Kent. He is a handsome man. I sure would like to meet someone that good-looking who would become interested in me. I'd marry someone like *that* in a minute!" (Her observation that he was a noteworthy reporter was correct, as he gained a considerable amount of exposure in the years that followed.) Valeri prayed for a quick end to the Gulf War.

One of the things which delighted Valeri was to buy little gifts for her godchildren, Andrea and Brian. She would say, "Dad, it's so much *fun* seeing the expressions on their faces when I give them some small thing. They always give me a hug and a kiss. To me, that's worth a million dollars. Of course, I always buy something for Alex, because it seems Alex is so close to me that I like to give her little surprises when I drop her off or pick her up from school."

We enjoyed eating at home much more since Nikki and Alex came to live with us. In the past, Marietta, Val, and I would often go out to various restaurants, because it was more convenient when Marietta worked. Valeri often offered to cook, but Marietta would reply: "No, forget it, Val. We're just going to go out to eat." But now Marietta was cooking more, and Valeri was helping, and so was Nikki. We were enjoying family suppers together and sharing events of the day.

It was time again for Val to receive a transfusion. She showed the same symptoms she'd had for over twenty-nine years: feeling weak and tired, and having a pale complexion. Through experience, we learned to appreciate the transfusions and relied on them to help her feel stronger and regain her energy. The transfusions were her only salvation. We counted on them totally when Val was in a run-down condition.

I took her to the hospital on a Saturday. Nurse Teresa was on duty. Teresa was one of the four nurses who were very efficient and caring, and who knew Valeri so well. The transfusion was started, and it was moving along normally when I mentioned to Teresa that Valeri had experienced a fever the last transfusion or two. I explained that Marietta thought it was maybe due to the special filter that had been used, instead of the "washing of the blood cells method" used in the past. Today the blood was being "washed," instead of using the special filter.

Teresa acknowledged that she knew about Valeri's problem and would watch Valeri very closely. After Val had received most of her second pint of blood, Teresa took Val's temperature. Teresa observed: "Val is beginning to run a temperature again. I'll keep checking it and call the doctor to see what course of action I should take."

When she spoke with Dr. Carion, he directed: "If Valeri's temperature increased within fifteen minutes, stop the transfusion. If the fever remained steady, Teresa can continue the transfusion until this pint of blood was finished, but Valeri is not to receive a third pint." Val's temperature did drop and Teresa permitted the second pint to be transfused. After removing the IV needle and the Desferal needle from Valeri, she suggested that Val rest for about a half hour and she would take her temperature again. When Val's temperature was checked again, Teresa noted that it was almost back to normal. She said, "I'll call the doctor and see if Valeri can be released." Dr. Carion gave his permission for Val to be discharged, with the orders that she was to rest for one day.

As all this was going on, I thought to myself: "I hope this is not something that is going to complicate future transfusions. This is her lifeline." Of course I did not relate my thoughts to Valeri. I could see that she was already worried.

We went through the usual discharge procedure. Val dressed in her street clothes. Meanwhile Teresa gave her a carnation from one of the vases (a common practice) and had her transported down to the discharge door in the front of the hospital. I went to get the car from the parking lot and drove to pick her up. It was always such a happy feeling for me as I pulled the car up and saw Valeri get out of the wheelchair and get into the car with the help of a nurse's assistant. We would have happy conversation on the way home. This time though, she was quiet. I interrupted her thoughts. "Valeri, your temperature went down, so that apparently is a good sign. I'm glad you got the two pints."

"You know, Dad, I feel kind of bloated."

"That's normal with all fluids that you receive. You will eventually get rid of the fluid-waste through urination," I explained to her.

"Yes, that's usually what happens. You're probably right. It's just that this time if feels a little different."

# 31

# Good Medicine:
# Florida Sunshine

THE following week Marietta and I left for Florida on our annual, one-week vacation each February with George and Jeannie Kordas. As Valeri wasn't feeling up to par, I hated to leave her, thinking perhaps we should drop everything and begin the chelating immediately. But, Valeri insisted that we go. "Don't worry," she said. "Call me, or I will call you every day. I'll be with Nikki and doing my job with Alex, and everything will be fine. Have a good time."

We spent a wonderful week in Florida. I called Valeri almost every night. She'd answer in a very jovial tone. "Hey, things are going fine. I'm having a great time. Wish you were here."

"Wait a minute Val," I'd reply. "*I'm* supposed to say that."

"No, Dad," she insisted, "I am having a great time. Maybe Nikki and Alex and I will have one of our famous wild parties while you're gone!"

A few days after we returned, Val reminded us that it was time for her to leave for Florida with Rena and her daughter, Andrea. "Generally, I feel well, and I think this trip will do me a lot of good. You know how I love to be in the warm climate during these long, hard Michigan winters. I get a little tired once in a while, but it's probably because of the cold weather. Once I get into the Florida sunshine, I'll get all my energy back again. I know the ten days I spend at Lake Worth with Rena and her parents will do me a world of good, so I will definitely go and have a good time."

The morning that they left for Florida was hectic. I volunteered to drive them to the airport. After packing Valeri in the car with her suit-case - one of those big, heavy ones as Val always liked to have a good supply of clothing with her on a trip - we went to pick up Rena and

Andrea. I finally got them all situated in the car and off we went to the airport. Val was feeling quite well and was talking cheerfully all the way there. It was a relief for me to see them walk into the airport with the porter managing all their bags, and knowing that they were off to Florida to have a good time.

Later that evening, Val called to let us know they'd had a safe plane trip and that Rena's father, Jim, had picked them up at the airport and driven them to their condominium in Lake Worth. As usual, Valeri's cheerful, upbeat tone of voice on the phone made me feel good. My final comment was, "Val, make sure you take all your medication I prepared in your little pill box." She agreed that she would. (Usually when Val went on a trip she never took her little pump along. She would stay off the Desferal chelation treatment for that period of time.)

When she called us every night to let us know how things were, she always sounded upbeat and cheerful. The ten days she spent on vacation with Rena and Andrea turned out to be a great deal of fun, and as usual, they made Valeri very happy. She spent much of the time playing with Andrea, who enjoyed Valeri so much. Rena said to Val: "I don't know how I would take care of Andrea if you weren't here, Valeri. You're doing a great job for me."

Rena and Valeri spent much time at the pool sunning themselves, while Rena's parents took care of Andrea during the day. One highlight of the trip was when they all went to the ocean for a swim and to sunbathe. Val loved swimming in the ocean, and she had great fun when the big waves would knock her over and roll her around. Once she even had to be helped to her feet as the wave was so big.

Val mentioned to Rena that she was establishing a new schedule on this trip by getting up early in the morning with the rest of the family and going to bed early, which was far from her normal routine. "But I'm getting lots of sleep and I'm having a great time." What really pleased Valeri was the fun she was having with Andrea. "The hugs and kisses that Andrea gives me are a big bonus, much like frosting on a cake," she confided to Rena.

One day while at pool side, Rena was thinking about the future: "What are we going to do for your thirtieth birthday in May, Valeri? We have to do something really special."

Half-chidingly and half-seriously, Val replied: "I don't know, Rena. I hope I'm still around when my birthday comes up."

"Oh, Valeri! Quit talking silly! Why would you say something like that? You and I are really going to live it up on your birthday!"

"Well, Chris wants me to go out to L.A. to celebrate, but you and I will do something special before I leave."

Rena reflected on Valeri's comment about not being around for her next birthday. She was disturbed, noting that Val did not want to do a lot of walking, and when she did, she would tire easily. Rena wondered whether there was a connection.

On another afternoon, when they all went to Worth Avenue, the exclusive shopping area nearby in West Palm Beach, Valeri asked Rena and her parents, "Would you mind if I just walk and do some shopping by myself? I'd like to be alone for awhile, if you don't mind."

Of course they all agreed and said, "Sure, Val, you go ahead and do your thing." Rena thought this was an unusual request from Valeri and wondered about it to herself. She noticed that Valeri seemed sad. Val went on her little walk and shopping tour. Upon rejoining them, she still seemed very sad.

One evening at the very end of their vacation, Valeri and Rena went to the Abby Road Bar, a hot night spot for young people. Rena knew that Valeri wanted to go out and celebrate one night by dancing and enjoying music instead of a quiet time at her parents' condo. It so happened that as they sat enjoying a drink at the bar, a young man came up to Valeri and asked her to dance. He said he would be right back because he had to tell his friends that he was going to talk to Valeri and Rena. Val asked: "Do you think I should dance with him, Rena? I do have a little problem moving my leg and maybe I would be embarrassed."

Rena replied, "Don't be silly, Valeri. You have always danced and you look great. You go ahead and dance."

So when the young man returned, he and Valeri began to dance. They ended up dancing for two hours straight. He spent the rest of his evening with Valeri. His name was Jim, and he wanted to get together with Val again when she and Nikki and Alex would be returning to Orlando. He gave Valeri his telephone number where he would be working that particular week and insisted that Val call him, promising that he would show her a very nice time. He was counting on her to contact him. Valeri replied, "I will definitely try to get in touch with you when we come back down. I have had a wonderful time with you tonight." Jim hugged Val, kissed her on the cheek, and said good-night.

On the way home, Val said, "I'm sorry I didn't keep you company tonight, Rena."

"Don't worry about it, Val. I enjoyed watching you dance and have a good time," Rena replied.

Vacation was over and it was time to return to Grosse Pointe Woods. The two friends packed their suitcases and Rena's dad loaded them into the car. Rena and Val finished dressing and came downstairs and headed for the car. En route, Val stopped and looked back at the condo, scanned the nice golf course behind it, and began sobbing. She told Rena she was so sad to have to leave Florida and this beautiful place. Rena comforted her by saying, "Don't worry, Val. We're going to come back next year." Val looked at Rena and began to cry again. "What *is* the matter, Valeri?" asked Rena, and began to cry herself. Val continued sobbing until they walked around the side of the house to the parked car where Rena's parents were waiting with Andrea.

Val was very quiet on the way to the airport. After they said good-bye to Rena's parents, they boarded the plane and prepared to fly home. As the plane left the runway, Val began crying again. Little Andrea looked at her and said, "You're crying. Is Nouna sick?"

Val answered, "Oh, no, Nouna's fine, don't worry." Val hugged and kissed her. "Everything is fine, Andrea." Val cried again a couple of times during the flight home, but made sure it was while Andrea slept.

After arriving home and unpacking her bags, Val told us about some of the nice things they did in Florida. She said she'd had a wonderful time and appreciated what Rena and her parents had done for her.

Two days later, the Philoptochos Club was going to hold its annual Macaronatha dance. The Macaronatha is a traditional dance and party held just prior to the beginning of Lent each year. No other social event of that magnitude is permitted in our religion until after Easter Sunday. As you can imagine, it was to be an enjoyable affair, with delicious food, American ballroom dancing, and Greek dancing - tremendous favorites with our parishioners. The antics involved in Greek line dancing while following a leader performing all kinds of fancy gyrations to enjoyable music were a popular pastime with that group.

Val's good friend Harriet Stoukas was president of the Philoptochos, and Valeri was a member of the set-up committee. Val very much wanted the party to be successful, and she was willing to do the required work that went into the planning of such an event. The night of the Macaronatha found a crowd of over four hundred attending. Val did much of the work in the kitchen and served the food. She also sold tickets for the raffle, in addition to other small details that needed attention during the evening. She loved working with Harriet and the other Philoptochos members. It was an outstanding evening for her, as she always enjoyed helping to make this a successful event.

Valeri had always enjoyed the Greek dances, and this one was special, as she played an important part in it. After the dance had ended, Val and Harriet plopped down near where we were sitting and looked at each other. Harriet exclaimed, "Oh, boy! It was a great one, but we are tired."

I expected to hear Valeri say, "Well, let's go, Harriet. Get some of our guys and let's go to Greektown." But, I did not hear those words.

Marietta glanced at Valeri and asked, "Aren't you going to celebrate your successful dance?"

"No, Mom, not tonight. I think we'll just kind of take it easy. I'll go home with you."

Harriet looked at Valeri in amazement: "I can't believe it. Usually I'm the one that can't move, just like now, but Valeri drags me downtown. Here she's the one saying *she's* not interested in going - which really might be a break for me, too!"

Valeri laughed. "No, I just feel like going home and relaxing now." After hugging Harriet, she left with us.

On the way home, I thought that Valeri must not be feeling very well if she turned down an opportunity to go to Greektown to see many of her late-night buddies. Val said to Marietta, "You know, Mom, I am getting a little old for that kid stuff. After all, I am almost thirty years old, so I think I'll just take a rain check and relax at home."

Marietta, concerned, asked, "Are you feeling okay?"

"Oh, yeah," Val answered. "I'm just a little tired, but I'm feeling good. I did spend ten days in Florida and just got back a couple days ago, you know. I feel I should rest up a little and catch up on the news with some of my other friends, especially Sue and Jill. I think I'll go up to my room and make a couple phone calls, watch David Letterman, put my chelating pump on, read the Bible and get some good rest tonight."

About two mornings later Valeri came down to the kitchen where I was loading the dishwasher. She sat down and said: "Why can't Billy Skuras stop drinking and doing drugs? You know he was in a rehab center for a month. He was clean for a while after his release. Then it was back to alcohol, then to drugs, and now he's right back in the same mess he was in before. Rena is very upset and wishes she could do something to help him. His mother and father keep trying to help, but he just won't cooperate. No one knows where he is as of now. He just seems to want to stay with his addiction and not make contact with anybody. Why can't he change? He's such a wonderful young man in so many ways. He has always been very good to me through the years. I wish he could change. I've always felt I knew something about human behavior, but this confuses me. I wonder why he won't change?"

I listened to her tirade, and finally said, "I don't know, Valeri. I don't know."

By then, Marietta had come into the kitchen. She volunteered her thoughts. "Billy is a nice young man heading for trouble. Let's hope and pray that he will change in the near future before something very serious happens to him."

Valeri shook her head and said, "I hope so, Mom and Dad," and went back to her room to dress before visiting Sue.

The trip to Orlando with Nikki and Alex was scheduled for the middle of March, which was coming up rapidly. Nikki was going to attend a dermatologist convention to promote her product, Sigvaris Surgical Socks. She wanted to take Alex with her so they could enjoy a vacation in Florida for five days. Nikki also wanted Valeri along to care for Alex while Nikki worked at the convention. The three of them would visit Disney World and take in other sights, as well as enjoy the pool and other hotel facilities. Nikki and Valeri also planned to do some shopping. It sounded like an ideal setup for them, especially since Nikki was also going to pay the airfare and hotel for Valeri.

They finalized the plan several weeks prior to leaving. Valeri felt she should have a blood transfusion before leaving, so that she'd have extra energy and feel strong while in Orlando. She made arrangements with Dr. Carion to have a transfusion two weeks before the trip.

Valeri was finding it physically tiring to fulfill her much-loved routine of taking care of Alex, which now included helping with homework assignments. Often they would play games or each take a nap until Nikki arrived home. One of Val's favorite pastimes was to visit one of her friends while Alex was in school, and another was to work out at Vic Tanny's. It was a busy, hectic schedule. Valeri was limiting her evenings out, electing instead to stay and keep Alex company, to watch television or to rent a video. It was still common for Val to rent a video for the family to watch together. She seemed to know all the good films and would bring one home that we could all enjoy.

A new routine would soon be started, as Jill was moving back home. Jill was looking forward to doing the town with Valeri, and sent little notes or a card saying: "Fourteen days to go until I'm home for good," or "thirteen days . . . " and then a humorous comment would be added. Val was happy about the thought of Jill's return, because they'd always had so much in common.

With the time nearing for her departure to Florida, Valeri said, "I'd better get a transfusion fast. I'm feeling tired again, and generally feeling punk. Remember, I just had a transfusion two weeks ago, and I only received a pint-and-a-half of blood because I developed a fever. Nurse Jeanine, who took care of me, worried about it so much that she called the doctor. Soon my temperature rose one degree, and the doctor told Jeanine that if it rises more than two degrees during either the first or second pint of blood, we will stop the transfusion. If you recall, this took place before the second pint was finished. Then, when I contacted Dr. Carion a couple days later, he suggested that I come in within two weeks for my regular two or three pints. He was still baffled as to why my temperature continued to rise during the transfusion."

So Valeri went to St. John Hospital to have the transfusion about a week before she was going to Orlando. I drove her to the hospital. Marianne Thomas was on duty. She was aware that in the last several weeks Valeri was running temperatures during transfusions. Marianne said she would be very careful in monitoring Val during the transfusion. Hopefully Val could accept at least two pints of blood that day.

As sure as clockwork, it happened again. About the middle of the second pint of blood, Valeri began running a temperature. It shot up to over one hundred degrees. Marianne said, "Let me call Dr. Carion and see what he might suggest. Meanwhile, we'll observe Valeri closely."

Although Val had a temperature, she seemed to be feeling relatively well. Dr. Carion said that if Valeri was feeling reasonably well, to continue until the second pint of blood was finished, but at that time to stop the transfusion. That is exactly what they did. The temperature seemed to subside slightly, and Valeri felt better. At least she was able to accept the second pint of blood. Now her blood count would be high enough for her to regain her strength for the trip to Orlando.

I asked Marianne if she had any idea why Val was experiencing this problem with the temperature. She answered that the doctor still did not know, but felt that the process was not really harmful to Val and not to worry too much about it.

Again, as after recent transfusions, Val told me that she felt very bloated and it bothered her, but she would probably feel much better once she got home and relaxed and was able to get rid of some of the fluids in her body.

Although Val rested for the next two days, she still found herself feeling very tired. By the next week, however, she was feeling much better and looking forward to her trip on the thirteenth of March. As was a custom with Valeri in the past, she put a suitcase on the floor in her room and began slowly packing clothes each day. She firmly believed this was the way to make sure that all her clothes were clean, and that the proper ones would be packed without a great deal of pressure at the last minute.

The Thursday before she left on the trip, Valeri told Marietta that she wanted to see Dr. Carion before leaving because she hadn't been feeling up to par for the last day or so. We called his office. Dr. Carion was not available, though Dr. Benvenuto had an opening. Since Valeri preferred to see Dr. Carion, she asked the receptionist for an appointment later that week or early the next week with Dr. Carion.

Later that day, Valeri still was not well. She was very tired, so we suggested that she take the appointment with Dr. Benvenuto. Upon calling again, she found that the appointment with Dr. Benvenuto had already been filled, and that the next appointment with a doctor was the following Monday, when Dr. Carion would be in his office. She set one up with him for Monday.

That evening, she was feeling worse, so Marietta suggested we go to the "Quickie Clinic" at St. John Hospital. This new Quickie Clinic would see patients with virus infections and other illnesses that could be treated immediately, thereby avoiding long periods of waiting. Valeri agreed: "Okay, I'll go to the clinic, but I do not want to go to the Emergency Room and spend four hours lying on that uncomfortable cot."

So, we took Val to the clinic that night. After a few tests, it was found that Valeri did have a slight fever, though it did not appear to be anything serious. One of the doctors came in for a final check, looked at Val, and announced: "Hey, you are jaundiced. I think we should admit you to the hospital."

Marietta very angrily said: "I do not think so. I do not think she is jaundiced. She has a fever and might have a virus or a bladder infection because she has complained about her lower abdominal area."

The doctor answered, "There are no signs of a bladder infection, but I can give her an antibiotic if you want to take her home. I'm worried, though, about her jaundiced appearance."

Marietta retorted: "This pale complexion is common for Valeri from time to time because of her illness."

"Go ahead, you can go home. But, I suggest you talk to her doctor tomorrow and try to see him tomorrow, if it's possible," the doctor urged.

The next day we called Dr. Carion and told him what the emergency doctor had said. He told us he would check with them and call back. He returned the call a short time later and said, "They did mention that she might be jaundiced, but of course they do not know Valeri's complexion. I will prescribe an antibiotic for her."

"I did check her throat with a flashlight," I told him, "and she did have some white spots in the back of her throat. Maybe it's a throat infection."

"Well," Dr. Carion replied, "I'll prescribe the antibiotic. I want to see her early next week."

Later that day, Valeri started the antibiotic. She still felt sick through the weekend. On Monday when she called to verify her appointment with Dr. Carion, the receptionist said he was not available as he was at Partridge, the other medical center in Clinton Township. This upset Valeri, as she had wanted to speak with him before going to Florida.

She was still not feeling well in the early evening, so she decided to call Dr. Carion at home to see if he would see her the next day. "Dr. Carion, I'm trying to get an appointment to see you. I'm going to Florida on Wednesday, and would like to come in to see you before I leave."

He said, "Valeri, you are on the antibiotic. It seems like everything is going to be fine. Just make sure you take your medication and if you feel a little tired and perhaps dehydrated, make sure you drink lots of fluids."

"You don't think it would be possible to see you?" she asked again.

"No," he answered, "it isn't. Not before you leave, but have a real nice time in Florida anyway."

Valeri hung up and looked put-out as she complained, "I am really disappointed as I wanted him to examine me. I am just not feeling well."

Later that evening Valeri confided to Marietta, "I hope nothing happens to me while I'm with Alex down in Florida, Mom. I'm very worried, as I am not feeling well."

"Well, Valeri, if that is how you feel, let's make some other plans. You don't have to go to Florida."

"Oh, no! I really **do** want to go, Mom. I want to go with Nikki and Alex. I know it'll be a lot of fun, but I am rather concerned."

That night when Valeri was going to bed, she said, "Please, Dad, no pump for chelation tonight. You remember what happened two nights ago, when I was feeling quite good and we decided to put the pump on for a night or two. I woke up in the middle of the night and could not urinate, so I took the pump off. I really have not been feeling well ever since. How about no pump?"

"Oh, of course, Valeri, no more pump until you get back from Florida. In fact, when you get back, we will begin the aggressive chelating that we've been discussing." I personally felt that this was one way for Valeri to get rid of the iron and that it would help her feel so much better.

The next morning, Tuesday, Val was still not feeling well. She mused, "I probably should see the doctor, but he can't see me. What do I do?"

That's when I said, "Hey, how about going to see Dr. Tapazoglou? He will see you if he's in his office."

I called Dr. Tapazoglou at 11:45 a.m. The nurse answered and I explained Valeri's situation. "Wait a minute," she told me. After a slight delay, she said, "Bring her right in, because the doctor is going to be leaving at twelve-thirty."

We went to see Dr. Tapazoglou. He immediately said, "Let me take some tests, Valeri. The first will be an electrocardiogram, another will be an x-ray, and then a blood test. I will be able to do this within an hour. I'll cancel my appointment downtown and reschedule it for later on." After the testing was done, he called us both into his office and said, "Valeri's blood test is good. Her blood count is a little over ten, which is good. However, I looked at the x-rays and it shows that Valeri has a *very enlarged heart*."

"Oh, we've known about this for years," I reassured him. "We've had doctors tell us about that before."

"Okay, but it is quite enlarged. When I checked the electrocardiogram," he went on, "it was beating in sinus rhythm, though, and it seems that she is doing quite well."

"Do you think the bladder infection she had, along with a slight virus, could be causing dehydration?" I inquired.

Dr. Tapazoglou replied, "No, I don't think so. But just keep treating her with the antibiotic."

"Valeri wants to go to Florida for five days. Do you think she is well enough to go?" I asked him. He looked at me very seriously, paused before he spoke, then answered, "I think she is okay to go; however, make sure she gets a great deal of rest. Val, sitting around the pool is okay, but do not do anything very strenuous." Looking toward me, he continued, "I want to see her as soon as she comes back next Monday."

"That'll be fine," I agreed. "Do you think we can talk seriously about her aggressive chelation therapy at that time?"

"Of course. That's exactly what I want to talk about." He turned toward Val and said, "Have a nice time, Valeri."

She looked at him and said, "I want to thank you so much for examining me, Dr. Tapazoglou. I think that it is wonderful that you were so receptive. Thank you so much."

When we went home and explained to Marietta what had happened, her reaction was: "Well, it sounds very good. Perhaps you should go, but Nikki began making other plans in case Valeri could not go. Maybe Michelle, Debbie's oldest daughter can go, or maybe Debbie or Dad, but Nikki said she really wanted Valeri."

"Let's have Valeri get to bed early tonight and get a good night's sleep. We can decide tomorrow morning," I suggested.

Late that evening I went into Valeri's room. She was still awake so we began talking. "I'm worried, Dad. I hope that I'll be in good condition and able to take care of Alex and do what I'm supposed to when I'm down there."

"Don't worry about it, Val," I calmed her. "If you're not up to going tomorrow morning, just stay home. If you feel good, you can go."

"I really want to go, Dad!"

I took her pulse. Her heart seemed to be beating evenly, at about seventy-five beats per minute, which seemed very normal. After spending a little more time with her, I said, "Let's both get a good night's rest."

We all woke up early the next morning. I was busy packing the car to drive Nikki, Val, and Alex to the airport while they were getting dressed and ready to go. Val announced she was feeling pretty well that morning, so it was decided that she would go on the trip. I did ask her to sit down after she finished dressing so I could take her pulse. Again, her rate was very steady, around seventy-five to eighty beats per minute, without any skipping. I took this to mean that she was basically feeling quite well. After breakfast, the four of us got into the car and I drove them to the airport. Valeri was quieter than usual, but she still took part in conversations and seemed to be doing okay. "Dad," she admonished, "quit staring at me. It makes me feel uncomfortable. I am feeling pretty good, really."

Once we arrived at the airport I parked my car in the short-term lot, after dropping them off at the Northwest Airlines door. I ran into the lobby to see if everything was going well and saw a long line of people getting ready to check in for that particular flight. Nikki, Alex, and Val were standing by an airline flight attendant on the side of the counter. "Dad, I completed check-in arrangements. We're going to have an electric cart take us to the airplane so Valeri doesn't have to walk," Nikki told me.

We then went through security and Valeri said, "Dad, I'm very, very thirsty. Please get me some water."

"Sure," I replied, and ran over to the Burger King nearby and asked one of the young workers for some water. I ran back to where Valeri was standing. The electric cart was ready to take them to the boarding gate. Val stepped on the cart with Nikki and Alex. I gave Val her water, kissed all three of them good-bye, and told them to have a good time in Orlando and to get some extra rest. Val waved and gave me a half smile. Alex and Nikki waved good-bye.

As I drove home I worried. "Was I smart to permit Valeri to fly to Florida? How sick is she? Is it really something serious? She had mentioned to her mother that she did not feel as good as she would have liked. Wild thoughts raced through my mind. Finally, I decided I would call Dr. Peomelli in New York to find out about aggressive chelation, and to let him know that Dr. Tapazoglou would call him for chelation regimen information, so that we could begin treatment immediately.

Once home, I told Marietta how Nikki had secured the cart for Valeri to be driven to the boarding gate. "Oh, that's great," she said, but sounded worried, as well.

In fact, we looked at each other and I admitted, "You know, it is a worrisome time for us, and I'm hoping that Valeri is going to be okay."

"Yes, I'm quite concerned, too," Marietta concurred. "We'd better get that aggressive chelation going fast."

"Marietta, Dr. Tapazoglou was very considerate in examining Valeri yesterday. I really think that displayed much feeling on his part. He's a very fine doctor."

About two hours later, I looked at the clock and announced, "Well, they're in Florida now. I hope they're enjoying the sunshine and the pool, and that Val is getting some rest, even while taking care of Alex."

The weather for the first two days of their visit was typical of Florida in March: sunny and warm with a light, cool breeze. Valeri and Alex spent time swimming and lying on the lounge chairs by the pool. They'd get up late, eat a light breakfast, and relax by the pool for most of the day. Then they'd walk through some of the shops in the beautiful Hilton Hotel. Later, they would meet Nikki, who had finished her work at the exhibit booth at the convention, and she would treat them to supper in one of the hotel restaurants.

The only problem, Nikki thought to herself, was that Valeri was not eating very much. Val usually had a very good appetite, and enjoyed eating in fancy restaurants with large assortments of food. Now she was only taking in tiny morsels and eating soup. Nikki tried to encourage Valeri, saying, "Why don't you eat a little more?"

Val would reply, "Well, I've eaten enough. It's really good, thank you, Nikki."

The second night in Orlando, after going to bed, Valeri developed a bad case of the itches all over her body, and it prevented her from sleeping very soundly. She'd scratch and scratch, trying to get rid of the itch. When Valeri called us early Friday morning, she told us about her terrible case of the itches. She did not know what to do. I suggested that she try not to scratch unless it was absolutely necessary. "Dad," she patiently explained, "I do not think you understand how itchy my skin is. I've never had this type of feeling before, even when I had the allergic reactions to the blood transfusions years ago. It was never like this. In a way, it's funny. This is a dermatologist convention, and I have the itches! It just so happens that Nikki met one of the doctors and told him about my situation. He prescribed some medication which I'm going to pick up later today. I sure hope it helps me."

"I hope so too, Val." The medication did relieve her to some extent. However, the itches were the least of her worries that day. Valeri now felt very tired and lacked energy. Somehow or other she got through the day, and she and Alex enjoyed themselves, even though the weather had changed drastically, as it had begun to rain.

Val called us again that evening. "Dad, I'm feeling somewhat better as far as the itches go, but I feel so tired. We had another wonderful day with Alex, but the weather is just not cooperating. Fortunately there are many things to do in the hotel, and Alex and I are entertaining ourselves again." Then she added, "Remember, Dad, tomorrow you and Mom are going to Rena's to celebrate Andrea's first birthday. Last week I bought gifts for Andrea and I want you to make sure to take them with you and give them to her. I'm planning to call her tomorrow night during the party and talk to her."

Saturday morning was relaxing for Val and Alex. Nikki had to work one final day at the convention in her exhibit booth. Val and Alex were lying around in bed watching TV and just being carefree most of the morning. Suddenly Alex looked out the window and said, "Look, Valeri. It's raining again. Darn it! My mommy says she's going to take me to Disney World later on this afternoon. It's going to rain the whole time we're there."

Val tried to comfort her by saying, "No, it might stop, sweetheart. Let's just hope that it does." Unfortunately, the rain did not stop. But Nikki still took Alex to Disney World anyway. Val elected to stay in the room and rest.

Later that evening they met at the hotel and ate supper together. Once again, Val was not very hungry and did not eat much. This concerned Nikki, because she knew how Valeri loved to eat. Val tried to be cheerful when Alex was around. She didn't want to worry her in any way. But Alex was observant and noted: "Valeri, you're not eating much again. How come?"

Valeri replied, "Oh, well, I'm just not too hungry tonight. I ate enough, though."

About ten o'clock that night Valeri called Rena's home back in St. Clair Shores. We were all at the party celebrating Andrea's birthday. Andrea was the cutest little baby - a wonderful little one-year-old with a big smile and dark, curly hair. Val spoke to Rena briefly, and then Andrea was put on the line. As soon as Andrea heard Valeri's name, she cried out: "Nouna!" She yelled out again, "Nouna!" and repeated again, "Nouna!" and smiled. "Nouna" in Greek means "Godmother." Andrea was excited to recognize Val's voice. After all, Valeri had spent much time with her in recent months. Valeri talked to her for a few minutes and enjoyed listening to Andrea jabber with her baby-talk. Rena then gave me the phone.

Valeri told me she was feeling a little better as far as the itches were concerned, but she still felt very tired. She was glad to be returning home the following day as the weather was rainy and not as pleasant as it usually was in Florida. She said, "I hope that tomorrow will be a sunshiny day so we can spend a little more time at the pool before leaving for home. Say hello to Mom. In fact, let me talk to Mom for a couple minutes." Valeri talked to Marietta for awhile before hanging up. We were all happy that she had called Andrea, but I think Valeri was probably the happiest, as she had spoken to Andrea on her first birthday.

The next morning, Valeri, Nikki, and Alexandra got up. "Valeri, get dressed because I'm going to treat you to a nice lunch in a very exclusive restaurant before we go to the airport to go home," Nikki announced.

Val was rather excited and answered, "That sounds very nice, Nikki." When they were ready they took a cab and went quite a distance from the hotel to this exclusive restaurant Nikki knew about. The cab fare was thirty dollars.

When Nikki ordered her meal, Val just said, "I think I'll just have a bowl of soup."

Nikki looked at Valeri. "Valeri, I brought you here purposely, as I want you to have a nice, big lunch before we get on that plane."

"Well, I'm really not that hungry, Nikki so there would be no need for you to spend all that money if I'm not going to eat the meal."

"Valeri," coaxed Nikki, "I want you to eat. Do you hear me?"

Alexandra looked at her aunt and said, "And I do too, Valeri."

Valeri smiled and gave up: "Okay," she said and proceeded to order a dinner. Unfortunately, she did not eat very much of it, even though it looked tasty. She did not feel like eating; and besides, she was very, very tired.

After lunch, Nikki, Valeri, and Alex took a cab directly to the airport. When they arrived, Nikki immediately asked for a porter to bring a wheelchair so that Valeri would not have to walk to the departure gate. The porter was not too receptive at the time. "I'll be back in a few minutes," he told them, but he did not return.

Nikki became a little upset and went to another porter and demanded, "Look, I want some service here. I want a wheelchair." She then walked over to the ticket window and said, "I want to get our tickets verified immediately, my luggage taken care of, and a wheelchair so my sister can be wheeled to the gate where we are to board the airplane."

The woman at the desk was very nice and offered, "Okay, I will help you."

Nikki was somewhat mollified and said, "Thank you, because I am not getting much cooperation around here right now." A few minutes later a porter showed up with the requested chair and Valeri was wheeled to the gate as Nikki and Alex walked alongside.

Upon boarding the plane, Valeri was not seated next to Nikki or Alex. Nikki complained to the flight attendant, who made arrangements to have Alex and Nikki sit next to each other, but nothing could be done to help Valeri. "Don't worry, Nikki," Valeri said. "I'll just kind of relax and maybe sleep on the way home." Nikki was still a little upset, but Valeri calmed her down and they were ready for the flight. Nikki checked on Val several times and found her sleeping each time.

Meanwhile, I had driven to the airport to pick them up. Their plane arrived a few minutes late. After a large group of people had de-boarded the plane, I saw Nikki walking beside Valeri in a wheelchair being pushed by a porter. Alex was sitting on Valeri's lap, and Val was holding a bag of oranges. "Hi guys!" I greeted them. "How are you doing?"

Val looked very pale and appeared to have no energy. Nikki answered, "Oh, we're not bad, Dad."

"I'm feeling very tired, Dad," Valeri added. After we moved over to the luggage conveyor, Nikki came to me and said, "Dad, Valeri is not feeling very good, and I'm terribly worried."

"Val, I'm going to call Mom and have you admitted to the hospital tonight. I think we should have Dr. Carion check you out and get you good and healthy, so we can begin the aggressive chelation."

Valeri just sort of nodded and responded, "Okay, Dad," very quietly.

As I walked to the phone across the hall, I thought about my phone conversation with Dr. Peomelli. When I had explained to him how Valeri was feeling, he'd said to me, "Mr. Samaras, Valeri is a medical emergency. I suggest you call Dr. Schwartz in Philadelphia, who is an expert on chelation for Cooley's Anemia victims, and make an appointment to fly her there as soon as she gets back from Florida."

Medical emergency. Those words rang in my head, over and over again. I finally got to the phone and called Marietta. "Valeri is not feeling too well. Please make arrangements for her to be admitted at St. John Hospital tonight. I think she'd better get into the hospital and receive some medical treatment very fast."

Marietta replied, "I will take care of this, Bob. You come home and we'll go to the hospital together with Val."

I went back to meet the girls and to secure their luggage off the conveyor. The porter pushing the wheelchair for Valeri said, "I'll take care of the luggage. Let's just go to the car." We walked across the street to the short-term lot to my car, loaded it, and Nikki and Alex sat in the back seat while Valeri sat up in front with me. I looked over at her. She did not look healthy. On the way home, she did not take part in the conversation unless we intentionally asked her a question. She just stared off into space. This was not like our amiable, outgoing Valeri with the infectious laugh.

Upon arriving home, Valeri said, "I want to go into the house. We can wait for Mom to get ready to go to the hospital with us."

"Fine, Valeri," I said, and helped her walk into the kitchen, where she sat down in her familiar chair, where she so often sat to eat, relax, and read the paper. Meanwhile I took all the luggage inside. Nikki went up to her bedroom with Alex to prepare her for bed. Marietta was getting dressed to go to the hospital with us. Alex and Nikki came down to the kitchen to talk to Valeri for a few minutes.

I whispered to Marietta: "Valeri does not look good. I'm very, very worried. Incidentally, how did you get her admitted to the hospital without going through emergency?"

"I couldn't reach Dr. Tapazoglou," she answered, "but I reached his associate, Dr. Burrows. I asked him if he could please make arrangements for Val to be admitted. He answered that he didn't know Valeri and was unfamiliar with her case. On what basis would he admit her? I told him that I didn't care how he did it, but to please contact Dr. Tapazoglou and make arrangements so I can have her admitted. Fifteen minutes later," Marietta continued, "I received a phone call from the hospital asking me to please bring Valeri there as soon as she arrived home."

I went back down to the kitchen to wait for Marietta and sat with Valeri. When Marietta came down, Val said, "Mom, do you think I am dying?"

Marietta scoffed. "Oh, Valeri! Don't be silly. We have been through this many times before. They are going to fix you up very well in the hospital and we are going to have that aggressive chelation. You are going to regain your health and go on your way again."

Val gave a faint smile and said, "I hope so, Mom." I helped Valeri walk to the car and the three of us headed for the hospital.

We arrived at the emergency door and I jumped out of the car, ran inside and got a wheelchair and brought it out. Both Marietta and I helped Valeri get into it. Marietta wheeled her to the admissions desk and filled out the requisite forms. I parked the car in the structure and went back to meet them, just as an orderly was pushing Val towards the elevator. Marietta and I walked with Val to her room.

I noticed the room number on the door as we entered. It was number 438. It was customary for me to notice what room number Val was in whenever she went into the hospital so I could inform her friends and relatives. A nurse quickly came in and helped Val change into a hospital gown. She took her temperature and did all the necessary formalities that a new patient received.

A resident came in after a little while and examined Valeri. She told him about her symptoms of feeling very weak and lacking energy. She also told him that she'd had a recent viral infection, and maybe that was the cause of her not feeling well. The resident seemed very concerned, but did not say too much to us. He asked Valeri if she was having difficulty breathing. Valeri said, "Yes, I am having some problems."

"I think I'll get you hooked up with oxygen for tonight, to help you feel more comfortable and allow you to rest more easily," he told her.

"Also, I've had this itchy feeling for the last few days," Val mentioned.

"I'll give you a medication to help you relax and hopefully to eliminate that feeling. I'll inform Dr. Tapazoglou. He will be here in the morning to begin recommending tests that should be taken."

By now, Valeri seemed very comfortable in bed. She began talking. It was easy, even with that little tube with the outlets in her nose, which was giving her oxygen to help her breathe more easily. "Boy, I sure hope I can rest up and feel much better than I do now," she said. "I hope we can begin this aggressive chelation to help me get back on my feet very soon." Both Marietta and I said that we were sure she'd be feeling much better in a few days and be able to go home and begin doing her thing again.

As we sat there in the hospital, keeping Val company, I couldn't help but think of some of the past experiences we'd had in hospitals. Frankly, I was very worried about this experience, as the problem seemed to be the way her heart was functioning. On one hand I felt somewhat optimistic, but on the other I was quite concerned, remembering Dr. Tapazoglou's comment about her heart being very enlarged. I thought: "We still have that 'ace-in-the-hole' - the aggressive chelation to remove the iron from Valeri's body and allow her heart to function better again. Also, her other organs will function better, too. I was really quite confident that Valeri's condition would be reversed, and that she would regain her health.

It was around one o'clock in the morning when Valeri directed, "Please, Mom and Dad, you two go home and let me rest. I'll feel much better knowing that you are resting too. I know you and Dad will be here first thing in the morning, the way you always have been with me at times like this for almost thirty years. Please, go home and rest. Okay?"

Both Marietta and I took turns hugging and kissing Valeri and telling her how much we loved her and that she was such an important part of our lives. Marietta repeated: "We love you, love you, love you!"

Val smiled and said, "I know, Mom and Dad. I love you too. I'll tell you what I'm going to do. I'm going to try to get some rest, and feel much better in the next few days." We said our good-byes and left for home.

En route Marietta and I expressed our concerns, and admitted to each other how worried we were. However, on the other hand, we were still quite optimistic that something could be done to help Valeri.

When we walked into the house, Nikki heard us and asked, "How is Val?"

I answered, "She was not feeling too well tonight, Nikki, but we have high hopes at this point."

"I hope so, Dad, because she was not feeling very good in Florida, and I'm really worried about her. I love my sister so much. I hope and pray that something can be done to help her this time."

We all began crying. Marietta finally said, "I know Valeri is going to be okay. Let's get ourselves some rest so we can go to the hospital early tomorrow with Dad."

We all went to bed, feeling reasonably optimistic that something could be done for our lovely Valeri.

# 32

# Nine Fateful Days

WE WENT to the hospital around eight o'clock Monday morning to see Valeri. To our surprise, Dr. Tapazoglou had already been in to visit and exam her. He ordered a series of heart tests, as well as liver and kidney-function tests. He told Val that he felt these would give him a complete picture of what was taking place in her body. Val said he planned to begin aggressive iron chelation therapy immediately after receiving results of the tests. Val's eyes lit up when she talked about receiving the aggressive therapy. She said: "I think it's time for this, Mom and Dad. It will do me much good, I'm sure."

Both Marietta and I were optimistic about her comment regarding the chelation therapy. We felt it was time, and its aggressive nature would lower the iron count in her system, allowing her body to regain some of the strength that it had lost.

Val was uncomfortable, however, and very worried. She was still itchy. We noticed that she was very tired, but also active. She would get out of bed and walk to the bathroom on her own. She could move around the room quite easily. Dr. Tapazoglou's orders were for her to get up and out of bed, to go to the bathroom, to move around and sit in a chair for awhile, but to stay in bed for the greater part of the time.

It was a little unusual, but Val didn't particularly want to watch any television. She looked at us and explained, "You know, I really don't want to have any visitors for a few days, either. Probably the best thing for me now, would be to get lots of rest, get the test results, and then begin the aggressive chelation." Later that morning, Valeri was taken from her room to begin undergoing some of the tests.

I went to Wayne State University to teach a community health class (my part-time teaching assignment) later that morning. By the time I returned to the hospital at about one-thirty in the afternoon, most of the testing was completed. A bit later, Betty Rothis and her daughter Angie came by the door of Val's room and wanted to visit with her. Marietta went into the hall and explained to Betty that Valeri really wasn't in the mood for any visitors. Val heard her mother talking and said, "Invite them in, Mom. It's okay."

Betty and Angie spent a few minutes talking with Valeri. Angie, who always made funny comments that would crack Valeri up, finally looked at Valeri and said, "You know, Val, you really do look pretty good. I hope you feel much better in the next couple days, go home, and get back into your famous, fun-time routine." Val thanked her, and then the two of them left.

Minutes later, Valeri got up, went to the bathroom and looked into the mirror. "You know what, Mom?" she said when she came back, "I don't think I look very good. Look how pale and ashen I look."

"Oh, Valeri, you know you have that kind of ashen appearance when you're run down. You look very good."

Later that afternoon, Valeri was hooked up to a second IV to keep a vein open should they need to give her blood. She was already receiving an antibiotic through another IV. Val complained about the itchiness, which was still quite bothersome. A nurse called Dr. Tapazoglou. He prescribed a medication called Tylox, which would minimize or eliminate the itchiness. He visited Val again later in the day. He said he would make it a habit to visit her several times a day, until further notice. Dr. Tapazoglou ordered the oxygen therapy continued and told us that it would be much easier for Val to breathe, her heart could have a rest, and she would have more energy.

Some of Valeri's friends began telephoning once they found out she was in the hospital. Valeri said she didn't want to speak with anyone on the phone. She seemed very irritable that day, and rightly so. She was feeling tired and ill. That afternoon she reflected: "I came in the hospital yesterday, the seventeenth of March. It was St. Patrick's Day. You know I've always had a lot of great times celebrating St. Patrick's Day, but yesterday wasn't a very good one for me. I hope next year I'll be able to go out and really make up for yesterday."

When Dr. Tapazoglou saw us that evening he told us about notifying Dr. Carion's office, to let him know that Valeri was in the hospital. He also requested Dr. Reyes, a cardiologist who worked out of Dr. Carion's office, and Dr. Patel, a gastroenterologist, to see Val. He wanted these doctors to assist him in working with her for the next several days.

As I sat in Valeri's hospital room later in the evening, I thought to myself, "I'm sure Valeri's going to be okay. I was very confident that somehow she'd get over this crisis, as she had all the others." I was sure that the aggressive chelation would make Valeri much stronger, and she'd return to a reasonably healthy status. I was still quite hopeful that everything was going to be fine.

It was almost midnight when Val said, "Mom and Dad, here I am napping and resting, while you're just sitting there doing nothing. Why don't you two go home and come back to see me in the morning?" We took her advice.

Dr. Carion visited Val on Tuesday morning, before we arrived at about 8:30 a.m. Val let him know that she was upset that he hadn't seen her before she left for Florida. "Maybe if I had seen you I wouldn't be in this condition today," she scolded. Dr. Carion responded that, whether he had seen her or not, it wouldn't have made a difference. Valeri pretty much accepted this. Though she had this continuous fondness for Dr. Carion, she still felt it was her place to complain to him about the unmade appointment before her trip.

There was more testing done that morning on her kidneys and liver, as well as a series of daily blood tests. I gave Valeri a sports update on the Pistons and the Tigers. The Pistons were fighting to qualify for a third World Championship title and the Tigers were now entering their last phase of spring training. She was very interested to hear how both teams were doing. "I hope my Pistons do it, but they don't seem to be playing very good basketball lately," she said.

Val was still very tired, irritable, and at times, itchy. She still had no desire to watch television or to answer phone calls from her friends. She was definitely not feeling well, and she was concerned about her health, which was evident through the expressions on her face. "I hope they start the aggressive chelating soon, Mom and Dad. I want to get this thing going because it sure would be nice to feel better than I do now." Then she added, "The way I feel right now, I don't even know if I'll make it to my thirtieth birthday in six weeks." (Today was March 19th, and her birthday was on May 16th.) She laughed then and said, "Oh, well, I'll just have me a biggie. I know I'll be okay."

Her doctors visited Val throughout the day, and the nurses were very attentive, doing all they could to keep Valeri comfortable. Early that afternoon, Val arose from bed to go to the bathroom. A few minutes later, she called Marietta. "Mom, I don't feel very good. Would you please come and help me get back to bed?"

At about the same time, the telephone rang. Marietta ran to answer it. It was Chris, calling from Los Angeles. "Valeri, Chris is on the phone. What do you want me to tell him?"

Valeri answered, "Mom, I feel dizzy. Please help me back, and ask him if he would mind calling later today or tonight."

Marietta did, then rushed over to Valeri, who was hanging onto the sink in the bathroom. "Gosh," Marietta exclaimed, "I didn't realize you were feeling that weak, Valeri." She helped her back into bed and rang for the nurse, who came in very quickly.

The nurse said, "Please don't let Valeri get up anymore unless I'm with you." Once in bed, Valeri felt much better and the dizziness passed.

Later that day, I went home to check the house, read our mail, and run some errands. When I returned to the hospital, both Marietta and Valeri looked very sad. A few minutes later Valeri took a nap. Marietta and I went out of the room and into the lobby. She began crying. "Dr. Tapazoglou talked to me a short while ago about Valeri's condition. He said that her heart is very enlarged, and that there doesn't appear to be any hope for Valeri to regain her health. He told me that Valeri may not last more than four to six weeks."

I was stunned by this news. She added, "He said that Dr. Reyes is prescribing a special heart medication. If it works, it will help her considerably, for a while. If it doesn't, then they don't know exactly what the prognosis will be." Marietta and I both took this to mean that Valeri didn't have long to live, but would be okay and strong enough to come home for another month or two.

Marietta continued, "I saw Dr. Reyes a little later. He mentioned that we'll know more tomorrow, when he plans to confer with us. I told him you would go to Wayne to teach a class and be back about 1:30 p.m., and he said that would be a good time to meet with all the doctors present."

I asked Marietta: "What should we tell Valeri?"

"Dr. Reyes said we should let Val know how ill she is. It would only be fair for her to know."

When Valeri woke up from her nap, she asked, "What did Dr. Tapazoglou say about the aggressive chelation, Mom?"

Marietta looked very sad and carefully answered, "Valeri, Dr. Tapazoglou said that you are having some serious heart problems. They are going to give you a new medication which, hopefully, will resolve them and be very helpful for you. He can't think of aggressive chelation until he makes sure that this medication is working properly. Dr. Reyes told me it's up to you and your body to fight this thing, and with hope, the medication will work so you're strong once again."

Valeri looked worried. She seemed confused and upset, and yet after a few minutes she looked at us very hopefully and said, "I hope this medication works!"

While sitting there with her, I reflected on some of the comments made by several of the doctors throughout the years. When I'd asked Dr. Graziano who worked at the medical school at Columbus Presbyterian Hospital in New York about how an anemia victim dies, whether it was a rapid or slow process, he'd responded that the condition is a slow deterioration of health, until the patient expires. I asked myself: "Is this the beginning of this slow period? Or the end of it?"

Then I remembered that a hematologist at Children's Hospital had once told me that some of her young patients would come in so very anemic and suffering from congenital heart failure, that they were barely able to move. Then, after a week or so of treatment, they would walk right out of the hospital. With some hope, this was what would happen with Valeri. Perhaps the medication would work and she would be okay - at least for a short time.

Occasionally, Marietta would leave the room to get some coffee from the cafeteria. She would come back and her eyes would be swollen, and I knew she had been crying. But she never cried in the presence of Valeri, and Valeri never cried during this time. Even though Val was very upset, she just lay there in a hopeful, positive mood, thinking that things would still be okay.

Late that afternoon, Valeri tried to get up and go to the bathroom, but she was just too weak and was suffering from the dizziness again. The nurse suggested that she get back into bed and they would bring a bedpan for her. During the evening visiting hours, between seven and nine o'clock, Debbie and Nikki came to the hospital to keep Valeri company. She was very happy to see them, but she still didn't want any other visitors. Several of our family members showed up that evening, as did a few of her friends. They sat in the lounge with Marietta and me. We talked while Debbie and Nikki were with Valeri. The relatives said they wanted to be there for Valeri and for us, and to see what was taking place.

Before we left, again around midnight, an intern came into the room. He inserted a catheter into Valeri's urethra to help her urinate into an attached bag. He explained, "This is so she doesn't have to get out of bed to go to the bathroom, since she is experiencing dizziness and feeling very weak." This was a little demoralizing for Valeri, because she was hoping to get back on her feet the next day and begin moving around to maintain her strength.

On the way to the hospital Wednesday morning, Marietta and I both began crying when we thought about what the doctors had said about our Valeri not living much longer. Once in Valeri's room, I again gave her the sports report for the day. She talked a little bit about her Pistons and how they'd better start playing better than they had earlier in the week. She was very tired and would doze off from time to time. I was worried, because the doctors were going to hold our conference later on that afternoon, when I returned from my class at Wayne State.

After teaching my health class, I headed back to my car in the parking lot behind the Old Main building, about a tenth of a mile away from the classroom. I had to walk through the center of campus, near the Student Center Building. I couldn't help looking around at all the wonderful young people, so happily bouncing in all directions, to different places and classes. I thought about this beautiful, sunny day. It felt so good to be alive and to be a part of this wonderful world. I thought about the dynamics of attending college and securing an education, and about Valeri, who was close to getting her master's degree at Wayne State, and how much she had enjoyed taking part in the activities at the Student Center when she was a student here. I looked at the cars whizzing by on Warren Avenue and felt the life on the campus surrounding me. It suddenly occurred to me that Valeri was nearing the end of her own life and would not see these things much longer - perhaps never see them again. I thought of how much Valeri loved life.

Shortly after I arrived at the hospital, the doctors came into her room and asked Marietta and me to step out into the hall with them. Marietta and I joined Dr. Reyes, Dr. Tapazoglou, Dr. Carion, and Dr. Patel in the hall. As I left the room, I glanced back at Valeri, who was looking very apprehensive and worried. It reminded me of the times I would walk out of the room to talk to Dr. Charbeneau in the hallway when Valeri was a youngster. I couldn't help thinking of the quote in her diary:

> *There goes Dad again. Going outside to ask Dr. Charbeneau all kinds of questions without me hearing what's going on. I hate it. I wish they would consult with me, too.*

But in this case it was the doctors' choice to speak with us in the hallway rather than in Valeri's room. Dr. Reyes looked at us gravely and said, "Mr. and Mrs. Samaras, it appears as though Valeri might have had a silent heart attack in recent months, as indicated on her electrocardiogram. But worse than that, it appears that her heart is failing. She is suffering from congestive heart failure. It can't pump out even thirty percent of the necessary blood that her body requires. If the medication we are giving her doesn't help, then your daughter is not going to live more than a few days."

Both Marietta and I just stood there silently, in shock. Finally, I asked, "A few days, Dr. Reyes? When I take her pulse, her heart seems to be pumping so evenly and nicely at fifty-five beats a minute."

He agreed, "Yes, but eventually it will beat forty-five, forty, and thirty-five times a minute, before it will fail completely. Which is going to happen."

Dr. Carion interjected quickly, "I didn't realize she was that ill. I knew that she had a gallop in her pulse rate, but I didn't think her heart was that weak."

I asked him what Val's iron count was. He said it was up around 18,000; which was not a true indication, because she did have an infection in her body also. Dr. Reyes then said, "Let's hope that the medication works. But, she must eat to regain her strength. Let's see what happens in the next day or so. The treatment will continue as of now."

I glanced back into the room and noted that Valeri had her ear turned toward the hallway, trying to catch what was being said. Marietta asked Dr. Reyes, "Should I tell Valeri the truth about how sick she is?"

"Yes," he answered, "You owe it to her to tell her. I think you *must* tell her." With that, all the doctors said good-bye and left.

Marietta and I turned in our stunned state, and walked back to Valeri's bedside. Valeri asked, "What did the doctors say? Did I have a heart attack? Is that what has happened to me?"

I answered, "No, Valeri. They think that the electrocardiogram might have displayed a heart attack in the past."

Marietta then took Valeri by the hand and said gently, "You are sick, Valeri. It's up to the medication and your body to make a turnaround so you can get well."

"Am I going to die, Mom?" Valeri asked quietly.

"We're all going to die someday, but right now it's up to you to try to turn this thing around so you can go on living."

Valeri became very quiet. "I don't want to talk anymore, Mom and Dad. I want to take a nap."

I said, "Valeri, let's keep trying to turn the corner, honey. Let's keep working at it. You're going to have to eat and get your rest, and you're going to receive the medication. Let's try, sweetheart." She turned her head away and closed her eyes.

Marietta went out of the room and into the lounge. She broke down and cried. I was still dazed, not believing what I had heard. "Could this really be happening? Is our daughter's condition so serious that her life is going to end in a few short days?" I asked myself.

After Valeri awoke from her nap, we walked back into the room, sat down next to her, and held her hands. Marietta held one; I held the other. Valeri asked, "Am I really dying? Am I really dying or am I going to be able to live?" We didn't answer. "I don't mind if I die, Mom, but there won't be anybody up there in heaven with me."

Marietta quickly responded, "Valeri, there's John Kapotas, Ernie Kastran, Bob Vickrey, and so many other friends that we have. Also your grandmother, grandfathers, and quite a few other people are up there in heaven."

Val looked at us. "Yes, I guess I won't be all alone in heaven."

Then I quickly said, "Hey, Val, let's try to turn this thing around. Let's pray and hope that you can, and that the medication will accomplish its mission."

A little while later, as we sat there holding Valeri's hands, she looked sadly at Marietta and lamented, "I was never married, Mom. I never got married." When she said this, I remembered all the times I used to talk to Valeri about being healthy, optimistic, and happy; how things would all fall into place. I would tell her that she would meet someone who would love her and want to marry her. I thought about what a fabulous wedding we were going to have for her - it would be the best! - walking Valeri down the aisle and giving her away to her fiancé *would be the proudest moment of my life.*

Marietta gently consoled her: "Valeri, the relationship that you and Chris Garkinos have had through all these years is the kind that very few couples ever acquire in marriage. To have the companionship of a friend like Chris, and to do the things that you two have done, is more than one could actually expect in a marriage."

Val looked at her mother with tears in her eyes. We were all in tears, as we just sat there for quite a while before any of us said anything. Then Marietta and I both kissed Valeri and told her, "Valeri we love you so much. You're such a wonderful, wonderful daughter."

She looked up at us and said, "You know what? Chris didn't call back and I didn't call him back. I think I'll have to call him tonight or tomorrow morning when I feel stronger." Suddenly she cried, "I want to live, Mom and Dad! I want to live! How about my chelation? I wonder if they will reconsider giving it to me if my heart medication works?"

That night, Valeri still didn't want to see any visitors other than her two sisters. She had a restful evening and slept very soundly. Marietta and I spent much of that night thinking about her heart medication, and what would happen during the next couple of days. We sat there wondering what heart-shattering event could possibly happen next.

When we arrived at the hospital early Thursday morning, Valeri was taking a nap. She had been given a sponge bath, was offered breakfast, and had had two doctors visit her already. The patient-care routine in the hospital always began very early in the morning. It was common for Valeri to follow the early morning hospital routine, and then try to catch up on her sleep.

When she awoke from her nap, she greeted us with an upbeat: "Hi, Mom and Dad! You're here pretty early again."

"Yeah," I responded, "we wanted to get here and see how everything was going, Valeri."

Val looked out the window and saw the bright, shining sun. "Gosh, it looks beautiful outside!"

"Yes, honey," I said. "It's the first day of spring. It's been kind of warm lately. It's a very nice day today."

"Yes, that's right, springtime, sunshine! It's definitely top-down weather in my convertible, with the radio blasting!" she commented excitedly. But, then she turned her head away and looked very sad.

I brought her up-to-date on the sports world which, again, she seemed to enjoy. During this stay in the hospital, Valeri didn't watch television or listen to the radio. She seemed to be too tired and too weary to listen to or watch either one. "Yeah, Dad," she said, "those Pistons are floundering. I'm starting to worry about them."

"Don't worry," I reassured her, "they're going to get on the winning track again and be very tough in the play-offs."

"I had a restful night, Mom and Dad," she announced. "I'm feeling pretty good this morning, except that I feel very tired." Then with her beautiful, big eyes wide open she stated, "You know, Mom and Dad, I am quite ill. I realize that. But, I want to live. I love my life and I want to keep on living. I want to live. Ask the doctors what I have to do to turn this thing around so I can go on living."

Right around that time, Dr. Patel, the gastroenterologist, entered the room and walked over to her bed. He looked at her and asked, "Val, how are you feeling this morning?"

"Fine," she answered, "doing just fine." It was her stock answer. No matter what the doctors would ask and how badly she was feeling, that's what she would automatically say. She asked Dr. Patel, "How can I help myself get better?"

"Well," he began, "one of the keys is that you have to eat to regain your strength."

"Will I receive an IV, so that I can be fed that way?"

"We can use the IV, but I would rather see you eat food instead. It would be much better for you," he told her.

"I really don't feel that hungry for regular food," she said.

"Well, I'm going to order this special malted milk for you, which has many of the necessary nutrients. You try to drink it. Let's get you back on some sort of eating schedule."

"Okay. I'm certainly going to try." A short while after he left, a nurse brought the special malted milk drink in and gave it to Valeri. Slowly, she began to sip it through a straw. "Oh, boy! This is good old chocolate. You know how much I like chocolate!" But after taking two or three sips, she pushed it away. "I really don't want any more, Mom and Dad. I'll just put it down here and try to drink some again later."

Valeri seemed to be holding her own at this time. She could sit up in bed, but she didn't seem strong enough to get up and sit on the chair, as she had the day before. She preferred to lie there, and occasionally she would doze off. The itchiness was gone, and she seemed much more comfortable. The nurse often changed the bed position so Val could sit up comfortably. As in the past, she struck up a friendly relationship with all the nurses. Whenever they did something to help her, she would smile at them and say, "Thank you very much." She was not a demanding patient. In fact, she never pushed the nurse's button. She didn't seem to be bothered by the oxygen tubes in her nose, as the oxygen helped her breathe more easily.

By early noon, flowers and gifts began pouring in for Valeri. Obviously word was getting around to her friends and other relatives that she was in the hospital and not doing well. She was always so appreciative of the gifts and flowers that were sent to her when she was in the hospital. She received several cards from the volunteer mail person. One of them was from Jill, who wrote: "Hey, Val! I'm going to be back for good within a few days! We're going to light up that town, so you'd better start feeling better!"

That afternoon Father Kavadas visited Val with Father Makrinos, who had been visiting each day. Father Kavadas and Valeri were very good friends. She was happy to see him. He stayed and spoke with her for several minutes, and then he turned to Father Makrinos on the way out and stated, "I think Valeri should receive Holy Communion tomorrow when you come to visit." He went back and spent a little more time with Valeri before leaving. Val had much respect and love for Father Kavadas and Father Makrinos. She appreciated that they had come to visit her. Marietta and I walked both fathers to the elevators. We spoke of her condition. All of us had tears in our eyes.

Early that evening Valeri was very pleased when Nikki and Debbie came to visit her. Nikki brought Alex along. Alex sat on the bed next to Valeri during her entire visit. They talked to each other, laughed, and kidded around. They used their own set of communication signals, like slapping hands when they said something they both enjoyed hearing, winking whenever they agreed on something, and blowing kisses back and forth whenever Alexandra would leave the room and then come back. Alex's presence seemed to give Valeri an emotional boost.

Meanwhile, there was a constant parade of friends and relatives coming to visit, and they all were told that she was not having visitors at the moment. They would stay out in the patient lounge and visit with us. When told about them, Val said, "I would like to start seeing my friends and relatives, Mom and Dad." We realized that it probably was best to have only two or three people visiting in the room at one time; otherwise it would become too tiring for Valeri. So we set up a procedure, and Valeri really enjoyed talking with her visitors.

After visiting hours ended, Marietta and I sat with Valeri until nearly midnight. She commented, "You know I do want to get well, Mom and Dad." It was the same, wonderful, determined look in her eyes that we had seen so many times in the past when Valeri was tackling a very difficult obstacle in her life.

I thought to myself, "If there's any chance of Valeri turning this thing around, she will do it."

On the way home from the hospital, Marietta and I were both quiet and downcast. Finally, Marietta broke the silence. "Valeri seemed to be very anxious to try to do things that would help her regain her health." She looked at me, with tears in her eyes. "I hope that she'll have that chance. She did seem a little stronger today, at times." Both of us were thinking the same thing: unless the medication worked, this was a no-win situation; but who knew what could happen?

Our brief moment of optimism was shattered early the next morning. On Friday, Dr. Tapazoglou reported that it appeared that Valeri had contracted pneumonia. We had noticed that Valeri was having a little difficulty in breathing. When she was told this, she exclaimed, "Oh, no! What next?" At first, during her hospital stay, Valeri didn't believe that she was seriously ill. After a couple of days, she expressed some anger about her situation. Later, she bargained with the idea that if she ate she would get better. Now, Valeri started to get depressed.

Later that morning she turned to her mother and asked again, "Mom, am I going to die?"

Marietta gave her our stock answer. "Valeri, let's work and see if we can turn this thing around, honey." Val looked at us very sadly, then closed her eyes and fell asleep.

She took brief naps during the morning and early afternoon. When she would wake up, she would stare at the calendar and clock on the wall opposite her. She had a rather strange and questioning look on her face. Finally, after about the third time this happened, Marietta asked her: "What are you staring at, honey?"

"Oh, nothing. I'm just looking at the time and the date." It seemed as if Valeri was looking to verify that she was still on this earth, living with us, by looking at the time of day and the date, and then looking to see that we were still there with her.

As I sat there, I became very upset, deliberating over what our Valeri must be thinking and feeling at this critical time. She had to be fearful about dying and leaving this world and going into the unknown. These thoughts and feelings must be excruciatingly painful. Additionally, she was experiencing physical pain and suffering along the way. I became very depressed about the emotional and physical pain that Valeri must be undergoing. It was devastating to see how upset Marietta was, as well as Debbie and Nikki. The whole scenario was one of uncertainty, fear, and sadness.

That afternoon Father Makrinos came to visit Valeri and gave her Holy Communion. Father Makrinos administered it to both Marietta and me, as we thought it would be less worrisome for Valeri if she saw us both taking Holy Communion, too. At a time like this, Holy Communion, in a way, represented the last rites for a person. Valeri thanked Father Makrinos for administering Communion to all of us.

A short while later, Valeri extended her hands out to Marietta and me. She wanted each of us to hold one of her hands. As we sat there talking, she squeezed them and looked at us and said, "Mom and Dad, I love you two so much! You're such wonderful, wonderful parents! I just love you so very, very much!" She continued to squeeze our hands and to impress on us how much love she felt for us.

At intervals, Marietta and I would say to her, "You know how much we love you. You are our wonderful, wonderful daughter."

As I wandered through the hall a little later on the way to the elevator, I ran into a friend of mine, Dr. Ted Pantos, a urologist. I explained to Dr. Pantos that Valeri was quite ill. He understood, because being Greek, he knew quite a bit about Cooley's Anemia. He told me he'd like to visit Valeri for a few minutes. We went back to her room. Val was awake. "Hi, Dad. How are you doing?" I introduced Dr. Pantos to her. He very gently shook hands with her. He talked to her for a couple of minutes in a very encouraging voice. After she fell asleep I walked out into the hall and had a brief discussion with him about her condition. He expressed deep sadness at seeing Valeri in her weakened state. I thanked him for his visit, and he waved and left to see other patients.

Later in the afternoon, I went home to check the house, and to jog my usual two miles. Exercise was my way of trying to relax, and reduce my anxiety and stress. Meanwhile, Marietta walked to the gift shop and then stopped at the hospital chapel, leaving Valeri alone with Debbie and Nikki. Val asked both of them: "Am I really dying? Am I going to die, Debbie and Nikki?"

They were at a loss for words. Nikki finally gently scolded her: "Look, of course you're not going to die, silly. You're going to get well."

"I hope you're right, Nikki," Valeri said a little skeptically. "You know, if I *do* die, I think Mom is going to be okay, but I'm not so sure about Dad. I'm worried about him."

Debbie said, "Let's not talk this way, Val. Let's just try to get you well."

In the early evening I noticed that Valeri was having a difficult time breathing. I called for the nurse. When a nurse came in, Valeri said, "I'm having a hard time breathing."

Marietta was on the other side of her bed. She looked at Valeri and said, "Val, you're okay. You're just a little anxious and excited." She took Valeri's hand and said, "Now Valeri, I want you to breathe with me. In . . . out . . . in . . . out." Marietta continued this very deliberate breathing and speaking at the same time. After about eight to ten minutes, Valeri appeared very relaxed and was back to feeling good again. The nurse just stood there and watched. She realized that, with her marvelously quick reaction, Marietta had gotten everything under control.

The nurse later told us in the hall that Valeri had just experienced a terrible anxiety attack, which happens to people who are seriously ill.

When we returned to the room I looked down at the little bag which collected urine from her bladder, and realized that it wasn't filling up as rapidly as it had been. This was disturbing to me, as I knew that if the kidneys ceased to function, a patient couldn't survive for very long. But the bag did contain some urine, which meant that they were still working, even if at a low level.

Many people visited Valeri that evening. She seemed to show a little spark of interest when they would enter the room, two at a time. She was especially happy to see Rena, Sue, Harriet, and Roula, as well as some of her cousins. Of course, Nikki and Alex were always there by her side. Later that evening, Valeri remarked, "I haven't heard from Chris in several days. I wonder what has happened?"

Nikki stated, "Well, I'm going to find out what happened. I'll make sure that he calls you tomorrow, Valeri."

Marietta looked at me and said, "You know, Bob, I think we should stay with Valeri tonight." I agreed.

Val protested: "You don't have to, Mom and Dad. You can go home."

"No, it's all settled, we're staying," Marietta said firmly. She went to the nurses' station to inform them of our intent. They thought it was a good idea. Arrangements were made to have Val's roommate and bed moved to another room, so that a cot could be placed in the room for Marietta and me to use during the night.

Around eleven o'clock, Valeri once again informed us that she wasn't feeling too well. I went to the nurses' station and requested that a resident come to see her. Within minutes, a female resident arrived and looked at Valeri. "Okay, I'll take care of this," she said, and left the room. She returned shortly.

Marietta and I walked outside the room into the hallway and began questioning the resident on what she was planning to do. As we were speaking, two medical assistants came up with a large machine. "I'm going to hook Valeri to a respirator. I'm going to take emergency action right now because she's quite ill."

We looked at each other and Marietta stated: "You are not going to touch Valeri at all. We only asked you to check her for a minute to see if anything could be done within reason. You are not going to put her on a respirator or any other kind of machine, or stick tubes down her throat or into her neck. We refuse to have that done!"

The resident looked back at us and replied: "That is my job. I made that decision."

"You will not do that," Marietta retorted. "I will not allow you to." I supported Marietta.

The resident responded, "The only way you can prevent me from doing this is to have your doctor order me not to. He left no message as to what is to be done, and it is my responsibility."

Marietta turned and said, "Well, let's go to the nurses' station to phone Dr. Tapazoglou. I will call him and he will talk to you. Meanwhile, Bob, you stay here and don't let anybody go in and touch Valeri."

Nikki and Debbie were still with Val when I walked back into the room. "What's Mom yelling about now, Dad?" Valeri asked.

"Oh, nothing. She's just trying to straighten out some things with the resident."

Later, when I was recollecting these events, Valeri's question reminded me about the comment she had once made in her journal:

For years whenever a treatment was not going the way Mom thought was correct, she would go down the hall screaming and hollering to the nurse, until things were rectified properly.

"There goes Mom again, huh, Dad?"

"Well, you know your Mom, she'll take good care of things. I'll go help her in a minute."

Debbie and Nikki stayed with her while I went to the nurses' desk. Marietta and the resident were still arguing. The secretary was trying to place a call to Dr. Tapazoglou. I told the resident: "We're not going to put Valeri on any machines. We will wait until Dr. Tapazoglou informs you that you cannot touch her."

The doctor answered the phone and I explained to him what was happening. He asked me to put the resident on the phone, which I did. Dr. Tapazoglou spoke with her and told her that Valeri was to be left alone, and just kept comfortable. The resident responded, "Okay, I will do that for now, but I think you and the parents will have to sign the form that we have in the office." We agreed to sign the form.

As we were looking the form over, Dr. Tapazoglou called back and cautioned us, "Please don't do anything or sign anything until I get there in about half an hour."

When he arrived, he conferred with Marietta and me. We decided that it would be better if we just kept Valeri comfortable. There were to be no machines or blood tests. She was not to be tortured with needles stuck in her arm or instruments stuck in her neck. She was not to be hooked up to any machines. Dr. Tapazoglou agreed with our decision. He had the secretary fill out the proper papers and we both signed them. The resident said, "Everything is all set now and I will stay out of the picture," and she left.

Dr. Tapazoglou empathized, "I know this is very, very difficult, but I think it's best if we quit doing anything except feed her, give her oral medication, and keep her comfortable." We thanked him.

Then Marietta and I headed back to Valeri's room, crying along the way. We felt extremely sad, but knew that we had made the right decision. Marietta said, "You know how terrible it is to put a youngster on a machine with all those needles and instruments stuck in her - and then we'd only be allowed to visit her for five minutes every hour? Especially one of those tubes stuck down her throat preventing her from talking - no! Our Valeri doesn't need that. I think we made the right decision to keep her as comfortable as possible during her last few days."

Unfortunately, the heart medication was not working. Therefore, there was no reason to keep the IVs on or to take any blood test, which would cause pain to her. Marietta quietly repeated, "Let's just keep her comfortable until it's all over."

When we returned to the room, Valeri said, "Hey, Mom! Just like old times, you really let them have it. Whatever it was, I know you won the argument." Debbie, Nikki, Valeri, Marietta, and I laughed. Then she said, "I don't think you've ever lost an argument, Mom." We laughed again. Valeri could find humor in almost any situation.

A little later, Debbie and Nikki left for home. Val seemed very tired, and again was having difficulty breathing. When we mentioned this to the nurse, the nurse said she would send a respiratory therapist to give Valeri a treatment. This particular treatment consisted of a mask that covered Valeri's mouth and nose. The mask was connected to a tube that was connected to a machine. The procedure cleared out some of the mucus that was causing the problem. After the treatment Val could breathe easier and was more comfortable.

We decided that perhaps Marietta should sleep on the cot and rest. I would sit next to Valeri, keep her company, and watch a little television while she slept. I insisted that Marietta sleep on the cot, because she was extremely tired. I knew it was difficult for her to sleep on the lounge chair alongside Valeri's bed. I had more of a penchant for dozing off in a lounge chair, and thought this arrangement would be more convenient for both of us. I also felt it would be easier for me, a light sleeper, to get up and help Valeri should she wake up during the night and need anything.

Both of us stayed up with Valeri until after 1:30 a.m. as she slept very comfortably. Marietta finally lay down on the cot and fell asleep. I sat there for a while, then put my head down on Valeri's thigh, held her hand, and fell asleep in that position for most of the night. Valeri awoke a couple of times, wanting to sip a little bit of water. As she was lying there, going back to sleep, I told her what Marietta and I had often said during these last several days: how much we loved her and what a wonderful daughter she was. I told her to keep working to turn this thing around.

Our desire to stay overnight in the hospital as long as Valeri remained critically ill made it mandatory for Marietta and me to set up a new routine. Marietta refused to go home while Valeri was in this condition; rather, she insisted on staying with her around the clock. I was to go home to check the house, shower, shave, change clothes, maybe jog, then bring different clothes for Marietta to wear. Meanwhile, Marietta would visit the chapel each morning and pray for Valeri. The chapel at St. John Hospital is a beautiful place to visit. Both Marietta and I had found comfort there over the years, especially so during this crisis. After returning to the hospital, I'd spend the rest of the day there, except for occasional errands.

Following my visit home that Saturday morning, I returned to find Valeri extremely weak, tired, and unable to speak above a low whisper. We could barely hear her. Her vital signs were showing a change for the worse. Her heart had slowed down to less than forty-five beats a minute, her blood pressure was very low, and she had difficulty breathing. Her breathing was uncoordinated. It seemed like she was breathing twice instead of just once with each breath. I also noted the urine bag alongside her bed contained very little fluid.

As the day progressed, Val seemed to become somewhat stronger, and she was more responsive to what was going on around her. I gave her the usual sports report and, to my surprise, she was able to communicate with me. Her voice was strong again. Her condition seemed to go in spurts - she showed sporadic strength, followed by severe weakness and weariness. She also took naps more frequently.

All four of her doctors visited. Again, every time they asked Val how she was doing, she would say "Fine," then would perk up and talk to them.

Early that afternoon, a strange thing happened while she was napping. I had gone out to run an errand. Only Marietta was sitting with Valeri, who was asleep. Suddenly, Val said, very loudly: "Mom! Mom!

Something wonderful is happening! I see beautiful light! It's just wonderful. It's a beautiful, bright light." Marietta looked at Valeri and noticed she was still sleeping.

Later on, when Valeri woke up, Marietta asked her about the light that she had talked about. Valeri just looked at Marietta strangely. "I don't know what you mean, Mom."

"Valeri, you were talking about a beautiful light that you saw," Marietta insisted.

"Honestly, Mom, I can't remember anything about seeing a bright light."

While walking down the hall a little later I saw my friend Dr. Al Santino, a urologist. He asked what I was doing at the hospital and I told him that Valeri was critically ill. He had seen Valeri on one or two occasions professionally when Dr. Carion wasn't available. Dr. Santino urged, "Come on. I want to visit her." We walked into her room and he greeted her, "Hi, Valeri. How are you doing?"

She looked up at him and gave her usual, "Fine, Dr. Santino."

He took her hand, held it, and told her, "Valeri, I think you're going to make it. You just keep trying." He gave her a nice smile, then left. Val was very pleased that Dr. Santino had taken the time to talk to her.

On another occasion that day, I saw my friend Dr. Pozios, who had treated Valeri when she had her stroke. Dr. Pozios is also Greek and very familiar with Cooley's Anemia. I mentioned to him that Valeri was critically ill; he was very sympathetic. He looked at me and said, "You know, Bob, maybe it's time to let go. Maybe it's time to let Valeri find peace. She has suffered so much, and for so long. Maybe it's time . . . She's been a very courageous young lady, but the suffering has really taken its toll."

It was depressing for me to hear Dr. Pozios' words, especially when, upon returning to Val's room I heard her say: "Mom, I sure would love to live. I wish I could do something. I want to live."

Visitors were coming up at all hours now. There were no restrictions on the number of people who came or at what time they visited. The reception room was loaded with friends and relatives. Nikki and Alex visited Valeri for long periods of time each day, as would Debbie and her husband, Brian.

That afternoon, Nikki told Valeri that Chris was planning to visit her tomorrow, on Sunday. He would leave Los Angeles early in the morning and arrive somewhere around four-thirty or five o'clock in the afternoon to see her. Nikki explained to Val that he would have been here today, except that communication was fouled up. Nikki informed us that Chris had been told that Val was not seriously ill, and there was no need for him to come at this time. He did not realize that Valeri was critically ill and near death. He called on Saturday morning when Nikki was home and asked her what was going on. Nikki told him that Valeri was very critically ill. He was extremely upset, and he told her he would make a reservation immediately and come in on Sunday.

Chris also called Valeri late that afternoon to tell her he was going to be in the next day to see her and he hoped that she was feeling better. This pleased Valeri very much. She said, "I sure will be happy to see you, Chris." Later Val reminded us how both she and Chris were very interested in the Academy Awards program which was going to take place on Monday night. "I hope he's here so we can enjoy the awards on TV together, as we've done in the past."

It suddenly occurred to me that we had neglected to contact two people whom Valeri loved very much: Debbie's daughter, Michelle; and her son, Phillip. Both children were living with their father, Joe Bellomo. I turned to Debbie and asked, "Debbie, don't you think we should call Michelle and Phillip?"

"I think that's a great idea, Dad," she answered. "I'll do it right now." Five minutes later, she returned to the room and announced, "Dad, they're going to come down here. Joe will have them at the new entrance to the hospital, and you can go meet them and bring them up to see Valeri."

A short while later I met them in the lobby. Phillip and Michelle came upstairs with me to visit their aunt. "Hi, Poochie!" they said, and each one kissed Valeri and held her hand. She seemed very pleased to see them.

Michelle told her, "I made the honor roll, Poochie! I just got my report card. I'm very happy about it, and Phillip did very well, too."

Valeri's face lit up. She smiled and quietly said, "That's great, Michelle and Phillip. I'm proud of both of you guys." Valeri always encouraged them to work hard at school.

Michelle and Phillip visited with Val for about an hour. Their departure was very emotional. Both children had tears in their eyes as they kissed Valeri and bid her good-bye. I walked them back to the main lobby. They both sobbed all the way. "We love our Poochie so much! We hope she's going to be okay, Pa Poo," Phillip said.

Michelle added, "I know she's going to get well. Poochie just has to get well." Once in the lobby, I thanked Joe for bringing them to see her. He asked how Val was doing and I told him that she wasn't doing very well. He was very sad.

Upon returning to the room, Valeri amazingly showed her sense of humor again. She looked at me and commented, "I must be dying if Joe made time to bring the kids to the hospital to see me. Too bad he didn't come upstairs, too."

It was interesting to Marietta and me that as long as the visitors were coming into the room two or three at a time, Valeri seemed to perk up. After everyone had left for the evening, including Debbie, Nikki, and Alex, Valeri was really tired and very uncomfortable. She requested another respiratory treatment, which again seemed to help her relax.

Marietta and I talked about many different subjects while watching TV as Valeri slept. Eventually Marietta went to sleep on her cot, and I again slept with my head on Valeri's bed, holding her hand, with my head occasionally on her thigh or leg. I felt very stressed out and worried, but was comforted by the thought that Chris was going to visit Valeri the next day.

When I returned to the hospital after completing my chores at home the next morning, I was pleasantly surprised to find Valeri feeling quite good, sitting up, and actually being chipper. It was a paradox, since she had seemed lethargic and sluggish when I had left. She greeted me with a very happy, "Hi, Dad, how are you doing? How's everything at home?"

"Valeri, how are you feeling?"

"Pretty good, Dad," she replied. "A couple of the doctors stopped in to see me. I told them I was feeling somewhat better today."

"Did you eat any breakfast?"

"Not really, Dad, not very much. I tried to drink some of that malted milk, but I just couldn't handle it." Marietta sat on the opposite side of the bed and seemed to be very happy about Valeri's resurgence.

A short time later during an ensuing conversation centering on life and health, Valeri looked at us, and in a semi-humorous yet sad tone, lamented: "Don't tell me I went through all this just to die. I do *so* want to live." She put her head back down on the pillow and then stared into space.

Marietta quickly chided, "Don't be silly, Valeri. We're going to work hard and pray that you turn the corner and regain your health."

I couldn't help thinking to myself what a dynamic statement Valeri had made: "Don't tell me I've gone through all this just to die." I thought about the more than five hundred times she'd had to go to the hospital; of the nearly one thousand pints of blood she had received during several hundred transfusions; of all the illnesses along the way; and then her horrible stroke, followed by months and months of therapy; of her fractured shoulder and her fractured leg; of her arthritic knee; and of the mental anguish that she'd undergone, as well as the emotional abuse by peers during her school years, when they made fun of her because of her appearance when she was run down and needed transfusions. All this she had suffered, in addition to the discrimination she had endured while looking so hard for a professional job. Her twenty-nine years and ten months were loaded with a variety of enormous life problems. Still, there she was, lying in bed, dying, yet asserting, "I want to live!" She had met all her problems and adversities with courage, fortitude, enterprise, and bravery. She loved life and was willing to endure pain to continue her pursuit of happiness. How beautiful it would be if our prayers were answered and she could have a reprieve.

My thoughts were interrupted when Dr. Tapazoglou entered the room to see Valeri. "How are you doing today?" he asked her.

"Oh, fine," she answered, as usual.

He gave her a warm smile and then said, "I'll see you later this afternoon or tomorrow morning for sure," and he turned and left the room.

This period of feeling good for Valeri lasted into the early afternoon; then, once again, she showed signs of being very weary. Even more visitors were showing up at the hospital today, probably because it was Sunday and many people were not working. There had been a steady stream of friends and relatives since ten o'clock that morning. The visitors were very patient with the two-at-a-time system that we had established for them to see Valeri. Again, Debbie, Nikki, and Alex stayed with her in the room at all times.

Valeri spent most of the afternoon napping and talking with her visitors. About 4:30 p.m. she awoke from one of her naps. It happened that I was the only one there at her bedside at that moment. She looked very pale and weary. I asked her how she was feeling and she answered, "Not so good, Dad. I'm suddenly feeling very sick."

I held her hand and comforted her: "Well, you'll probably feel better in a few minutes, honey."

"I sure hope so, Dad. I just don't feel good." She stared into space, suddenly looked at me, and said vacantly, "Dad, I think it's time for me to go to heaven. I think it's time for me to go."

Although I felt panicky, I quietly said, "Valeri, sweetheart, hang on, honey. Chris is going to be here in about half an hour. I'm sure you're going to feel better. Just close your eyes and rest a little more. I'll sit here holding your hand while you rest, but please, honey, hang on." I thought to myself how awful it would be if something happened and Chris didn't get a chance to see Valeri alive one more time.

She fell asleep for about fifteen minutes and suddenly I felt her squeezing my hand. Valeri opened her eyes and looked at me with a pleasant smile on her face. "Dad, I feel better. I'm so happy Chris is going to be here in just a few minutes." I was so relieved to hear her say that.

I looked at the clock and thought, "Gosh, it's 5:15 p.m. Chris should be here any minute now." Marietta entered the room and I went out to the lounge for a while to talk to Nikki and Alexandra.

Just as I said to Nikki, "I think it's about time for Chris to show up," I spotted him at the far end of the hall, walking towards us. I quickly got up and ran toward him. "Hey, Chris, here we are. We're down here."

He walked quickly over to me and said "Hi, Mr. Samaras," and we hugged each other. "How is she doing?" he asked.

"Gosh, Chris, am I ever glad you're here! She's up and down, but she seems to be feeling pretty good right now, so let's go in and see her."

Chris walked into the room quickly, hugged and kissed Marietta, then looked at Valeri and said, "Valeri, sweetheart," and hugged and kissed her, too.

"Oh, Chris!" cried Valeri, "I'm so very, very happy that you're here!" All four of us had tears in our eyes.

Marietta and I decided to go into the hall to join Nikki and Alex, and leave Chris and Valeri by themselves. As we walked out of the room I heard Valeri's infectious laugh. It was the first time I'd heard that wonderful laugh in a long time.

Chris sat in the room, holding Valeri's hand as they talked about old times and things they wanted to do together in the future. For the next several hours, he only left the room once, to go to supper with Marietta and me while Debbie, Nikki, and Alex stayed with Valeri.

After six o'clock other visitors began arriving. It was about eight o'clock when Valeri awakened from a fifteen-minute nap and Marietta told her, "We have quite a few people in the lounge waiting to see you."

"Mom, bring them all in the room please. Bring them all in right now!"

Marietta looked at her in surprise and asked, "What did you say?"

"You heard me, Mom! Bring all my friends in the room right now. It will help me cope."

So I went out with Marietta to inform the visitors. "Come on," Marietta invited, "Valeri wants to see all of you together. We're all going to sit in her room." The visitors scurried around and found chairs in the hall and in the lounge, and everyone entered the room, greeted Valeri, and sat down.

Valeri's eyes lit up. She was smiling from ear to ear. Our "people person" Val was thrilled to have so many friends in her room with her at this time. All of the visitors seemed very sad, and some were trying not to cry. Valeri looked at her friends Sue, Rena, Harriet, Roula, Chris, several of her cousins, her Uncle George and Aunt Mary, her grandmother, her sisters, niece Alex, Godmother Dolly and husband George, and several others. "Gosh," Val said, "it's so *quiet* in here. I have never seen all of you so darn quiet."

Just then, Chris said, "You know what? I've got to tell you a funny story about Val and me. When Val visited me for her last birthday in San Francisco, I took her out to this very nice restaurant to eat. I secretly ordered a cake with the initials 'V.S.' on it. Just as we finished our meal I saw the waiter walk by with a birthday cake with the initials 'V.S.' I looked and thought, 'Hey, that's *Valeri's* cake.' As he took it over to a table on the far side of the room. I jumped out of my seat and said, 'Hey, that is *your* cake, Valeri,' and ran across the room to talk to the waiter. I interrupted the waiter: 'Excuse me, but that is my friend's cake. I think you've delivered it to the wrong table.' The waiter looked at me strangely and replied, 'Please, sir. You're bothering us. You're bothering these people. This is their cake.' I insisted: 'No, it *isn't* their cake' loudly enough to be heard across the room. The waiter protested again, '*Please,* sir, you *must* stop bothering us. This is *their* cake.' I was reluctant to leave, but turned to look at Valeri and suddenly saw another waiter going towards her with a cake and a candle on it. I ran back to the table and *it* was Valeri's cake. So obviously the other cake did belong to the other people. Valeri said, 'Oh, thank you for the cake!' and she and I could not stop laughing. All the people in the room began to laugh, too!"

Chris' story broke the ice, as one by one, each of us began telling little stories about incidents that had taken place. The whole room turned into one big, casual, fun-loving party. I looked at Valeri and could see how happy she was. Of course, she told several hilarious stories too.

There was suddenly a prevailing calmness and happiness among everyone in the room. All the attention was centered on Valeri. *She was making all of us feel at ease.* I could not help recalling her phrase from years ago: "Mom, if you stop crying, I'll stop crying." Valeri was putting us at ease. She wanted everyone in the room to accept her fate, as she had accepted it. She wanted us to be happy along with her. Even the nurses entering the room periodically, and the security officer who came into the room asking us to please be a little quieter, seemed to be involved in the happy spirit that prevailed. Our gathering lasted for a little over two hours.

As the guests began leaving, one by one they kissed Val, touched her hand gently, smiled at her and said, "We'll see you tomorrow." She smiled back and thanked each person for being there to help her enjoy the moment.

Soon the room was quiet again. Only Marietta, Chris, and I remained. Chris held Valeri's hand as she dozed off and took a brief nap. Obviously she was very tired from the excitement. She awoke again and began talking with Chris, mentioning something about the Academy Awards. Marietta and I left the room in order for Chris and Val to be alone for the next couple of hours.

When we returned, Valeri fell asleep again. I spoke with Chris about my desire to write a book about Cooley's Anemia and some of the medical advancements made against the disease. I also wanted to include some of the highlights of Valeri's courageous and exuberant life. He thought it was a good idea, and offered, "If there's any way I can help you, please feel free to call on me."

It was about midnight when Valeri awoke again. Chris hugged and kissed her and then said, "I'll see you tomorrow, Valeri," then turned and left.

Her eyes followed him until he left the room. Then she spoke: "I'm so happy that Chris came to see me. He is such a wonderful, wonderful person. He plans to leave tomorrow afternoon for Los Angeles. He must get back to work, but he'll spend several hours with me tomorrow before leaving."

Marietta was quite tired, so she went to the cot to sleep. I was holding Valeri's hand as she rested, with her eyes closed. Then she opened them and looked up at me and said, "You know, Dad, what I said about it being time for me to go to heaven? A woman does have the right to change her mind. I would like to stay on this earth and live for a while longer." Both of us began laughing.

I squeezed her hand, hugged and kissed her, and said, "Valeri, I love you so much. You're such a precious daughter."

She looked wistfully at me. "It has been a wonderful evening, Dad. You should get some rest, too. You and Mom should go home tonight."

Marietta, who had awakened, heard Valeri. "No way, Valeri. We're going to stay with you, sweetheart, but I think it's time for you to sleep and get some good rest tonight."

"I think you're right, Mom."

Marietta made Valeri comfortable in her bed by straightening her wrinkled sheets and pillow. Val turned her head to the side and fell asleep. Marietta returned to her cot and fell asleep, as I again slept with my head next to Valeri's thigh. When I checked her in the middle of the night, she appeared to be sleeping comfortably. She actually had a very restful night.

Although tired in the morning, Valeri seemed to be very happy. She remarked, "This is a typical Monday morning, Mom and Dad. I am tired and weary from my heavy weekend." But Marietta and I were quite concerned because Valeri napped most of the time. Even when she was awake, she seemed to be very, very tired. I again noticed the urine bag with its limited contents. Of course, this was a bad sign.

Nikki called and reported, "Gosh, Mom and Dad. We've been getting phone calls by the dozens wanting to know how Valeri's feeling. Tell Val that Chris called to say he would be there around 12:30 p.m."

I told Marietta about the many phone calls the girls were receiving at the house. "I'm sure Father Kavadas mentioned Valeri's name in church yesterday," Marietta explained, "and that she was not feeling well. He must have mentioned that she was at St. John Hospital." (It was customary for Father to tell the congregation when a parishioner was ill or in the hospital.)

We conveyed the message from Chris to Valeri. She responded, "Oh, good," then looked at us sadly and told us, "he's leaving to go back to Los Angeles at 5:00 this afternoon. He is new on his job and it's hard for him to get too much time off right now, but he does plan to return next weekend for a couple of days."

Dr. Patel entered the room a bit later and asked, "How are you doing today, Valeri?"

"Not so good." He was astounded to hear her say that. In fact, he looked quite worried, as he was so used to hearing her say "fine."

"Well, try to eat something today," he directed her with a half smile. "I'll see you tomorrow."

Marietta and I noticed that Val's arms were swollen. Her breathing was still uncoordinated and labored. Marietta asked the nurse to turn Val's oxygen supply up a degree or two, which the nurse did.

Chris showed up a little after 12:30 p.m. He sat down and held Valeri's hand. Marietta and I went to the cafeteria to eat lunch. The afternoon seemed to be flying by.

Later, when Marietta and I were sitting out in the lounge, she remarked, "You know, Chris will be leaving in another hour or so. His being here has been so good for Valeri. She seems to perk up and to be so much happier when he is with her. She is slipping, Bob."

I was in the room at about five o'clock when Chris said, "Mr. Samaras, I'm going to leave soon. Would you mind leaving Valeri and me alone for a few minutes?"

"Of course not, Chris." I quickly walked out of the room to join Marietta in the lounge.

Chris hugged and kissed her. "Good-bye, Valeri. I'm going to come back and see you next week." They both were sobbing when he said good-bye, as they both realized that they would never see each other again. "I love you, Valeri. Keep feeling better until I see you next week."

A few minutes later he emerged from the room, crying. Both Marietta and I broke into tears. We each hugged Chris and said, "Thank you so much for coming. We'll keep you posted on what is happening. Take care and have a safe trip back to California." He left.

Marietta and I looked at each other and both had the same thought: That was probably the last time Chris and Valeri would see each other. The thought was almost unbearable.

When Marietta and I walked back into the room, Valeri was crying quietly. Suddenly she stopped. "I hope Chris has a nice trip back. I'll get to see him next week anyway." Then she said, "I think I'll take a nap, Mom and Dad. I'll pass on supper. I just don't feel like trying to eat anything."

Marietta objected. "No. I'm going to get the food for you and keep the malted milk here. When you wake up, I'll give it to you."

Valeri gave her a little smile. "Okay, thanks, Mom." Then she fell asleep.

Visitors were arriving intermittently, and we would take them in to see Valeri. Sometimes Valeri would wake up and talk to them, and at other times she would continue sleeping. If she was sleeping, they would sit and talk with Marietta and me, then leave.

Around eight o'clock, Valeri once again requested, "Hey, Mom, you are going to bring all my visitors in to see me, aren't you?"

"Of course, Val. I'll go get them right now." So once again, we had a room full of people. They would converse amongst themselves or with Valeri; then Val would talk for a short time. At times one person would speak while the entire group listened, and at other times, several conversations would go on at once. It was a pleasant, relaxing atmosphere. Valeri, although very tired, would wake up and smile and talk for a while, then doze off again. Sometimes it was funny when someone would comment about an incident that had taken place, and she would wake up and add some humorous detail to it. Many of her old standby friends were in the room again, as were some of her cousins.

Soon it was after nine o'clock and time for the visitors to leave. Marietta and I felt that Valeri should rest, as she appeared very tired. So again, one by one, the visitors bade Val good-bye. When most of them had gone, Rena and Sue said their good-byes and began crying as they left the room. Roula, the last to leave, leaned over Valeri and with a warm, affectionate smile said, "I'll see you tomorrow, Val."

With a sparkle in her eyes, Valeri smiled back and affectionately nodded her head and replied, "Okay." Then she closed her eyes and fell asleep as Roula left the room.

It was very quiet. Marietta and I were both very disturbed. I noticed that Val's arms seemed to be swollen. The urine bag was almost empty: the kidneys were barely functioning, if they were functioning at all. Valeri would bravely open her eyes, hold our hands, and smile at us. We would say "I love you" to each other, and she'd fall back asleep.

At about 9:30 p.m. Valeri opened her eyes and whispered, "Mom, Mom, put on Channel Four. Put the Academy Awards on."

Marietta was happy to hear Valeri's request, especially since through this whole ordeal Val had not watched any television. She knew how much Valeri loved Academy Award night, and she was elated that Valeri wished to see how the ceremony was progressing. But, Val was unable to watch the program for very long, dozing off after only a few minutes of watching. I sat there viewing the program while Marietta went to the cot to lie down.

Val awoke and whispered, "Dad, put the ear plug in my ear so I can hear what's going on." I quickly jumped up and honored her request. However, after a few minutes she again began dozing off and on, then woke up and whispered, "Take the ear plug out, please, Dad. It's too uncomfortable." I knew it must have been very irritating for her because of her weakened condition.

Meanwhile, I kept watching the award presentations. When Valeri would open her eyes, I'd tell her about the presentation and who had won the award. Jeremy Irons won the Best Actor award for *Reversal of Fortunes*. I thought to myself, "I've never even heard of this person."

When Valeri awakened she asked: "Who won the Best Actor award?" I replied, "I don't know. I forgot his name. He was in the film *Reversal of Fortunes* or something like that."

"Oh, Dad," she chided, "that's Jeremy Irons!" and then she fell asleep again. Soon the award for Best Actress was presented to Jody Foster for *Silence of the Lambs*. Again, when Valeri awakened for a few minutes I told her who won. She gave a small smile and said, "Super! Jody deserved it for her fine acting in that movie." Later, when *Dances With Wolves* won the Best Picture award, I waited again for Valeri to wake up so that I could relay the information to her. She smiled and reminded me, "I didn't see that movie. Remember, Dad, when you went to see it? I didn't feel like sitting for over three hours or else I would have joined you. You were right about predicting that movie would win." Then she fell asleep.

I noticed she was experiencing further breathing difficulties, so I requested another respiratory treatment, which was given to her about twenty minutes later. After that treatment she began wheezing slightly and fell sound asleep.

Marietta woke up and we looked at Valeri and noted that her arms were more swollen. Both of us began to cry. A nurse entered the room. Marietta asked her, "What happens when a victim dies? What will happen?"

The nurse was sympathetic and understanding. She replied, "They slip into a coma, usually. Then they quietly pass away." She hugged Marietta, who began sobbing. The nurse had tears in her eyes, too. I turned my head and started crying, also.

Soon the nurse left. Marietta said, "Bob, you get a couple hours of sleep. You haven't rested at all and it's almost one o'clock in the morning. I'll stay awake with Valeri." I reluctantly agreed and lay down on the cot. I slept for about an hour. I awoke and insisted that Marietta go to sleep on the cot. I slept in the chair, in my usual position with my head on the bed. Marietta fell asleep; she was so worn out and tired. I felt so sorry for her because she hadn't left the hospital for four days. She insisted on staying near her daughter every minute of the day and night.

As I sat holding Val's hand, listening to her wheeze with each breath, watching her uncoordinated breathing, and looking at her swollen arms and hands, a thought suddenly struck me: "I should recite a prayer or two for her. This could help both Valeri and me spiritually." I said a little prayer, and then I began The Lord's Prayer. "Our Father, who art in heaven . . ." and Valeri began reciting the prayer with me, even though she seemed to be asleep. Then she opened her eyes and we both completed the prayer together. I said another brief prayer. She looked at me kindly, then fell asleep again.

A short while later, as I sat there, Valeri opened her eyes, looked at me, and asked, "How are you doing, Dad?"

"I'm doing fine, Valeri. How are you doing?" She just smiled and her eyes began wandering around the room.

Suddenly, she focused her eyes on her extremely swollen right forearm and hand. She looked at me, then back down at her arm, then at me again and stated: "Dad, I'm dying. I'm dying, Dad."

I felt like a lightning bolt had just struck me. I quickly jumped up, kissed her hand, kissed her on the cheek, put my head next to hers and said, "Valeri, Valeri, sweetheart, we love you so very much! You're such a wonderful, wonderful daughter! You've given us so much happiness in our lives. We love you, Valeri." I kissed her again, held her swollen hand and put my head next to hers. She fell asleep almost immediately.

Words fail me when I try to describe how devastating it was to think about her words, "I'm dying, Dad." I said to myself, "Gee, what frightening, terrible thoughts must be going through her mind right now." The dreadful feeling and the thoughts of dying, leaving this earth, going into the unknown . . . nothing could be done to save Val . . . Her words: "I'm dying, Dad," haunted me. My wonderful daughter was dying. Then I thought to myself, "Maybe with Valeri, she's thinking of being with God and in heaven with Him, because God loves her so much." This thought comforted me, that Valeri would be in heaven with God.

I was quite tired and sleepy by now, so I lay my head down next to Valeri, held her hand, and fell asleep. I woke up intermittently during the night and noted that Valeri was still wheezing but seemed to be sleeping comfortably. Finally, I fell sound asleep, holding Valeri's hand and resting my head next to her thigh.

Both Marietta and I woke up simultaneously Tuesday morning at approximately 7:15. Valeri was sleeping quite soundly, so I told Marietta that I was going to race home to take a shower and bring some clothes back for Marietta. "Please hurry, Bob," Marietta said. "I feel very uncomfortable for some reason right now."

So I drove the three miles home, took a bath, picked up some clothes for Marietta, and was back at the hospital by about eight o'clock. When I walked into Valeri's room, Marietta reported, "Bob, there are two nurses aides about to bathe Valeri and make up her bed. Why don't we go down to the cafeteria and have breakfast?" Valeri was lying there asleep.

I answered her, "Marietta, I don't feel very comfortable about going down for breakfast right now. Why don't we stay in the room for a few minutes?"

"No, Bob. Let the aides do their job. We can go down, and be back shortly." This was against my better judgment, but I acquiesced. We got down to the first floor and walked off the elevator, when Marietta suddenly looked at me, panic-stricken. "Bob! Bob! Something is wrong! We have to go right back up to Valeri's room. I've got this dreadful feeling that something is about to happen."

I looked at her and nodded, "Okay, you go up to the room while I go to the men's room. I'll come up in a minute."

"Okay," she said, then reentered the elevator to return to Val's room.

When Marietta walked into Val's room, a hospital volunteer brought in some flowers with a note. It was from Jill Haley, who had written, "I'm all through here, Valeri, and will be home immediately." Marietta took the flowers and walked around the two nurses' aides who were finished and preparing to leave. She said, "Valeri, these are from Jill." Val gave no response. Marietta turned and put the flowers on the table.

As Marietta turned back around to look at Valeri, a young nurse had just walked into the room and asked: "Is Valeri still asleep? Let me take her pulse to make sure everything is okay."

Marietta and the nurse were on the left side of Valeri's bed. I walked in and went to the right side. Marietta observed, "Something is wrong. She's really not breathing very much." I looked at Valeri and noticed she hadn't taken a breath for several seconds. Finally Valeri took a deep, gasping breath, and there were seconds between the next gasping breath. I realized that something was drastically wrong.

Meanwhile, the nurse was trying to find a pulse in one of Val's carotid arteries. After several seconds, Valeri seemed to struggle to take a deep breath, then suddenly exhaled air with a loud gasp and went limp. The nurse looked at her and exclaimed, "Don't go, Valeri! Don't go, Valeri! Don't go!"

Marietta put her head next to Valeri's and repeated, "Don't go, Valeri! Don't go! Don't go!" She began sobbing hysterically, and continued to scream "Don't go! Don't go!"

I realized that Valeri had died. It was all over. Her life had ended. I began to weep as Marietta kept sobbing, "Valeri, we want you to stay, honey! Don't go! Please, please don't go! Stay with us!" Marietta hugged and kissed Valeri and kept repeating the words over and over: "Stay with us, Valeri! Don't go! Don't go!"

I kissed Valeri several times and pleaded, "Sweetheart, stay with us, baby!"

The nurse, stunned, could only stand and stare at the action that was taking place. Suddenly she gathered her wits and asked, "Mrs. Samaras, are you okay?"

"Yes, "I'm okay, but I don't want her to go! I want my baby to stay with us! I want her to stay *here*! She can't go! She can't!"

Another nurse entered the room and then left very quickly. A short while later, Sister Dianne Donican, a chaplain, came into the room. She stood alongside Marietta. The nurse said, "Let her do whatever she wants to. Let her grieve. This is a terrible time."

Marietta straightened up and looked at Valeri. She directed, "Look, Bob. She's got a smile on her face and she's very relaxed. It's as though she's saying, 'I'm out of pain now, Mom and Dad. I'm going to heaven where I will find peace and happiness permanently.'" How beautiful she looked! She appeared so relaxed, with a partial smile on her face. Marietta continued, "My beautiful, beautiful daughter. You have left us to go to a place of rest and peace." Then she began crying again. She looked up at me. "Bob, call Father Makrinos. I think we should have him here with us right now. Also, call Debbie and Nikki right away. I called them earlier this morning and asked them to come here because I just felt something was going to happen this morning. They are probably getting ready to come to the hospital."

I went to a phone and called our church office and told them what happened. They said that Father Makrinos would be right over. I called Debbie's home, but she wasn't there. I called Nikki and said, "Hang on, honey, but Valeri just passed away."

Nikki cried, "No! No! No! It can't be, Dad. She couldn't have died! She's in a coma! Don't tell me she died! I know she's in a coma!"

I tried to calm her and said, "Okay, honey, okay. Just be careful, but come over to the hospital as soon as you can."

"I'll be right there."

I called Marietta's sisters Mary and Toni. Toni, who lives with her mother, would notify her. Everyone said they would come to the hospital. I called Rena. She was very, very upset and began crying hysterically on the phone. She asked me, "Should I come there?"

"No," I replied, "you take care of your daughter, Andrea. I'll keep you posted."

I called Sue who broke down and began crying. I promised to keep her updated on our plans. I also called Mike, Marietta's brother, and told him what had happened. As I finished making the calls, I went to the right side of Valeri's bed again and turned around to see Dr. Schwartz. He said, "I came to see Valeri."

"Valeri just passed away, Dr. Schwartz." He looked shocked.

After a few seconds he regained his composure and gave us his condolences. "I'm so very sorry. Valeri was such a fine and courageous young lady. She was so very, very sick. I am so, so sorry." Then he turned and left.

Marietta announced, "I don't want to leave. I want to stay here with Valeri."

The nurse replied, "Oh, you can stay here all you want, Mr. and Mrs. Samaras."

Sister Donican moved toward Marietta and assured her, "Mrs. Samaras, there is no rush. You take all the time you need."

Father Makrinos, who had arrived a few minutes earlier, also said, "Just take your time. There is no hurry. Give your family a chance to get here. You have plenty of time this morning."

I thought to myself how fast things had happened. Valeri died on March 26th at 8:20 a.m. The resident doctor pronounced her dead about ten minutes later, at which time Dr. Schwartz walked in. Phone calls had been made, and relatives were on their way to the hospital. Things were happening quickly, almost too fast to comprehend what was taking place.

By 9:30 a.m., the family began arriving, one by one. As each family member arrived, they walked up to Valeri, touched her, and began crying. Marietta refused to move away from the bed. She just stayed there, holding Valeri's hand, occasionally kissing her, and talking to her. I stayed next to Val, too, although I did leave to make more telephone calls. The chaplain said a beautiful prayer for Valeri. Father Makrinos followed with a beautiful, customary prayer for the deceased.

Marietta still sat next to Valeri, holding her hand and stroking her hair. She spoke, "My beautiful, lovely, courageous, wonderful daughter. You have left us and we find it unbearable." She looked up at me and asked, "Doesn't Valeri look so relaxed and so beautiful?" I nodded. Then Marietta suddenly realized, "Debbie's not here yet. Try to reach her again."

I telephoned Brian at work. He affirmed that Debbie had been notified and should be at the hospital shortly. Brian said he was coming too.

"Marietta, you know I'd better call Mike Flannery at Peter's Funeral Home to inform him that Valeri has passed away." Marietta and I had decided that we would have the wake at the well-regarded Peter's Funeral

Home, which was near our house and convenient for so many friends and relatives. Mike, who worked for the funeral home, had been a basketball player in one of my camps some years earlier. I called him, and he assured me he would make arrangements to take Valeri's body to the funeral home. We could make plans for the wake later that afternoon.

Debra finally arrived at the hospital a little after ten o'clock. She walked up to her sister, kissed her, and began sobbing. Debbie, Nikki, Marietta, and I all stayed close to Valeri, holding her hands and crying from time to time. The presence of all the family members there helped us get through those terrible moments.

Three hours after Valeri died, at approximately 11:30 a.m. Marietta said, "I think I'm okay. I think it's time for us to go, Bob." We informed the family that it was time to leave. One by one the family members paid their final respects to Valeri and left the room. Finally, when Marietta, Debbie, Nikki, and I were alone, we cried and said our final good-byes. We walked into the hall to join the rest of the family.

As we walked toward the elevators, George Backos, who was late arriving, came up to us and said, "I sure would like to see Valeri for the last time."

"I'll go back with you, George," I said, and we headed towards her room. Once there, George began crying, as he had many times in the past when she was ill. Valeri loved George very much. He was a favorite uncle. After he paid his last respects, I once more held Valeri's hand, kissed her on the cheek, and left the room with George.

I just couldn't accept or believe that our Valeri was gone, and that she would not be with us any more on this earth. As we walked out the back entrance to the hospital, en route to our cars in the parking lot, I saw a silver hearse which was to transport Valeri's body to the funeral home. I had seen that hearse so many times in the past when I went to the hospital whenever Valeri was ill. It was shattering that this time it was for our Valeri.

To our amazement, when we arrived home, Terry Vickrey, Christine Cheolas and Betty Rothis had brought food and were already preparing lunch for anyone who would visit to pay their condolences to our grief-stricken family.

# 33

# *The Many Lives Val Touched*

A FEW minutes after arriving home from the hospital, I went out to get something from one of our guests' automobiles. I noticed my neighbor, Bill Mestaugh, in front of his house. Bill, a retired principal, was a good friend. We had spent many hours over the years discussing athletics and world problems in his driveway. He yelled across to me, "Hi, Bob. What's going on with all the people coming over to your house?"

I quickly walked across the street. "Bill, Valeri passed away a few hours ago."

Bill was stunned. All he said was, "Valeri died?" Then he threw his arms around me and began crying. "I can't believe that wonderful girl is gone."

We both cried for a little while, then I thanked him for being so supportive and said, "I'd better get back to my guests. But I'll give you more information and the details about her wake a little later on." Bill was still looking at me and crying when I turned to walk away.

It was now close to 2:30 in the afternoon. Marietta came to me and said, "Bob, let's get Brian and go to the funeral home to consult with Mike Flannery regarding arrangements for the wake."

I went to the kitchen to ask Brian if he was ready to go with us. "Sure, let's go," he said. Marietta and I had asked Brian to accompany us as he was a take-charge type of person who could take responsibility and expedite pending business in a very professional manner.

Mike Flannery was extremely helpful in making all the arrangements with us. He arranged for Valeri to lie in state in the large room on the second floor of the funeral home. When plans were finalized, Mike looked at us with tears in his eyes. "I feel so badly about Valeri, Mr. and Mrs. Samaras. I remember her from basketball camps at Notre Dame High School, and I also saw her several times in recent years. She was a wonderful young lady. If there is anything I can do for either one of you in these next three days, please call me immediately." We thanked Mike for all his help and left for home.

En route, Marietta talked about the arrangements we had made. Wednesday and Thursday Valeri would be at Peter's Funeral Home. The funeral would be at our Assumption Church at 11:00 a.m. on Friday, which happened to be Good Friday for other religions, but not for ours. Marietta thought out loud: "Valeri's going to be buried on Good Friday. Even though it isn't our holiday, Easter was one of her favorites."

The afternoon was spent with many people visiting us to offer their condolences and support. So many people showed up that we really didn't have much time to be alone until nearly midnight.

I woke up early the next morning after a very restless night and decided to attempt to cope with my anxiety and stress the best way I knew how, by taking a two-mile run. While jogging on Marter Road, just ready to make a turn and head for home about a half mile away, I saw a car pull in front of me onto a driveway. Someone in the car yelled, "Hey, Bob!" I stopped and looked to see who it was. Out jumped Phil Koufas, the maintenance man at our church and educational center, and also a good friend. He came running towards me and said, "Bob! Bob! I heard the terrible news!" and he threw his arms around me and started crying. He continued, "I'm so sorry. I loved that gal. She always talked to me whenever she saw me at church. I know I'm going to miss her very much."

I began crying, too, and thanked Phil for being so thoughtful. "She enjoyed talking with you, too, Phil," I told him. He returned to his car. I wiped away my tears and continued to jog.

Mike Flannery greeted us at the door of the funeral home. He took us up to the room where Valeri's body was lying in a beautiful mahogany casket. Marietta, Nikki, Debbie, and I all cried when we saw how beautiful she was. On the table near the casket they had set up some mementos commemorating Valeri's life : her graduation caps and tassels from both the University of Michigan and Grosse Pointe North High School, her diploma from the University of Michigan, a few pictures and other articles, and the yearbooks that were printed when Valeri was the yearbook sponsor.

Flowers began arriving almost immediately. The room eventually would be filled with all kinds of beautiful flowers. A lovely fica tree that was sent to Valeri was one that we took home with us following the funeral. She had always appreciated flowers, and the room was filled with gorgeous plants. She would have been very pleased. Many of our visitors said they had never seen so many flowers at a funeral.

Another flower arrangement we would later take home was one sent by Sue Schucker, Valeri's wonderful, long-time friend. Sue had come over to our home and had taken one of Val's favorite large hippo dolls and had the florist put it in a basket surrounded by flowers. It was a lovely arrangement. Sue knew that Val had a life-long love for hippos. The arrangement was so appropriate for the occasion.

Marietta and I requested that donations be made to the Greek Assumption Church, or the AHEPA Cooley's Anemia Foundation Association. Several thousand dollars were donated and divided between the two organizations.

The *Detroit News* printed a picture and nice article about Valeri, thanks to the efforts of our friend, Georgia Gianopolis. The *Detroit Free Press* also had a good article written by Lori Mathews, thanks to an assist by Val's former employer and our friend, Angie Bournias. *The Grosse Pointe News* contained another article on Val the following week.

Over a thousand people visited the funeral home during the two days Valeri was there. Family members, relatives, friends from her elementary, junior high, high school, and college days came to visit. Teachers from Grosse Pointe North; teachers from the elementary school she'd attended, including her first grade teacher; doctors and nurses who had helped her through the years - all came to pay their respects. Parishioners from our church turned out in large masses. Several of her dearest friends who played basketball for our church team came to tell me how much they were going to miss Valeri, who was one of their most avid fans.

Rena, Sue, Roula, Harriet, and so many of her other friends spent time during both days in the funeral home. They would talk for awhile, and cry on occasion, but they wanted to be there near Valeri.

Father Kavadas and Father Makrinos presided over the special memorial service that was held early Thursday evening. The room was completely filled with people during the service. Near the end of the evening, there was a sudden hush among the people. I looked up to see what was happening. There was Rena Skuras, escorting her brother Bill to the casket. Bill had not been seen or heard from for several months. His parents and Rena had not known where he was. It was a shock for everyone to see him walk into the funeral home.

As Bill stood at the casket looking at Valeri, he suddenly did a quick two-or-three-step dance, looked at her and said, "Maraca, Salsa!" He continued to look at Val for a few more minutes, with tears in his eyes.

Then he turned around, said good-bye to Rena, and left the room without talking to anyone else.

Rena walked over to Debbie and Nikki to explain what the little dance and the two words meant. Later, Debbie explained to us, "Mom and Dad, you know that little dance that Bill did in front of Valeri's casket? That is how Bill and Val greeted each other the last couple of years. It originated in Arizona, when Val and Rena visited Billy a few years ago. Valeri would hold two things in the air like they were maracas and she would say: 'Maraca, maraca' and Billy would do a little dance, step back and say: 'Salsa! Salsa!' It was a silly thing, but it was their own fun way of communicating with each other."

Billy attended the funeral the following day. He also went to the cemetery, put a rose on Valeri's casket, then dropped out of sight again for a long time. (He has since gone to another rehab center, and is a recovered alcohol and drug addict.)

During the evening, one of the assistant funeral directors came into the room and asked me, "Gosh, is this some sort of celebrity?"

I looked at him and explained, "Well, to *me* she is a celebrity. She is my lovely daughter."

As he walked away he mused, "Wow, she sure must have been quite a gal."

The comments made to Marietta, Debbie, Nikki, and me made us realize that Valeri had touched so many lives. We had no idea that she influenced so many people. She had always lived her life to the fullest. Very few people realized that Valeri was so ill, and that living with death was a constant part of her life. They deeply respected her fighting spirit, and particularly her upbeat attitude. Her constant cheerfulness, and the fact that she never complained about her disease, had deceived people into thinking that she was not seriously ill. After all, Valeri was usually the life of the party. This was a revelation to us, because we had always felt maybe Valeri was a little *too* reserved. Her friends saw her in a different light - the true light - and we were very pleased.

As the crowd began to thin out, Marietta turned to me and said, "I feel bad that Chris didn't return for Val's funeral - but, I can appreciate his feelings. He was extremely upset about losing Val. It was nice he sent a dozen roses to his mother for Val and requested that she place them next to Valeri's casket. He told his mother it would be too hard for him to handle seeing Valeri lying in the casket. He loved her very much."

(Note: Later, when we visited Chris in London, England, he told us, "I wish I would have married Val. We could have had two years of happiness together before she died." Chris was on special assignment in England for his new job with the Walt Disney Company.)

Marietta looked at Debbie, Nikki, and me with a half-smile and said, "You know, I placed a rose from Chris, a hippo, a panda bear doll, and a picture of our immediate family, including the grandchildren, in the casket with Valeri." Hearing this, we smiled approvingly. After the crowd left, Debbie, Nikki, Marietta, and I took a final look at Valeri in the casket and said a prayer. As we walked to our car, Marietta commented, "The last two days have been very sad and difficult, but tomorrow will be the worst. The funeral will be the worst day of all. We better get home and get some rest in preparation for it."

There were still many visitors at our home when we arrived. They began departing rapidly after a little while, each urging us to get some rest for the impending funeral. Although we intended to follow their good advice, we stayed up into the late hours before going to bed. They were hours well spent, however, because Marietta, Nikki, and I reminisced about the past. We also talked quite a bit about some of the things that had happened in recent days. This seemed to help us relax.

Still, neither Marietta nor I could sleep much that night. Losing our Valeri was almost unbearable for both of us.

# *Epilogue*

IT HAS been over three-and-a-half years since that terrible Tuesday morning when our valiant Valeri died. The pain of losing her is still with her friends, her sisters, Debra and Nikki, and especially with Marietta and me. At first the pain was nearly intolerable, but several things happened that helped us cope with our loss. The more than three hundred cards and letters we received from her friends and our friends were very consoling. Comments in letters from Dr. Wonke, Dr. Graziano, and Dr. Peomelli helped us deal with our grief. The donations to the Cooley's Anemia Foundation and to our Assumption Church were also very greatly appreciated.

Marietta and I have made frequent visits to Valeri's grave at Clinton Grove Cemetery, both alone and together; the visits seem to bring peace to both of us. We have visited there as many as three or four times a week since she died. In the spring, summer, and fall we visit constantly. Just sitting and reflecting on things that happened in her twenty-nine years and ten months of life are soothing to us. The fact that Val is buried adjacent to our good friend, Bob Vickrey, who passed away three years before Valeri, somehow helps put our minds at ease.

It is common for friends to visit Valeri's grave, and to plant a little flower, or even in one case, to leave a chocolate chip cookie on her tombstone. Chocolate chip cookies were Valeri's favorite. Crying from time to time also seems to comfort us. It is hard for me to really believe that Valeri's life is over. She fought so long and so hard to live.

After her death, it was very difficult for Marietta and me to think that Valeri was gone. Although she had lived almost thirty years, when in the beginning doctors speculated she might only live two years or at best into her teens, we still felt that somehow she would overcome her disease and be able to live a long life.

Being in Valeri's bedroom, which she loved so much, seeing pictures of Valeri, packing and storing away some of her belongings and seeing the creative, artistic things she did around the house was - and is - like a double-edged sword. On one hand, it eases our pain, because it reminds us of so many nice and happy things that she did. On the other hand, it is sad, because we know that Valeri is not around to enjoy these things anymore. When we sold Valeri's car and watched the woman who bought it drive away, both Marietta and I cried, knowing how much Valeri had loved that little convertible, and knowing how much fun she had with it. There it was - gone out of our life - for good.

On the morning that Valeri died, when both Marietta and I were so grief-stricken, Marietta had put her head close to Valeri's and whispered quietly, "Valeri, I will not ever be able to rest in peace unless I know that everything is okay with you in heaven. Please send us a sign that you are doing well. I must know that you are okay. Please do that, sweetheart." Marietta told me about this request at the funeral. I remarked at the time that I thought it was a good idea, because it would make both of us feel very much at ease, knowing that Valeri was happy in heaven.

We both feel, that there have been some phenomenal signs indicating to us that somehow Valeri is, in her own way, communicating with us, and that everything is going well for her. One omen took place when Debra called Marietta on Valeri's thirtieth birthday, May 16, 1991. "Mom, did you see the short presentation on television today about the St. Phanourios icon?" Debra asked. "There is an icon of St. Phanourios at the church that was adjacent to the spot on the expressway where you had that terrible auto accident, when Phillip and Michelle and I were in the car with you back in 1982. Remember how you felt as though someone was watching over you, because you could have bled to death if it hadn't been for that little bone in your cheek that closed off the artery that was bleeding so badly? Well, on the day that Valeri died, it was discovered that on their icon of St. Phanourios, a large halo engulfed St. Phanourios' upper body and head. They called it "the miracle icon" and people by the hundreds are visiting the church so they can see and touch the icon and hope for miracles to happen."

This hit home immediately with Marietta. St. Phanourios was a saint who had been persecuted and suffered all his life, trying to preach Christianity to the people in his village on the Isle of Rhodes, Greece. He died at a very young age. The original St. Phanourios Church was located on the Greek Isle of Rhodes, the birthplace of Marietta's parents, Ianthie and Nick Christofis.

Marietta and I went to St. Phanourios Church in Roseville to see the icon. Marietta felt that, along with the parallel suffering that St.

Phanourios and Valeri had endured, the icon showed very fine features of the saint. Actually, Valeri resembled him in looks. Sure enough, the icon had a halo around it. Marietta whispered to me, "Bob, I almost feel like this saint and Valeri are one and the same person."

On the fortieth day after Val's death, Marietta visited Val's grave. In our religion, the fortieth day is when the soul of the deceased leaves the earth permanently and goes to heaven. While sitting next to the grave and meditating, Marietta suddenly heard a loud sobbing. She quickly looked around, but saw no one. The sobbing stopped a few seconds later. She thought to herself that it was her Valeri leaving the earth for good and that was Val's way of letting Marietta know that she was leaving. Her soul was now in heaven.

One evening, Marietta, Nikki, Alexandra, and I were eating supper when we heard a radio in Valeri's room. We ran upstairs to see what it was. To our amazement, it was Valeri's clock radio. It was tuned to a religious station and a religious speaker was delivering his message. To our knowledge, Valeri never listened to that station. We all just looked at each other and turned the radio off. It went on several times during the next week. It was a happy event. "Gosh, that's another sign from our Valeri," Marietta declared.

One day when Marietta went by Valeri's grave before meeting her golf league at Gowanie Golf Course, she stood over Val's grave and said, "Valeri, I cannot stay very long today because I have to hurry to make my starting time at the golf course." It was a calm day up to this point. All of a sudden, the wind became very gusty, and for the next few seconds, it swirled around Marietta. At first, she was a little frightened and then realized that this was a sign by our Valeri. Marietta remembered how Val used to say, "Oh, no, Mom! You're not going golfing again today! How come you don't stay home and make lasagna and cherry pie like other mothers do?" Valeri always laughed after making this remark. Marietta looked at the headstone and whispered, "I get your point, Valeri," and began laughing to herself as she left the grave site to go to her car.

Another time, Marietta and I went to the cemetery. As we sat there praying, a bee started flying around our heads. It kept buzzing around and finally landed on one of the rosebushes on her grave. We found it interesting, because it just kept buzzing and buzzing, flying around and not intending to sting us. It was just there, and finally landed gently on the bush. We chose to interpret that as a message from our Val that she was doing well.

After golfing one day, I drove out to the Clinton Grove Cemetery to visit Valeri's grave and to do some gardening. I trimmed the bushes, cleaned the headstone, and smoothed out the soil around the flowers and bushes. I was kneeling down to say a prayer when, to my astonishment, I looked down and noticed a four-leaf clover in the grass next to the rosebushes. One four-leaf clover, and no other clover around. Just grass. Definitely it had to be some sort of sign. I put it by Valeri's picture, near the icon in our religious corner in our home.

Last summer we visited the Isle of Rhodes for the fourth time. Our first venture was to seek out the St. Phanourios Church, which was located in the old city inside the city of Rhodes. We wandered through many streets and asked several people for directions before finally locating that church. It was tiny. An archaeological monument, it had a seal of antiquity from the Greek government. The story behind it was that it had been buried for centuries, but rediscovered by an archaeologist, who also found several buried icons. All of them were destroyed except St. Phanourios, which was almost as new as the day it was first painted. The church was later restored, with much of the original belongings left inside. The original icon of St. Phanourios was beautiful. As we looked at it, again Marietta claimed, "Look! I swear Valeri and this saint looked alike." (Phanourios in Greek means, "from dark to light.") It was also interesting that the church's pastor's name was Vasilou, named after St. Vasilios: the same saint for whom Valeri was named. It was a wonderful experience visiting St. Phanourios. Both Marietta and I felt Valeri's presence in that church.

Late last fall, Marietta and I found a white rose in the bush near Valeri's headstone. Why was this significant? Simply because it was growing on a red rosebush. The rosebush was planted by my nephew, Dean, one of Val's favorite cousins. Dean's mother, Mary received the bush as a gift when Dean was born over thirty-five years before. Mary and her husband, George, took the rosebush with them and replanted it when they moved to their new home. Dean took care of the flowers each year, and they flourished. He thought that planting this bush at Valeri's grave would be a nice gesture to his wonderful cousin. He loved the way this rosebush blossomed each year, with bright, beautiful, red roses. So, when Marietta and I saw the white rose among the red, we thought surely this had to be yet another sign from our Valeri.

Marietta and I definitely feel that the incidents I have mentioned are signs by Valeri that everything is well with her in heaven. These little signs along the way have been very influential in giving us peace of mind and the ability to adjust to our tremendous loss. We have received much comfort at the Clinton Grove Cemetery. Beside Val's grave are four large, beautiful trees. Upon her grave is a lovely headstone, which Marietta designed with the help of cemetery director Jim Krause. Its novel design magnifies our Valeri, and the inscriptions on it are of priceless comfort to us.

Inscribed on the middle of the stone is Valeri's name, and below it, her birth date: May 16, 1961. Below that is the date she died: March 26, 1991. In the upper right-hand corner is a design of a graduation cap with the letters "U of M" inscribed, and above the cap is the year "1983." Of course, this signifies the wonderful years she spent attending the University of Michigan, and her pride and joy in graduating from that school. Also centered on the headstone, in large letters, is the phrase "Seize The Day," in reference to how Valeri learned to make every single day count in her pursuit of a happy and fulfilling life. It was a lesson she taught our family and many others.

Mike Utley, a tackle for the Detroit Lion's football team, who became paralyzed after suffering a neck injury in a game, was later to use this slogan in his attempt to recover his health and ability to walk again. If Valeri were alive today, being a football fan, I know she would have said, "Mike, go for it. I know you can do it, and good luck!"

Marietta and I wanted to donate something to our church in Valeri's memory. There was money available for a project, as well as our willingness to offer other monies if necessary. We decided, with the help of Father Kavadas and iconographer George S. Papastamatiou, to have George paint an icon in her memory. This project was completed several months ago. It is an icon of St. John baptizing Jesus in the Jordan River. It covers the entire back wall of the baptismal sanctuary and is located behind an altar. The baptismal fountain is in front of the altar. When people attend a baptism, they face the fountain where the baby will be immersed in the water and can view the beautiful icon of Jesus being baptized. Mr. Papastamatiou created a very masterful piece of art, which is now being appreciated by all our parishioners. I know Valeri would love this icon, because it is located in the sanctuary where children, whom she loved so much, are baptized and accepted into our Orthodox religion. Since Valeri had the honor to baptize her two godchildren, Brian Dittmer and Andrea Venettis, at this very place, we know she would have been happy with this icon, and we are very proud of it.

The effort of trying to cope with losing Valeri and making adjustments in our lives without her has been very stressful throughout the many months since she passed away. There are two thoughts that give us comfort and make it easier for us to go on. The first is that we know that Valeri would want us to continue with our mission in life, even though she isn't with us. The second is that both Marietta and I feel that Valeri is happy and at peace in heaven with God.

Still, there is a tremendous void in our lives. We miss Valeri's great sense of humor; the wonderful conversations we had after arriving home in the evenings or coming back from a trip or when Valeri returned from a trip; her watching the soaps that she had taped earlier in the day; gathering together late in the evening to watch the movies she'd rented, ones she knew we would enjoy, because of her knowledge of them; and, watching the Academy Awards with her. We miss attending family outings together and hearing and watching her happiness as she enjoyed them. We miss hearing Valeri laughing in her room while watching television, and her laughter as she talked to Chris in his far-away apartment in California. Marietta, of course, misses her shopping trips with Valeri at the various centers around town. I miss the insightful counseling Val would give me whenever I was upset about something and wanted someone to help me analyze the problem. Marietta and I miss the wonderful, happy expression on Valeri's face as she would drive up in her little convertible, sunglasses on and music blaring.

Most of all, we miss the priceless and irreplaceable companionship she gave us day in and day out. We often think if we could hug her just one more time, how wonderful it would be. Yes, God knows there is a tremendous void in our lives that can never be filled.

Marietta and I both know that we must try to have as much courage as Valeri did throughout her life, so that we can continue and go on with our lives. If Valeri were able to talk to us today she'd say, "Often throughout my life I told you: I'll stop crying, if you stop crying. Now I am at peace. I have stopped crying. It is time for you to stop crying."

Okay, Valeri, we will stop crying. But no matter what, the pain is still in our hearts - and it will remain there until we are with you forever.

# APPENDIX

May 6, 1991

Mr. Bob Samaras
930 Canterbury
Grosse Pointe Woods, MI 48236

Dear Mr. Samaras:

Although your letter was obviously very saddening to me, I am most grateful to you for sharing your feelings with me. Unfortunately, for many of the older patients, Cooley's anemia is not curable. Our hope lies in the future, for the very young patients.

Valeri's wonderfully warm human qualities transpire from your letter and the article. Although I never met her, in my experience with this disease, I have always been impressed by the remarkable grace of these patients, who somehow always project faith and hope in their lives.

As a doctor and a father, I share with you this very difficult time.

Sincerely yours,

*Sergio Piomelli, M.D.*
James A. Wolff Professor

# BIBLIOGRAPHY

Chirban, John T., (edited by). *Thalassemia: An Interdisciplinary Approach.* University Press of America; Maryland, New York, London, 1986.

Giardina, P.J.; Grady, R.W.; Ehlers, K.H.; Burstein, S.; Graziano, J. H. ; Markenson, A.L.; & Hilgartner, M.W. "Current therapy of Cooley's Anemia: A decade of experience with subcutaneous desferrioxamine." *Annals of the New York Academy of Sciences.* 612:275-85, 1990.

Giardina, P.J. "Update on Thalassemia." *Pediatrics in Review.* 13(2):55-62, 1992 Feb.

Hoffbrand, A.V., Wonke, B. "Results of long-term subcutaneous desferrioxamine therapy." *Baillieres Clinical Haematology.* 2(2): 345-62, 1989 Apr.

Masera, G. *International Directory*, Thalassemia Internal Federation; Information Center, Monza, Italy.

Nash, K.B. "A psychosocial perspective. Growing up with Thalassemia, a chronic disorder."*Annals of the New York Academy of Sciences.* 612:442-50, 1990.

Nathan, D.G., Piomelli, S. "Oral iron chelators." *Seminars in Hematology.* 27(2):83-5, 1990 Apr.

Piomelli, S., Loew, T. "Management of Thalassemia Major (Cooley's anemia). *Hematology-Oncology Clinics of North America.* 5(3):557-69, 1991 Jun.

Vullo, Rino, and Modell, Bernadette. *What is Thalassemia?* Printed by the Cooley's Anemia Foundation, Inc., New York, NY.

# ORDERING INFORMATION

**Mom, I'll Stop Crying, If You Stop Crying**

If your local bookstore is unable to obtain this
book, you may order directly from:

## Publishers Distribution Service

**CONSUMER ORDERS:**
1-800-507-2665

**TRADE ORDERS:**
Phone: 1-800-345-0096
Fax: 1-800-950-9793

**MAIL ORDERS TO:**
Publishers Distribution Service
6893 Sullivan Road
Grawn, Michigan 49637